Wildcat

Book One of the Caledon Saga

J.P. Harker

Testimonial

'I had great pleasure reading Wildcat. Apart from your obvious talent as a writer I have such admiration for your meticulous research. Please accept my thanks and appreciation for your talent and hard work. Best Wishes.'
James Cosmo

Prologue

'Taran!'

Rhia screamed the War God's name with a joyful rage as hot blood spattered on her face. Rhia was small and the Gorvic was big, but he was already on his knees thanks to the axe she'd left lodged in his stomach. At first his hands had clutched at the haft, trying to drag the weapon from her grip or else pull it from his wound, and for a moment Rhia had lost her balance. But then she'd simply abandoned her axe and grabbed a fistful of blonde hair, yanking his head back hard before her knife opened up his throat. Bright red now sprayed both on Rhia and on the grass below, and the young woman felt the thrill of battle rise up in her like a flood, erupting from her mouth in another bellowed warcry;

'Taran!'

The Gorvic's body jerked and twisted in her grip and she let go the hank of hair, leaving the dying man to collapse on the muddy ground. When they'd arrived at Broken Stream the fields had been nothing but a vibrant green on both sides of the water. Belenos had been shining overhead when the two warbands first faced each other across the little ford, and the stream had been clear and bright and gurgling merrily along its way.

Now the sky was overcast and warriors from both sides lay dead or dying all around. The ground had been churned up into a treacherous mire of mud and the stream was now tainted by the blood of wounded fighters. The scene might have been another world entirely, somewhere far away from the tranquil valley it had been this morning. Though the change in its image was as nothing to the change in the sounds of this once-quiet place.

This morning Broken Stream had known little noise but the trickling of the waters and the singing of the birds.

Then the Gorvicae had come and they and the Caderyn had traded insults and boasts, jeers and challenges, and the air had been alive with the voices of warriors, all daring each other to attack first. Then the two sides had charged, and the insults and challenges had changed to warcries and screams, and the sound of iron meeting iron and of iron meeting flesh had combined to fill the valley with the dreadful song of battle. And Rhianwyn, daughter of Carradan, revelled in it.

She cast her eyes around to find another Gorvic to fight, her eyes wide and almost feverish, her hands shaking in anticipation. This was her first true battle, the first time she had taken the field to defend her people, and the fear she'd felt before it had melted away into something like lust as she sought out another victim for her long knife and narrow axe. Remembering that the latter weapon was still embedded in a Gorvic's guts, she crouched down and began working it free of its fleshy prison, all the while looking around her at the carnage.

Even with her limited experience Rhia could tell the Caderyn had all but won, and she screamed out in wordless triumph as her axe came free of her enemy. She held the weapon high above her head as she looked around the bloody field. Nearly all the Gorvicae were fleeing back across the stream, only a few dozen still fighting of the two hundred who'd come here this morning. Rhia saw Caderyn fighters encircling the few who were still refusing to run away, and her breath caught in her throat as she took in the long iron swords and rigid white hair of their warrior elite. These were the Gadarim: The Mighty.

The finest of the Gorvicae fought with their hair twisted into spikes and bleached blindingly white with lime and Rhia knew that, like the Gadarim of her own people, the patterns on their skin were made of more than simple woad. Rhia, like every warrior on that field, had painted

4

her body with swirling shapes of bright blue, to attract the favour of the gods and inspire terror in her enemies. Twin snakes writhed up her arms from wrist to shoulder, one of them continuing up her neck and around the ear to cover her cheek. She was liberally sprinkled with blood and grime by now, and sweat and struggle had caused much of the warpaint to smudge or fade, risking the chance of the gods losing sight of her in all the chaos. The men of the Gadarim had no such concern.

Though they had painted over them before the battle to make them brighter, the spirals and whorls on their bodies had been tattooed there to shine forever, ensuring that Taran and Mabonac would never lose sight of their most favoured warriors. For the most part only their faces had mere woad to decorate them today, the honour of permanency there being reserved for the greatest of fighters. Rhia wondered for a wistful moment if she might know that honour someday, but she shook her head at such a foolish notion. Female Gadarim were a rare thing. Instead she settled for looking around for more Gorvicae to kill. She spotted one, a lad of about her own years, who seemed torn between running back across the stream and running forwards to where the Gadarim fought. She decided to make his mind up for him.

Rhia screamed as she raised the axe and sprinted towards the Gorvic, whose eyes widened as she charged him. The thrill of battle was pulsing through her like blazing fire in her veins, and she grinned fiercely as she saw how that fire was absent in her enemy. The boy was pale beneath his woad and he shrank away as her axe swung for his head. The resulting miss caused Rhia to stumble and a bolder fighter might have taken advantage of it, but the Gorvic simply backed away further, apparently forgetting the iron sword held in his hand. The Caderyn regained her balance and swung back at the sheepish man, who raised his sword in a clumsy block which barely kept the axe-blade from his neck. Rhia thrust her long knife at his stomach. It was shorter than the Gorvic's sword, but that was still holding off her axe, and she came within a hairsbreadth of gutting him before he twisted away.

The two broke apart and Rhia watched the man eagerly, her eyes as wide with excitement as his were wide with fear. He was licking his lips nervously, his grip on the sword clearly tenuous, and the daughter of Carradan smiled, licking her own lips with glee as she sprang forwards at her enemy. She swung the axe in three quick blows at his head, forcing him to cower behind his sword. Rhia kept on striking, screaming out in what was either rage or passion, though she had no idea which one, and each time it seemed the axe came a fraction closer to splitting his skull.

Finally the hammering strikes became too much for the feeble man, and the sword fell from his nerveless fingers. Rhia bared her teeth and put all her weight into a swing that would cave in his head, but the Gorvic ducked and rolled before the blow could land. Once again Rhia stumbled off-balance, dropping to one knee this time. The man took a coward's advantage of the pause and was soon sprinting towards the stream for all he was worth. Rhia made to follow but after only a few paces she knew it would be no good. The man was already in the water and he would cross it and be among his own people before she could catch him up. She screamed after him;

'You bollockless piss-drinker!'

A few chuckles from nearby told her that her fellow Caderyn were appreciating her wit. She turned to see Barden and his wife Peira laughing with the others as they watched the Gorvic run. Peira was beautiful, she thought without envy, and the blue and red that covered her only accentuated her looks. *Not that she'll be out here to wear those colours for long now, not once her belly starts to swell.* War was no place for new mothers.

A quick glance around her showed that nearly all of their enemies had been slain or had crossed the ford and, after sweeping up her former opponent's sword, Rhia joined her comrades as they gathered in a half-circle to watch the last fights, leaving space beside the stream so that the fled Gorvicae could watch too. Her belted tunic was splattered with mud and blood and she paused to wipe the gore from her axe and knife. She was disgusted to find that her newly-won sword was completely clean, but she supposed that at least it meant that no Caderyn had been struck by such a coward. *I should probably give this a name now that it's mine,* she thought. *Doubtless it'll see better service with me than it did with that craven bastard!*

There were only four foes left who'd neither fallen nor run, all of them with the limewashed hair of the Gorvicae Gadarim. One man had already been dealt a wound that left his right leg a red mess, and he now sat on the edge of the circle, a Caderyn warrior putting pressure on the gash. Another of them now stood in front of his two remaining comrades, and Rhia watched in awe as one of her own Gadarim stepped forth to meet his counterpart.

Like the Gorvicae's elite, the Caderyn Gadarim tattooed their battlemarks onto their bodies and painted over them for war but, unlike the Gorvic warriors, the Caderyn men left their long hair dark and bleached their moustaches and beards to shining white. The man currently taking the challenge, Madoc, had pulled his long beard into a single sharp spike, and was twirling his sword casually around his wrist as he moved forwards. Madoc was arguably the best swordsman of all the tribes and Rhia had no doubt that the Gorvic knew his reputation. The white-haired warrior showed no fear however and bellowed his name as he stepped up to face him.

7

'Face me and tremble; I am the Leaping Wolf!'

He pounded his chest with one fist and Rhia saw thick muscle shake under the impact. Madoc made the same gesture and then spread his arms wide.

'Face me and tremble; I am the Smiling Fox!'

His lip curled upwards and he moved towards the other man, his long sword held at the ready. The Gorvic called Leaping Wolf didn't wait for him and lived up to his name by springing at his adversary, his iron blade pointed forwards in a lunge towards his chest. Madoc swayed to his right and parried the sword down, leaving his left hand outstretched to slam the forearm into Leaping Wolf's face. The Gorvic saw it coming and pulled back just in time, swiping his blade low at Madoc's legs as he did. The Caderyn fighter hopped back out of range and then went forwards again, this time hacking down at the Gorvic's right shoulder. The man blocked the cut and shoved his palm into Madoc's chest, forcing him back. The two Gadarim paused for breath, their eyes locked.

Rhia was cheering herself hoarse for her champion, the nervous energy of the fighting still pulsing through her body. She screamed for the Smiling Fox to batter down the Leaping Wolf, to win the day for the Caderyn in a welter of bloody gore. She watched the finest warrior of her people and almost forgot that he'd seen forty winters of this world, more than twice how many she had seen. Right then she felt a stirring for him, as no doubt did every other woman there, as he moved forward and started hammering hard at his enemy once again.

The Gorvic managed to block and counter several times, and more than once it was only Madoc's inhuman speed that saved his head from being struck from his shoulders. Leaping Wolf was a strong man and clearly an exceptional fighter, swaying and cutting with immense skill and dexterity. But Madoc was the greatest swordsman that anyone could remember and it wasn't long before the Gorvic was forced onto the defensive. Rhia cheered and cheered again as Madoc swiped his attacks aside and swung blow after fearful blow at his fellow Gadarim, until something happened that was so fast that even Rhia's young eyes missed it. Later, she was told that Madoc had feinted a thrust and then twisted away, slicing the Gorvic's forearm and then whipping the blade back across his torso. All Rhia saw was Leaping Wolf dropping his sword in surprise and then a thin line of red appearing on his painted chest.

Madoc stepped back and his opponent dropped to one knee and the shouting from the Caderyn redoubled in volume, even as cries of dismay could be heard from the Gorvicae across the stream. Rhia looked forward keenly even as her own voice joined the others, eager to see if Leaping Wolf had been killed. The man kept his head down for a moment but then Rhia almost groaned in disappointment, for it seemed the cut was shallow and Madoc himself offered a hand to help him up. The Gorvic took it with a nod and heaved himself to his feet as Madoc spoke, loud enough for everyone to hear.

'Enough?'

Rhia wanted to scream out *no*, she wanted to call the Gorvicae back across that damnable stream and keep fighting until she'd killed her fill of them. She wanted Madoc to take the bastard's head, not take his bloody hand! All around her was silence as she was certain many others shared the same thoughts that she did. The air, which until moments ago had been full of the sounds of battle, was now eerily still and the tension was almost something physical that she could reach out and touch with her hands.

The man called Leaping Wolf bowed his head a little to the Caderyn who'd bested him.

'I am Gawan son of Dearg.'

Madoc returned the bow solemnly.

'I am Madoc son of Derfel.'

There was another pause, another moment of terrible silence as four hundred men and women stared at them, waiting for the next words to come from the Gorvic's mouth. He cast his eyes about the field and when he spoke his voice was clear and strong, even in his defeat. He gave a single nod.

'Enough.'

The field erupted in another round of cheers and even Rhia raised her voice as unexpected relief overrode her disappointment. Her eagerness to keep killing was dimmed to almost nothing as a wave of happiness and, more palpably, weariness washed over her. Her legs felt almost hollow and her shoulders ached horribly, and she realised she didn't really want to keep fighting after all. She wanted to sit, to drink, to sleep, to laugh with her friends and celebrate their victory.

Across the stream the Gorvicae marched sullenly away, their heads bowed, while Gawan son of Dearg and Madoc son of Derfel embraced each other like brothers, the other warriors cheering all around them. Tonight, the Gadarim of both sides would drink together at one fire, and then the Caderyn could go back to their farms and villages, and the land the Gorvicae had tried to steal would be securely theirs once more. Rhia looked down at her clean new sword and smiled at what looked like good craftsmanship. Within a few days she would be home again. And her father would surely be proud after his daughter's first taste of battle.

Chapter 1. Back Home

The ride back to Bryngarth was a quiet procession, mainly in sympathy to the pounding headaches suffered by most of the little war party. The village at Broken Stream had provided them all with roast mutton, fresh bread and a seemingly endless supply of thick-tasting beer, and every warrior had fought hard to outdo his neighbour in its consumption. Rhia kept her eyes shut as much as possible as she rode, certain that her pony, Neida, had somehow doubled in weight, or else she was deliberately stamping her hooves down on the track. Every impact with the ground sent unpleasant judders up to Rhia's skull and even hidden by the clouds, Belenos was uncomfortably bright.

She tried to remember how much she'd had to drink last night, but gave up as thinking about it just caused her head to ache more. She remembered there'd been a lot of singing; that much she was certain of. She remembered matching horns with Domnall near the end of the night, each one drinking until the ale was slurping down their chins to soak into their tunics. Rhia took a tentative whiff of her garment and the strength of the odour made her jerk her face away, a movement her head told her was not desirable at present.

Her eyes still squinting against the damnable light, she looked around at the surrounding countryside. Grass spread out in all directions in an ocean of green, and beyond the fields she saw the rolling hills that meant they were not far from home. No doubt once they reached Bryngarth her father would throw a proper feast for the returning warriors, along with the Gorvicae Gadarim they were bringing along, and she could look forward to another night of drinking and laughter. *And then another bloody morning like this one!*

Rhia decided she would take it easier next time. Her head felt ready to split open and her eyes felt like they were on fire. A breakfast of greasy sausages and fried bread had done a little to calm her roiling stomach but all the same, she was wary of every hiccup and belch as they made their lazy progress along the road.

She tried to look on the bright side of things, to take her mind off her sorry state if nothing else. The Caderyn had won a great victory against their neighbours and her father, the High Chieftain of the Caderyn, would be proud of her. When he'd first said that she'd be joining the war party sent to face the Gorvicae, Rhia had to admit she had been nervous. Though she'd practiced with her siblings, and even with Madoc a few times, she'd really not been sure of how well she could fight and had approached Broken Stream with her heart fluttering in her chest. But all it had taken was her first warcry, the first feeling of her axe thudding home in a man's torso, and that fear had shrunk down to a shadow of what it was. The thrill of battle had overcome her, just as Madoc had said it would, and for all that she was not fool enough to have abandoned fear completely, she also yearned for the opportunity to taste violence again, to test herself as a warrior of her people and bring greater pride and honour to her clan.

Up ahead of her she saw the lime-bleached hair of those Gorvicae Gadarim who were coming with them to Bryngarth. Gawan and the others had drunk with Madoc and the Caderyn Gadarim last night, as though they'd all been friends for years and not men who'd been trying to kill each other only that morning. It was all a part of what made them Gadarim she supposed, though Rhia confessed she found it hard to understand. Though the warrior elite might fight each other, and kill each other when their tribes fought, a certain respect and courtesy was always extended to another man who had made permanent his battlemarks. Madoc and Gawan had been moments away from sending one another's spirits to the Otherworld that day, yet by the time the night had fallen the two were drinking and joking like brothers. It was strange. The Gorvicae would almost certainly raid or steal from them again and yet for a brief time last night, they had ceased to be the enemy. *Perhaps for the Gadarim. To me they will always be the enemy. The enemy of my father and the enemy of my people, no matter how much damned lime they rub into their hair.*

Rhia stared at the back of Gawan's head for a while and wondered how it might feel to smash her new sword through his skull. She'd decided that Silverbite sounded like a fine name for it and it would be good for the blade to taste some Gorvic blood. But even hating was too much like hard work for her this morning, and she soon went back to keeping her eyes half-closed and fixed blankly on Neida's mane. Peira came trotting up beside her before long, her own mount's hooves sounding intolerably loud. The pretty new-wed smiled at her.

'Feeling as groggy as I am?'

Rhia tried for a smile but it seemed her friend would have to settle for a smirk.

'Worse. At least you have it in you to *pretend* to be cheerful.'

Peira smiled again.

'A good rutting, that's what you need to take the edge off these things.' Her eyes travelled over to Barden and the two exchanged a wink. 'A nice thick one in the night may not be a cure but I find that it definitely helps.'

Rhia couldn't help but smile.

'I thought you'd already missed your blood? Don't you have something already on its way?'

She'd tried to sound chiding but doubted if she succeeded. Peira leaned in a little closer.

13

'You and I might know that but Barden doesn't! You know how superstitious men are about bedding girls once they're carrying. I want to hold off telling him as long as I can.'

Rhia didn't really have an answer to that but fortunately Peira carried on.

'Anyway, you'll get to find these things out for yourself soon enough. When is it you and Bevan will kiss palms?'

Rhia shrugged her shoulders.

'If and when Father says so. I think he wanted me to get blooded first. I understand. I'd like a few more fights to my name before I actually become a *mother*, but I think Father wanted at least one done before we wed. Just in case I wound up with a child in me straight away.'

Peira nodded understandingly and then leaned in close again.

'You can tell me though; have you two already been together?'

Rhia shook her head, and regretted it straight away as her skull filled with more throbbing pain. To lie with a man before marrying happened often enough, but if a girl gave birth before she'd kissed palms then the child would not be blessed by the gods, and Rhia hated to think what her father would say if his first grandchild by her was a bastard.

'We've done some other things but that's all, neither one of us wants to take the risk.'

Peira grinned.

'And is it a good one?'

Rhia felt somewhat embarrassed to admit it but she had very little basis for comparison. Not that Peira was much better informed than she was.

'It's bigger than Ailin's, that's all I can really say.'

Her friend gave an exasperated look.

'I don't know why it is we let that man anywhere near us. Barden's is bigger as well.'

Rhia nodded, very slowly and carefully this time, and thought of pretty young Ailin. Through some method of charm she still didn't understand, the young man had convinced half the girls of Bryngarth to taste his seed at some point, despite most of them knowing his manhood was nothing to fuss about. Rhia remembered the feast day long ago when she'd been the one to go behind the barn and unlace the handsome boy's trews. She'd been very drunk at the time, as she suspected most of Ailin's girls had been, but all the same, her willingness had been baffling. *But then he is such a handsome boy, and there's just something that draws us to him, I suppose.*

She shrugged again and put it down to magic of some kind. His uncle was a druid after all and it could be he'd learned some trickery to lure the girls into doing it. Though whatever it was, his charm rarely lasted longer than one sampling. The moment Rhia had met Bevan all of Ailin's charms had fallen on deaf ears, and the exact same thing had happened when Peira had met Barden. *Perhaps the gods sent us boys like Ailin just to give us something to compare them to? So we'd know a decent man when we finally met one?*

She put it from her mind and tried not to think of Bevan. It would only make her frustrated, and both her home and her would-be-husband were still a fair way away. She turned to face Peira again.

'Have you spoken to Madlen yet about your child?'

She shook her head.

'Only to tell her I suspected. She said to wait another moon's turn to be sure I'm definitely *having* one. I'll get a blessing then and see what she has to say after that.'

Rhia nodded. The druids might be masters of ceremonies but it was the herbwives that girls went to when they found themselves with child. Madlen had delivered both Peira and Rhia, along with both of Rhia's brothers and all three of her sisters, though the last one had died only a year later. She had come along too early and that winter had been hard. Rhia didn't like to think about it.

'I'll have Father make an offering for it after you decide to tell everyone.'

Peira smiled gratefully.

'Thank you,' she gave another mischievous look to her husband, 'but let's keep things quiet for now. I want to make the most of Barden's ignorance.'

Rhia returned the smile and tried not to feel envious of her friend. She'd see Bevan before long and they could enjoy each other's bodies at least a little once they were alone. And before much longer they would kiss palms and move into a home of their own, and then every night they would enjoy each other as befit a husband and wife.

The smile stayed on Rhia's face as they plodded along their way, her pounding headache somewhat lessened by the promise of what was to come.

*

Depending on what story you believed, either Garth had been a giant who had lain down as he died to form the great hill at the heart of Caderyn territory, or Bryngarth was simply a word from the Ancient Tongue meaning 'broad hill'. Rhia was never quite sure which of those stories was true, but if it was the latter then while it might not have been the most imaginative of names, no-one could say it wasn't accurate. The bank and ditch around the summit enclosed a huge flat plain, with the great town of the Caderyn set squarely in the middle. Countless round houses breathed smoke from their chimneys, the yellow thatched roofs seeming to shine in the sunlight.

The longhall was hidden from view from where Rhia rode, but she knew that fires would be burning there too and that food and ale was being made ready for them.

The war party rode slowly towards the fort and passed more than one little village on their way. Men in checked trousers of a dozen bright hues and women in long skirts of red and blue came out from their houses to greet them, and Rhia had clasped wrists and exchanged smiles with what felt like a hundred people before she reached the base of the hill. She looked at some of the women who came to greet them and envied them what they were wearing. Rhia was still dressed in her stinking battle-gear and though she had nothing against the practical tunic and trews, the easy comfort of a clean dress would certainly be welcome.

They rode up to the first line of defences, the ditch around the vast hill with an earthen bank thrown up behind it. No men guarded the perimeter today but in times of trouble the surrounding clans could all be gathered up in the empty longhouses inside the fort, and the banks they now approached would be lined with warriors. The hill-fort was so large that unless the entire tribe decided to go there at once, the whole perimeter could never be fully manned, but then Rhia could not imagine any army large enough to surround Bryngarth's hill anyway. Besides, a small band of good men in a fort could defend against many times their number of attackers. That was what the bards and the Gadarim said anyway; such an emergency had not been known for generations. Since the time of Rhia's grandfather the Caderyn had been the dominant tribe for more than five days' ride in any direction, and neither the Gorvicae to the north or the Breiryn to the south had the power to challenge them in their own land.

The riders plodded along up towards to the flat top of the hill. A horse might not be able to move up the slopes that quickly, but their ponies were sure-footed and could make it easily at a walk. Rhia longed to leave the saddle and have a wash and a change of clothing. She hadn't minded her aching limbs when set beside her pounding headache but now that the agony of that had receded, and the prospect of another night's drinking was no longer quite so distasteful, her muscles and joints had taken over as her primary discomfort, and she hoped someone up at the longhall would be heating some water for them.

By the time they reached the summit her legs and rear were killing her, far more than they really should have done after only a few days of riding. But then Madoc had always said that nothing quite compared to the fatigue that came from battle, and the soreness all over Rhia's body bore testament to his wisdom. Trying to ignore the ache in her neck and shoulders, Rhia turned in the saddle to look back the way they'd come. From up here she could see an endless sea of green grass, ploughed fields, shining rivers and dozens of little towns. The land of the Caderyn stretched out all around and the beauty of her home was as breath-taking as always. The sky above was blue with barely a cloud to be seen, and Belenos' sunlight shone down in golden rays.

Rhia took in a deep breath of clear air and enjoyed the view for a while, and around her she saw other warriors do the same. All of them, she was sure, felt the same swelling of pride and love as they saw the beauty of their homeland, and wordless smiles were exchanged all around before they headed into the town.

They rode through the houses of the central dwelling-place of the Caderyn, yet more men and women coming out to cheer their victory. Rhia kept an eye out for Bevan among the crowds but she doubted if he'd be there. He was the son of a headman from the other side of the White Rush and he was probably still on the road. *He'll be there for the feast tonight though*, she thought. *Or he'd bloody well better be!*

*

Rhia resisted the urge to actually groan aloud as another jug of water was poured over her. She, Peira and Meghan were sitting with their knees drawn up in the big wooden tub in a back room of her father's house. It was a little cramped but the feeling of the water was magnificent, and Peira actually *did* moan as more liquid was poured over her back. Meghan sighed as she rubbed soap of yellowy sheep's-fat under her arms.

'I've needed this since the moment that Madoc called an end to the fighting. I've been stinking like a dog and aching like I've seen a hundred winters.'

Rhia nodded to her as Gwen, her younger sister, poured another jug over her tender shoulders. Though the girls were all fairly young, Rhia knew that she for one had felt much older on the ride. She looked at the many bruises that Meghan was sporting and was thankful that she herself was at least less *obviously* battered. Meghan, red-haired, long-legged, curvaceous and pretty, would normally have been the best-looking of the trio in the tub, but today her slender forearms were liberally smattered with blue and black, and one cheek was dominated by an ugly purple bruise. But it would heal, Rhia thought, and then Meghan would be the beautiful one again.

Both Rhia and Peira had been described as attractive by people before, but Meghan was something else and it was a minor miracle that no man had wed her yet. At least four young men of Bryngarth had tried to tempt her into accepting them, and only a moon ago two of them had come to blows over it. But Meghan had not chosen any of them, and rumour had it that she was infatuated with Dane, one of Rhia's brothers. Given that her father was no headman there was every chance that the High Chieftain would not approve, but Rhia hoped that she could talk the old man around. Dane would hardly say no to a girl like Meghan becoming his wife, and with her height they might finally have some tall children in the family!

Neither Carradan nor any of his offspring could be described as towering, and Rhia was nearly always the shortest girl in any group. Dane and Ewan weren't exactly diminutive, they were of good stocky build like their father, but there were plenty of women of the Caderyn who stood taller than they did. Gwen poured a jug over Peira and Rhia saw how her sister was standing tiptoe to reach over her. Even Olwyn, the eldest, would not have stood much taller.

Rhia reached for some soap and started rubbing it on her skin, washing away the days of sweat and grime that had built up on her.

'I know what you mean, Meg. I don't know which smelt worse by the end of it, me or the horses!'

Peira splashed her playfully.

'I was sleeping next to you last night and I can tell you; it was you!'

Rhia splashed her back before rubbing some more soap into her hands, and she slowly ran them through her long black hair. Gwen had combed out the tangles before they'd sat down in the tub but it still felt dry and dirty and, she massaged her scalp liberally as they chatted.

'If you fight harder, you sweat more,' she smiled, 'clearly *I* was fighting harder.'

This led to yet more splashes from the others and both Gwen and Erin, Meghan's sister, caught a fair amount of water as well. It was Peira who got the first objection in.

'Two of their men and three of their bitches between us, me and Meg got!'

20

Rhia smiled back through her splashing.

'I'd have got four men if that last one hadn't pissed himself and run.'

Meghan raised an eyebrow.

'He probably got a whiff of you and sprinted at the smell!'

Rhia switched her splashing aim from Peira to Meghan, and the three were laughing as they mock-fought when Rhia's father came into the room.

The High Chieftain of the Caderyn was heavily built, even if he wasn't tall, and his strength had been the stuff of legend in his youth. Now nearing fifty winters much of that strength was still there, though his belly had grown rounder recently and his brown beard had a streak of grey down the middle. As a young man he had been a part of the Gadarim, and spiralling tattoos covered his arms right down to the fingers, and his face showed a single blue star above one eye.

He was dressed in a fine tunic of red wool trimmed with black and his stomach was held in by a wide leather belt. He smiled at the group as he approached.

'Wasting good hot water on fighting each other, girls?'

Rhia smiled up at the old man.

'Just re-enacting the fighting at the stream, Father.'

Carradan nodded to Meghan's impressive chest.

'Had I known it would have been like this, I'd have come along!'

The girls smiled and Meghan stuck her tongue out at the chieftain.

'I'm surprised your heart hasn't given out at the sight!'

Rhia's father continued to smile. He'd known all the girls for years and none of them felt any real embarrassment. They all had to wash after all and he was a married man; it was nothing that he hadn't seen before.

'My heart always threatens to give out around you Meghan, perhaps you should keep your charms hidden around old men?'

The red-haired girl shook her head impatiently, though she failed to hide her smirk and did nothing at all to cover herself. The chieftain gave a bark of laughter.

'You really want me to collapse right here and now don't you?' he turned to look at Peira, 'and you are no less a culprit in that murder!'

Rhia's fellow brunette glanced down at herself before giving her chieftain a chiding look.

'These are for Barden to enjoy father, just you remember that.'

Peira wasn't Carradan's *actual* daughter of course, nor even an adopted one, but as a chieftain and an elder she called him so out of respect. The bearded man sighed as he sat down on the tub's edge.

'He's a fortunate man, Peira. Should you ever grow weary of him, you let me know.'

Both Peira and Rhia splashed their chief at once and Rhia spoke in mock indignation.

'Something tells me that Mother would have a thing or two to say about that?'

Carradan tilted his head in thought.

'That is true, and I *sleep* beside her as well. No offence girls, but it's not worth the risk of waking up one morning to find my manhood's been fed to the dogs.'

Meghan gave an exaggerated sigh of disappointment, first glancing down at herself and then raising one eyebrow with a smirk.

'Oh well, if you are sure it's not worth the risk?'

The chief smiled back. It was clear he was enjoying the view but equally clear that he had not been speaking seriously. He loved his wife dearly, and Meg and Peira were both long-term friends of Rhia and her sisters, which made the two practically family. Not close enough to family that he didn't *look* of course, but his words were all in jest, and they knew it.

'I'm afraid so. I am sure you can find some other man to make so fortunate.'

Meghan's playfulness almost faltered and she looked away for a moment, and Rhia tried to spare her any awkwardness.

'Meg has too many of them to choose from, Father. You should start telling people that only the best men can be candidates for her hand.'

Carradan looked at Meghan's long legs and gave a mock-wistful sigh.

'Only for the best men indeed...'

He was rewarded by another splash from the redhead. For all his manner, Rhia wondered what he'd say if Meghan ever actually *offered* to sleep with him. *Probably panic and stammer and then run to rant at her father for not bringing his daughter up properly!* The old man laughed and turned to face Rhia.

'Anyhow, the reason I came in here was for you, daughter. I'll want to hear all about your battling later on, but I thought you'd like to know that I have spoken to Reaghan and he agrees that the signs are ripe for you to wed. You still have your heart set on young Bevan?'

Rhia felt her spirits start to soar and nodded as a beam spread over her face. Ever since Bevan had asked for permission to marry her she'd been filled with a dread of her father or the druid refusing him. All her aches and pains seemed to vanish in an instant and she knew the bath alone could not take credit for it.

'I do, Father.'

The old man beamed back.

'Then it is settled. I will speak to him and to his father and all being well you two will kiss palms here at the next full moon.'

Rhia leaped to her feet, slipped a little, and had to lean hard on Gwen to stay upright. She practically tore the towel from her hands and quickly wrapped it around her before running to her father and throwing her arms around him. She knew that her hair would be dripping on his tunic but the old man didn't seem to mind and he squeezed his daughter back. Rhia felt his booming voice vibrating from his chest.

'I'm glad that you are happy, Rhianwyn.'

Rhia hugged him all the harder as she realised that she was. She was happier than she'd ever been in her life. She'd fought her first battle and fought it well, her friends and her sister were voicing their congratulations and waiting their turn to embrace her, and within ten short days she would be married to Bevan! And their life as husband and wife could begin at last.

Chapter 2. The Feast

The longhall of Bryngarth was filled to bursting point as the warriors who'd fought at Broken Stream were feasted to their hearts' content. The massive fire-pit at the hall's centre was on its second round of roasted meats, with three whole pigs turning slowly on their spits, and fresh barrels of beer were being rolled in from outside. The air was thick with smoke, though the smell coming from the pit was delicious. Rhia took another bite of the portion in her trencher, the apple sauce that drenched the meat dripping down onto the floor. Bragger, one of the many dogs wandering the hall for scraps, started licking happily at her hand and Rhia snuck him a piece of meat under the table. Beside her, her father tutted as he sipped his mead.

'That animal will grow fat, the way you spoil him.'

Rhia shrugged.

'You keep saying that of me and it hasn't happened yet.'

Carradan gave her flat stomach a pat before slapping his own growing paunch.

'Give it time my daughter and these things will catch up to you.'

Rhia tore off another strip with her teeth and spoke through a mouthful of pork.

'Then I should make the most of it while I can.'

The chieftain sighed and reached for the jug beside him. He refilled her horn to the top and smiled.

'I can't argue with that, I suppose.'

Rhia smiled back at him and washed down her pork with the drink, enjoying the sweet taste of honey in the ale. Even though Bevan had not yet arrived the evening was off to a fine start. Cael, the chief bard of Bryngarth, had already composed a ballad about their victory at Broken Stream and he and two of his juniors were singing sweetly to the room, accompanied by others on harp and pipe.

Along the benches scores of Caderyn were eating, drinking and laughing, and Rhia waved to where Peira and Barden sat together, the wife sitting comfortably on the lap of her smiling husband. Both waved back and Rhia took another sip of sweet mead.

Bragger was pawing at her leg and Rhia threw his next treat a little further away. Her red dress was clean, comfy and almost newly-made, and she had no desire for claw-marks on it, no matter how much she might love the greedy hound. Bragger dived for the meat and almost knocked Gwen from her seat beside her sister. She was looking pretty today in a blue and red dress and she wore a golden pin exactly like Rhia's on her shoulder, the whorls of the metalwork reminding her of battlemarks.

Her elder sister, Olwyn, was away at the village of her husband about to give birth to their third child. It worried Rhia only a little that Madlen wouldn't be there to deliver it, but Olwyn had assured her that the herbwife at Penafon was very good and besides, her mother and Ewan were with her. Hopefully the child would be born, and healthy, by the time of the full moon. It would be good to have Olla and her mother and brother there when she married. *Assuming my damned husband-to-be ever gets here!*

Rhia looked across to where the man who would perform that ceremony was sitting and talking to her father. Druid Reaghan, his greyish-white robe held in place by a silver pin, was a man both loved and feared by every man, woman and child of the Caderyn. He must have seen sixty winters if he'd seen one, and his hair and beard were both whiter than his robe. His face was long and was dominated by a beak-like nose, but for all his clothing and sombre features it was his eyes that told you who he really was. Those bright blue eyes that could be merry or stern, that could twinkle or could blaze, those eyes that spoke of a lifetime of study and wisdom and told anyone who saw

26

him that this man was a true druid; that he was learned and just and blessed by all the gods.

As a child Rhia, like every other child of the tribe, had been terrified when she had first encountered him. Now, though she still had a healthy fear of his powers, she felt relaxed around the old man who was a second father to them all. Right now he was chatting quietly with his chieftain, but on seeing Rhia looking at him he turned those bright blue eyes to her.

'Madoc tells me that you blooded yourself well at Broken Stream, child?'

Another man calling her that, perhaps with the exception of her father, would have received a glare and a reprimand for his cheek. But they were all Reaghan's children in a way, so Rhia didn't mind. She swallowed a mouthful of pork before speaking.

'I like to think so, father. I sent a couple of Gorvicae to the Otherworld, and some others will be smarting hard from meeting me!'

Carradan smiled from the great chair that was set between the high table's two benches.

'I've no doubt of it, daughter. You have the blood in you.'

Reaghan's voice was slow and sombre as he nodded.

'The Caderyn raise warriors well I think, and I am glad that you have proved yourself as a fighter. Though always it saddens me to know of Lurian killing Lurian.'

Rhia shrugged.

'It was the Gorvicae who started it, stealing fields of good grain from Merwyn's clan.'

The druid nodded again, though he continued with his point.

'True, the Gorvicae needed to be shown we are not weak, but men and women who might have given greatly to the land now lie dead for the sake of a few stolen fields.'

27

Carradan chipped in, and like Rhia he kept his voice respectful even as he argued.

'They would have contributed nothing to the Caderyn, father. I do not enjoy inflicting death but their contribution would have been only to our neighbours.'

The druid gave him a look of mild reproach through his thick white brows.

'Come now Carradan, you know full well that we trade with the Gorvicae, and the Breiryn and the others, far more than we do fight with them. Those who died at Broken Stream might have helped in that trade. Besides which, all of the world is nourished by our lives and our devotions, from Caderyn and Gorvicae and all Lurians alike.'

Rhia had a limited understanding of the gods but she knew the druids' preachings that the earth and air was filled with swirling currents of their magic, and that the magic was created by life and the worship and works of decent men. How much she was convinced by that she wasn't sure, but she knew Reaghan to be unquestionably the wisest man she knew, and so was happy to take his word for it about most things. All the same, the Caderyn should surely come first?

'Even if the Gorvicae *do* enrich the world and help us trade, they tried to steal from us. That is reason enough for killing a few, I think.'

The druid made a tiny gesture.

'I do not say they should not be stopped, nor that the Caderyn should not defend their home and lands. But that does not make the dealing of death a pleasant thing. Madoc is the First Man of our Gadarim and even he takes no delight in killing men.'

Rhia had to agree with him on that, even if to her the Gorvicae were not worth fretting over. She'd seen Madoc as he helped his wounded enemy to his feet and the relief on his face that they no longer had to fight. That Madoc was no coward was as true as grass was green, yet he had not wanted to keep on battling any longer than he had to. Reaghan seemed to sense her conflict and gave one of his rare smiles.

'My words are true, child, but it makes me no less proud of how you and the others defended our tribe.' He nodded towards the chieftain. 'Besides, from what your father and I have discussed, you may need to make the most of battling whilst you are still suited to it.'

Rhia smiled at that, thinking of Bevan and what would happen in a matter of days. It was true she regretted the notion of less fighting to be done; she was fairly sure she had a good aptitude for axe and blade and she now had Silverbite to carry with her. All girls were expected to know warfare before they married, but once they had children most women stopped going to war if they could avoid it. Once she'd borne Bevan's sons, and *that* thought made her belly flutter a little, she would have to wait until they were old enough to manage on their own before she could disappear off to battles again. But the Gorvicae could be relied upon to cause mischief somewhere else before long, and she would probably get the chance to fight them again before she fell pregnant. *Though I fully intend to try damned hard at the process. If bloody Bevan ever turns up!*

She beamed at the druid.

'True, father. I am glad that the omens for it were good.'

Reaghan nodded sagely.

'I was examining the clouds and birds only yesterday, child. I saw two doves flying from opposite directions, one from the east, one from the west, to land on the same bough of the Great Oak. They stayed apart for a while but soon the one flew close to the other, even as a wisp of cloud drifted over the tree and then away to the north.

After this the two doves flew off together beyond my sight.'

He gave her another small smile.

'It means that you are right to be married, and though a trial will face you, you shall both emerge from it together, and stronger.'

The mention of a trial made Rhia nervous for a moment, but she soon abandoned her worries and embraced the joy inside her. The gods were happy for her to marry Bevan, who was coming here to her from the west even as she was returning from the east. Or northeast anyway. Even if some hardship or another awaited them later on, the fact that they were meant to be together, and that they would come through it still as one, made her forget all her worry about what that hardship might be. *It's Bevan. Whatever it is, we will weather it.*

She inhaled to speak her thanks but Carradan got there first.

'I was so pleased when I heard of this, father.' He looked over to his youngest. 'Only Gwendolyn left to go now.'

Rhia's sister smiled uncertainly. She was barely thirteen and had yet to have a woman's blood, but it was never too soon for fathers to start speculating about potential husbands. Gwen had confided in her once that she thought Ailin was very handsome but Rhia had nipped *that* thought very much in the bud. Earlier that evening Peira had nodded to her and flicked her eyes across the hall and, sure enough, pretty Ailin had been sneaking outside with a girl from Glynderyn who Rhia knew by sight but not by name. For all that she could hardly judge, the thought of her baby sister on her knees before that man was enough to make Rhia want to punch something. Hard. Ideally Ailin. So she'd told a half-truth that he was already involved with someone, she didn't mention it was with anyone he could get his hands on, and had discouraged her affections as much as possible.

Gwen spoke in a voice so quiet that the older men had to lean forward to hear her.

'I'm in no rush to find someone, Father. And Rhia's waited long enough to be with Bevan.'

The High Chieftain smiled gently.

'I am teasing, my love. I keep my eyes open for you but I am in no hurry to lose you either.'

Reaghan agreed, his voice sage and kindly at the same time.

'I look forward to standing there when you kiss palms Gwendolyn, but your father's house will be the dimmer once you are gone from it. You are right, there is no hurry for you at all.'

Gwen smiled at the old man and Carradan nodded his thanks to him. Rhia was trying to think of something nice to say to them when the great doors at the far end of the longhall banged open, and the man who would be her husband made his appearance at long last. Her heartbeat quickened. Though leaner of build than her brothers Bevan was both tall and strong, his jaw firm and his eyes deep. His hair was light, bordering between brown and blonde, though his trimmed beard was a slightly darker hue. He had tied his long hair into a single plait and was dressed in a fine tunic of sky blue, a well-made grey cloak held at his shoulder with a golden pin.

Rhia knew that she really ought to wait for him to approach but her joy at the sight of him, coupled with the knowledge that their wedding could go ahead, was too much to make her care for the formalities. *And Father has never really been that bothered with them anyhow.* So, though she suspected the reaction might draw some disapproval from the druid, Rhia sprang to her feet, leaped clean over the table, and after a very short sprint slammed into her future husband so hard that he was almost knocked into a beer barrel. His arms wrapped around her and hers wrapped around him and she felt him squeeze so tight she thought her ribs were about to cave in. Laughter and whistles came from the people on the benches but Rhia didn't care, and when Bevan planted a kiss on her mouth, her heart felt like it might burst. Her love smiled down at her.

'I've missed you!'

Rhia beamed back and kissed him again before replying.

'I've missed you too!'

They held each other tight for another moment before Rhia turned to where the bards were playing. Fortunately Cael had finished his latest song and so she didn't feel too rude when she shouted to one of his disciples.

'Ieuan, play us a dance!'

The younger bard smiled, nodded, and began *Rusty Rabbit Run* on his pipe, soon accompanied by the others on harp and horn. Rhia and Bevan began to dance in the open space between the tables, and Peira and Barden came and joined them. Before long a dozen other couples were leaping and hopping to the music and Rhia, the warrior who'd been killing Gorvicae only days ago, felt light-headed and girlish as Bevan pulled her to him and kissed her whenever there was pause enough in the dance. When the music was over she wrapped her arms around him and squeezed him again before leading him by the hand towards the high table and her father.

Carradan and Reaghan nodded greetings to the headman's son and Bevan bowed his head to both of them.

'Lord Carradan, Druid Reaghan, it is an honour to be here.'

The chieftain smiled at the younger man.

'We both of us know you well enough to be merely called "father", my boy. My daughter has seen fit to ignore the formalities, I see no reason to pretend to heed them now.'

Even the druid did not seem too disapproving and Bevan smiled back at his elders.

'Then I am glad to be here, fathers.'

Carradan nodded to him.

'And you are welcome here, my son. Be seated.'

He indicated the bench to his left where Rhia had been sitting and the two of them moved there to sit down. She felt Bevan give her thigh a little squeeze as he shuffled in and the gesture was not unnoticed by her father.

'If you two can keep your hands to yourselves for a while, I have good news for you, young Bevan.'

Bevan, for all his passion for Rhia, was a well-mannered man and had the grace to look contrite.

'I'm sorry about that father, it's just we've just been apart for a while.'

The old man laughed and poured a horn of mead for his new guest.

'My boy when Myrna and I were your age they had to pry us apart every time we saw each other,' he grinned boyishly and leaned a little closer to his guest, 'she was well worth the trouble though!'

Rhia threw a chicken bone at him.

'We don't want to hear about what you and Mother got up to before you got old!'

The chieftain chuckled at her as the bone bounced from his chest.

'Old? You listen out in the night when my wife gets home and you'll see how old we are!'

Rhia twisted her face up in distaste that was only marginally exaggerated. In a way she supposed it was sweet that her parents still loved each other, but that sort of activity was not something she wanted to picture, and certainly not something she enjoyed hearing about. More than once she'd run out for an involuntary night-time stroll when she'd heard noises coming from the next room, and the image them doing what she did with Bevan... she shuddered.

Fortunately Reaghan stepped in to change the subject before her father could torment her any further.

'Was there not the matter of your news to him, Carradan?'

The chief nodded his head to the druid before turning to Bevan.

'Yes indeed. You will be glad to know, Bevan, that Rhianwyn has fought well in her first trial of combat and Reaghan has agreed that the omens are favourable. If you both still wish to marry, you may kiss palms when Leu is next at her full.'

Bevan's already smiling face split into a grin and he hugged Rhia close to him as he replied.

'Thank you, father!'

His voice was full of joy and he turned on the bench to face Rhia. His dark eyes met her blue ones and Rhia felt her heart start to quicken again as he spoke, his voice serious.

'Will you still have me, Rhianwyn?'

It was odd to hear him use her whole name like that and she felt a bubbling inside her chest. She wanted to say something witty to him but she couldn't find it in her and settled for a simple answer.

'Of course I will.'

His smile came back with a vengeance, transforming a face that was already handsome into something beautiful. Rhia found she couldn't keep the grin from her own face and she grabbed him in another hug and kissed him hard on the mouth. Her father's voice came from along the table.

'Well, I'm glad that's settled, though you can both calm down at least for now.'

There was no real disapproval in the old man's voice but they obeyed anyway, settling for simply holding hands under the table. Rhia was thinking she should probably say thank you again to her father, but before she got the chance she saw that Madoc had left his place on the other side of the druid and had walked around to stand in front of his chieftain. The lime in his beard had been mostly washed away and the hair was back to its natural brown. Like Bevan he was built on the tall and lean side, and he was dressed in his best tunic of red and blue wool, the favoured colours of the Caderyn, though his trousers were patterned with green and brown squares. He spoke loudly to both Carradan and the druid, his voice carrying across the hall to drown out all the others.

'My lord, I would present to you my fellow Gadarim of the Gorvicae tribe.'

Rhia's father nodded, his expression turned to something more serious. He may not have minded impropriety between his daughter and her betrothed, but rituals like these were an important tradition, and his words now were slow and heavy.

'Let them come forward.'

Madoc bowed his head low and reached an arm out to beckon to the Gorvicae Gadarim who'd been seated at the table below him. The first man to step up was the one Rhia had seen suffering from a leg wound at Broken Stream, and he moved across the floor with the aid of a short staff. Despite his frail appearance his posture and voice were both strong, and he looked up at the chieftain with pride in his face.

'I am Bradan son of Conyn. The Howling Hound.'

The second and third men of the Gorvicae stood from their benches and followed his lead. All of them had

35

washed the white lime from their hair, though patches and clumps still showed here and there, and all wore their green cloaks over one shoulder. As Gadarim they'd been permitted to keep their swords at their sides, and to anyone watching they must have seemed more as guests than as prisoners. Which to an extent, Rhia thought, they were.

The next two introduced themselves as Duran, the Flying Hawk, and Nuallan, the Running Boar. Carradan greeted them each with a cordial nod before the last one stood up and approached him; Gawan, the man Madoc had fought last at Broken Stream. He was a heavy-set man and, like the others, his arms and neck were decorated with blue tattoos of battlemarks. In Gawan's case they spread all the way up his arms and neck, curling over his ears to reach down to his heavy brow. Now the lime was no longer there to colour and stiffen it, his hair had returned to an almost pitch black and fell down to his shoulders in messy curls. His beard was the same colour and was both thick and bristly, and the grey eyes that looked up at them were cunning and keen.

'I am Gawan son of Dearg. The Leaping Wolf.'

Madoc stood beside him and addressed the chieftain.

'Gawan is the First Man of the Gorvicae Gadarim. He fought bravely and with skill at Broken Stream.'

Rhia wondered at Madoc actually *praising* the man who'd doubtless killed several of his comrades, but she said nothing. The Gadarim's traditions were their own.

Her father nodded his head to the man.

'Then I am honoured to meet you, Gawan son of Dearg.'

The Leaping Wolf bowed his head.

'As I am to meet you, and to meet Madoc son of Derfel.'

The Gorvic slowly drew his iron sword out of its scabbard and the three other men copied the movement.

'We are defeated by him, and so by your people. We offer you our swords.'

It was all a part of the rituals of the warrior elite and Rhia was unsurprised when her father shook his head.

'You are Gadarim. You may give your swords to Annwn when you go to meet the gods, where no man shall have need of one again.'

Gawan nodded and sheathed his sword.

'Then accept this instead, great chief.'

He reached his hand to the golden bracelets adorning his left arm and selected two of the thickest and heaviest-looking of them. He took them off and handed them to Madoc, the other Gorvicae following his example. Madoc took them with a nod and then held them towards his chieftain.

'Instead I present you with these trophies of war, my chief.'

Carradan raised an open hand and spoke to his First Man.

'The victory was yours, Madoc. The spoils are also yours.'

Madoc bowed his head again and placed the bracelets on his own arm. He would probably give one or two of them to Owain or Arthfael, or whichever of the Caderyn's Gadarim had fought best in his eyes. Rhia looked on in silence as her father spoke again.

'Tomorrow you shall return to your own people with honour. Tonight we drink together to the spirits of the fallen,' he placed his palm over his heart, 'may they cross the bridge unharmed.'

All around the room people echoed both words and gesture, and Rhia and Bevan touched hands to their chests and added their voices to the blessing.

'May they cross unharmed.'

It was said that the Bridge of Souls, the passage to the Otherworld, spanned a chasm that teemed with evil spirits and the ghosts of wicked men. The more a man had pleased the gods, so the druids taught, the wider the bridge would appear for them. The worse his deeds in life, the narrower it would become and the risk of being grabbed or of toppling into the Pit was that much higher. There they would spend hundreds of years clambering over and around the other unfortunates until they finally reached the bridge to try again.

The solemn moment was broken by Carradan smiling at the warriors and raising his cup in front of him.

'Drink with us for tonight, we are friends!'

The room filled with cheers and Gawan approached the high table to clasp wrists with the chieftain. Carradan's genuine smile stayed in place as they did so, though Rhia frowned in disapproval. They ought to have taken their damned swords and sent them all bootless home, not taken their hands and given them food and drink. Neither her father nor the Gorvicae's First Man seemed to notice her though, and the chieftain was first one to speak.

'A fine name you have, Leaping Wolf, how came you by it?'

The other man shrugged.

'Years ago one of our headman's dogs was killed when a wolf attacked it during a hunt. I was too young and stupid to do anything else so I ran at it, jumped from a fallen log and crushed its skull with my axe. The chief seemed impressed by it and our First Man gave me my name then and there.'

The gigantic Arthfael passed him a drink and the Gorvic sipped his mead before continuing.

'No need to ask the same of you of course, Lord Carradan. Every Lurian must know the saga of Charging Bull.'

The chieftain brushed off the compliment.

'It was a long time ago, my friend. Snoring Bull might be more accurate these days!'

Rhia felt a little indignant as the Gorvicae laughed at the comment and felt someone ought to speak up for her father.

'This Charging Bull could still flatten a Leaping Wolf, I'm sure.'

Her father seemed a little embarrassed by that but Gawan spoke before he could say anything.

'Perhaps so. I prefer his chances of it to those of a dancing kitten.'

He smirked and Rhia felt anger well up inside her but again, the Gorvic spoke before anyone could comment, this time addressing Carradan again.

'Though this daughter of yours did fight well at Broken Stream. Perhaps Dancing Wildcat would suit her better?'

Her father laughed, clearly interpreting it as an apology for the first remark, but Rhia saw through the smug bastard straight away. He was still mocking her. She knew well how very few women ever became Gadarim and that she would never bear a warrior name, no matter what might be suited to her. Gawan was making fun of her for enjoying her meeting with Bevan and was reminding her that no matter how high the station of her father or husband, she would never enjoy the merited prestige of a Gadarim like him.

She wanted to hurl back an insult but with her father and Reaghan there she didn't want to cause a scene, and she would not let this damned outsider spoil her night, not now that Bevan was here and her dreams were about to come true. But that didn't mean she was going to stay quiet either.

'This wildcat will just have to settle for carving up a few more of our enemies and then breeding some sons to do the same thing in a few years. We women can do both, you see.'

There were good-natured sounds of approval from nearby tables, most people probably thinking it was all being said in fun. They didn't see the real dislike behind her words. Gawan answered in exactly the same tone; feigned jest hiding the real mockery.

'We men can make sons readily enough as well, and our part is done quicker than the women's. It means we can get back to the fighting that much sooner.'

A few of the drunker warriors pounded cups on the table in approval but Rhia got her answer in quickly.

'I know that *some* men are very fast when it comes to that,' she stroked Bevan's arm, 'others like to take their time over things.'

She'd never fully given herself to Bevan and likely everyone who was Caderyn would know that, but there was every chance that this Gorvic didn't and besides, a chorus of whoops and laughs, mostly from females, told her that her remarks had been approved of. Bevan himself was smiling quietly amidst all this, content to let Rhia fight her own fight. She loved him for that.

The Gorvic scowled a little but kept his voice light for the benefit of the hall.

'Perhaps you think us too fast because we're too eager to find our next girl? Perhaps we should do as the Seiriae do and take as many wives as we want? Not that I'd relish the noise of them!'

There were more approving noises, this time mostly from men, though Rhia enjoyed the sight of several women, Peira amongst them, giving their husbands disapproving glares or slaps when they voiced their agreement. She decided to keep going. She was enjoying this.

'I doubt if many of them make much noise when *you* are on top of them. I suspect they're just bored waiting for the Wolf to leap off them!'

Her father guffawed and most of the hall joined him in laughter. Gawan seemed ready to retort with something unpleasant but then seemed to remember he was surrounded by Rhia's family and friends, and thought better of it. He settled instead for a grumbling answer.

'That is a treat you will never get to experience, Wildcat.'

Rhia didn't hesitate.

'Thank the gods!'

More laughter. Another subtly hidden glare came from the First Man of the Gorvicae, though this time he did not answer but simply trudged away towards his bench. Carradan spoke to him before he got far, a smile still on his face.

'If you and my daughter can keep from knifing each other, you are welcome to pull a stool up to our table, my friend.'

He was only being polite to his captive-guest but Rhia was far from sure she'd be able to keep quiet if he sat too near. Fortunately he placed a stool close to her father and began talking to him and Madoc, firmly ignoring her, which was fine as far as she was concerned.

Their topic of conversation seemed to revolve around the fact that the Gaians were apparently interfering with the Bearnicans. The mighty empire had conquered half of the continent already but had ceased its expansion a generation ago. The Carrocks of the Canwyns had stopped their advances cold, and an untrusting peace now existed between the Carrocks, the foreigners and the various Lurian tribes.

But apparently they were now leasing out their trained warriors to the Rydicae, one of the neighbouring tribes to the Bearnicans, in exchange for a share of the tribute the Rydicae would extract when they beat the Bearnicans. The northern part of the Canwyn Mountains fell within Bearnican territory and parts of it were known to be rich in silver. Both the Rydicae and the Gaians stood to make a small fortune if the Bearnican warriors were beaten.

Her father and the Gadarim went on about this for some time and on another night, Rhia would have been interested. Warfare was to be her trade until she fell pregnant after all, and it was wise to know what was going on in the world. But Bevan was here now. The man who would be her husband was sitting beside her and holding her hand. She knew him to be strong, he'd fought off Dariniae raiders on the coast more than once, but his touch was gentle on her hand and Rhia forgot she was a warrior and remembered she was a woman. She forgot all about Gawan, Gorvicae and Gaians and squeezed his hand back and leaned her head down onto his shoulder. Tonight he was all that mattered. Tonight, Rhianwyn was in love.

Chapter 3. Udergosc

The night was falling fast and still there were bodies left to be carted to the pits. The battle, or the organised butchery it had become, was long over now and the only task left was to clean up the mess. Severus watched with minimal interest as tribesmen were sorted from decent Gaian soldiers, the former to be simply piled up in the next field ready for the fires, the latter to be buried with a little more dignity outside the town. What the subjugated Basiae would normally do with their dead, he neither knew nor particularly cared.

General Severus Lepidus, commander of the glorious Tenth Legion, looked back at the retaken town of Udergosc, or Oderosc, or Undergosc, or whatever ridiculous name the Basiae had for it, and pitied the poor fool who would be given governorship of the place. Not only was it an ugly slag-heap that these savages actually saw fit to call a *city*, but he would doubtless be universally hated by the locals for what the legions had done today. The rebellion of Tangerix had been short-lived but the tribes surrounding Udergosc had been his greatest supporters, and no doubt they would like to cause trouble for their reinstated Gaian rulers. *Not that they'll dare to rise up in arms against us again. Not after today.*

Severus turned in the saddle and surveyed the darkening field again, the sights warring with the smells for which was the uglier reminder of the day's carnage. The smell of blood and offal assaulted his nostrils savagely, and he found the choking scent of smoke a welcome relief from the awful stench. Around him, the bodies of eight hundred Gaians and almost twelve thousand Basiae littered the field before Udergosc's hill. Legionaries were wandering everywhere among the mass of corpses, ostensibly to find living Gaians and finish off wounded tribesmen, but

43

Severus knew perfectly well that most of them were there for loot.

Basiae, and barbarians in general, seemed fond of displaying their wealth upon their bodies, and all around him torques, rings and bracelets were being pulled and cut from corpses. He saw one soldier hack away at a warrior's hand to free his rings, only to find with a start that the man was not wholly dead. His stomach was opened to show the grey ropes of his intestines and his painted face and torso were a red mess of blood, but apparently the Basian was not quite finished yet. He grunted and punched the soldier in the ear, knocking him sideways into the mud. Two other legionaries saw the commotion and within seconds they were stabbing at the wounded man, the Basian not even having enough left in him to cry out. In a few moments it was all over and the first man's rescuers began jeering at him for his clumsiness.

Severus heard screams coming from somewhere to his left, and he turned his head away from the looters to see another group of soldiers dragging a figure into the trees. It was hard to tell with their kind but he was reasonably sure it was a Basian woman. The barbarians allowed their wives and daughters to fight alongside them as equals, and Severus suspected that this one at least would soon be regretting that custom. The women of the town were not exactly *safe* from rape but there was a degree of organisation going on up there at least, and whichever general or politician fancied the idea of ruling the place would probably try to keep such things to a minimum. Not so out here.

A lock of grey-and-brown hair fell over his eyes and Severus was reminded of his dire need of a haircut. The Tenth and Fourteenth had been force-marching for nine days and civilised things like proper haircare and shaving had become secondary priorities. He irritably pushed the strands back over his ear. Severus had been a soldier all his life. He'd made a name for himself expanding the Gaian Empire into Avidia and now approaching his thirtieth year with the legions, he knew full well that victories were more important than personal decorum. But nonetheless, he was beginning to look positively bestial. *I probably smell like one of them too by now.* He tried not to think about how long it had been since his last proper bath and instead thought back on today's battle. If it could be called that.

Having seen the Gaian reinforcements approaching their precious stronghold, the Basiae had decided for some idiotic reason that they were better served taking the fight out to the enemy rather than risking protracted siege. Thirty thousand of their warriors from half-a-dozen tribes had charged towards the legions like a wave of ragged fury, only to break themselves on the solid lines of the Tenth and Fourteenth Legions.

Severus held back a smile; it wouldn't do to show emotion in front of the men. Despite the brutal downsizing that the legions had suffered since the civil war, between them the two units had fielded some four thousand men, to add to the same numbers from the First and Second Legions already engaged. Eight thousand trained soldiers, along with a few auxiliaries, against thirty thousand Basiae who'd come howling for their blood. *And the fools did not stand a chance.* Their solid wall of shields, discipline and cold iron had once again proved completely unbeatable, and the legionaries had seen off the tribesmen in a textbook display of Gaian efficiency.

The general almost smirked as he remembered how the Basiae had come at them without even a basic knowledge of tactics. The disunited rabble had spread out to allow room to swing their weapons, and had predictably been crushed by the tight formations of professional Gaian soldiers, stabbing out with short blades and cutting down warriors by the score. The tribesmen had held for longer than Severus had expected but eventually they'd broken and fled as they were always going to, having caused no real damage to the legion shieldwalls. The incredible elite of the Gaian soldiery had then charged into the chaos as they ran, and barbarians had been mown down like grass before a scythe.

And just like that Tangerix's rebellion was over, his city taken, his armies scattered or destroyed, and the man himself stripped and beaten in front of the other prisoners, ready to be taken back to Gaivia in chains. And Lepidus and the Tenth Legion would now doubtless be sent to fight whatever new uprising threatened the Emperor's peace. *The joy and curse of being the best is that one is always in demand.*

Severus looked over to where the camps were being erected, upwind of the stench and smoke of the battle. He saw the eagle standards of the four legions that had fought today, each with its own badge sewn onto the banner beneath it. The banner of the Fourteenth, who'd marched with him, showed a prowling black panther above the words; 'Vulco's Claws'. Their hosts, the First and Second, were camped just to the south of them, one banner showing a black bird, the other a capricorn, with 'Unto Death' and 'Blood and Iron' written under them in gold letters.

But it was his own mighty legion, the glorious Tenth, that drew the eye of the general across the field. He saw the golden eagle of their standard placed exactly in the centre of their straight lines of white tents. The banner of his legion showed a single roaring lion, above the apt words that made up the Tenth's motto; 'Justly Proud'. Severus ignored the foul smell of war and death around him, and focused on the standard of the greatest legion in the

Empire. Soon he and his men would be on the march again, he thought, and who knew what fresh glories might await them on the horizon?

Chapter 4. The Next Day

Rhia's head didn't pound nearly so much the next morning as it had after that night at Broken Stream, but then she hadn't drunk *quite* as much this time. *And at least I don't have three days of bloody riding ahead of me.*

She rolled slowly from the straw mattress and reached for the little jug she kept nearby. There was a clean twig next to it, and she used it and the water to rub the sticky feeling from her teeth before she heaved herself up and stretched. Across the room Gwen was snoring quietly and Rhia was tempted to see if she could sneak Bevan in while she was still asleep. For the sake of avoiding awkwardness, and because she couldn't be sure they could limit themselves to their usual antics, she'd not invited her future husband to come to bed with her last night, but she knew that he'd be sleeping in another room of her father's longhouse, along with the other important guests. She could maybe creep in there and wake him, then bring him back here for a little quiet fun before her sister or the others woke up?

But she thought better of it. She knew how embarrassed she would feel to wake up and find Gwen or Olwyn doing things like that, so she fought down her urges and got dressed sullenly. She put on the same red dress she'd worn the night before, it smelt a little bit of smoke but it was otherwise clean enough, and she could fetch herself something cleaner after breakfast. She slipped on her soft shoes and made her way out of the little room she and her sisters had always shared. It had been odd indeed when Olla had left this place for her husband's house, and it would be odder still when Rhia left. She'd be excited to be living with Bevan of course, but it would be strange to leave this place behind. And Gwen would be so lonely.

She pushed the sad thoughts away and trudged towards the main hall. Apparently she was not the only early riser today, and Madoc was sat chatting with the other Gadarim over fried bread and honey. Rhia smiled as sweetly as she could at Noden, the cook, and he passed her some breakfast of her own on some of yesterday's flat bread, the butter and honey dripping onto her fingers. She had no real desire to sit with Gawan and the other Gorvicae but it would look rude to go and sit on her own and besides, she could always chat with Madoc or Arthfael instead. Rhia lowered herself with a sigh onto the bench beside the big man, and Madoc passed her a cup of water to go with her breakfast. On another morning she and the others might have drunk milk but Rhia had learned early on that milk after heavy drinking was not a good idea, and she nodded her thanks without a word.

Fortunately it seemed that Gawan was just as keen to avoid her as she was to avoid him, though he gave her a brief glare as she sat down. She locked eyes with him for a moment until Madoc continued the conversation they'd been having, and then Gawan proceeded to ignore her.

'My father always said they weren't good fighters on their own, but that they cluster together, hiding behind their shields and stabbing out with short swords.'

One of the Gorvicae, Nuallan, Rhia thought, shrugged his shoulders.

'It hardly matters. They don't dare to come past the Canwyns and leave the Carrocks to their rear. They gave them all a pounding last time they tried.'

Madoc gestured with his cup as he answered.

'True, but then the Carrocks keep to their mountains. So long as they're left alone the little folk don't care what happens to others.'

Arthfael grinned at him.

'Better not let a Carrock hear you call them that, my friend! They're fierce enough bastards and they don't take insults well.'

Madoc shrugged indifferently.

'I've not even *seen* one in twenty winters, I'm not too worried about them overhearing.' He sipped his drink. 'Besides, they *are* little.'

Rhia couldn't resist jumping in.

'So am I.'

Arthfael, the biggest man in Bryngarth, if not of all the Caderyn, laughed.

'True, and I'd not cross Rhianwyn given the choice. She's a vicious one when she's a mind to be!'

There was happy laughter among the Gadarim, though Gawan stayed sullenly silent. Rhia was trying to think of something funny to say when she heard steps behind her and Bevan walked in. There were more chuckles from the warriors and Madoc nudged her in the ribs.

'You try not to knock him over this time!'

Rhia stuck her tongue out at him and waited for Bevan to pick up some bread of his own, then she gave Madoc a shove and the First Man smiled and shuffled along the bench to make space. Bevan sank down between them and gave Rhia a quick kiss. It was a lovely feeling and she wished again that she could sneak him off into her room, but it was too late for that now. Bevan nodded to the others at the table but held on to Rhia's hand as he talked.

'So apart from sore heads, what are we talking about?'

The Gadarim smiled at him, apart from Gawan of course, and gave a quick summary of their discussion. Bevan contributed only a little, his own experience of war was limited to fending off Dariniae raiders. Their chieftain, the infamous Ierryn the Black, periodically sent ships to harry the coastline of Caderyn and Gorvic alike, and the need to keep him contained was one of the few things both tribes agreed upon. Bevan mopped up some honey with his bread.

'I'd heard somewhere that Gaian leaders fight among themselves all the time, and murder one another to gain power.'

Most of the warriors at the table seemed shocked by this but Madoc and Gawan looked unsurprised. It was the Caderyn man who spoke.

'I remember hearing the same thing. Even their elders will plot and scheme against one another, and the whole people lose their direction.'

Rhia shook her head. What fools! Chieftains were sometimes challenged for leadership but it was rare indeed and was usually settled by combat, or by a meeting of the druids and headmen. To fight among your own people was to make them weak, surely the Gaians could understand that? But then from what she'd heard, there was very little that they understood.

The men spoke on for a while about what dreadful fools the Gaians were, the general superiority of the Lurian race, and the usual shared complaints about Ierryn and his raiders. After allowing him a few derogatory comments of his own, Rhia decided to lead Bevan away from the table. They might not be able to get any real privacy, but at least they could take a walk together. Bevan didn't argue and the two left the hall hand in hand, leaving behind them a dozen smiling faces and a single dark frown.

Outside, Belenos was still hugging the eastern horizon and his heat had yet to make itself felt. Rhia didn't quite shiver but Bevan knew her well by now, and within moments had whipped his cloak off and wrapped it around her slender shoulders. Bevan was no giant but still the cloak felt massive on her, and Rhia felt very small and snug as they walked through the town together. All around them people were getting their day underway, opening up shop-fronts, setting out wares, stoking their fires and sweeping out floors. The few town-folk who worked on farms would already have left for the fields and the people they saw in the streets were mostly tradesmen. Blacksmiths, goldsmiths, tanners and cooks, tailors, cobblers, bakers and butchers were all hard at work to begin another day of earning their keep.

Rhia and Bevan walked arm in arm, sharing smiles and words of greeting with those they passed. Her betrothed spoke to her in that soothing voice she'd missed so much.

'So, how did you like your first taste of combat?'

She knew that he would have been worried for her, but equally knew that he'd wanted her to do well.

'I wasn't hurt beyond the odd lump and bruise, not like poor Meghan, and I took down my share of Gorvicae, I think.'

Bevan nodded slowly as they walked.

'Yes, but how did it *feel*?'

With some people she might have hidden it, but she had no secrets from Bevan.

'I was scared at first. On the way there I thought of all the bad things that could happen to me in battle, and when the morning came I was actually shaking with the fear of it. Peira and me struggled to get our battlemarks on straight.'

Bevan said nothing but simply nodded again, gesturing for her to continue.

'When the horn sounded I felt a chill all the way down my back and I felt like I wanted to be sick. But then…then we cried out to Taran and we ran into them and I…I sort of forgot it and I got caught up in the thrill of everything. It wasn't like the fear was gone, it was just that it didn't matter as much as the fighting. Does that make sense?'

Bevan nodded again.

'I remember when I first saw one of Ierryn's blackwood ships approaching the coast. I was so scared of getting killed or crippled or something if I went down there to fight them. But once we got going, with Garan and Derwen beside me, I just got lost in the thrill of it like you did. I'd still be afraid when I saw a sword come at my head but mostly I was thinking about cutting at my enemies. I didn't want to stop.'

He turned his head to look off into the distance, his expression suddenly confused.

'The strange thing was that, after it was all over, the fear seemed to come back again. Even though we'd won and I knew I was safe, my hands started shaking and my stomach was twisting inside of me.'

Rhia bobbed her head, glad that she'd not been the only one. In between the battle ending and the drinking starting she'd felt the same cold feeling that she'd had before the fighting, and had sat down on a rock for what felt like an age, completely unable to stand up. She shared the memory with her husband-to-be.

'Something like that happened to me as well. It doesn't make sense.'

Bevan shrugged, his concern dissipating.

'Maybe we had enough fear to last through the fighting but just put it off somehow until we were done?'

Rhia smiled at the notion but Bevan spoke again before she could pass comment.

'I suppose this fight puts you ahead of me in experience, being a proper battle and all?'

He spoke without any sign of envy and Rhia wondered if he might be right. She had only seen combat in one engagement to his three, but each of his had been against minor raids of a boat or two of raiders, never facing much more than maybe twoscore of his enemies at a time. Broken Stream had been a proper battle, arranged by challenge and with hundreds of warriors lined up on either side. *Does one proper battle beat three little ones?* She wasn't really sure but decided to tease him anyway.

'I suppose it does. But don't worry – as a war veteran I will be sure to keep you safe once we are married!'

Bevan smiled and put an arm around her waist.

'You mean you'll stay up all night to guard me while I sleep?'

Rhia's lips turned up in mischief.

'I'll be keeping *you* up as well, my love. You'll get no more sleep once I'm your wife.'

He grinned back and reached a hand around to squeeze her buttock.

'I cannot wait.'

She gave him a playful slap.

'I just might make you.'

The grin widened.

'Don't pretend you can wait for it either.'

Rhia knew perfectly well that she couldn't, and the instant they were past the last buildings of Bryngarth Town she dropped a hand to his trews and started stroking. He was hard within moments and they increased their pace towards the open area beyond the houses. There were plenty of old buildings here set aside to house the clans in times of emergency, and Rhia wondered that she hadn't thought of this earlier on. But then Bevan was so rarely at Bryngarth and the last time he'd been here, Gwen had been away and their room had been available. Without that option, Rhia had resigned herself to their having to sneak into the big barn or out into the woods to take their pleasure. But this, this was much better.

They sped up their walking even more and the moment there was a wall between them and any watchers, Bevan had a hand down the front of her dress and was massaging away, kissing her hard on the mouth as he did. The feel of his skin on hers was incredible and Rhia fumbled frantically with the ties of his trousers as Bevan pulled the dress over her head. As soon as she was naked in front of him he put his mouth to her breast and she gasped aloud, her breathing quickening even further as she finally removed his trews and grasped his manhood in her hand. Bevan groaned as she started stroking again and Rhia grinned as she whispered in his ear.

'You were right. I couldn't wait.'

*

Rhia was reasonably sure that she'd been missed by now, and equally sure that her father and sister had a good idea what she'd been up to, but she didn't care. It had felt so good to touch, and be touched, and she walked back through the town with a smile on her face, hand in hand with her beloved. They approached the longhouse, Rhia expecting to find her father glaring half-heartedly at them. Instead she was greeted by a scene that somehow made her even happier than she already was.

Olwyn was standing outside their father's house along with their mother and Ewan, their older brother. Both Olwyn and Myrna, their mother, had the exact same blue eyes as Rhia and Gwen, though Olwyn and Ewan shared their father's brown hair, with only Rhia inheriting the black locks of their mother. Myrna was looking as she always did; fair-faced and still slender for her age and with barely a sliver of grey in her hair.

Eogan, Olwyn's husband, was standing there as well and in his arms was a tiny bundle, with Gwen cooing softly over it. Rhia hurried over to them and wrapped up her sister in a hug.

'Olla!'

'Rhia!'

They beamed at each other and Rhia shared a quick hug with their mother as she spoke again.

'Boy or girl?'

Olla smiled happily.

'A girl this time, and as beautiful as any of them.'

Eogan traded grips with Bevan and smiled.

'What did you expect?'

Bevan grinned at him.

'You never know, there's always the danger that they'll take after your looks and not your wife's.'

Eogan gave him a friendly shove.

'Let's hope when you and Rhia get some of your own that they favour their mother as well. I hate to think of being lumbered with a blonde-headed nephew.'

Bevan embraced Olwyn just as Eogan hugged Rhia one-handed.

'Better that than inflicting a face like yours on an innocent child.'

Their bantering would probably have continued if Rhia's mother hadn't stepped in, her voice tired if not really cross.

'I do hate to interrupt you boys but some of us have just travelled a very long way, and with a six-day-old child to take care of as well.'

Olla nodded along. She was clearly happy to see them but there were dark rings under her eyes and her skin was looking pale. Rhia cuffed Bevan's arm.

'You'll have to forgive him. He's far too full of joy because he's finally allowed to marry me.'

For all their weariness the women's faces positively glowed and a fresh round of hugs for the couple followed. Eogan passed the child over to Gwen and put his arms around each of them in turn.

'Congratulations to you both. Who'd have thought a straw-head like you could entangle so nice a girl?'

Bevan was about to retort but Rhia smacked him on the arm again before he could.

'You two can chatter away later on, the hardworking womenfolk want to get inside for a seat and a drink.'

Olla and Myrna smiled at her and they started walking into the longhouse. The elder sister motioned to Gwen.

'Give Rhia a hold of her, she'll need to get a feel for this.'

Gwen seemed a little reluctant to let the child go but she passed the girl over without a fuss. Rhia had to manhandle the bundle a little to get her leaning comfortably in her arms. As usual with babies she was shocked by how tiny they were, and by how much she wanted to keep hold of them once she held them. Rhia wanted children of course, but she'd never been one of those girls that cooed over every baby they came across, or played with ragdolls that were made to look like newborns. When Rhia had been a child her favourite toys had been stick-swords and she'd spent more time batting about with her brothers than she had mooning over children.

But holding her new niece, just as she had done with Olla's other children, she felt such an urge to be a mother herself, to have children of her own with Bevan beside her, the proud father. The infant had the same blue eyes as her mother and Rhia gently placed a finger into the bundle, and felt a little surge of joy as a tiny hand grabbed hold of it. She smiled.

'She is beautiful.'

Olla nodded.

'Her name is to be Siriol.'

Rhia was going to ask what had made them choose the name when her happiness was marred a little by the appearance of the Gadarim, both Caderyn and Gorvicae. Madoc, Gawan and the others were coming out of the longhouse just as they were about to go in, and while most of the warriors smiled pleasantly at the women and babe, the Gorvic leader kept up the scowl he'd had on earlier. Arthfael, the big Caderyn man, spoke first.

'Marna's blessings; a fine-looking child.'

The other men all nodded and both Caderyn and Gorvicae offered the goddess' blessing to the newborn. All save Gawan, of course. Madoc may have noted the impoliteness but he didn't mention it, instead addressing the Gorvicae with friendly words.

'Well, go in peace my friends, and may it be some time before we have to meet again.'

The four men all clasped wrists with him, and then with Arthfael and Owain, and set off towards the path that led down the hill. Three of them favoured the women and the child with nods or smiles. One of them did not, and simply glared at Rhia for a heartbeat before he trudged off on his way. Rhia wanted very much to say something cutting, or simply hand Siriol over to Bevan and knock the bastard's teeth out right there. But a glance at her new niece was enough to take the anger away, and she walked back into the longhouse without a thought for her beaten enemies. She felt Bevan come in beside her and she smiled down at the child. *Blessings on you, little Siriol, welcome to the family. Maybe soon you'll have a cousin you can play with!*

*

The ten days between getting home and Leu finally growing full had seemed to take forever, and yet somehow they were gone in an instant. Rhia had yearned for the day to finally arrive but had been so busy that the time had flown right past her. On the first day she'd been busy getting Olla settled in and taking turns with Gwen and the other girls to look after the new baby. The second and third days had been spent sending messengers here there and everywhere to gather together hers and Bevan's friends and relatives, not to mention all the clan headmen and their families who would want to be there to see their chieftain's daughter married.

She'd spent a long and boring afternoon with Reaghan discussing what would be expected of them, as if they'd never seen a wedding before, and she and Bevan had placed their hands on an oak and sworn to him and to two other druids that neither one of them was already wed. Bevan had then set to getting their new house up and ready for them, while Rhia's mother and sisters had roped her into helping them as they either made new or repaired old wedding robes for them to wear, and she was certain she'd have gone blind if she'd spent another day staring at white cloth. Rhia had then spent most of a day with Cael the bard as he took her through the steps of what would be her first dance with Bevan as his wife. It wasn't as if she couldn't dance well enough already, but the Wedding Dance was one you only learned when you were about to kiss palms, and the footwork had been complex and tricky. Though at least she'd had Bevan with her for that.

For at least three days she'd not seen her betrothed at all. Two of them he'd spent riding to escort guests from Gwaelmyn and on the third Rhia had been down at the long lake from dawn until dusk. She, Peira and Meghan had gone down to the water, with Gwen tagging along with them, and had gone through Mehine's cleansing rituals that maidens were expected to complete before they married. Rhia couldn't really say she felt any closer to the gods but she knew that she'd been on the verge of freezing by the time they were done.

Now, with the ceremony only hours away, there was still endless work to be done and though Bevan was there with them there was no time for intimacy. Rhia was standing just outside of Bryngarth Town, helping Gwen and Peira as they set up posts adorned with ribbons to mark the route down to the Great Oak. The ones they were putting in the ground were little more than sticks with strips of blue and red cloth tied to them, but at the entrance to the town six mighty pillars were being erected, each one hung with half a dozen coloured trails.

Arthfael was heaving one of them into position using only his massive strength and he winked at Meghan playfully as he dropped the post into its hole. The redhead smiled back but that was all. Her bruises had all gone and her hair was shining in the sunlight, and Rhia had lost count of how many boys and men had gawped at her so far. Including Dane, though he'd been too shy to say anything.

Dane was a year younger than Rhia, and a moon older than Meghan, and had ever been a nervous one around girls. He was pleasant enough to look at, even if he shared the family's traditional lack of height, but Rhia suspected he would sooner face a bloody sword than approach a pretty girl. He'd wanted desperately to come with them when they'd gone to fight at Broken Stream but his ankle had still been weak from when he'd come off his horse at the gallop, and even now he favoured his right leg quite heavily. *I'll need to make sure he has a staff or something for the wedding procession.*

Rhia was in danger of yet again becoming distracted by the preparations in her head, but she shook herself out of it and beckoned to Bevan, who was merrily wasting time throwing a stick he was meant to be planting and letting Bragger chase after it and bring it back to him. Rhia was extremely tempted to whack him with one of the poles from her own pile but his smile melted away at least *most* of her annoyance, and she settled for a brief kick to his shin. It wasn't hard, and it only made her betrothed grin even further, and Rhia couldn't help but kiss him before she spoke.

'Go and get Dane to talk to Meghan. He's been eyeing her all day and she likes him too, he needs to get on with it.'

Bevan looked over at them and shrugged.

'Most men have been eyeing her, it doesn't mean anything.'

Rhia scowled at him.

'Does that include you?'

Bevan was good at saving himself from things like this and Rhia was unsurprised by his answer.

'I look at pretty girls, the same as any other man, but there's only one girl in the world I want to marry.'

He wrapped an arm around her and Rhia was infuriated at how she couldn't stay angry with this man, even if she tried. It didn't stop her from shoving him off her of course but Bevan kept his smile up as he staggered.

'Just keep your eyes on me, my love, and get Dane talking to Meghan.'

Bevan cocked his head.

'How do I go and get them talking if I have to look at you the whole time?'

He made an exaggerated performance of walking away while still staring at her, and Rhia bit back a smile and made to throw one of her sticks.

'Don't make me come over there!'

Her husband-to-be winked.

'Promises, promises.'

Rhia turned away before he could see her smiling and went back to planting her sticks. Some subtle side-glancing showed her Bevan practically dragging Dane to where Meghan was struggling with an armful of flowers, and she saw her brother's face turn red as he offered his help. Meghan accepted graciously and Bevan left the two of them to it, and Rhia hoped that Dane would just relax and talk to her. Who knew, if they could talk the old man

61

into accepting it, they might have another wedding to prepare for before long? Rhia snapped herself out of it. They hadn't even had a proper conversation yet. *And you have your own wedding to be preparing.*

Morning gave way to afternoon and both Rhia and Peira cursed the hill as they clambered back up it, having prepared the whole route down to the Ring of Stones. Rhia was certain the slope hadn't been this steep coming down it, and she had all this walk to look forward to again before long. Peira was looking red in the face and Rhia reluctantly decided to stop for a few moments. The two girls sank down onto the grass-covered bank and Rhia felt the aching in her legs subside a little.

'You shouldn't be doing so much, you know. Not if you're carrying.'

Peira shrugged.

'It will all be done soon and then I can get some rest. And Barden can cook his own damned supper tomorrow!'

Rhia smiled at her. She remembered a few moons ago when Peira and Barden had walked along this route. There hadn't been *quite* this much fuss and bother made about it, Rhia being the chieftain's daughter and all, but it had been a lovely day nonetheless. Peira was a pretty girl anyhow, even if none of them were as stared after as Meghan was, but she'd looked beautiful that day, and Rhia put it down to the sheer happiness she'd been feeling. *If being happy is what makes you beautiful, I must be radiant today!*

She fought back a grin but failed and Peira smiled back at her.

'Don't even pretend to hide it around me, Rhia.'

Rhia felt a little embarrassed.

'I'm not trying to hide it, I just...I didn't want you to think I was showing off or anything.'

'Because your wedding is about to happen and mine has been and gone?'

Peira finished off the thought for her. Rhia nodded, a little ashamed of herself. Her friend put a hand on hers.

'Rhia, my wedding was a wonderful day, it really was, and I was as happy as I've ever been when I kissed palms with my Barden,' she gave the hand a pat, 'but it's the life *afterwards* that matters. We all complain about our husbands but the truth is I'm happier now than I was then. I know it's not been long but I know in my heart that we'll keep getting happier as we go on.'

Peira smiled sweetly at her. The two were almost exactly the same age but Peira somehow managed to sound so much older than she was. Rhia felt her awkwardness start to ebb away.

'I hope the same is true for me and Bevan.'

Her friend nodded.

'You'll disagree about things and argue, but the two of you love each other, just like Barden and I love each other. As long as you keep that foremost in your thoughts, everything else will just wash over you.'

Rhia remembered the omen that they would face hardship and overcome it and she smiled back at her friend.

'If we ever get back up this damned hill to start it all!'

She heaved herself to her feet and offered a hand to Peira, who took it and pulled herself up to stand beside her. They eyed the remaining slope with a sigh.

'Come on then, but I'm not racing you!'

Belenos was slowly dipping towards the west when the two reached the flat top of Bryngarth. The town was now heaving with people and Rhia saw that her Aunt Eleri and Uncle Aeron had arrived, along with her cousins Pryder and Merrion, and their wives Eluned and Kira. Cerridwen, their sister, was chatting with her own husband, Natan, who was looking as red-faced as Rhia felt after her climb up the hill. They must not have been there long.

She was about to approach them when she saw another face and instantly turned to look somewhere else. People from various clans all over Caderyn territory had come to see the daughter of Carradan married, but all the same, she'd forgotten that Delyn would almost certainly be coming. Delyn was the third son of the headman of Durolwg and had been a keen suitor for her a year ago. He wasn't a bad sort, not really, but Rhia had felt no interest in him, not even a spark that might turn into real affection one day, and her father had turned down his proposal at her request. They'd not really spoken to one another since then, and Rhia gave a quick thank-you to the gods that he seemed not to have noticed her arrival, and plodded on into one of the houses where other guests were being squeezed in.

Rhia looked around to see if Bevan was anywhere in sight but if he was then he was lost in the crowds. She did note with a smile that Dane and Meghan were still together, though the redhead seemed to be doing most of the talking. Peira smiled at her conspiratorially and Rhia drove a knuckle into her palm for good fortune. The two started to walk towards the now overfull town, but Rhia paused for a moment to look out, over the buildings and towards the distant west. The sky was still pure blue but Belenos was riding ever closer to the horizon. She'd better get inside and get changed into her robes. Soon the sun would be setting in earnest. And her wedding would be finally underway.

Chapter 5. The Wedding

The procession began at the longhall of her father. The High Chieftain was wearing his finest clothes with a bright red cloak about his shoulders and his massive winged helmet on his head. With him stood Madoc and the Gadarim of the tribe, the only men there to carry swords in their belts. All Caderyn were warriors, and always would be, but today was a day for the gods and for love, and only those fully pledged to the Gods of War would bear arms for the procession and rituals.

Next to Carradan stood Myrna, looking beautiful in a long dress of dark blue, a matching cloak held at her shoulder with a shining golden pin. Beside her stood Ewan and Dane, dressed in all their finery, while Olwyn, as a married woman, stood behind them with Eogan, tiny Siriol sleeping quietly in her arms. Gwen, as a maiden, was standing at the front with Meghan, and both wore dresses and long robes of pure white, as Rhia did. On their heads were intricate garlands of colourful wildflowers, while the bride-to-be wore a crown of white-berried mistletoe.

Rhia choked down a grin as she looked to the man who would soon be her husband. He looked handsomer than ever in his own white robes and headdress, his long bright hair braided just as carefully as hers had been, and tied in place with the same coloured ribbons of red and blue. He gave her a little smile and raised his eyebrows, clearly nervous, but equally clearly happy that the time had come. She knew how he felt.

Rhia's hands were shaking just as they had at Broken Stream and though the evening air was cool, her palms were sweating. She resisted the temptation to wipe them on the robe and tried to stop clenching and unclenching her fists. Her heart was pounding as though she'd just sprinted down Bryngarth's hill and back up again, and it felt as though it might suddenly decide to leap into her throat. It was strange; she knew so well that this was everything she wanted, yet still she felt something very akin to fear, and could already feel the sweat beneath the robe and dress she wore. She shuffled her feet nervously, hating the waiting more than anything else, and it seemed like forever before her father gave the word and called for the procession to begin.

Belenos was sinking fast into the west, but it was still light enough to see the brightness of the ribbons on the poles that marked their way, and Rhia was certain that the hill had never looked so beautiful. She wanted to hold hands with Bevan, walking beside her, but she knew they weren't supposed to now until after the rituals were done. It was difficult, her heart was still fluttering and she knew his would be as well, but sometimes the formalities were there for a reason and so she went back to balling her fists whenever she thought no-one was watching.

At the very front of the party walked two of the younger druids, Meryn and Bael, the rings on their staffs jingling with every step. Behind them went Gwen and Meghan with baskets of coloured flowers that they flung on the ground before the couple, and Rhia wondered how many baskets they would get through before they were done.

Though there were rumblings of quiet conversation from the following crowd, at the front all was silent but for the chanting of the druids, the jangling of the rings, and the sound of their feet brushing the grass. It was all wonderful, but also eerie as they made their way down the hill, and the light became redder and redder. Rhia thought back to Olwyn's wedding, more similar to this than to Peira's smaller affair, and tried to remember how she'd felt back then. It was before she and Bevan had begun courting each other and Rhia's principle memory had been of boredom. She'd been happy for her sister of course, but with no prospect of her own marriage and with a very long time before the drinking could start, Rhia remembered how she'd been almost sulky on this walk, just counting the steps until the ceremony was done.

This walk could not have been more different. They reached the base of the hill and followed the ribbons towards the woods and not once in that long walk did boredom ever threaten her. Her mind was a whirl of hopes and of dreads. It was finally here, the day she had dreamed of, but what if something went wrong? What if she tripped and fell flat on her face in front of everyone she knew, and had to carry on the ceremony in a dress and robe drenched in mud? It was hardly damp underfoot but who knew what might happen? What if they reached the Ring of Stones and Reaghan was not there, or he was and had decided that the omens were no good after all, and that the wedding would have to be cancelled? What if Bevan, her own dear Bevan, was seduced by some girl in the crowd or enchanted by a dryad or sylph of the forest, and abandoned her just as they kissed palms? What if…what if…what if…?

Every few steps she shook away these feelings and the warm joy of the moment would fill her again as she looked at her soon-to-be husband, tall and handsome in the red light, or at her sister and Meghan as they smiled at her and threw more flowers. Then the dread would hit her again and her legs would feel weak and hollow. And then the joy would come again and the urge to run and shout and dance would be almost irresistible. Rhia almost laughed out loud at herself. If there was one thing this long walk was not, it was boring.

It seemed as if no time had passed at all before they were pausing at the edge of the trees and Rhia and Bevan slipped the shoes from their feet. The witnesses might be permitted footwear in the forests but for tonight the couple would go barefoot as the druids did, and Rhia gripped onto the cold grass with her toes as they waited. Then Meryn and Bael lifted their hands as one and the huge wedding party surged forward into the trees, and Rhia felt her chest begin to flutter yet again. She looked at Bevan and his smile was like golden sunlight and though her heart still raced wildly, her nerves seemed to dissipate. A little.

The light was fading fast as they entered the woods and by the time they had followed the poles and ribbons to the glade, Belenos had fully gone and Leu was on the rise. The sky went slowly from red to darkest blue and soon the soft grey light of the full moon was all that bathed the sacred Ring of Stones.

The stones themselves, each one greater than the height of a man, were set upright in a perfect circle, each one the exact same distance from the next. On the faces of the stones the ancient druids had carved markings and runes that Rhia could not even begin to understand, and in the centre of the ring, stretching up into the night, was the Great Oak. Before the Great Oak, stood Reaghan. The elder druid was dressed in his usual white robes, though tonight they seemed to shine in the silver light, as did the rings on his staff and the sickle at his belt. The old man beckoned them forward with a gnarled hand and Rhia and Bevan stepped inside the sacred circle.

The moment she crossed the boundary of the first moonlit stone, the whole world seemed to change in an instant. The Ring of Stones had been a sacred site for the Caderyn, and indeed the Luriae in general, for longer than even the druids could remember. For generations these stones had seen the sacrifices of goats and bulls, the last funeral rites of long-dead men and, like tonight, the sacred rituals between two lovers to declare themselves one before the gods. The moment these particular lovers had stepped within its boundary, a wind that seemed to come out of nowhere began gusting around them, not so strong as to howl and buckle them, but with something in it that spoke of power which Rhia could not explain. She approached the Great Oak in silence, the only sound the rushing of the leaves in the sudden wind. Her heart was hammering and her sweating hand was desperate to catch hold of Bevan's, so close beside her. She took a deep breath and closed her eyes for a moment. *Soon.*

The two betrothed stood before their eldest holy man and Reaghan, in his deep and mellow voice, began to sing above the whistling of the strange new wind. He called out in the ancient language now only spoken between the druids and the gods, and Rhia almost shivered as he spoke. The wind seemed to increase in its intensity, though none of the onlookers she saw seemed bothered by it. Their clothing seemed barely to stir. To Rhia, it felt as if every spirit of the sacred woodland was dancing around them in the moonlight, as if all the gods of the ancient forest were now with them as witnesses, and she felt a sudden fear at the thought of them watching her. She thought of all the stories she'd heard of the awesome power of the gods, and the legends of the Sidhe who communed with them and had disappeared into the forests long ago. The idea that such beings were in the air around her right now, looking down at her and *through* her made her skin feel oddly cold and her legs feel weak and empty.

Rhia had been to this place many times in her life, but never had she stood within the circle beneath Leu at her full. She'd always known that the holy place was home to all kinds of gods and spirits, but never until now had she truly felt their presence. Rhia had known the gods only through the warmth of Belenos' light on her face, or the love of Marna and Camelas in the eyes of her parents or, more recently, the wild thrill of Taran and Mabonac as she battled with her enemies. This was an altogether different experience of the gods and Rhia was as intrigued as she was scared. It felt as if Mehine, the Lady of the Woods, was galloping around her, invisible yet unmistakable, and that dryads, naiads, sylphs and sprites were running and dancing in her wake. She risked a sideways glance at Bevan as the druid went on with his chanting and the sight of his face, looking pale and beautiful in the grey light of the moon, somehow made her feel safe and warm, even when surrounded by the phantoms of the forest.

Reaghan was still singing his chants and blessings over them and the wind seemed to accentuate his words more than it drowned them. He built to a crescendo of music and volume and the spirits around them seemed to harmonise with him, then he suddenly struck his oaken staff on the ground, and all sound around them died but for the jangling of its rings. The silence was eerie and Rhia wished that she could say something, or do something, but she knew she was to be silent until she was spoken to. She could be wilful enough when she had a mind to be, but the gods were watching tonight, and she had no wish to displease them.

The voice of the druid came forth again, this time in a language that Rhia could understand.

'The forest has gathered to watch you, my children. You have come here before the gods and before the eyes of the Caderyn, to become one with one another in this most holy place?'

Rhia's heart began to calm a little, though she still felt it hammering in her chest. This part at least, she was more or less prepared for. Both she and Bevan answered as one.

'We have.'

The white-haired man continued.

'You have come here to receive the blessings of Camelas, God of Fathers, and of Marna, Goddess of Mothers, that you may bear strong children and raise them in love?'

Rhia kept her eyes on the druid and again, the betrothed spoke in unison.

'We have.'

Reaghan nodded solemnly.

'You have come here to set aside that which you both were and to embrace what you shall become, to no longer be as two souls but as one soul, one heart, one flesh, forevermore?'

Once more, Rhia and Bevan spoke with a single voice.

'We have.'

The druid nodded his head again and stepped back, gesturing with his hands spread wide apart. Rhia bowed a little and took a step towards the Great Oak before sinking down to her knees, Bevan doing the same thing next to her. Once again she wished that she could hold on to his hand but she resisted the urge and kept her eyes fixed ahead of her. Bael entered the circle and pulled a tiny piece of bark from the great tree before crushing it in a silver bowl with a pestle. As he did this, Meryn took a cup that Rhia knew he had filled from the little stream that trickled nearby, and slowly poured water onto the dirt before the oak. Bael then sank down to his haunches, muttering prayers all the while, and put a handful of the newly-soaked earth into the bowl with the tree-bark.

Once this was done, the silver bowl was handed to the elder of the holy men and Reaghan approached the kneeling couple in silence, his bare feet making no noise on the grass. The winds around them were still whirling with their strange, intangible power but now the earth seemed to join them in their dance. Rhia was sure she felt the ground throb for a moment, like the beating of some great creature's heart, and she wondered if she were actually hearing Mabonac, the giant green dragon who lived beneath the world. It was a frightening feeling, but she shook herself clear of it. Now was not the time for fear.

The old druid placed his thumb into the silver bowl and leaned down from his great height to mark each of their foreheads with the dirt and oak-bark. The mud was cold on her skin and Rhia worried for a moment that it would run down into her eyes, but the wet earth stayed in place and she kept her breathing steady. It was almost time.

Slowly, Reaghan took out the tiny sickle from his belt, a golden blade no longer than Rhia's thumb. Rhia could almost feel the anticipation on the wind, from both the dancing spirits and her watching family. Without a word, she and Bevan each presented a hand, the man showing his right, the woman her left. Reaghan's stunning blue eyes showed nothing but reverence as he made quick, shallow cuts to each of their hands, on the fleshy pads just below the thumb. The cut stung but Rhia knew better than to flinch, and in the corner of her eye she saw that Bevan was still as stone. Dearest Bevan. Her Bevan.

She stayed as motionless as she could as Reaghan poured a little of the dark liquid into each of their hands, and her heart almost stopped as he gestured once more and the great moment of the ceremony began; the Kissing of Palms. The pulsing earth and dancing winds seemed to urge them on and as one, Rhia and Bevan placed their cut hands together, and spoke with a single voice as blood and sacred earth was shared.

'I vow before all who look upon me here that I shall be ever true, ever loyal, ever loving. May our gods and kin bless us, may our children grow strong, may the love we have last all our lives, and beyond this life into the next.'

Rhia remembered hearing her sister and Eogan saying those words, and Peira and Barden, Arthfael and Cerys and she knew not how many others over the years. She had dreamed of speaking these words with Bevan a hundred hundred times but now that it was here, the words were so strange she found she barely got them out. Suddenly, for the first time, she really understood what they meant to both of them, and she fought to bite back tears as joy threatened to overwhelm her.

Reaghan stood above them and smiled a fatherly smile.

'Bevan son of Bradan, Rhianwyn daughter of Carradan, you are one with the land and one with the gods.' He raised his arms high and then brought his hands together. 'Be one with each other.'

Rhia leaned forward just as Bevan did the same and as they kissed, the winds gave one last howl, the earth's heart gave one last beat, and the glade around them erupted in five hundred cheering voices. The feel of Bevan's lips on hers was both soft and hard at once and Rhia only stopped the kiss because she couldn't hold back the grin, all her tension and fear vanished in a heartbeat. She laughed aloud even as the tears came to her eyes and she saw Bevan, her husband, laughing as well. The man she loved grabbed her and wrapped his arms around her and the cheers seemed to redouble as their witnesses urged them on.

Reluctant as they were to part, Rhia sensed the presence of Reaghan above them. They each took a hand of his and the old man heaved them up. He was stronger than he looked, and he wrapped their cut hands in white linen before warmly embracing them both.

'Congratulations, my children. The gods bless you both.'

Rhia hugged him back with enthusiasm before turning to look around her. The winds had died down to a bare whisper through the trees, drowned out by cheering voices from smiling faces. Bevan took her hand, his own face grinning uncontrollably, and led her from the circle to their families. To their one family. Bevan's father Bradan and Felmid his mother were the first ones to reach them in the rush to embrace the new-weds. Then came Rhia's own parents, both glowing with pride and joy, followed by Ewan, Olwyn, Gwen and Rhia's two new sisters, Aerona and Elisedd. Rhia hugged them all tightly, the smile plastered to her face, and the line of friends and kin went ever on: Peira and Barden, Madoc, Arthfael, Owain and all the Gadarim, then Kira and Natan, Merrion and Cerridwen, Pryder and Eluned, and then Meghan and Dane, her brother still sneaking shy looks at the redhead.

Behind Aeron and Eleri came Delyn and for a heartbeat Rhia worried that some awkwardness might ensue, but her former would-be suitor simply smiled at them both, and his words to them were spoken without malice.

'I cannot say I am not envious, but the gods have blessed you tonight. I shall try to be happy for you both.'

Bevan embraced the other man before Delyn turned to Rhia. The hug was brief and she was spared from having to think of what to say by her new husband's kindly voice.

'I am grateful, my friend. I hope that you find such happiness of your own before long.'

Rhia nodded and placed a hand on his shoulder.

'And you will, I am sure.'

Delyn smiled again at them both, doing his best to sound convinced by his own words.

'I am sure.'

And with a final nod he slipped away to disappear into the crowds. Rhia felt a tiny moment of sympathy for the man, but then that sadness was swept away by another wave of joy. She looked up at pale Leu overhead and wanted to thank the gods aloud for the wonder of tonight, but the druids had gotten there ahead of her. Meryn and Bael had started to sing out blessings in both the old tongue and the new, and Reaghan motioned for the procession to begin again, back along the long path of ribbons through the trees. This time there was no nervousness, no sense of expectation or reverent silence. This time the crowd sang along with the holy men, or chatted or laughed happily amongst themselves, exchanging blessings and back-slaps with the couple and with each other.

Rhia kept her hand in Bevan's the whole time and her new husband grinned at her as they walked.

'Were you as scared as I was through all that?'

Her seemingly-permanent smile widened as relief flowed through her.

'I'm sure I was scared, but I'm just as sure it was less than you were!'

Bevan prodded her playfully in the ribs and Rhia jerked away with a giggle. There weren't many things that could make Rhianwyn daughter of Carradan giggle, but Bevan was one of them. She strongly suspected that was the main reason she'd fallen in love with him. He understood the part of her that was a warrior for her people, but he could bring out the girl and the woman in her as well, and all of it without trying, just by being who he was. Just by Bevan being Bevan.

As soon as they broke the treeline pipers and drummers struck up tunes, and the chanting to the gods gave way to merry songs of love and summer. Half the population of Bryngarth sang and danced their way along the path leading back to the longhall. The ribbons of red and blue now seemed grey in the moonlight but the drinking and dancing would go on until dawn, and the colours of the Caderyn would be bright once again.

The walk back up the hill should have left her tired but for some reason Rhia didn't feel it. Before she knew it, she and Bevan were walking through the doors of her father's house, the sudden change from pale moonlight to the bright yellow of roaring fires making her blink in shock, and the wave of heat almost suffocated her as she went inside. Those few who'd not come to the ceremony had not been idle, and the smell of roasting meat was enough to make her mouth water. In all the excitement Rhia had forgotten that she'd not eaten in what amounted to a day and a half, and her stomach rumbled loudly at the sight and smell of the food.

The walk to the high table seemed to take longer than the whole trek to the grove and back, and her father's kind words to the hall felt longer than a bad winter. But eventually, after her stomach had growled loudly enough for the whole damned hall to hear it, the High Chieftain of the Caderyn raised his bowl of wine in front of him and said the only words that Rhia cared about right now.

'And now, let us eat!'

The new bride almost forgot about her new husband in her urgency, and had swept up half a chicken the moment she'd heard the word *eat*. She heard Bevan laughing beside her and managed to give him a quick smile before tearing into the meat. The skin was crisp but the meat inside was soft and tender, and Rhia wanted to groan out loud but there was a danger that it would slow down her chewing. A cup of apple wine appeared from somewhere and she emptied it without pausing for breath before turning back to the food again. Joints of pork and beef and venison were all trotted out to her, the new-weds being given first choice of anything brought to the top table. Pigeon's wings, buttered vegetables, breads and cheeses and beers and wines all came to Rhia and Bevan before anyone else, and the young bride took full advantage of the tradition.

Rhia's sense of elation and love wasn't diminished as the night went on, far from it, but now that the rituals were over it felt as if all the things she'd pushed out of the way as unimportant were coming back to her in a flood. She bit into another grease-dripping sausage as she thought. Her hunger was certainly the first and most obvious thing to make itself felt, but a close second was definitely her feet. Rhia had walked barefoot around most places in her life but the procession through the trees had been hard and chilly, and even sitting indoors with her shoes back on, her toes were aching and tender.

Cael was playing something especially beautiful and Bevan took her hand to lead her up to dance, but she shook her head at him before he rose.

'Later, my love.'

He gave a little smile.

'Alright, but we're doing it before you've eaten much more. It might spoil the mood if the bride vomited on the bards mid-dance.'

She gave him a playful prod in the ribs.

'If it comes to that, I'll be sure to aim for you!'

Bevan looked as if he was about to jest back, but his eyes flicked up to something over her shoulder and Rhia turned to see her mother standing behind her. Her new husband nodded politely.

'Mother.'

The older woman smiled back at him.

'My son. Have your feet warmed up yet?'

She looked at them both but Rhia answered her first.

'On their way to it. My toes are still cramping something fierce, mind.'

Myrna gave a knowing smile.

'When I married your father I thought my feet would drop off by the time we reached the longhall. My wedding dance was the clumsiest I've ever moved.'

Bevan nodded his head in sympathy, and Rhia assumed that his feet were as uncomfortable as her own, but before he got the chance to complain about it, Madoc had plucked at his arm and began questioning him about their new house. With her husband distracted, Rhia leaned a little closer to her mother. Through all her euphoria she'd still been curious, and a little concerned, about the whistling winds and throbbing earth when they'd stood within the Ring of Stones. She couldn't remember ever seeing or feeling anything so powerful at anyone else's ceremony.

'Mother, can I ask you something else about your wedding?'

The older woman sighed and sank down onto the bench beside her, her voice calm and patient.

'I'm sure that you and Bevan have been intimate with each other in some ways but the act itself is very different.'

Rhia had made the mistake of taking a mouthful of wine after she'd spoken and so couldn't speak again in time to stop her mother.

'You'll have to make sure he takes his time, to warm the oven first so to speak, before you start. Even then it hurts at first but I soon found…'

Rhia quickly swallowed her drink and motioned as frantically as she dared without causing a scene.

'I didn't mean that!'

Her mother frowned a little.

'You've not already been doing such things, I hope? Granted, nothing's come of it but it's a bad example to set for Gwendolyn.'

Rhia shook her head, keen to be off the subject.

'No we haven't.'

Myrna was not convinced.

'There's nothing wrong with doing other things before wedding of course, but some things ought to be kept special,' she took a sip from a cup of wine, 'why, I remember one time when your father and I disappeared for a whole afternoon in that little woodland beside the lake and I…'

Rhia made another frantic gesture. The Caderyn, like Lurians in general, were normally free enough in their talk of the carnal but there were limits, and as far as Rhia was concerned this definitely went past them. She spoke very quickly, her voice low.

'Yes we have been intimate and no, not as in the act itself, yes I know what you and father have done and no, I don't want to hear about it!'

She paused for breath but didn't let her mother start again. *I swear she and Father talk about these things just to aggravate me.*

'I wanted to ask you about the ceremony itself, when you were inside the Ring of Stones.'

Myrna smiled, clearly enjoying the discomfort she was inflicting on her daughter, but she answered the question plainly all the same.

'Of course, child. What do you want to know?'

Rhia took a deep breath before continuing.

'Did you feel…like the winds suddenly picked up when Reaghan was speaking his blessings? Like there were spirits around you or something?'

Her mother's brow furrowed a little.

'It *is* a place of the gods. I remember feeling a sort of tingling all through me when Reaghan was speaking and yes, the winds were whipping fast all about us. I thought at the time it was a sign from the gods and if it was, it seems to have been a good one; five healthy children and twenty summers together; your father and I can hardly complain.'

Rhia smiled back. It was good to hear that her mother had felt the gods as well but all the same, it didn't sound quite like what she and Bevan had experienced earlier. She pressed her gently.

'Did you notice anything like that tonight?'

Her mother shrugged noncommittally.

'Well my heart was pounding hard, my daughter was marrying after all, and there was wind as well I suppose, but nothing unusual. Did you feel something special from the woods?'

Rhia felt a little embarrassed to speak of it.

'It felt strange. As if Mehine herself was riding around us, or Mabonac's heart was beating below us. I was almost afraid of it.'

She looked away for a moment but when she looked back her mother was smiling.

'I don't doubt that the gods were with you tonight my love, and if you weren't nervous at your wedding you are the first bride I've known not to have felt so.'

She placed a hand on her arm.

'Mehine watches over maidens, Rhia. If she was there she was there to bless you.'

The young bride nodded, feeling only a little better, and her mother rose slowly to her feet.

'Meanwhile I shall leave you two alone. Doubtless you'll want to feast and dance your fill before heading to your new home.' She leaned down with a wicked smile and spoke quietly to her. 'Your father couldn't wait to get me back to his bed of course, he all but...'

Rhia found herself fighting off a grin as she put her hands over her ears. It might not be what she wanted to hear, but her mother's teasing brought a smile to her face nonetheless.

'I-don't-want-to-know-I-don't-want-to-know-I-don't-want-to-know!'

Myrna smiled again and flicked a lock of Rhia's hair over her face. She'd done that for as long as Rhia could remember and they both smiled at the familiar gesture before the older woman took her leave.

Rhia went back to the serious business of eating while her husband continued to be interrogated by the Gadarim.

The conversation with her mother had made her feel slightly better, knowing at least that other people felt the gods too when they stood in the Ring of Stones, but it still sounded like what had happened tonight was somewhat out of the ordinary. On another day she might have sat and pondered that for a while, but then Bevan turned back to her with a little spit of roast goat, and the combination of love for her husband and the smell of the food drove all other worries from her mind. *There will be time enough for worrying tomorrow*, she thought, *for tonight and tonight only, I am a bride*.

*

The first rays of the dawn were creeping into the sky when Rhia and Bevan left the longhall. The feasting and drinking would carry on of course, but everyone knew that the couple had more important business; a marriage unconsummated was no marriage at all and they had walked from the hall amidst whoops and jests, with Bevan's friends especially shouting encouragement and advice. Now outside, Rhia felt the air was chilly after the stifling heat of the hall but Bevan put his arm around her as they walked to their new home. The sky above them had barely a cloud in sight and a handful of stars could still be seen in the west. Rhia looked at them and hoped that the gods were still looking down on them, and a tingle of nerves ran through her again at what was soon to come.

The roundhouse was not far from the house of her father but it was a strange feeling nonetheless that when she spoke of 'home' from now on, she'd be speaking of this place, or of a house in Bevan's home town. They paused at the doorway, and Rhia felt that Bevan was just as nervous as she was but she took his hand in hers and he gave it a squeeze, and then ducked his head under the lintel and led her in. Inside the house was spacious, divided into two rooms by a screen of twined wicker. Here in the first one were benches large enough for five people each provided they bunched up tight, along with two tables, a cooking spit, and a heap of useful gifts given them by friends and relatives. A part of her wanted to pause to take it all in but Bevan simply led her onward, and Rhia did not object.

Past the wicker wall there was their bed room, a brand new cot waiting for them with a freshly-stuffed mattress of clean straw. Bevan picked up flint and tinder from the table and lit the kindling in their little hearth. The yellow light showed a few other odds and ends of furniture but Rhia paid them no notice as her husband turned to face her. He was beautiful, the long braid of his near-blonde hair falling down over one shoulder, his bearded face happy but not truly smiling, merely looking at her with undisguised longing.

He leaned forward and placed the first kiss on her lips, and Rhia felt her pulse quicken as his hands found her waist. She began kissing back and placed her own hands on his shoulders, feeling the solid muscle even through the white wedding robe. Bevan began to run his hands across her body, caressing her legs, her hips, her back and her buttocks before gently brushing across the swell of her breasts. She gasped a little and felt his hardness pressing against her, and wasted no time in grasping hold of him and stroking slowly through his clothes. Her new husband moaned a little and within seconds he was drawing the robe over her head. Rhia began struggling with his as well and after a few moments of tugging and what sounded ominously like a rip, the two new-weds stood naked before each other.

Rhia had seen Bevan without clothes on before, as he had seen her, but every other time it had been either out at the lake when everyone else was naked too, or it had been a frantic fumble in some secret place, with no time to truly appreciate it. Now, with all the time in the world, she gazed at the man she loved in wonder, and sensed him feel the same thing as his eyes wandered over her. It was strange how she almost felt shy as he looked, but then her boldness came back to her, and Rhia grabbed hold of her man and pulled him into another hard kiss. Bevan was strong, a glance at his body or the feel of his grip was enough to tell anyone this, and he held her tightly as he kissed her back. The two dragged each other with equal fervour down to the cot.

Her breathing grew heavy as she felt Bevan's hands exploring her. Rhia had never thought of herself as particularly feminine in her body, having been built very much on the slender side, a stark contrast to Meghan's eye-catching curves. Though she'd been told by her friends that her hips and breasts were nicely shaped, there was no denying that neither aspect of her body were exactly prominent, and for all her confidence with words or weapons, Rhia had always felt a little self-conscious about herself. The warrior in her found comfort knowing she was clearly built for battle, being lean and strong and fast, but at the same time a part of her longed to feel like a woman, as Meghan and Peira must do. Bevan made her feel like a woman tonight.

Rhia's new husband kissed her neck and then moved down to her breasts, his hands massaging gently and his lips and tongue soft and wonderful. Rhia took his manhood in her hand again and stroked his hardness as Bevan kept on kissing. They tried, and tried hard, to follow the advice that they'd heard earlier and take their time before actually starting, but Rhia had yearned to feel her husband inside her from the moment they'd left the longhall and Bevan was clearly just as eager as she was.

They kissed and fondled for only a few more heartbeats before Rhia guided him forward and the two began making love.

Her mother had been right; it did hurt at first, and Rhia had to bite her lip to keep from crying out, but Bevan took his time and was slow and gentle for all his lust, and soon both of them had lost themselves in the ecstasy of the moment. Nothing, not any of their frantic fumblings nor any words from her mother or her friends, had prepared her for what this feeling was, and Rhia knew she would never be able to describe it. It was bliss. It was joy. It was life.

Rhia had no idea how long they'd made love for but when they were done, and husband and wife lay quiet and panting in one another's arms, all she wanted was for this feeling to never end, to keep doing this day and night for the rest of their lives. Bevan leaned across and placed a tiny kiss on her forehead and Rhia cuddled into him, feeling as warm and safe as she could ever remember feeling.

'I love you, my wife.'

She found her voice was very small, and yet the words that came out were somehow strong, as if they were the most powerful words she'd ever speak.

'And I love you, my husband.'

Chapter 6. Married Life

Even five of Leu's turns after they kissed palms beneath her light, Rhia sometimes found herself grinning at the thought that she and Bevan were actually *married.* Whether waking up together in their little house or lying with him at night, or simply sitting at the fire in a comfortable silence, a bowl of steaming stew in her hands, Rhia still kept finding herself smiling for no clear reason, and she'd seen Bevan do the same thing more than once. It was as if their joy from that night, rather than fading, just continued to glow inside them, and Rhia wondered if that would ever go away. She hoped not.

She gave a copper coin to Arian for the eggs she'd just bought and strode on through the street where the shopkeeps sold their wares. Though summer had come and gone and autumn was upon them, the day was still bright and warm, despite the clouds looming in the north. Rhia walked briskly along her way, not pausing to browse but only picking up what she'd come out for. She'd left her cloak at home and only wore a woollen dress, and had no desire to be caught out if the rain should come as she shopped.

Every trader in the town seemed to be out this morning, all vying with each other for the coin of passers-by, and the street was alive with enthusiastic voices. Gronow the Tallow was calling to all who would listen about the high quality of his candles, while Rhisiart the Beef praised his steaks and joints to any potential consumers. Dawood the Smith roared at his apprentices as they hammered out shovels and ploughs, while Saer the Gold showed off torques and bracelets in the open-fronted house next door.

More butchers and bakers, horse-traders and carpenters, smiths, farmers, fishmongers and seamstresses lined the street all around her, each one trying to catch her eye to sell her something from their table, and giving up and moving on to the next face the moment she'd walked past. Rhia was striding as quickly as her legs would allow her, determined to get this done before the rain came, as it surely would. She only had Jeston the Saw to visit now, since Bevan had tripped over the little table in their room and somehow managed to splinter all four of its legs. She was reasonably sure he could never have done that deliberately, but in his clumsiness he had reduced one of their few items of furniture into little more than nicely-shaped firewood.

Rhia had nagged him about it at the time but in truth, she wasn't really angry. It was inconvenient and annoying but when it came down to it, she was the daughter of the High Chieftain and he the son of his own town's headman, and they had silver enough to get themselves a new table. As she walked along the street, heavy with the smells of meat and fish and bread, she wondered how long it would be before they left their snug little house and moved into the longhall at Mobryn. Bevan would be a headman there one day after all, and the move would be inevitable once his father died.

A little wave of sadness hit her as she wandered through the crowd. She would miss her family when she moved of course, but it wasn't so much that she would pine for Bryngarth, it was the fact that they'd spent the last five moons making their simple round house into a home. The insignificant things they'd done to make the place that little bit special; her painted vase beside the door that Bevan filled with wild flowers, or Bevan's massive bear pelt that in summer she'd found foolishly heavy, and was now finally beginning to appreciate. Things like the coloured blankets they'd hung as an inside doorway between the two rooms, or the places on the wall where she'd put her hand out in the dark and would recognise every pit and bump in it as though it were her own skin. She loved their house. It was a place where they were happy, and for all that they would have a larger living space when Bevan was a chief, Rhia would be sad to see the place go after all the memories they had shared there. *And speaking of those memories...*

Rhia hadn't just come out today to buy some eggs and get a table. She'd been hoping to run into either Meghan or Peira and it seemed that the gods were on her side this morning. Even as she'd thought of them she saw the pair coming out of old Leathan's pottery, the redhead carrying a new and heavy-looking vase. Peira of course was in no condition to carry anything and Rhia rushed over to them with a smile, her hand instantly going to the brunette's swollen belly.

'Is he kicking today?'

Her friend returned her smile.

'He stopped just as dawn came but he'll probably start again before long. He's keen to be out.'

Rhia grinned and tried to feel for any movement but apparently the little fellow had tired himself out for a while.

'Are you two off to anywhere interesting?'

Meghan shrugged her shoulders and indicated the vase in her hand.

'I only came out for this, we were going to head back to Peira's for some leaf.'

Rhia cocked her head.

'What do you have?'

'Thyme or rosemary.'

Rhia pondered on that. Bevan was expecting her back before long and she still had Jeston to visit, but the thought of a cup of leaf was a pleasant one. And besides, she had news to impart. She persuaded the others to come with her while she saw the carpenter and, after a few choice words

87

about the clumsiness of her husband, she purchased an almost identical table to the one that he had broken, and Jeston promised his boy would bring it around the next day.

Her errands run, Rhia took her basket of eggs over to Peira and Barden's house. It was only slightly smaller than the house Rhia shared with Bevan, though their scattered belongings bore testament to their having lived there for longer. Barden was out with the dogs, looking for game to sell to the butchers, and Peira began the process of boiling some water for their drinks before Meghan and Rhia whipped the pan from her and told her to sit down quietly. Peira looked grateful and only argued enough to be polite. She had confided in them already that her back and feet were killing her.

While the water slowly heated over the smoky little fire, the mother-to-be began a vain attempt to rub the ache from her feet, but Meghan was there in an instant. She had her friend's shoes off in the blink of an eye and started to rub at them herself. Again, Peira was thankful and smiled as her friend eased her tension.

'I must get myself with child more often. The making of it is enjoyable and once you're showing, people do everything for you.'

Her friends smiled as they went about helping her, not minding in the least putting in the effort. When one of them fell pregnant, they knew that Peira would be the first one to come and offer her help. *And speaking of...*

Rhia brewed up the leaf for them and they each took a clay cup, blowing on the steam before they drank the warming liquid. Rhia had always preferred rosemary to any other type of leaf and she enjoyed the savoury flavour, the rich smell reminding her of pine needles and resin. Why Meghan always felt the need to sweeten her leaf with honey was something Rhia had never understood but, she supposed, to each their own. They drank in silence for a few moments until Rhia couldn't hold it back any longer.

'I think I might be joining you before long!'

There was a heartbeat's pause before the other women realised what she meant and then huge smiles appeared on their faces, and Meghan abandoned Peira's feet and rushed to wrap Rhia in an embrace.

'Congratulations!'

Peira made as if to stand but the other two went over to her instead and Rhia shared another hug with her friend.

'How sure are you?'

Rhia shrugged. She'd almost been afraid to confide in her friends for fear of jinxing her chances of really being pregnant, but the pressure of keeping quiet had just been too much.

'Not sure, but I've missed my blood by ten days now and... it just sort of *feels* like I am. Does that sound foolish?'

Peira shook her head.

'Each time my mother was with child she knew it in her heart even before she missed her blood. I can't say I was exactly the same but I know what you mean. It is hard to explain.'

Rhia nodded. She had no idea exactly why she thought she was carrying, and she couldn't have described the feeling to anyone, but she felt as if somehow she just *knew*. Meghan chipped in.

'Have you been to see Madlen?'

Rhia shook her head.

'Not yet. I wanted to wait until I'd not bled for two moons, just to make sure.'

Both women nodded sagely.

'Have you told Bevan?'

Again, Rhia shook her head, but this time it was with a smile.

'No,' she looked at Peira, 'I see now why it was you took so long to tell Barden. I'm enjoying our nights together too much to risk him stopping them.'

Peira smiled conspiratorially but Meghan frowned and spoke with obvious frustration.

'Bloody wives!'

Peira put a hand on the redhead's arm.

'Your time will come as well, and soon.'

Rhia took her other hand.

'You and Dane are getting along well though, aren't you? Give it a little time and I'm sure you'll end up wed.'

Meghan smiled a little. For all his initial shyness Dane had finally begun to court the lovely girl in earnest, and Rhia was sure that their father had noticed. Hopefully, the good marriages made by his other children would be enough to make him consider a bride for his younger son who did not come from a prominent family. Besides, Carradan was a man who cared for his children's happiness. If the gods were good he had seen how contented Dane and Meghan were together and would give his blessing to their union before long.

'I just hope he doesn't wait forever before asking me, if he both wants to and can that is. Remember Gandwy and Irwen? *Two years* they courted before they finally kissed palms.'

Peira shrugged with a wise expression on her face.

'Better that than to do it too soon. Think about what happened with Pyrs and Arwen.'

There was a brief silence between the three as they thought about the unfortunate couple. Pyrs had asked Arwen to kiss palms with him only five days after meeting her. Like a fool Arwen had accepted him, gained her father's consent, and they had wed a mere eight days later. Reaghan had counselled them both to wait a while but they had not heeded him, insisting that their love was true and strong enough for anything, and the druid had grudgingly allowed it. It was ever his place to advise, not to command. *Strange that almost everyone would obey the command of a druid if he gave it, but that none of them ever command us to do anything.* Perhaps that was why it worked; all knew that they held great power and chose not to use it, thus showing their wisdom and humility and ensuring their advice was always heeded. Well, almost always anyway.

As it had turned out, Pyrs was over-fond of strong beer and Arwen over-fond of strong men, and they'd been fighting day and night only a moon after the ceremony. The separating of a couple joined by the gods was extremely rare, in all his years and among all the tribes Reaghan had only known it happen twice before, but in this case it was clearly necessary. Rhia hated to think of what rituals the gods demanded for such an insult to their power, but both Pyrs and Arwen had returned from the woods wide-eyed and pale-faced, revealing nothing of what had happened there to anyone. The resulting scandal of their failed marriage had essentially ruined any future prospects for either of them, and both had moved to separate villages where their shame was less well known. Rhia had no idea what had become of them.

Peira's tone became a little lighter.

'But a blind man can see that you two are besotted with each other, and probably always will be.'

Rhia nodded.

'Very true. And if my brother takes too long about it I'll have Gwen put eels in his bed until he does.'

The others laughed. Outside the wind was picking up and Rhia thought she'd best be making her way home before long, but she was enjoying herself so much among her friends. It wasn't as if she didn't love married life, or that she didn't see Meghan and Peira all the time, but cosy moments like this seemed to be rarer than they used to be, and Rhia missed them. She wrapped her hands around the cup of leaf and listened as the others continued to talk. She'd stay for one more cup after this, then she'd make a move and head back. Just one more cup.

*

Three cups of rosemary leaf and a handful of oatcakes later, Rhia emerged from the little house into the wind. Midday had come and gone and the dark clouds had reached Bryngarth, and Rhia felt the first tiny droplets of rain hitting her face. She didn't have a cloak with her and she'd not yet got into the winter habit of wearing trews under her dress, so she decided not to dawdle on her way back. The hugs and repeated congratulations with Meghan and Peira were brief, and Rhia headed off across the town towards her house.

There were still people about but the street was far from crowded and Rhia walked with far less dodging and weaving than she had done that morning. Before long she was past the traders and striding between quiet houses, the majority of people likely still out about their business. She thought about whether she ought to speak to Bevan about her suspicions when she got back. He'd be wondering what had kept her and his annoyance would be tempered nicely by the news that he might soon be a father.

The rain was getting heavier and Rhia ducked her head down as she upped her pace. Perhaps it was best not to tell him just yet, not until she'd seen Madlen at least, there was no point in getting his hopes up if it turned out to be nothing. Besides, there were other ways to get rid of his annoyance, and like Peira had said, she ought to make the most of such pleasures while she could. Some men were happy to still couple with their wives when they were pregnant, but most were superstitious about harming the child in some way and there was every chance that Bevan would be no different.

The rain increased into a light but steady shower and Rhia was glad when she saw the longhouse and her own little home steadily nearing. She wondered if Bevan had built up a fire where she could dry her clothes. She'd make sure to take them off as soon as she got under cover, partially because her mother would have berated her at length for keeping on a wet dress, but mostly as a distraction for her husband. If she was naked before he managed to get any words out, he might forget to be irritated that she'd taken half a day to order a table and pick up some...*damn and buggery!*

Rhia cursed under her breath as she pictured exactly where in Peira's house she'd left the eggs. The rain was getting heavier but she knew she ought to go back and get them. It wasn't fair to Bevan to make him wait around for her and not even bring back what she'd gone out for. Her dark hair threw droplets of water everywhere as she whipped around to go back the way she'd come.

For the most part the walk was not too muddy, the ground in the town was much stonier than the rest of the hill, but all the same the rainfall was softening the earth under her feet, and Rhia heard a definite squelching as she hurried back to Peira's. The usual walk meant going around a few of the larger buildings and so she decided to cut behind them in her rush to get out of the rain. She'd be tempted to accept her friend's inevitable invitation to come in for another cup of rosemary until the weather cleared up, but she told herself firmly that she'd politely say no to one. She was running late enough as it was.

It was only because of her decision to take that shortcut that Rhia saw the fight between the boys. Through the silver-grey haze of the rain she spotted Gwyr, Madoc's son, thudding brutal-looking punches into another boy's midriff. Gwyr had almost fourteen summers and the other boy was clearly smaller than he, and Rhia called out to them at once.

'Stop that!'

The noise caused Gwyr to turn from his pounding and Rhia, striding towards them, saw a look of shame flash across his face. It might have ended there with his apologising for his behaviour, had the smaller boy not seen his opportunity to fight back and slammed his knee into Gwyr's ribs while he was distracted. The older boy doubled over and coughed, and his former victim landed a punch on his jaw. Rhia was only paces away and shouted again.

'Stop it the pair of you!'

But this time she was ignored as Gwyr staggered and then grabbed his opponent's arm as he tried to strike again, before hammering a straight punch into the smaller boy's face. His nose seemed to burst with blood and he toppled backwards, but Rhia caught hold of Gwyr before he could follow it up, and she grunted as she dragged him back from the fallen boy. She shoved him away and stood between the two brawlers.

'What by all the gods do you think you're doing?'

The look of shame had gone from Gwyr's face to be replaced by stubbornness and anger.

'He started it! He insulted me!'

He tried to get past her to continue his fighting but Rhia caught him again and pushed him back.

'And that is reason enough to start beating a boy of half your size? What would your father say?'

Gwyr looked awkward but kept up his scowl.

'He'd say I was right.' he pointed behind her, '*he* said I'd only be a Gadarim because of Father.'

Rhia half-turned as the other boy spoke, his voice nasal and thick with blood.

'It's true. My father didn't get made a Gadarim just because Owain doesn't like him, it's not fair!'

Rhia turned to face Gwyr again but the younger boy dashed around her, knocking her sideways in the process, and grabbing for Gwyr's knees. Both boys fell to the floor and rolled in the mud, fists flying as they battered at each other. Rhia suspected that controlling both of them would be a challenge but then a man appeared from the rain and rushed towards the commotion. It was only when she heard his voice as he dragged the smaller boy clear, that Rhia recognised him as Delyn. Normally she disliked the awkwardness of his company, but she was glad of him today and quickly set about restraining Gwyr. Her former would-be-suitor berated his captive.

'Damn it Lorcan, calm down!'

The boy kept struggling but Delyn held him fast. Gwyr seemed to realise he'd have no more fighting today and stopped trying to escape from Rhia's grip. She kept her hold on him just in case though.

'Lorcan that is enough!'

The smaller boy slowly gave up his fight and settled for glaring at Gwyr.

'He hit me first! And then I was winning, he's nothing without his da!'

Gwyr leaned forward as he argued back, though he didn't really strain against Rhia's hold.

'You little bastard! You insulted my family you piss-licking little…'

But Rhia gave him a solid shake that interrupted his flow. Gwyr was as tall as she was and was strong for his age but Rhia had grappled with men who wanted to kill her, and holding on to a petulant youth was definitely easier.

'Neither one of us gives a cow's turd about why you did it!'

Delyn nodded as he joined in.

'You're both old enough to know better than to fight over something like that! What does Reaghan teach us?'

Rhia had to admit, Delyn had been clever there. The boys might have argued with them if they'd simply told them not to do it, but no-one dared to disrespect a druid. It was Gwyr who answered first, sulky defiance still evident in his voice.

'When a family fights itself, no-one wins. But he's *not* my family!'

He pointed at Lorcan with a sneer. For a moment, Rhia thought he might try to squirm free again but apparently he was prepared to settle for pointing. The rain was coming down even heavier now and was running through Rhia's hair into her eyes. Across from her, she saw Delyn's face was equally soaked.

'*All* the Caderyn are one family, does he not teach that as well?'

Rhia felt Gwyr shrug his shoulders and his answer was grudging.

'Yes.'

Delyn nodded and turned his attention to the boy he was holding.

'You understand what that means, nephew?'

It was hard to see through the rain but Rhia suspected that the smaller boy was still looking resentful. Nonetheless, he agreed with his captor through clenched teeth.

'That we shouldn't be fighting each other.'

Again, Delyn nodded.

'That is exactly what it means. Now, do we have your promise that if we let you go you won't fight any more?'

From the blood that still stained Lorcan's face despite the rain, Rhia was fairly sure that if they fought again, the smaller boy would come off worse. Nevertheless there was still fire in his eyes as he nodded, and she suspected he was eager to give it another try.

'Alright.'

Delyn relaxed his hold and looked over to Rhia, who spoke to her own captive.

'And you?'

Gwyr nodded his head.

'I promise.'

Delyn seemed satisfied with that, but Rhia decided to try going a step further as she let go of Gwyr's arms. They could break it up again if things got out of hand.

'Now I want you two to trade grips.'

Madoc's youngest turned to her with a look as if she'd just told him to eat manure, but Rhia matched his glare and the boy broke eye contact first. He turned to look back at Delyn and Lorcan and started shuffling reluctantly forwards. Delyn indicated that his nephew should do the same and Rhia watched them like a hawk as they closed in on each other. This gesture, one that bordered on the sacred among Lurians, might bring a level of commitment to the boys' promise not to fight each other. But it also brought the two youths within easy striking range, and Rhia saw that Delyn too was keeping a close eye on his charge, ready to spring forward should the brawling recommence.

For a moment it really seemed as if it might, as the two boys squared up to each other with twitching hands and sour expressions. Even through the downpour the air felt warm with tension, and Rhia bent her knees a little, ready to leap in and drag them off each other if needed. But slowly, Gwyr extended his hand. It hovered there for a dangerous moment before Lorcan raised his own and the two gripped one another's wrists. It lasted barely a heartbeat before they let go again and they stepped back from each other slowly, eyes locked.

Only once each boy was far out of punching range did they turn and face away. Delyn simply jerked his head behind him and Lorcan stomped off without a word. Rhia nodded to Gwyr before speaking to him.

'I'm glad you worked that out, now be off to your father.'

The boy nodded back stoically, fully aware of the clout his father would likely give him when he heard of this. For a moment it looked as if he wanted to say something, but then he seemed to think better of it and walked away through the rain. It was only once the boys had gone that Rhia remembered both the freezing cold water that was pouring down her neck, and the awkward silence that had fallen between her and Delyn. He had handled the boys well, and done her a good turn, but still she couldn't think of what to say to him now they were alone. The dark-haired man saved her the trouble.

'Well, now that's sorted out we should probably get inside.'

Rhia nodded.

'Yes, we should.'

She couldn't think of much else to say in response but it seemed to be enough and Delyn turned to leave. Rhia started off towards Peira's again but just before he moved from sight she called out to him.

'Thank you for helping.'

Delyn gave a very small smile as he nodded back.

'You too.'

Rhia smiled a little and then turned away again. She felt better for having acknowledged his assistance but it was still awkward to be around him, and it wasn't just the weather that made her hurry along her way. She found herself thinking that even though Delyn would never have been right for her, he was the sort to make a good husband to *someone* at least. That made her feel happy for him, even through the grimness of the weather.

By the time she reached Peira's she was soaked to the skin, and for all her protests about brevity she was practically force-fed oatcakes and leaf, and was given a dress and cloak of Peira's to wear for the walk home. Her friend had sighed that there was no great hurry to bring them back; they didn't exactly fit her well at the moment. Rhia tried not to smile as she thought of her own suspicions. *With the help of the gods, they soon won't fit me either!*

Chapter 7. The Challenge

It was hard to tell because of the weather, but Rhia felt the light was fading by the time she finally reached her own home, carrying a basket of eggs and wearing another woman's dress. She walked in to see Bevan sitting in the corner and for half a heartbeat, he didn't notice her. The fire had been made and a pot was hanging over it, and Rhia could smell the beginnings of a stew bubbling inside. On the low table was a bloody pile of bones and fur and from the scent coming from the pot, she guessed that Bevan was cooking rabbit for their supper.

The man himself was dangling a ribbon over a bundle on the chair beside him, and Rhia smiled as she saw little Siriol's hands grasping helplessly at the cloth, giggling out squeakily as Bevan twitched it away from her. In that moment, Rhia wished she could tell him her suspicions about herself. She had never felt so in love with him as she did at that moment, watching him smile happily back at his niece as he played with her. The danger of raising his hopes prematurely seemed foolish now and she laid down her basket of eggs and drew in a breath to tell him the good news. But then his eyes shot up and she saw this was not the time.

'Where have you been?'

He didn't raise his voice but Rhia could tell he was annoyed, she was after all supposed to have been back here some time ago. She spoke softly.

'I'm sorry love, I got to chatting with Peira and then got caught out in all this.'

She waved an arm to indicate the rain that was still pouring down outside. Bevan frowned a little.

'I was worried you'd slipped down the hill and snapped your neck or something.'

Rhia raised an eyebrow.

'And you're annoyed that you've had to start making supper on your own?'

But Bevan, if not exactly *angry*, was not in a playful mood.

'I'm annoyed that I spent my morning hunting for fresh game and was confronted with a tiny child to entertain the moment I got back, and *then* had to start making supper on my own.'

Rhia squirmed a little. She'd forgotten that she'd asked Olla if she might have Siriol over for the evening. It would be good practice for her and Bevan and also give her sister a night of peace and quiet. And, truth be told, Rhia had fallen in love with Siriol the moment she'd set eyes on her and was keen for any excuse to spend time with her.

Of course, she'd not counted on being so late back that Bevan would be greeted by an empty house and then by his sister-in-law presenting him with her child. Rhia tried to sound positive.

'She's behaving herself well, isn't she?'

Bevan frowned again.

'She was bawling her eyes out when the rain started up,' he waved the ribbon a little, 'fortunately your husband has his methods.'

The tiny hands grasped for the ribbon again and Rhia saw to her relief that Bevan was struggling to keep up his bad mood. She moved towards him and put a hand on his arm.

'I'm sorry I was so late. I saw some boys fighting in the rain and had to stop to break them up. It only got me more wet so I went back to Peira's to change into something dry.'

She held up a part of the skirt, which was now very damp but not quite so sodden as her own clothes had been. For a moment she wondered if she ought to mention Delyn's role in separating the brawling boys but decided it was best to leave him out of it. Bevan might not like to hear talk of his former rival. *Not that he ever was one, not really.*

Bevan grunted and touched her hand. Rhia squeezed his fingers and smiled down at him, her lips twitching with mischief.

'Of course, with the rain coming down like it is, these are pretty wet now too.'

She ran his hand along the hem of the dress, which was indeed damp from the rain, but then guided it up underneath the skirt to touch the cool skin of her leg. Bevan turned to face her and stood, one hand still on the flesh of her thigh, the other arm wrapping around her to pull her into a kiss. Rhia felt his hand slide up further and, after a brief glance to make sure Siriol was alright in her bundle, drew him away towards the second room of their little house.

The two kissed slowly but with passion and Rhia felt no hurry as she unlaced Bevan's trews. Her husband moved his kisses to her neck and he paused in them only long enough to pull Peira's dress over her head. When she'd left her friend's house she had considered asking to borrow some leggings as well, given the weather, but now she was immensely glad that she hadn't – it would only have slowed things down.

Bevan removed his own tunic and Rhia enjoyed the feel of his skin. It was still cold, but touching him she felt warm to the point of feverish and she placed kisses of her own on his chest and arms. His hand had found her womanhood and she fought back a gasp as he began pleasing her, his mouth moving down to her breast. Gently, her husband started easing her down to the bed but Rhia held up a finger in front of him.

'Not yet.'

Her voice was barely a whisper and she bit her lip playfully at his frown.

'First things first my love, I shouldn't have kept you waiting.'

Without another word she sank to her knees and took him in her mouth. Bevan groaned appreciatively and Rhia stroked his hardness with her hands as well, enjoying the control that she held over his pleasure. He began to run his fingers through her hair and Rhia felt certain this evening was going to be another great night of married life.

And then her stupid bloody brother appeared at the doorway, gave a high-pitched yelp of embarrassed surprise, and fled from the house again. Both husband and wife started at the sound and looked towards the door that poor Dane had only managed to half-close in his flight. The young man was clearly still standing outside, his feet shuffling awkwardly, and Rhia struggled to hold back a laugh as she called out.

'Sorry about that, Dane!'

Her brother's voice didn't quite shake but his nervousness was painfully obvious.

'I should have called out first.'

Rhia smirked as she started scrabbling for clothes and indicated to Bevan he should do the same. She worried a little at how long it would be before he and her brother would meet one another's eyes again, and tried not to find the whole thing quite so amusing. Bevan scowled as he dressed, clearly irritated at the interruption, and Rhia sympathised with her husband. They'd barely gotten started after all. She called out to her brother as they dressed, though she noticed that Siriol had fallen asleep and so she took care not to shout.

'It could have been worse – remember when Olla walked in on Mother and Father?'

Dane managed a laugh from outside.

'I'm sure *she* does! Is it safe to come in yet?'

Rhia nodded, then remembered that he couldn't see her and called out.

'Yes.'

Bevan was half clothed and Rhia had only just picked up a fresh dress, but Dane wouldn't be concerned about mere nakedness. He was family after all and had seen all his siblings as the gods had made them, but what a husband and wife did together was supposed to be something private, something intimate, and his red face was apologetic as he walked back in.

'Sorry to have intruded on you.'

Bevan rubbed his hands awkwardly on his trews before clasping wrists with him.

'Sorry to have inflicted the sight of me on you!'

Dane managed a smile, though Rhia was sure it was more courtesy than genuine relief. She pulled the dress over her head and spoke through the fabric.

'What brings you barging in here anyway, brother?'

Dane's voice became serious.

'There's been trouble with the Gorvicae. A rider came to the longhall with a message for Father. I don't know any details but he sent me to find you and Bevan straight away.'

Rhia frowned but Bevan spoke up first.

'A raid at this time of year?'

Dane shrugged, clearly just as baffled as Bevan was.

'It seemed strange when I heard about it but that's what it sounds like.'

Rhia was confused. It made no sense for anyone to be out fighting at the tail-end of autumn, not unless stores for winter were dangerously low, but the Gorvicae were a huge tribe and clans could doubtless support each other. A single clan might have chanced stealing from their Caderyn neighbours, but something so small would not need the attention of the High Chieftain. What were they up to?

Bevan was already dressed and ready by the time Rhia had slipped on cloak and shoes and he was holding Siriol, wrapped up in her blue blanket, waiting for her to join him at the door. They exchanged nods before Rhia turned to her brother.

'Let's be over there then.'

Dane nodded and led them out into the rain. It wasn't hammering quite as hard as it had been but it was enough to wake the baby and she was soon wailing pitifully, with Bevan trying in vain to sooth her and to keep her as dry as he could. For the sake of some different noise as much as anything else, Rhia nudged Dane as they hurried.

'Peira and I saw Meg today. Apparently she's envious of us wives!'

She was teasing and Dane knew it but nonetheless he flushed red once again.

'I want to marry her, I do, it's just getting to Father and finding the right time.'

Rhia looked at him through her brows, though she couldn't keep it up as the rain got in her eyes. He wasn't much taller than she was but it still meant looking *up*.

'You see Father all the time and you see her all the time, I'm pretty sure you've had some opportunities to ask them both!'

Dane twitched his mouth as they sloshed their way towards the longhall. The whole world seemed to have gone from blue and green to a black and grey, but a flash of yellow light up ahead showed them it was not far to their destination.

'Father is busy more often than you'd think and I don't often get the chance to be with Meghan alone.'

Rhia raised an eyebrow at his excuses.

'And when you do, you'd rather be doing what you just saw me and Bevan doing than asking the poor girl to marry you?'

Dane tried to look offended, then embarrassed, and then gave in to a very boyish smile. He was only a year younger than Rhia in terms of seasons, but he would always be her baby brother in her eyes.

'I'm amazed any man finds time to propose to a girl when those are his choices!'

Rhia frowned a little and Bevan's voice came from behind them.

'It's because eventually that first option gets rarer, and if you don't get on with the second option before long, you stop being offered it altogether!'

Dane's eyes darted back and forth between them, looking genuinely concerned.

'But... she knows I'm *going* to ask, doesn't she? I mean, you're her friend, you could...'

Rhia raised a hand as they approached the longhall.

'I am not instructing my friend to go on pleasuring you regardless, if that's what you're about to ask!'

Dane shook his head just as they got under the shelter of the hall's entranceway, sending droplets of water flying from his hair.

'Of course not! Just... you could tell her I'm finding a way to speak to Father about it, tell her what my intention is?'

Rhia took off her cloak and then held Siriol as Bevan removed his. The tiny girl was still squirming uncomfortably but had given up on her wailing for now, and Rhia rocked her gently in the hopes she would go back to sleep. It was strange and yet wonderful how heavy she was getting.

'She knows it's what you *intend* Dane, but I would get on and do it were I you.'

Bevan nodded along, handing his cloak to one of the women who ran the longhall for Carradan.

'You don't want a girl like that growing tired of waiting and looking around for a more eager man to share her affections with.'

Dane shook his head again.

'No... no, of course not!'

Rhia exchanged a sly wink with her husband. They both knew how much Meghan was in love with Dane but it was fun to scare him a little. *Besides, it will do him good not to take her for granted.*

They might have continued to torment her brother for a while but Owain, one of the Gadarim, appeared. The stocky warrior had only a couple of summers on Bevan but his face was as grim as an old man's.

'Your father would speak with you all, come.'

He beckoned them to follow him into the main room of the longhall and Rhia saw that all the Gadarim of Bryngarth, along with Reaghan the druid and half-a-dozen headmen of prominent clans, were already in the hall waiting for them. Carradan was sitting in his usual seat, his normally cheery face sombre and grave. He waved them forward and the trio moved to stand next to a man Rhia didn't recognise, whose soaking cloak and hair made him look even more bedraggled than the rest of them. The chieftain spoke.

'We are all of us here now, I think.'

He turned to Reaghan with a worried frown and the druid gave him a nod before he continued, speaking in short bursts as if he wished to get it all out as soon as possible but didn't know how to say the words.

'Nantwyn has been attacked by a Gorvicae warband. No challenge was sent, no ground arranged. Aedan is dead and many of our people fell with him defending the town.'

The silence in the hall was eerie but it lasted only a heartbeat before angry voices began shouting. Ordinarily, Rhia might have expected Madoc or Owain to be among the loudest of the shouters but the two men merely looked on with sombre faces, and she guessed that they'd been told of this already.

Arthfael, the largest of the Gadarim, made himself heard.

'How many of ours were killed?'

The soaked man spoke up in answer.

'We are not certain, comrades, but my count would have been some five hundred, perhaps more.'

This time the silence lasted longer, and the sounds of Gwen and the other women as they helped him from his drenched clothes became something almost deafening. Rhia found herself gawping at the man. *Five hundred?* Surely there were barely seven hundred Caderyn *living* in Nantwyn? There was no chance that so many of them had been fit for war. Bevan put a hand on her shoulder as he spoke into the silence.

'How many of the nearby clans had gathered up to join them?'

The messenger looked at him directly and it seemed to Rhia that the man wanted to weep but could not find the tears.

'None, comrade. There was no time to send for them.'

'Then how…' Bevan began but then he stopped himself, and a heartbeat later Rhia reached the same conclusion. A cold feeling crept into her gut. The messenger spared them from saying it aloud.

'Between two and three hundred of those slain were warriors. The rest were simply those who lived in the town. Only we who fled survived the battle, all who remained were killed.'

The cold feeling began to squirm inside her as Rhia thought of what that meant. *The old and the slow… the lame cripples and nursing mothers. All those too weak either to fight or to run.* Despite herself she felt tears well up behind her eyes but she forced them away. The messenger hung his head a little but then raised it up again.

'Before he died Aedan sent me to find the High Chief and warn him, or I would have stayed there to die with them.'

He had perhaps meant for the words to come out as defiant, or as a challenge to any who would call him coward, but the fact was that he just sounded tired. It seemed as if simply standing up was a challenge for him, and when the women offered him a seat to help him change into dry clothes, the man almost collapsed onto the floor. He was exhausted. Arthfael spoke again from the group of Gadarim, his voice thick with emotion.

'Where are these bastard Gorvicae now, comrade? What place do I need to destroy to avenge this?'

There was a chorus of approving growls but the messenger simply blinked at him.

'They are still there, my friend. They took the town from us and now they keep it, and fortify it further against attack.'

This caused even more blank faces to stare back at him and Rhia found her mind whirring in confusion. What did this mean? Plenty of times the Gorvicae or the Dariniae had come to raid or steal from their villages, and occasionally, as had happened at Broken Stream, they tried to take some farmland on the edges of their territory. But once the fighting was done, for the most part, both sides would go home again. There was no sense in taking large amounts of territory like what Nantwyn represented; it was a hill fort that commanded a great tract of land in the northeast, and the Gorvicae simply didn't have enough people to farm so much land effectively in addition to their own. Had they beaten the Nantwyn warriors in a properly challenged battle they could have forced them to pay a tribute that would be much more manageable. Why just *take* the town?

Rhia was clearly not alone in her confusion and it was Gaetan who spoke up for them.

'Why would they do this? And why kill those who are not warriors?'

The messenger was silent a moment and Carradan spoke in answer.

'It is believed that Baercban has allied himself with the Gaians. Gaian soldiers were seen fighting at Nantwyn, in great numbers and fiercely armed.'

Rhia felt her confusion mount even through her horror, but was spared from feeling foolish by Dane asking her question first.

'What's a soldier?'

Rhia's curiosity was smothered by the wave of pity she felt as both her father's and Reaghan's faces grew so solemn she might have thought her brother had just dropped dead in front of them. A number of those in the hall looked on quizzically and the druid answered their looks.

'You are all of you too young to remember when last the Caderyn faced the Gaians, and even then we faced them but little. But I and my brethren have communed on this matter before and I will tell what I can. A soldier is a type of warrior; one who fights all the time and has no farm or trade to go back to when the battle is done. He simply moves on to the next place that his chiefs tell him to fight, and he is given food and coin for his fighting.'

A curious murmur began but it was silenced as the druid continued.

'Each time they fight, rather than return home they keep the land for themselves, have other men farm it for them, and settle their own people on that land. They then use what they reap from that land, in farmed food or traded goods, to pay for their soldiers to fight another tribe and take more land. By doing this they have conquered most of the land across the sea, and it is how the eastern part of Henys was taken by them.'

Most of the Caderyn had only a basic knowledge of this and even Rhia, who thought herself well-informed, struggled to understand it. She'd known that the Gaians were a people from over the water who had beaten or made alliances with various tribes east of the Canwyns, and that many of them now lived there and continued to fight amongst themselves and with the eastern tribes. She remembered that Reaghan had once told her that the Gaians believed that all the territory of the east was theirs, but that didn't make sense because the land was filled with Duronii, Seiriae, Averyn and others. She had said at the time that these Gaians must be fools but the druid had just smiled at her and had let the matter be. Now...

Dane was still confused.

'So, does that mean the Gaians keep taking tribute from people, but... just forever? And live on their land if they want to? Why haven't the Duronii and the others stopped them?'

The druid spoke patiently to him.

'Because the Gaians will send their soldiers to kill them if they try. Not to fight with their warriors but to kill *them*, do you understand?'

A hollow, sickening sort of feeling in Rhia's stomach told her that she might be beginning to, and Dane opened and closed his mouth a few times without speaking. He was not the only Caderyn in such a state. Carradan spoke into the silence.

'Whatever their methods, it seems that the Gaians have tired of fighting with the Rydicae and Bearnicans and are now offering their soldiers to the Gorvicae. And between them they have killed our people and stolen our land. This is all that I need to know of them.'

Reaghan leaned closer to speak to him.

'Perhaps so my chief, but we would be wise to find out *why* the Gaians are lending their assistance to Baercban and his people. They cannot be trusted.'

Carradan nodded.

'It would indeed, father. But who knows what havoc these dogs will wreak across our lands whilst we look into *why* they are doing it? I would ask you and your brethren to ask what questions you can with your tongues,' he turned to Owain, 'and you to send men east to ask questions with their eyes,' he turned back to the druid, 'meanwhile I shall do what a chieftain must do before all else; I shall look to the safety of my people.'

Reaghan's face was without expression as he nodded, and Rhia wondered if he approved or disapproved of how her father was speaking. Either way it didn't matter. Rhia knew what Carradan would do and the rest of the hall knew it as well. Details would be needed but they could wait. Right now there was only one course of action. She locked eyes with Bevan who gave a grim little nod before looking around at the Gadarim who were watching their chieftain in silence. The battlemarks on their arms looked black the firelight and she could see Owain and Arthfael standing behind Madoc, almost willing their chieftain to say the word.

Rhia looked up at her father as well. He seemed sad, and troubled, but both of these were far outdone by the rage that burned behind his eyes. Slowly, the High Chieftain of the Caderyn rose to his feet and the horrible, cold feeling that Rhia had felt in her gut began to burn into something bright and terrible. The chieftain turned to his Gadarim.

'Gather your brothers. Assemble the clans.'

He turned to face the rest of the hall, and Rhia saw it had slowly filled up behind her with Caderyn men and women coming in to hear what had happened. They all looked up to their chieftain in hushed expectation and Carradan spoke once more, his voice loud and boiling over with determination and righteous fury.

'We go to war!'

Rhia's voice, and Bevan's and Dane's, joined with countless others as the Longhall of the Caderyn erupted into a roar.

Chapter 8. Gathering the Clans

Rhia was just one more rider in a column of hundreds on the long road towards Nantwyn. The headmen of almost every clan of the Caderyn had flocked to Bryngarth over the last few days as word of Carradan's command spread through the land. Each chief brought with him as many warriors as he could spare, and in most cases offered to fight in person alongside them. Some of the older men were unable to of course, though being true Caderyn men they'd have been keen to if they could, and had instead sent their sons to represent them on the field, along with their own elite Gadarim. Plenty had been left behind to defend their homesteads of course, raids from the Dariniae were still a constant threat along the coast, but nonetheless the numbers that had gathered here were vast, and Rhia had never seen so many people in one place.

Depending on their size, each clan had brought anything from thirty to five hundred fighting men and women, and Bryngarth itself had mustered seven hundred warriors. Rhia looked back along the column at the endless mass of people and almost pitied the Gaians and Gorvicae for the hammering they would soon be taking. She patted Neida's neck. The ponies of the Caderyn might not be beasts of war but they were numerous in the mountains and valleys of her homeland, and nearly all of the war party were travelling mounted. Rhia turned to look at Bevan, riding beside her.

'Ready for your first proper battle, husband?'

She smirked as she mocked him, and Bevan returned the smile.

'As ready as ever. Though I'd hoped for a little more time to enjoy married life before setting off for this.'

He gave her leg a quick squeeze. Rhia shook her head.

'We should be setting an example for Gwen, it's her first taste of a proper fight too.'

Her younger sister was riding only a little way behind them and was fidgeting at her reins, clearly nervous. Bevan gave a glance back and shrugged, still with his hand on Rhia's leg.

'We've days yet to set a good example. Right now I'm missing my wife in my bed, is that so wrong?'

Said wife sighed though she wasn't really annoyed. It was nice to still be wanted and in truth, she was feeling much the same way as he was. *Though before long you'll have to settle for your old games for a while, my girl. It's been well over a moon since you bled by now and from the way your chest is starting to swell, you won't keep it from him forever.* Rhia had a brief flash of worry for the battle ahead, and wondered if she should be fighting in the condition she suspected she was in, but she brushed the thought aside. Peira had gone to Broken Stream when she was all but certain she was pregnant and no harm seemed to have come of it. Rhia felt a pang of guilt that she might miss the child's birth, and hoped that all of this would be over before too long. She had a definite hunger for battle but she looked forward to her homecoming all the same, to seeing little Siriol and Olla, and holding onto Peira's hand as she brought new life into the world. *As she'll hold onto yours when your time comes.*

Rhia was about to start daydreaming about that when the sound of a slap in front of them, followed by Meghan's voice, drove the thought from her mind.

'You ought to watch your tongue, Madoc!'

She looked up to see the First Man shaking his hand as if it stung and sharing a grin with the pretty redhead. Like most of the Bryngarth men he liked to flirt a little with her, though they all knew that she would likely be a betrothed woman soon.

'I just thought that if you're still not promised to him, you might want a little company before the battle.'

Given that Madoc's wife, the fearsome Hefina, was riding just behind them, it was obvious that the offer wasn't serious, but Meghan enjoyed playing along anyway.

'Gadarim or not, you couldn't handle a girl like me, old man. And besides, Dane will ask me any day now.'

Madoc smiled.

'Perhaps I couldn't handle you Meg, but I'd enjoy finding out! And Dane had best get his arse moving if he wants to keep men like me from trying.'

Meghan shook her head and the two carried on their happy bickering as they rode. The whole column of riders seemed in good humour for the most part, and Rhia even heard Gwen laughing a little behind them, and turned to see that Ewan seemed to be sharing a jest with her. Rhia was glad that her big brother was able to put her at her ease. Gwen was a gentle soul at heart and would need encouragement before the battle. Rhia of course, though she had suffered the odd bout of anxiety, needed no such support and was eager to get to grips with the enemy. She patted the hilt of the sword sheathed at her belt and thought of the coward she'd taken it from. *Silverbite deserves to go to war with a decent master. Or mistress.*

From what news they'd had so far, it seemed that a group called a *legion*, meaning some fifteen hundred Gaians, was now occupying Nantwyn, along with as many Gorvicae and a few hundred Orugae fighters. Baercban, the Gorvicae chieftain, had been sighted there himself, along with his son, Sedryn. As Caderyn from the area fled southwest away from them, more news of the enemy was coming to the assembling force, and Rhia had been both overjoyed and enraged to hear that Gawan, the Leaping Wolf, had been seen at Nantwyn as well.

Rhia clenched her teeth as she rode and wondered what honour she might be granted for defeating a Gadarim. He might be good, but he'd lost to Madoc last time hadn't he? And that meant he could be beaten, and she might be the one to do it. She pictured his face, his ugly, black-bearded face, and dreamed how it would feel to ram Silverbite through his sneer. She could almost taste the victory on her tongue.

Rhia looked around at the green fields and sloping valleys of the lands of the Caderyn. Belenos was shining down on glittering streams and vibrant trees, and her love for her tribe and land swelled. They would win their territory back, she was certain of it. The clans would come together at Dunn's Vale in a day or two's time and from what Madoc had told her, their numbers would swell to some three thousand warriors, likely more. Ossian, the messenger from Nantwyn, had brought two hundred survivors of his town with him when he'd fled, many of whom were keen to return there and fight for their lands, and with more clans arriving with every passing day, the number of Caderyn fighters was truly vast.

Up ahead, leading the Caderyn to war, Carradan rode straight-backed and proud, with Reaghan and the other druids riding beside him. The holy men would not be doing any actual *fighting*, of course. Many had fought in their youth but now they played a far greater role; before the battle they would call upon the gods and on the land itself to lend victory to the Caderyn, and would put blessings and charms on the weapons of the warriors. For a moment Rhia wished that they might use their magics to help them against the Gorvicae, but quickly chased the thought away with a feeling of shame. Battles were to be proven by the courage and skill of warriors, and it had been lifetimes since the druids had unleashed their powers directly against their enemies. *Besides, if our druids start hurling real spells then the Gorvicae druids will do the same, and the gods only know what sort of chaos might ensue.* Rhia sighed and patted Neida's neck again. Courage and skill; that was what would matter, and the unity of the clans against their enemy.

Bel, Meghan's brother, rode up beside Rhia and Bevan and nodded to where his sister and Madoc still flirted.

'Dane is still yet to ask her to be his wife then?'

Rhia smiled at the red-haired young man.

'Still nothing.'

Bel shook his head and gestured to Bevan.

'Can you not get your own husband to encourage him or something? All we ever hear at home is Meg's lamenting at his delays.'

Rhia shrugged and her husband sounded amusedly weary.

'Don't you start on that as well! All I hear in *my* home is how I'm not encouraging him enough.'

Rhia looked upwards as if trying to remember something.

'Oh, I'm sure you give me more to complain about than that?'

Bevan gave her leg a playful slap.

'I wouldn't know, dear wife, I don't pay that much attention.'

He swayed away from her swiping hand and Bel laughed aloud beside them.

'You see? Dane and Meghan have all this to look forward to.'

Bevan grinned and Rhia smiled and shrugged her shoulders.

'It makes us eager for a good battle at least. It gets us out of the house and away from our quarrelling for a while.'

Bel gave a confident snort.

'Not that this will likely take long.'

Rhia grinned in agreement. The Caderyn were gathering nearly all of their fighting strength, and Carradan was a legendary war leader and well loved by his people. No town had held back any more men than they'd had to, and all were willing and able to do their duty for their chieftain. Apparently messages had been sent to the Bearnicans as well, to see if they were now willing to fight with them against the Gaians, but Rhia had no idea what sort of deal they might have struck, and few Caderyn held much hope of help from them. *Not that we'll need it. The Gorvicae are fighting us on our home ground. They cannot hope to win.*

She smiled to herself. Not only were the Caderyn clearly the better fighters, it seemed that rather than come out and find them, the Gaians and Gorvicae were hiding at Nantwyn, building up the fortifications and generally wasting time. It was a sure sign that they were no real warriors, of course. They must have heard about the gathering of the Caderyn clans, and real fighters would have come out here to meet them by now. *They are afraid,* she thought, and looked back again at the massive column, *and so they should be.*

*

There were almost no clouds to mask the stars of the night sky and on another night, Rhia might have been tempted to just lie back on the grass looking up at them. All her life she had never grown tired of the beauty of the stars, of staring up at the light from Camelas' daughters and wondering if any of them were looking back at her. But tonight there was something different for her to see, and she hoped fervently that Camelas' daughters weren't watching her now.

She was lying flat on her belly on a low ridge of grass, staring down at the circle of fires that she knew well she ought not to be looking at. Bevan and Dane and the others were all still eating at their fires a little way off but Rhia had seen Madoc and Arthfael gathering their warriors and heading away, and her curiosity had got the better of her. The rituals of the Gadarim were something most people only vaguely understood, and no outsider was ever permitted to actually witness them. A tiny part of her was worried that Taran would disapprove of her spying, but the warrior elite had fascinated her for years, and try though she might she couldn't bring herself to crawl away.

The yellow light from the fires cast eerie shadows all around them and the group of men who stood within it were grim and silent. Rhia recognised Owain and Bran and the huge shape of Arthfael standing motionless in the firelight, their battlemarks dark against their bodies. She was scanning around the warriors for the tall shape of Madoc, but then the First Man approached the ring of fire from outside with Ossian walking beside him. The Nantwyn messenger was naked and battlemarks had been painted all over his body, though his face remained clear and pale. He seemed nervous but his step was sure and his back was straight, and when Madoc asked his name, his voice was strong.

'I am Ossian, son of Lewyn.'

Madoc nodded to him and addressed the group.

'Brothers, Ossian son of Lewyn comes to us in the sight of Taran and Mabonac, that he would join us in the ranks of the Gadarim. Who will witness for this man?'

Rhia saw a figure she did not know step into the light, but she recognised him as one of the warriors who had come from Nantwyn.

'I will witness for this man. I am Elfed son of Grwn. I am the Running Stag.'

Rhia was straining to hear them over the crackle of the fires, and crept forwards a little on the ridge.

'Ossian son of Lewyn has long been a warrior of our people. He was charged by Aedan to carry his message, and to guide his people to Bryngarth because he knew the way better than any other. I was sent with him as guardian of Halwn, the son of Aedan, and I was with Ossian for all of our journey.'

The warrior held up three fingers in the air and continued to speak in a booming voice.

'Three times did Gorvic warriors seek to attack us as we went and three times did Ossian son of Lewyn defend us all with sword and heart. I say that his Test of Loyalty is done. I say that his Test of Strength is done. I say that his Test of Courage is done.'

There was a murmur among the warriors and Owain spoke up for them.

'We do not doubt your word, Running Stag, but only two of the Five Tests may be attested by a witness. One of those you have vouched for must be shown here among the others.'

Elfed nodded and turned to their newcomer.

'Very well. Ossian son of Lewyn, what test would you take once more?'

The slender man straightened his back and his answer made Rhia feel proud to call herself Caderyn.

'You may test all three.'

The next murmur was one of definite approval but Madoc spoke for them this time.

'A fine choice Ossian, but we all of us trust the word of Running Stag. Choose only one test to add to your others.'

The new man nodded, his jaw thrusting out.

'Then test my courage.'

Madoc nodded back and slowly drew his sword.

'Very well.'

He beckoned to Owain and to Arthfael and to Rhia's astonishment all three began moving around the Nantwyn man, and bellowed warcries as they swung their blades at his naked flesh. At the very last moment they stopped their blows from striking skin, but they were coming at him with great speed and power and Rhia held her breath in terror, certain that one of them would kill him by accident. But their skill prevailed as the three men moved and struck at him with their blades, though it was nothing to the nerve displayed by Ossian son of Lewyn. Though the voices and faces of the Bryngarth Gadarim made Rhia certain that they meant him harm, the Nantwyn man did not flinch even once. His jaw stayed grimly set as the swords came swinging at his body and Rhia sensed the approval of the men who stood watching.

After what seemed like an age to their hidden observer, the madness finally stopped and Madoc gestured to the crowd with an open hand.

'Does any man doubt the courage of Ossian son of Lewyn?'

There was silence around the circle before Madoc spoke again, this time addressing Ossian.

'Then prepare yourself for the Test of Focus.'

The slender man nodded and Arthfael led him forward and motioned for him to drop to his knees. Ossian did so and sat there unmoving for a while as Madoc and Owain waited behind him. Rhia squirmed a little and wondered what the next test might involve, and her heart leaped to her mouth as she almost missed it.

With no warning, Madoc silently sprang forward and slashed his blade straight down at the kneeling man in a cut aimed to split his skull in half. Ossian tensed for less than half a heartbeat and flung himself to the side in a clumsy roll before coming to his feet, his hands raised in fists before him. Madoc nodded as he sheathed his blade and once again addressed the crowd.

'Does any man doubt the focus of Ossian son of Lewyn?'

Again there was silence and Rhia felt her heart hammering in her chest as she watched. What would have happened if he hadn't moved in time? Would Madoc have stopped himself as he had done earlier? After Ossian had rolled away the First Man's sword had plunged downwards, cutting straight down to the dirt of the floor where he'd been kneeling an eyeblink earlier. Rhia doubted if even Madoc could have pulled back such a blow.

Fear and excitement flooded through the young woman as she gazed in awe at their greatest warriors. Madoc was speaking again as Owain approached one of the fires and thrust a sword into the flames.

'Prepare yourself for the Test of Will.'

Ossian nodded and once again it was the giant Arthfael who led him to his testing. Rhia shifted a little to gain a clearer view and saw the hopeful man sink to one knee before the flames, with Madoc standing opposite him. She stared down at the sword in the fire and remembered the scars she'd once seen on Madoc's hand, and both she and Ossian seemed to understand what had to happen.

The slender man did not hesitate for a moment and raised his right hand to grasp the sword but Owain, stood beside him, held him back. Rhia didn't hear what was spoken by him but she assumed that he said 'left' because Ossian lowered his right hand and grasped the hilt of the sword firmly with his left. The leather grip had cracked and pulled away from the iron, and Rhia was certain she heard his skin sizzle as it made contact with the metal. The man grunted in pain but did not cry out and Rhia thought she heard approval in Madoc's voice when he spoke again.

'Will you defend your land and your people with all of your might?'

Ossian's voice was strained but strong as he replied.

'I shall.'

'And will you balance fury and mercy as it pleases Taran and Mabonac?'

Rhia heard the clenching of the man's teeth as he replied, and she started grasping handfuls of grass in her fists as if it would somehow alleviate his pain.

'I shall.'

'And will you honour all Gadarim as your brothers beneath the gods, and live your life proudly by their code?'

Ossian's voice rose a little but still he grasped the burning sword.

'I shall!'

Madoc raised his own voice, addressing them all.

'Then Ossian son of Lewyn, I name you to the Gadarim, and may you live and die with honour!'

The men around all echoed his words.

'May you live and die with honour!'

Ossian nodded with a pained smile and Rhia saw Owain help remove the new Gadarim's hand from the sword and begin smearing it with what she assumed was grease and honey. Madoc produced another sword from somewhere and held it out with open hands.

'Rise brother, and take this gift.'

Ossian wobbled a little but stood up under his own power and took the sword from the First Man with his unburned right hand. Madoc raised his voice again.

'Ossian son of Lewyn, I name you the Hawk of War!'

Once more the crowd of Gadarim echoed him.

'The Hawk of War!'

The circle broke and Rhia looked on as the warriors gathered around to clap his shoulder and congratulate him, embracing their new brother with smiles and jests. She felt her pride swell again as she watched the Gadarim, the Mighty, the sons of Mabonac the Dragon who held no fear of death. She felt a warmth in her chest that her tribe held so many great men, and was glad that she had taken the chance to watch them. But nestled in amongst the pride was a sting of envy. Females among the Gadarim were practically unheard of and with a child on the way her chances of joining them had dipped from slim down to impossible. No mother could justify joining the warrior elite, no matter how well she might prove herself in battle. Rhia sighed quietly. The chieftain's daughter tore her eyes away from them and started shuffling down the bank, her pride and hope for her people's victory marred by her envy and frustration.

Chapter 9. Glyscoed Wood

The trees all around her looked dark and threatening, their branches reaching out like skeletal fingers, and Rhia struggled to remind herself that pines and birches were on *their* side. *There are no blackwoods in Glyscoed.* Leu's silver light was hidden behind the clouds Reaghan had called for, and the Caderyn in Glyscoed were now all but invisible. Rhia crept along in silence with the others as they floated like ghosts through the woodland, placing her feet carefully so as not to disturb the undergrowth. Their cautious pace was slow, such was the price of stealth, but they were finally nearing the first of the Gaian scouts, and Rhia had her first look at this new enemy of her people.

He was short. No taller than Dane and certainly shorter than Ewan. It was hard to tell colours in the blackness of the night but she thought his hair was dark, and had been cut very close to his head. His face made her think he was around her own age, yet for some reason he was wearing no beard. Rhia puzzled over that as she crept closer to him, her soft shoes making no noise on the grass. Plenty of Lurian men liked to shape their facial hair, the Dariniae were known for it, but to shave the beard completely was rare to say the least.

She moved closer still, careful not to stare for fear of his noticing her, and had to fight back a smile at the knowledge that this enemy had no idea that she was standing right in front of him. He was dressed in simple tunic and breeches, the fool had left his camp without even a sword on him, and she watched as he shucked the trousers down to his ankles and squatted beside a tree, blissfully oblivious to his danger. *Glyscoed won't welcome your little offering, foreigner, and tonight you can consider me its instrument.*

Rhia was so close to him now she was amazed he hadn't spotted her, and she was tempted to say something to this poor fool she was about to kill. He might be a Gaian and an invader, but it was hardly honourable to kill a man while he defecated. War should be about warriors facing each other in the open, not cutting men's throats in the dark. But Reaghan and Carradan had both stated that a night-raid on the scouts was necessary to give them some surprise for when they battled at Nantwyn. None of the Caderyn had been particularly fond of the idea but it had to be done and so here she stood, her long knife blackened with soot to dull its shine, ready to kill this man who had no notion she was there.

Her hand tightened on the grip of the weapon. This man had no business being here, he was no Lurian, not even a warrior by the looks of him, just a greedy outsider come to take what belonged to her people. This beardless foreigner was just a thief, nothing more, come to steal land and crops from others because he was too lazy to work for himself. His people had killed innocents at Nantwyn and would do so again if they were not stopped, and to stop the Gaians and the Gorvicae they needed the element of surprise. And to have that these scouts must be taken and killed. It was simple. Rhia looked at the young man and tried not to see his eyes, tried not to see the spirit behind the flesh, and poised herself ready to spring. But then he sneezed, just as any man might, Gaian or Lurian, and Rhia couldn't help herself. She coughed.

The tiny warning wasn't much, but it meant that the Gaian scout was at least facing her as the soot-blackened blade rammed home in his throat. Blood flowed and his bowels opened, and the stench was almost as bad as the sight of his panicked face as he flailed and gurgled, trying desperately to cling onto his life. He was not large and Rhia managed to lower him down to the ground, controlling his convulsions as best she could. The noise was not much but in the silence of the forest it seemed deafening, and Rhia was certain that she'd soon hear his comrades come crashing through the undergrowth towards her. But time passed and none came. The Gaian bled his life away in her arms and the trees stayed silent. After ten heartbeats his struggling stopped. Rhia sliced the blade across his neck and held onto him for another ten just to be sure.

When she stood back up she suddenly realised how cold the forest was, and her knife-hand was shaking as she wiped it on the grass. Her heart was hammering in her chest and she wanted to vomit from the smell, but she forced herself to breathe slowly and raised her other arm in a signal. From the darkness the other Caderyn approached in silence and when she saw Bevan she had to resist the urge to throw herself on him right there. She hated to admit it but killing the Gaian had shaken her, and she suddenly needed to be held by her husband and hear his voice telling her it was alright. Rhia almost approached to touch him but forced herself to focus on their task. With her husband had come Meghan, Bel and Gronow, though she knew there were a score of others spread about. They exchanged no words, only nods of grim determination over the motionless corpse, and the little group set off again into the night.

The next man they found they took down together. This one too had left the safety of his camp for a call of nature and had been pissing against a tree when the Caderyn had slain him. Once again, Rhia hadn't been able to bring herself to let him die with no warning at all and had deliberately snapped a twig as they approached, though Bevan's knife had found its mark by the time the man reacted. Bel helped him to control the body as another Gaian gave his blood to Glyscoed, and Rhia wondered if

Mehine might be watching them even now. Part of her was certain that she was, and that the goddess wanted these Gaians gone just as much as they did. All the same, Mehine's presence at her wedding had been a very different feeling indeed.

The orange glow and flickering shadows of a campfire was growing nearer, and Rhia suspected that they would soon be fighting openly at last, albeit after attacking from ambush. The Caderyn kept silent as they crept on towards it, and so quiet was the wood that Rhia almost jumped from her skin at the sound of a voice.

'Leander?'

The Caderyn froze in place as another Gaian, this one wearing an armoured shirt and with a sword at his belt, came tramping through the undergrowth towards them. He spoke again, presumably addressing the man they'd just killed, but his words were a stream of alien sounds and Rhia had no idea what he might be saying. Not that it mattered. Before Bevan could even twitch towards him an arrow transfixed the newcomer through his throat, and he dropped to his knees with a gurgle. Rhia and Bevan made towards him as quickly as they could, but Gwyr shot again before they were anywhere close and a second arrow thudded through his eye. The Gaian dropped without a sound.

Rhia looked back at Gwyr with disapproval. Had he missed, the man might have cried out and warned the whole camp of their attack, and while that might have assuaged a few consciences, it would have spelled ruin for the plan. Madoc's son came cautiously from the undergrowth, looking rather sheepish, and Rhia guessed that he had shot in panic or in fear for his companions, and she softened her glare. It was invisible tonight of course but she'd noted on the march that Gwyr now sported a beautiful black eye, testament to his father's intolerance for his son's bullying. Rhia wondered if Madoc's lesson on tribal unity had perhaps been taken too much to heart if the boy was taking such risks to protect his fellows. She exchanged nods with the young archer, and with Bevan, and they made a quick check of the body before beckoning the others and moving forwards again.

The only other men they saw before reaching the camp itself were a pair of armoured Gaians standing silhouetted in the firelight. They clearly hadn't heard any of their comrades' deaths and were leaning on their spears, chatting together in their queer tongue. Bevan began moving slowly towards the one on the left while Meghan began creeping up on the other. Rhia thought it strange, seeing Bevan like this. Meghan and Bel she had seen fighting at Broken Stream, and Gwyr looked enough like Madoc for his presence in a fight to seem natural, but Bevan she had never seen in combat. She knew that he had fought against Ierryn's raiders of course, but she'd never before seen him kill a man with her own eyes. It made her both want him and fear him a little all at once, as if she was seeing a part of her husband's spirit she had never truly known was there.

They were close enough now that they could see beyond the guards to where a group of beardless Gaians sat or stood around a fire, with what looked like one or two Gorvic warriors with them. *Probably came with them as guides. You should have guided them into posting more watchers in these woods, or come out here and done it yourselves.* It might not be their land but the Gorvicae at least would have known how dense and dark Glyscoed was, and how easily their little band might be ambushed.

Rhia stayed close behind Meghan as they closed in on the spearmen. It would be difficult to do, but if Bevan timed his attack well they might take both of them down at once and still be able to surprise those in the camp. Rhia's fingers flexed anxiously on the grip of her darkened blade and she determined to give no warning to these two. Honour or not, they might cost Caderyn lives if they cried out. She crept nearer to them, treading softly on the grass, and readied herself to kill a man in cold blood. But it seemed that Mehine or Karanon valued her honour more highly than she did, because just as Bevan rose up to grab the nearest Gaian, the hooting of an owl split the night's silence like a scream, and both the soldiers suddenly straightened up and looked about them for the noise.

Bevan was fast, and even as his man turned he sprang at him and bore him to the ground, the knife at his throat. The other Gaian gave a short cry of alarm but Meghan lunged forwards before Gwyr could send an arrow to silence him, and the two went down grappling into the undergrowth. Rhia and Bel leaped forward with knives ready, and it took only moments to finish off the startled guards. But it was enough.

Rhia rose from the bloody corpse of her and Meghan's making and saw that the camp was now alive with movement, with men reaching for weapons and barking out questions in the strange language of the Gaians. There were many of them, perhaps twice the numbers of the Caderyn who approached the little campsite, and Rhia stared for a moment and wondered if they should back off whilst yet they could. But then Bevan's voice sounded from behind her.

'Loose now!'

Gwyr's arrow flashed past her to thud home in a Gaian's chest, and a heartbeat later two more shafts flew into the crowd of men, the other Caderyn archers having heard her husband's cry. Rhia watched as arrows punched into flesh and bone as the confused Gaians grabbed for weapons and scanned the trees for the shooters. Men tumbled and fell, and before they could organise themselves enough to form a charge, Bevan screamed out again and the Caderyn echoed his bellow.

'Taran!'

Rhia let the War God's name howl out from her lips as she sprinted forwards into the chaos, thrusting her knife into its sheath and drawing free her axe and sword. She was the first of the Caderyn to reach the men around the campfire, and she screamed out the name again as her axe bit into a Gaian skull.

*

The Gorvic had been faster than she'd thought and he'd sprinted through the woods like a hare before a dog. Rhia, chasing after him, had been certain that he'd escape and tell his new masters what was happening, and she had panicked about what she should do but then, once again, she was reminded that the trees were on her side. The warrior's foot caught in a root and he cried out and stumbled, and Rhia seized the opportunity and hurled her axe into his back. It didn't quite make its mark but it was enough to draw a cry of pain and send him tumbling to the ground. Within heartbeats the Caderyn warrior caught up with him and she dragged her new sword across his throat. *Who's a dancing kitten now?*

She looked down at the bleeding man and felt a moment of fierce satisfaction. It wasn't Gawan of course, there had been no Gadarim in the scout party, but she pictured the arrogant bastard's face on the corpse's head, and felt the joy of battle pulsing through her at having brought down her enemy. The feeling was incredible, but it didn't last very long. The longer she looked at the body of the dead northerner the less she could convince herself that it was Gawan at her feet, and bile rose in her throat as she stared down at the man she'd killed.

Rhia turned away and, her legs unsteady, sat down under a tree and began wiping the blood from Silverbite. The Gorvic had led her a long way from the camp and she needed a rest before finding her way back. Her breathing was heavy and her hands were shaking, but she focused her mind on the task in hand and continued to clean off the blade. It was a fine piece of work, she thought. Good quality iron balanced nicely in the centre, with soft leather wrapped around the grip and swirling patterns on the guard and pommel. The man she'd taken it from at Broken Stream had been young and slim, and presumably the blade had been made for him because the sword was a little shorter and lighter than most, making it only slightly overlong for a woman of Rhia's build. *Silverbite is a good name*, she thought as she cleaned, *suits it. Light and beautiful, yet still deadly. Deadly...*

She worked the cloth over the iron until the red stains were gone and then kept rubbing long after it was clean. For some reason it felt important to keep running the rag up and down the blade in the same long, fluid movements, and Rhia lost all track of time as she sat under her tree, patiently wiping down the perfectly clean sword.

So absorbed was she in her task that when a voice came from the forest her heart leaped into her mouth, and she felt cold iron slice into her finger as her hands jerked suddenly in shock.

'I think it is clean by now, child.'

The cut was not deep but blood welled up from it and Rhia pressed the cloth to her flesh as she stood to face the speaker. The light was still almost non-existent but she made out the shape of a man, his back bent slightly with age, standing just outside the cutting range of her blade. He wore a heavy-looking cloak over whatever other clothes he had, and was leaning his weight a little on a gnarled old staff. His face was lined and grey-bearded, with bright green eyes and an expression that seemed only mildly interested, as if he found warriors and corpses on his way home every day.

Rhia ignored the sting of her cut hand and pressed the cloth tighter to the wound.

'What is it to you?' she replied, before politely adding, 'Father.'

The old man shrugged his hunched shoulders.

'Just noticing. I have noticed many things in my forest tonight.'

Rhia cocked her head.

'You are Caderyn?'

'I suppose, if that is what you call those who dwell here.'

Rhia frowned. She knew of no clan who lived in Glyscoed itself but there was always the chance that this man was a loner of some kind, perhaps an outcast or a criminal or the descendant of one. He didn't exactly look dangerous but all the same, she stayed wary.

'Well, I am Caderyn and I must get back to my fellows. The Gaians and the Gorvicae are coming and we have many of them to kill. You may wish to find somewhere safe for you and yours, father.'

Again the old man shrugged.

'I and mine are as safe as we are like to be.' He took half a pace forwards and his tone was conversational. 'You cannot kill the Gaians, you know.'

Rhia furrowed her brows again.

'I already have done tonight.'

The bright eyes of the old man stared into hers. He was barely taller than Rhia but his gaze was quietly intense.

'And it will do you no good. Caderyn and Gorvicae, Dariniae, Bearnicans, Averyn, Rydicae, Breiryn and all the others, you have been killing each other for years, this you are used to. But the Gaians are not like you. They do not live like you, they do not fight like you. You cannot kill them as you all kill each other.'

Rhia felt her anger start to bubble.

'You speak nonsense old man, the Caderyn can defeat anything.'

She knew she ought to be more courteous to a man of his years but his defeatism smacked of cowardice. The old man didn't seem offended but he shook his head a little, sounding disappointed more than angry.

'Young people nowadays. You would all be wiser to treat with these Gaians, not try to kill them.' He gestured upwards with his staff. 'I watch the stars child, and I see in their dance what may yet befall us.'

Rhia looked at him again. He didn't seem to be wearing a druid's robes and besides, all the druids nearby had come to Carradan's call to give council alongside Reaghan. This old man was clearly a would-be mage of some kind, and she decided she had indulged him enough.

'Thank you for your words, father. Now I must be gone. Once these Gaians are defeated I shall send word to any living in these woods that all is safe.'

With that she turned on her heel and started walking back along what she hoped was the way she had come. She would let the others know there was a body out here but there was no way she could carry the Gorvic back herself, and his bones would not be harmed by a day of neglect. Rhia had gone only a few paces however before the old man's voice came again.

'I saw in the stars many things, my child.'

Rhia kept walking but the man continued.

'I saw that the Gaians must be understood if the Caderyn are to survive. Your son might understand them, given the chance.'

Rhia froze. Slowly, she turned on the spot to face him.

'My son? I have no children.'

The old man raised an eyebrow.

'Not yet, but a son shall be born to you.'

Rhia resisted the urge to touch her stomach. She wasn't far enough to be showing yet, but Madlen had assured her that she was indeed with child. The man was guessing, surely? All young women planned to have sons at some point. Yet something in those shining eyes made Rhia doubt herself.

'With the gods' blessings I shall have sons, yes. Why should my son ever want or need to understand the Gaians?'

It was strange to hear herself say the words 'my son' but she tried not to let the little flutter in her belly show on her face. The old man kept looking straight into her eyes.

'Gaians often make treaties with nations they would rule. They make hostages of the sons and daughters of headmen and raise them up in their cities, hoping to make the conquered people more like them. If your son is sent to them, he may save your people much hardship.'

Rhia was confused, and more worried than she wanted to admit, and despite herself felt her hand hover over her stomach.

'My son will not be raised to be anything but Caderyn. We will crush the Gaians and the Gorvicae and they will beg to send *their* children to learn from *us*!'

She'd spoken more harshly than she had intended but still, the old man's face remained implacable.

'As you will. But I have seen both great good and great wickedness in those you would seek to fight, and a danger that threatens all of this land. If you would think on peace and not war, your people may prevail.'

Rhia was tired of the riddling warnings of this man, and the little shivers of fear that his words sent up her spine. All the way from Bryngarth her confidence in victory had been assured, and now his quiet words were sowing doubts in her head. She balled her fists, trying not to flinch as her cut started bleeding again, and she thrust out her chin defiantly.

'My people will prevail over the bodies of our enemies, and my son will hear the songs of it in his crib. You are a fool, or a coward or a liar to say anything else.'

Still the old man's expression showed only the mildest interest and he seemed to take no offence at Rhia's words. *He cannot be true Caderyn. No true Caderyn would stand to be so insulted.*

'Ignore my advice as you will, I care not.'

A little gust of wind whispered through the trees and Rhia saw the first flicker of emotion in the old man's face. An expression of impatience and irritation flashed across it, and he muttered his next words under his breath, his head turning away for a moment.

'Perhaps I care a little.' He raised his head and addressed Rhia again. 'I have given you my warning. Heed it, or do not heed it.'

He turned from her and started walking away, leaning his weight upon the staff. In the darkness his shape soon became indistinct among the trees and Rhia watched him go with relief, glad that this sower of doubt was leaving her. His words had been those of a fool and a craven and she could afford to have no doubts in her heart when she went to war. She watched him go, pondering on his warning despite herself and, for the briefest moment, she thought she saw the outline of a woman walking beside him. She strained her eyes that way but then a noise from behind her caused her to spin around, lifting Silverbite up to a guard.

Bel and Meghan were jogging through the trees, heads whipping back and forth, clearly looking for their missing comrade. Rhia raised a hand and the siblings nodded and made towards her, the relief evident on Meg's face even in the dark. Rhia smiled at her in what she hoped was a reassuring way, then turned back to look again at the old man. But he was gone. Whoever her strange companion had been he had disappeared into Glyscoed, and Rhia resolved to put his foolish warnings from her mind. He knew nothing of her, or of her son or of her people, and his cowardly whining was born of fear and ignorance. She was Rhianwyn daughter of Carradan, and a warrior of the Caderyn. And tomorrow there was a war for her to fight.

Chapter 10. The Battle of Nantwyn

Belenos shone brightly on the fields before the captured town, and the grass smelled clean and fresh on the early morning breeze. Across the plain, the hill of Nantwyn was green and bright, and the shining stream that ran down the west side of the mound was sparkling white and silver in the sunlight. The sky above was clear and the ground was dry and firm, and aside from a scattered few farmhouses the area between them and the town was all open, flat grassland. The time and place was perfect for a charge!

Rhia looked down from the little ridge and saw her enemy's full might for the first time. Directly across from her was a group of greyish squares made up of Gaians in their armoured shirts, all standing close by each other in tight groups of many hundreds. At the centre of each square was a flash of colour where a man held up a bolt of cloth on a shining pole, though it was all too far off for her to see any details. She wondered how the men there intended to fight, since it seemed to her that they were standing too close together to be able to use their swords properly. *But the swords the scouts had were quite short, remember. Maybe they don't know how to make proper long swords?*

The men in the squares were holding up heavy wooden boards as well, and it looked as if they planned to simply hide behind them in one big line and avoid having to fight altogether. *Well, more fool them when the Gadarim reach their lines and start cutting them apart!* Beside and in front of the grey squares marched the Gorvicae, a great dark mass of warriors with sunlight glinting from polished swords and limewashed hair.

Rhia took in another deep breath as she looked down at them. She'd not shared with the others her conversation with the mad old man, partially because it had been

139

confusing, but mostly because his talk had been all of defeat and surrender, and that was no talk to share with warriors. She was also a little ashamed that his words had worried her so at the time, though that worry was now evaporating faster than the morning dew.

Beside her on the ridge stood thousands of her kinfolk, men and women from every clan of the Caderyn armed and ready for the battle that was to come, with Reaghan and his disciples walking among them with their jangling staffs. The druids might not use their powers directly any more but they chanted blessings and good omens to the warriors of the Caderyn, and men and women held out their weapons to be touched by the holy men as they passed. Across the field, Rhia saw men in white were moving amongst the Gorvicae as well, and doubtless their own druids would be performing similar rituals. But everyone knew that Reaghan was without peer, and she could almost taste the fear of the enemy tribesmen, knowing as they must that the greatest druid stood with Carradan.

The robed men were still some way off, and Meghan and Rhia busied themselves about their battlemarks. She kept as still as she could as Meghan painted her face for her, and tried to focus on Taran and the spirit of battle as warriors were supposed to when their marks were being drawn. Her arms and neck were finished and Meg was now painting swirls across her cheek to sweep over one eye. Both wore sleeveless tunics to better show off their marks to the gods, and they had abandoned skirts in favour of tight breeches that they could run in.

All the way up the line and throughout the mass of Caderyn on the ridge, other pairs of warriors were engaged in the same activity. A little way from them Rhia spotted Ossian, his left arm and chest already tattooed with permanent marks, having his face painted by Owain. The tattoos were far more intricate than the finger-drawn paint, but much of their detail would be obscured when fresh woad was drawn over them. But then in battle it was most important to make the marks shine brighter in Belenos' light.

Meg put the last touch of blue paint onto her face and indicated that she was done so that Rhia could start on her. She dipped her fingers into the little wooden bowl and imagined venomous serpents as she drew shapes up the other girl's arms. A few drops fell from her hand onto the tunic and the redhead smiled a little at her.

'A pity it's not the old days, eh?'

Rhia smiled back and wiped off some of the stain.

'Even in this weather, I think I prefer this!'

According to Madoc their ancestors had fought their battles completely nude, the women as well as the men. Rhia strongly suspected that this was a fantasy of the Lurian men, but many of them insisted it was fact. In the unlikely event that it was, she pitied the poor fools for not having the sense to dress for battle, even without considering the weather, the notion of running anywhere while naked was not an appealing one. Rhia was hardly voluptuous but even she had wrapped her chest up tightly beneath her tunic to make running and fighting more comfortable. It had been a pleasant change when her breasts had swollen due to her condition, but the accompanying ache was highly unpleasant, especially when she'd been dressing for battle. But then, it could have been worse. Strapping herself tight might be wise for *her*, but for women like Meghan it was an absolute necessity. *The poor girl might knock herself out if those things were let loose!* Rhia almost giggled at the thought but Reaghan and Bael were approaching them and she put on a serious expression.

The two druids jangled their staffs and made strange gestures with their hands as Rhia and Meghan held their weapons out for blessing. Rhia mumbled a brief prayer to Taran and Mabonac for the battle, then to Camelas and Marna for herself and for Bevan. And for her unborn child. For some reason, the face of the old man in Glyscoed came back to her for a moment and she resolved once again that no matter what occurred, she would never give up this child. She asked Marna's promise that her son would be born and raised and live his life right here, and not as the hostage of some Gaian chieftain. Not that there was any danger of that. The men on the plain were moving slower than snails and the warriors of the Caderyn would soon sprint down there and crush them.

Once Silverbite and her axe had been blessed and returned to her belt, she pushed a knuckle into her palm and muttered another quick prayer to Mehine and Karanon for the sake of her land and people, just to be sure. Reaghan and Bael were about to move on when the elder druid spotted somebody behind them, and Rhia turned to see her husband offering Brackenthorn up for blessing. Bevan wore a similar sleeveless tunic to the other warriors, and his strong arms shone with blue woad from wrist to shoulder. Rhia had never seen him wearing battlemarks before and a stirring in her loins told her she liked it very much. The twisting marks that ran along his neck and across his face made him look fearsome to behold, and she felt proud to have such a man that she could call her husband. He smiled at her after the druid had spoken his spells over the sword.

'Ready to crack some more skulls?'

Rhia grinned back at him. Truthfully, as at Broken Stream, she'd felt fluttering nerves all morning as she prepared herself for battle, but now that it was almost here, and Bevan was here with her, all her fears seemed to melt away like icicles before the spring.

'Think you can keep up with us? It looks like more than a boatload of them down there so if you want to wait for me at home, I'll understand.'

Chuckles came from several Caderyn standing around the couple, and Bevan wrapped an arm around her waist and drew her close into a kiss. This only lead to more laughter and whooping and when he let her go, he addressed them all in a clear voice.

'You'd best all be keeping count today. If my wife kills more than I do I shall never hear the end of it!'

Their companions laughed even more and Rhia kissed her husband again, though she had to stop far sooner than she'd have liked as Carradan stepped forward from the line.

The High Chieftain of the Caderyn, the Charging Bull, wore a winged helm polished to a blinding shine and held Ironhorn aloft in his right hand. As leader of the tribe, he wore the ancient armoured shirt of bronze scales, brought back as a trophy generations ago when their ancestors had fought wars against the Grenn. Few Lurians of any sort concerned themselves with armour – skill and Taran's blessing would keep them whole if they deserved it – but the bronze shirt had been a symbol to their tribe for countless years, and it shone now like a beacon in the sun. The chief, for all his lack of height, looked both imposing and inspiring, with his beard bleached white with lime and his battlemarks freshly highlighted in blue.

Around him, their own marks and beards gleaming blue and white in the sun, the Gadarim of the tribe stepped forward to flank their chief. She saw Madoc and Owain, the Smiling Fox and the Stalking Fox, Arthfael and Bran, the Black Bear and Diving Raven, Bedwyr and Elfed,

Blackmane and Running Stag, and standing proudly among them their newest man; Ossian, the Hawk of War.

Carradan surveyed the field below and Rhia saw a gleam of anticipation in his eyes. Today they would wreak vengeance on the Gorvicae and their Gaian allies for the slaughter of good Caderyn people. The chieftain's sword-arm rose higher and Rhia shared a glance with Bevan as the tension mounted along the ridge. Her husband looked both handsome and terrifying in his battle-gear, and Rhia felt a surge of love for him as he smiled down at her and winked.

Carradan's voice was loud and clear, and he didn't bore them with any unneeded words.

'Warriors of the Caderyn, today we will have justice for our people. May Taran and Mabonac be with us all.' He pointed Ironhorn down the hill towards their enemy. 'Forward!'

A great cry went up from all around them and Rhia and Bevan added their voices to the shout as the warriors on the ridge began their walk down to the plain. Weapons were raised above heads, horns blew, and curses were hurled at the Gorvicae below, who Rhia saw were bringing their own Gadarim to the fore. *For all the good it will do them!* Rhia felt the lust for battle start to pound through her blood like the beat of a drum, and she shared another grin with Bevan before turning back to view the enemy. *Come on then,* she thought, *come forward and die!*

*

The ridge flattened out and they started walking faster as they closed on the Gaian squares. Over to the left Rhia saw the Gorvicae massing to charge their flank, and at a gesture from Carradan, Elfed and half a dozen Gadarim set off to lead some warriors that way. From what she could see, it looked like they were Durolwg men, and she whispered a quick prayer for Delyn and for his father Aeron, the headman of their clan. Straight ahead of them were the Gaians, hiding like cowards behind their wooden boards, their bodies grey and dull in their chain armour. The *shields*, as Madoc had called them, had been painted red, with what looked like a giant cat and a cross painted on them in yellow. The same symbol was on the cloth which flew from a pole in the middle of the square, a bird of prey cast in gold flying over it. Whatever gods they were supposed to be, Rhia was certain they'd be of little use to them here. These invaders were marching on Caderyn land and the sons of Mabonac, the mighty Gadarim, were closing on their lines.

Those warriors, with Carradan at their head, broke into a jog as they neared, and all across the field Caderyn fighters upped the pace. Rhia knew there would be no exchange of insults and curses today as there had been at Broken Stream. This would be warfare, plain and simple, and she gripped her weapons tighter as she lengthened her stride to keep up. Between her and the Gadarim she saw Ewan and Dane loping along as well, their faces blue with woad and their expressions determined. For a man who'd not seen battle before Dane was showing no fear at all, and Rhia was proud to be his sister as she watched him close with the enemy.

The line of Gaian shields was less than a bowshot away now, and Rhia's heart started racing as they drew nearer. What tiny amount of fear she felt was smothered by pride and rage, and she exchanged fierce grins with both Bevan and Meg as the pace increased again and the warriors began to run. Her feet ate up the distance with ease and then a cry went up from her father that was echoed from a thousand throats.

'Taran!'

Rhia bellowed the sacred name of the mighty God of War, though the sound of it was lost in the wall of noise that came from the Caderyn. Behind her she heard the warhorns blowing loud and long, and she wondered what terror these foolish Gaians must be feeling. They still advanced on them only slowly, no paint upon their faces or warcries to their gods, and Rhia wondered how on earth such men had ever beaten anyone.

The distance grew shorter. The Caderyn began to sprint. Rhia felt the wind rush through her hair as she pelted towards the Gaians and Mehine was surely on it for it seemed to fill her with courage, and once again she screamed out the name of the War God.

'Taran!'

From the square of Gaian men came a handful of thrown spears, but only a few of them hit their marks and it was too late now for the charge to be stopped. She picked her target in the line and readied her axe for a swing, Silverbite seeming to twitch in her other hand of its own volition, eager for blood and for vengeance. Rhia howled to the skies as she sprinted towards her enemies. And then the lines clashed. And chaos reigned.

Rhia's axe thudded hard into wood and she heaved back to pull the shield down, but before she could a stabbing blade came out of nowhere and she was forced to dodge back, parrying with her sword. She lost her grip on the axe-haft and tried to regain her balance, but the warrior behind her shoved her forwards again, and another blade lashed out towards her face. This time she ducked and drew her arm back for a thrust of her own, but another stab again came from the wall of Gaian shields, this one from a different man, and she was forced back on the defensive once more.

Beside her, Bevan was trying to cut down over the Gaian's wooden boards, but each time he raised

Brackenthorn a stabbing blade menaced his torso, and he too had no choice but to parry wildly to keep them from him. The Gaians were packed so closely together that each Caderyn warrior, having left space enough for his neighbour to swing his weapon, seemed to be facing two or three of the grey-clad men, all stabbing out viciously with their short-bladed swords. Rhia blocked another lunge and backed away a pace and she saw that further along the line, even the mighty Gadarim were struggling.

Madoc was fighting with a sword in each hand, his incredible skill allowing him to parry the attacks with his left while he struck out with his right. Rhia saw him crash his blade down hard on a helmeted head, and when the man crumpled down it seemed the wall of shields might be breached, but even as the Gaian fell his comrades dragged him backwards from the fight and another man stepped in smoothly to take his place. Madoc bellowed at them in rage and defiance and set about attacking again.

Rhia darted forwards as a man thrust at Bevan's flank, and she managed to score a cut on the Gaian's wrist. She'd not had time to put enough power in the blow to take off his hand, but the cut caused a cry of pain and the arm was withdrawn, the short sword falling to the grass. She saw her chance and pressed forward at the wounded man, but he hid behind his shield while the man beside him stabbed out at her, and yet again Rhia found herself forced to abandon attack for defence.

Frustration welled up in her and a trickle of fear mixed in with it as she saw Dawood the Smith rush forward at the Gaians, only to be stabbed by two of them at once as he drew back his arm for a swing. The big metalworker screamed as iron plunged through his belly, until another sword sliced through his throat and the scream was reduced to a gurgle. Meghan, on her right, took a stab clean through her biceps and then shrieked in pain as the short blade was ripped free. A heavy shield slammed into her beautiful face and she staggered back before collapsing to the dirt. To her left, Bevan had managed to knock a soldier from his feet but once again the Gaians pulled their man away before he could be finished, and fresh fighters appeared in the gap he had created, hacking at her husband with cold efficiency.

Rhia watched it all happen and felt as if her skin had been doused in freezing water. These Gaians were not large men, nor did they seem to have much skill with their iron blades, yet they were butchering the Caderyn with almost no loss to themselves. All around them warriors ran at the shields, or were jostled into them by their fellows behind, and the short blades whipped out and brave men and women died. It was like fighting a wall. A wall made of wood and iron and the occasional glimpse of flesh, though any time that flesh was pricked more wood and iron came in to replace it. Her easy confidence was pouring from her like water from a leaky bucket as she realised that they could not press on. And then the Gaians started to push.

High-pitched whistles sounded from somewhere in the grey square and the first line of men all shoved their shields forward at the same moment. In the heartbeat of confusion this caused, the next line moved past them to form a new front of fresh soldiers, and not only did these men begin hacking and stabbing that much faster, they also began to creep forward with tiny steps, the men behind them keeping close as the whole square began advancing.

Rhia tried to attack her new opponents but was forced backwards as stabbing blades came from all around her, and she stumbled into a Caderyn standing behind her as she dodged. It took only a moment for her to regain her balance and once again she sprang forwards, this time with Bevan at her side, but their blades met only dull wood and bright iron as they hacked at the wall to try to reach the men beyond. Rhia managed to shove her Gaian enough to open up his flank, but the soldier next to him menaced her with his short sword and she abandoned her attack to parry it down. The Gaians kept moving forwards, step by patient step, and the Caderyn were forced backwards once again.

Rhia could almost feel the resolve in her fellows start to waver as more warriors were cut down all around them. Further up she saw Carradan hammering blows down on a Gaian shield, furiously trying to batter his way through it, only for another soldier to lunge for the chieftain's side. Rhia's heart leaped to her mouth but Arthfael stepped in to defend his chief, shoving Carradan unceremoniously behind him and catching the Gaian by his forearm. The soldier tried to pull back again, but the giant Gadarim dragged him from his line and slammed a meaty fist into his windpipe. The soldier gagged and Arthfael lifted him bodily over his head. The big man hurled his opponent into the grey square and Rhia joined in as warriors cheered for him, and for just a moment she thought they might now start pushing back.

But the Gaian line was closing on them still, and three blades flashed out at the giant Gadarim. Two of them he parried away from his body but the third one stuck in his leg and he collapsed down to one knee. Madoc and Owain leaped forward as Arthfael pulled one of the Gaians down onto him to begin crushing him against his massive chest. The three Gadarim laid about them like madmen and Rhia was sure she saw Gaian soldiers fall, but the slow advance was unstoppable, and as the lines reached Arthfael she saw half a dozen short blades thrust down mercilessly into his body.

His brother Gadarim howled and Rhia felt tears blur her vision, but there was no way of reaching him and it was all that she could do to keep the stabbing blades clear of her own flesh. All around the Caderyn line was crumbling as warriors were pushed backwards, with no chances to attack as they desperately defended. Cold fear gripped Rhia like a hand around her heart and she was ashamed at her relief when Madoc's voice cut across the clamour.

'Back to the ridge!'

A heartbeat later she heard Owain echo the call.

'Pull back to high ground!'

The Caderyn began disengaging as best they could, though it was no easy task in the face of that murderous wall. Bevan tried to gain them time by dashing in and swiping at the soldiers, but a heavy shield-thrust knocked him to the dirt and Rhia panicked for a moment before Bel and Dane hauled him back to his feet. The Gaians were still coming slowly and the Caderyn retreat was swift, though many warriors were cut down as they tried to back away. Rhia hated it, but a shameful part of her was glad. This wall of men and iron was terrifying, it simply wasn't something they could fight, and they had to get away from it before it killed them all.

They managed to gain some space as they fell back, trying to keep together as the Gaian square shuffled forward. Rhia was tired but she jogged on all the same, and Bevan's voice beside her gave her hope.

'Come on, we'll get up the slope and cut down at them when they follow!'

She gave him the best smile that she could manage then ducked her head down and kept going. *If we can top the ridge they'll have to chase us. Then we can pay these bastards back for making us run! And for Arthfael.*

Her legs were heavy but she trudged on, and the ground was just starting to slope upwards when she turned to look behind her. Then panic hit her again. The line of Gaians was still edging its way forwards, but coming around them were hundreds of horsemen, not Gaians by the look of them but certainly on their side. They rode mounts that were slightly larger than Neida, but they didn't ride to attack the Caderyn as they retreated up the hill. Each one was carrying a short bow that seemed to curve awkwardly, and before Rhia could shout a warning the sky was filled with a hundred shafts. They fell amongst the warriors like iron-tipped hail.

Everywhere around her Caderyn were struck down as arrows sank into bodies, arms, necks and heads. Gwyr and those few others who had bows with them began shooting back at the horsemen, but they wheeled their mounts away and few arrows hit their marks. Moments later they cantered back around again and though one or two of them were shot down, many more brave Caderyn were laid low by the horsemen's archery. She saw a woman beside her take an arrow through her neck and fall to the ground with a gurgling cry, thrashing pitifully in the mud as she bled her life away. Rhia ducked her head and ran, sprinting for the ridge at the best pace she could, and the others around her followed her example. There was safety, of a sort, to be found up on the slope and all thoughts of battle left her as she pelted across the grass.

More arrows fell among them and she ignored them as she went, trying to keep in sight the blonde braid that marked out Bevan. But it was Dane she should have been watching. It was only when she heard her brother's voice cry out in pain that she whipped her head around to see the arrow protruding from his chest. The youngest son of Carradan fell to his knees with wide eyes, and Rhia felt her ankle wrench as she twisted on the spot to run back to him. Beside her she heard a scream of pure anguish and Meghan, her face a mess of her own blood, started sprinting towards where Dane knelt in the dirt.

The Gaians were still pressing forward but their advance was still slow, and Rhia was sure she could grab her brother and get him out of here. Bevan and Bel were both running with her and they were only heartbeats away from reaching him when the Gaian lines opened up.

From behind the wall of shields came men, giants of men, in heavy scale armour and wielding massive blades. The Caderyn were strewn about the beginnings of the ridge and the giants started wading through them as a man might wade through water, scything down men and women like they were no more than wheat and chaff. Their strength was incredible, and Rhia saw Gronow the Tallow carved fully in half by the swing of a heavy sword. Behind them the Gaian line still advanced steadily, shields close together, while the giants wreaked havoc on the scattered tribesmen.

Madoc, screaming the name of his god, launched himself at one of them, feinting high before cutting low. The giant was fast, parrying both blows before hacking down at the Gadarim. Madoc swayed away from the cut and lunged in again, but the heavy scales turned his blade and the huge Gaian struck the First Man's head with a vicious backhanded blow. Madoc staggered and fell, blood spitting from his broken lips. Rhia saw Ossian dart in to help him and it seemed the new Gadarim scored a cut on the giant's leg, but the armoured man seemed to barely notice it and his heavy blade hacked down into Ossian's shoulder. The slim man cried out as bone splintered beneath the iron, and a moment later a heavy boot slammed into his chest. Ossian flew backwards and then crashed to the ground, the impact drawing another grunt of pain.

Time seemed to slow as Rhia watched Caderyn die. Domnall, who she'd matched drinks with after their victory at Broken Stream, was lying motionless on the blood-soaked grass, a pair of arrows protruding from his torso. Arian, the girl who spent her days selling eggs and chickens, fought desperately against the wall of shields that had somehow caught up with her, and was soon bleeding from a dozen wounds as short swords plunged through her flesh. Rhia saw pretty Ailin, the youth she'd been so keen to keep Gwen away from, try to block the massive swing of a giant's heavy sword, only to have his weapon shattered by the blow and the blade hammer through his ribs and spine to rip out again through his stomach. He collapsed to the floor in two separate pieces, and it took Rhia a moment to realise that she was vomiting at the sight.

Gwyr and Lorcan, who'd been fighting each other so very recently, were now fighting back to back as the armoured monsters came forward, and she saw Lorcan shove his former rival from the path of a blow, only to take the force of it himself and crumple silently to the ground. He moved no more.

Rhia almost fell to her knees she felt so weak. All was lost. Her people were dying and there was nothing they could do. She felt herself begin to topple in fatigue and despair, but a strong hand took her by the shoulder and started pulling her away. She shook her head to try to clear it and realised that it was Bevan, and that he not only dragged her but was using his other hand to help Bel as he manhandled Dane. Meghan was still with them, trying to comfort her wounded lover, and Owain appeared beside her a moment later, the Gadarim facing away from them and keeping his body between the enemy and the son of his chieftain.

Carradan himself was bellowing at them all to stay together, though fear and panic had spread among the Caderyn like wildfire, and men and women were scattering in all directions. Rhia wanted to shout for warriors to rally to her and to Bevan, to join her father and the Gadarim and drive back at the advancing Gaians. But a look at her enemies showed her that the giants, sated for now, were heading back to stand behind the wall of shields, and that terrible wall was now moving forwards again.

Fear clutched at her heart once more as she thought of the child growing inside her fragile body. *I don't want to die. I don't want my son to die.* She squeezed tears of shame and grief from her eyes as she turned to face her husband. Bevan's face looked if anything even more distraught than hers must have, and with a nod that they both hated themselves for giving, they agreed what must be done. They turned around and they fled.

Chapter 11. A Lesson in Tactics

'You see Antonius? You see how they run?'

Severus pointed from atop his brown courser and indicated to the younger man where the barbarians were fleeing. For all that he resented being saddled with unblooded tribunes, the boy was from a very powerful family, and it always paid to be polite with such people. The new officer, the honourable Marius Dessidus Antonius, was a tall and dark-haired youth of some twenty years, with the slender build and sharp features that marked him as belonging to the higher patrician class. General Severus Lepidus was no plebeian of course, but the very fact that he had a mere two names to Dessida's three highlighted the social gulf that existed between them.

Young Antonius, his social superior and military junior, was clearly trying his best to look soldierly as he viewed his first battle, though to the lad's credit he looked less queasy than most of the new boys he'd seen.

'I see, general. May I ask a question of you, sir?'

Severus nodded, approving of the courtesy. When he'd first been told that the Tenth Legion would be heading for Daeria he'd been convinced that the Gaian society here would be little better than the savages they ruled, but this young man at least seemed to know his manners around his seniors.

'By all means, tribune.'

He nodded towards the battle.

'This appears to me to be some variant of Tactica Two. The detachment on the right was acting as a solid base for the Gorvicae to their flank, while the cohort on the left pushed the enemy tribesmen back and their retreat is harried on that flank by the Nomad archers. These actions adhere to standard doctrine. But why break open the shieldwalls to let forth these Aboran auxiliaries when the infantry were doing an admirable job on their own?'

Severus once again approved and was glad to have taken the boy under his wing. It was part and parcel of army politics to be friendly to socially high-ranking juniors, but this one he suspected would not be quite the chore that most of them were. He showed an intelligent understanding of tactics but was willing to admit to his lack of experience. And he showed a willingness to learn from his superiors.

'Much of our history has been forgotten, Tribune Dessida, and a great deal of it to our cost. In more ancient times such auxiliaries were far more commonplace within our military, and their use in such a way would have been standard doctrine at the time. I make a point, tribune, of ensuring that my officers are well-versed in military history, even that which is no longer commonly taught.'

The young man nodded respectfully.

'And I should be glad to learn, general. But I still do not understand the breaking of the shieldwall, since surely this risks compromising the formation?'

The general pointed vaguely towards the left flank, where the cohort was still driving the Caderyn back.

'Were we fighting defensively, this would be true. However, the tribesmen were already beginning to fall back and might have done so in good order were they permitted. For all that a legion shieldwall is unbeatable against a charge it is too often slow-moving on the advance, as it must be to maintain a tight formation. Unleashing the Aboran Destroyers incited panic in their withdrawal, thus making it more difficult for them to regroup, especially when factoring in the Nomad archers and their harrying. It also makes the tribesmen wary of attempting to attack the formation and then fall back, hoping to outmanoeuvre the shieldwall by striking and withdrawing, since they know that they will be pursued by the faster-moving Destroyers.'

Dessida nodded in understanding.

'I see. Thank you sir.'

Severus bowed his head back to him.

'Not at all.'

The general felt quietly pleased that his innovative tactics were working so well. Destroyers had not been utilised by the legions for centuries, and his peers had ridiculed the idea when Severus had first presented it. But the mighty Aborans, with their unnatural strength and intense training, had proved invaluable as shock troops, and Severus looked forward to the effect that these successes would have on his career. *That reminds me, I must speak to Praecus about their further enhancement.* The alchemist-sorcerer had used a mixture of exotic herbs and strange rituals to enhance the Aborans' already impressive strength, and the initial results were promising indeed.

He turned his attention back to the field. On the right the First Cohort, under the seasoned Tribune Cadmus, was pushing the Caderyn back and inwards, supported by the savage Gorvicae on their flank. The imbecilic tribesmen had charged wildly into the fray but they were killing the enemy quite effectively, and the more of their warriors who died in this fight, the less trouble they could cause later on.

On the left flank, directly before him, the Second Cohort was also wheeling slightly, looking to hem the Caderyn in and cause maximum casualties before they could withdraw. He remembered his Faustulus even today: *Always leave your enemy a line of retreat.*

It would be over soon, he thought, and then the tedious process of negotiations could begin as yet another tribe of savages were folded into the Empire. Not that they ever showed any gratitude. He raised a hand and a pair of aides rode up to the two officers.

'Send word to Tribune Titus to bring forward his reserves in the centre. And bring up a skin of wine for Tribune Dessida and myself.'

The two youths put fists to their chests before throwing their arms out in salute, and both hastened to do their general's bidding. Severus turned to face his protégée.

'Let us hope it is a decent vintage this time. The swill at Udergosc was beyond revolting.'

Antonius Dessida smiled a little but he was still watching the battle rage. Severus turned that way too, though he was bored of the sight of it by now. Another wild mob of tribesmen breaking themselves against the undefeatable Gaian legions. He sighed. Would these people never learn?

Chapter 12. The Battle Goes Ill

Her ankle burned as they ran from the carnage. The bowmen on horseback still peppered them with arrows, and were making it impossible for them to run straight back up the ridge. Rhia, Bevan and the others were forced to run, or hobble, at an angle in the hopes of gaining the high ground by a less direct route, and that angle was taking them across their own lines and dangerously close to where the Gorvicae were pushing their flank, supported by another Gaian square.

The Durolwg men were falling back and confusion reigned as chasing Gorvicae appeared among the retreating Caderyn, with the Gaians advancing slowly behind them, their shields still locked together. Rhia saw a pair of Gorvic warriors charging madly at her little group, and both she and Bevan sprang forward to meet them, glad to have an enemy they could at least meet blade to blade. An axe swung at her head but Rhia ducked beneath it and swiped a cut across the Gorvic that opened up his innards. The stench of offal hit her nostrils and the man screamed out in pain, but she silenced him a moment later with a crushing blow to his temple. Bevan had already dispatched his own opponent and more Gorvicae were approaching them through the panicked mob of Caderyn.

Rhia tried to lunge at the next man but her ankle buckled beneath her and she found herself falling at his feet. Bevan's sword appeared from nowhere to slash at the warrior's head, and as he brought up his guard to block it Rhia stabbed up into his groin. He shrieked as cold iron was thrust through his manhood and must have welcomed Bevan's second cut that caved in the back of his skull. Rhia leaned on Silverbite to push herself to her feet, but the dying man fell forwards and knocked her back down to the ground, pinning her.

The smell of him was horrid, but the earth was cool on her face and for a mad moment Rhia considered simply staying down and closing her eyes. It lasted only a heartbeat before she was cursing herself for her weakness, and she started shoving the Gorvic warrior from her. She was still struggling to shift his dead weight from her legs when the Gadarim of the Gorvicae came forward, and she could do little but watch as Duran and Nuallan, their hair bleached white and spiked into points, hacked their way through a handful of Caderyn before their eyes fell on her brother.

Dane was moving only with the help of Meghan and Bel, and Owain, who had been guarding them, was now embroiled with two other Gorvic fighters. Running Boar and Flying Hawk rushed the hobbling group, and Duran barely looked at Meg as he knocked her blade aside and punched her hard in the ear. The redhead tumbled to the ground and simply lay there, stunned. Bel let go of Dane for a moment to try to hack at Nuallan, but the Gadarim blocked the cut with ease and thrust his long sword through the Caderyn's torso. Rhia screamed in rage and struggled harder to free herself as Meghan's only brother toppled sideways into the dirt. Dane, the arrow still protruding from his chest, stepped in front of where Meg lay on the grass and bellowed out a challenge as he flung himself at Nuallan. The Gadarim parried away his thrust and grabbed for him, clearly hoping to take his sword away and capture him alive, but Dane was having none of it and he struggled like a madman.

Owain finally managed to bring down his other attackers and sprang to defend his chieftain's son, but Duran intercepted him and the pair began trading blows. Rhia had almost pushed the heavy corpse from her legs as Dane continued to flail wildly at Nuallan. For all the other man's skill, Dane's sword landed a glancing blow on his head and Rhia felt a swell of hope as Nuallan staggered back. But then Gawan came striding from the chaos that was that field, his blue battlemarks and whitened hair smeared liberally with mud and blood. And it seemed the Leaping Wolf did not like captives who fought back.

Dane managed a single clumsy swipe before the First Man of the Gorvicae took his arm off at the elbow, and his cry was cut off short as the iron blade reversed to ram under his ribs into his chest. He fell without another sound. Rhia's world seemed to turn upside down and inside out and she screamed wordlessly at the top of her lungs, finally shoving the Gorvic's body from her legs. She must kill this man. Nothing else mattered. Not the battle, not her people, not even Bevan or her child or all the gods of sky and earth. This man had to die, and she was going to make it happen.

She forced herself to her feet, oblivious to the world around her, and began dragging her twisted ankle as she closed in on Gawan. She didn't care that he was Gadarim, that he was the First Man of his tribe and one of the best swords on that field. This man had just killed her brother, and he would answer for it. She readied her taken blade, holding it low ready to thrust, and stumbled towards the warrior with murder in her eyes.

But her husband got there first, and he yelled out a challenge as he sprang past.

'Leaping Wolf!'

Gawan turned, his blade up and ready, and looked at Bevan with a sneer.

'You are no Gadarim. Best you run with the rest of your people.'

Bevan twirled his blade around his wrist.

'I can wield this well enough for you.' He pointed it at Dane's body. 'And that man was my brother.'

Gawan looked at him oddly for a moment, then recognition seemed to dawn on him.

'You married the Wildcat then?'

He turned on the spot and saw Rhia for the first time. His sneer became an evil grin as he turned to face Bevan again.

'What sort of noise does she make when you take her at night? Does she still spit out insults or does she moan when you're inside her?'

Bevan answered the Gorvic with a fierce grin of his own and brandished Brackenthorn.

'Almost as loud as you'll scream when this is inside *you!*'

Apparently that was all the bantering Gawan felt like indulging in today and he flung himself at Rhia's husband without another word. Rhia screamed a challenge of her own but another Gorvic appeared in front of her before she could get closer.

This warrior was female, a tough-looking bitch with half her face stained blue with clumsily-applied woad. She carried both a sword and an axe, Rhia's own combination of choice, and she lunged at the Caderyn fighter with the long blade. Rhia parried quickly and then ducked below the inevitable axe-swing. The momentum carried the Gorvic into a spin and Rhia chanced a stab at her exposed back as she went. The cut glanced more than it pierced, but it drew both a thin line of red and a shriek of pain from her opponent, and Rhia wasted no time in following it up, cutting down hard at the warrior's leg. The blade bit deep into her thigh and she swung wildly as she dropped to her knees. Rhia leaped back, ignored the burn in her ankle as she landed, then darted forward to swing another heavy cut at the woman's neck.

Some detached part of Rhia's brain was disappointed not to have decapitated her, but the sword passed through her throat far enough to scrape her spine, and the lifeless corpse tumbled to the ground nonetheless. Rhia felt a wave of weariness hit her like a fist to the belly, and her breath was coming out in ragged gasps. All around her men and women were either fleeing or battling for their lives but all the same, she had to take a moment to lean on her sword and try to breathe a little steadier before she could do anything else. Her hands and legs were trembling, and her ears were pounding louder than a drum.

The Gaian line was suddenly a lot closer than it had been a few heartbeats ago and Rhia staggered away from it as it edged its way forwards. She hated herself for how afraid she was of that unassailable mass of men, that wall that could not be cut or stabbed. She didn't know what she was the more afraid of; that it might carry on towards her and she'd be forced to fight the wall, or that it would open once again and the armoured giants would pour out. What she did know was how sickened she was at her fear of it, and tears of shame filled her eyes as she backed away from the line of shields.

She blinked her eyes a few times to try to clear them, and then suddenly remembered that her husband was busy fighting with a different monster, and she wheeled around to look for the pair of warriors. The field was a deafening confusion of blood and bodies but she soon found them again, duelling worryingly close to the Gaian line, but still she almost smiled with relief to see that Bevan still lived. His golden braid seemed to shine in the sunlight as he parried away the thrusts and hacks of Leaping Wolf, though the Gadarim did seem to be driving him back. Rhia limped closer, trying to block out the pain in her ankle, and her hope flared again as Bevan's sword nicked Gawan's left shoulder.

But that hope died a heartbeat later. Bevan was indeed a fine swordsman but Gawan had been right; he was no Gadarim. The Gorvic fighter barely flinched from the cut and he beat down her husband's sword before slamming a rock-like fist into his face. Bevan stumbled backwards and fell to the grass and Gawan, to his small credit, stepped back to allow him to stand. The Gaian line however, had no such compunction.

Rhia watched as first one and then two short blades stabbed at her fallen husband, and she screamed incoherently as she charged, all pain and fatigue forgotten as her world was filled with rage. She ignored the Gorvicae and leaped madly at the wall of men, grabbing a shield by the rim and yanking down with all her might. Rhia was not a large person by any measure, but the Gaian hadn't seen her coming and he was pulled off balance for a moment. Her sword rose and fell and the armoured man screamed as his collarbone was crushed beneath the iron.

Bevan was still moving on the ground at their feet and Rhia shoved the wounded soldier to stand over her husband, shrieking her defiance in the faces of her enemies. Short swords stabbed at her but she parried them away, her limbs somehow faster and stronger than they had been moments ago. She whipped out attacks and Gaians flinched from her blade, and slowly, so slowly, Bevan crawled away from danger. More Caderyn were coming from somewhere or another and the advance of the wall was slowed as warriors threw themselves into the fray. Rhia cut low at a man's calf and he cried out as he toppled over, and she bellowed the name of the War God into the face of the next man in the line.

'Taran!'

Her courage was beginning to come back through her fear, but then something struck her hard in the back of the head and it felt like her whole skull had split open. White light flashed across her eyes and she vomited again as she fell to her knees. She closed her eyes for a moment and when she opened them again someone was dragging her somewhere but she had no idea in which direction. Someone trod on her arm but she didn't notice any pain and then suddenly she was alone again, her face resting on cool earth. The smell of the soil and grass was surprisingly clean, and though she could still hear the battle as it raged around her it sounded quiet and muffled, as if she were hearing it from some great distance away. But she did hear it. People were shouting and fighting and screaming and dying, and for all that the sound was distant the black despair she had felt earlier washed over her once again.

The gods must have abandoned them to allow such slaughter to be unleashed on her people, and a part of her addled brain wondered if Taran or Mabonac had been offended when she had spied on the Gadarim's rituals. She began to whisper contrite prayers to them, until she remembered the sight of Dane balked in his own blood, and then her prayers turned into curses as she railed at the gods for what they'd done. She lay there, unmoving, and alternated between hating the gods and begging their forgiveness as the pain in her head seemed to intensify rather than fade.

Rhia had no idea how long it took her to stand up, her head was screaming every time she even moved it, but eventually she found herself on her front, then on one knee, then finally on her feet again, scanning around the chaos in an effort to get her bearings. All she saw was that the Caderyn now lay in droves upon the ground, and both Gaian soldiers and Gorvic warriors were hacking down her people like so much dead wood.

Suddenly a hand grabbed her from behind and even through the pain Rhia reacted instinctively, drawing her dagger as she whipped around and plunging it to the hilt in her enemy's side. Her wordless warcry became a shriek of horror as she saw the golden blonde braid of her husband on the shoulder of the man she'd stabbed. Bevan's eyes widened for an instant and he tried to say something, but only blood coughed out when he opened his mouth. Rhia's hand went numb and let go of the weapon, and Bevan staggered a pace before his legs folded underneath him. Her husband fell to the ground and moved no more, and Rhia dropped to her knees beside him and screamed.

*

Gut-wrenching grief was overwhelmed by blind panic and Rhia scrabbled to try to help him as he lay there in the dirt. Part of her brain knew there was no use in it but her limbs refused to listen as she reached for her husband's bleeding body. She'd barely touched him before another flash of pain went through her head, and she stumbled as her vision swam. Someone started pulling him away from her and she tried to clutch at them, but she missed and collapsed to the ground, her already pounding head thudding hard against the turf.

She must have blacked out because when she opened her eyes she was indoors. The battle's noise could be heard outside so she couldn't have been out for long, but her head still felt groggy and it was hard to think clearly. She saw that she was in a barn or stable of some sort, though beyond that she had no idea. Her eyes refused to focus on any details of her surroundings but it seemed her sense of smell was as keen as ever, and wherever she was it had housed animals until recently.

Panic struck her again as she remembered where she'd left Bevan, but a frenzied glance around her showed that her husband was here with her, propped up against a wall of wooden planks, his eyes closed and his clothing soaked with blood. For a wonderful, or hopeful, moment she was sure she saw his chest rise as he took in a breath, and she struggled to get up to go to him, but a firm hand on her shoulder held her back.

'Easy now. You've taken quite a knock, I don't know how bad you're hurt.'

She turned to see the speaker and was surprised to see Delyn looking down at her. The battlemarks on his face were smeared with his and others' blood, but he seemed to be unharmed and there was worry in his eyes. Rhia tried to speak but the effort of it was difficult, and as she tried to rise the world began to spin. Delyn eased her back down again.

'You're in no state to walk. Wait here and I'll get help.'

Rhia tried to object but before she could make the attempt the sound of splintering wood made both her and Delyn whip their heads around, and Rhia felt a horrible dizziness hit her again. Through the haze she saw a warrior stride into the barn, though whether Caderyn or Gorvicae she couldn't have guessed. There was no sign of lime in his hair or his beard so whatever else he might have been, he was no Gadarim.

From Delyn's reaction it seemed he wasn't of their tribe, because the crouching man drew his dagger and sprang towards him with a cry. She scrunched up her eyes in the hopes of forcing them to focus, but the best she managed was to see a vague blur of motion as the two men grappled with each other. Rhia closed her eyes again and took a couple of deep breaths. She had to get up and help. Bevan might still be alive. *Even after you stabbed him. You have killed your own husband, Rhianwyn. You have killed the father of your child.*

She ground her teeth and squeezed out a tear. *Delyn wouldn't have dragged him here too if he was dead. He is still alive and he needs your help. You'll have all the time in the world to hate yourself later on but damn it all, you have to get up and help him now!*

Rhia opened her eyes. Her head still throbbed and her vision was blurry but somehow she managed to clamber to her feet, leaning heavily on a wooden beam for support. Whoever the newcomer was he had Delyn pinned up against the wall and was slowly easing a dagger towards his face. The Caderyn warrior was snarling out curses but the Gorvic was pushing hard, and it was only a matter of time. Rhia's legs wanted to collapse under her again, but she forced them to obey and heaved herself across the barn.

The Gorvic was heavy but she caught him unawares, and she grabbed hold of his head and pulled back. Delyn still had hold of the arm which held the knife and he slammed the back of that hand against the rim of a barrel, the Gorvic grunting as delicate bones were snapped. Rhia heard the dagger clatter to the floor and kept dragging back as Delyn hammered punches into the man. The big warrior grabbed for him but Rhia's thumb found his eye, and he bellowed in pain even as she began shrieking in rage. He struggled and managed to shove Delyn away long enough to whirl on Rhia for a moment.

The warrior's left eye was a mess of blood but his face was blue-painted and fierce, and before she could reach for a weapon his fist had crashed into her cheek. Rhia was sent spinning and black dots flashed before her eyes. She managed to catch herself from falling by leaning on an oak pillar but she was certain she was about to pass out again. The Gorvic wasted no time in following her and his fist lashed out again, this time thudding hard into her belly. *No!* Her head was too fuzzy for her to fight back effectively, and she pawed uselessly at his face as blow after blow hammered into her body. After a few heartbeats that felt like years the attacks stopped and she fell to the floor again, retching pitifully but with nothing more to come up. She knew that the Gorvic would kill her, here and now, and there was nothing that she could do or say to stop him. Her weapons were lost, her head and body battered to a pulp, and her husband was bleeding to death only paces away.

She coughed and retched painfully again, waiting for the fatal blow, but when she lifted up her head it was Delyn standing above her, not the Gorvic. There was blood on his knife and when she glanced across the room she saw that Bevan now lay on his side, and there was no denying to anyone that he was dead. Tears ran down her cheeks as she screamed up at her former suitor.

'You killed him!'

He seemed puzzled and she lashed out at him, catching him a pathetically weak blow on his hip before collapsing to the floor and retching again. Only then did she realise that the Gorvic also lay dead on the ground, and that Delyn must have slain him just in time. She clutched at his leg and then at the hand that was offered.

'I'm sorry Delyn! I'm sorry, I didn't...I...'

But even as she struggled for her words she felt something in her stomach. Something *wrong*. She looked down at herself to see her breeches slowly soaking through with blood and she scrabbled back, her eyes flying wide with panic.

'No! No, no, no, no, no!'

Her hands flew to the ties and she struggled with the knot even as Delyn tried to make sense of her.

'Rhia what is it? What's wrong?'

But she wasn't listening. Rhia was back to her frantic praying, begging to all the gods to stop what was happening to her. *Not this too! Please dear gods above not this too! You have Bevan, you have Dane, don't take my child as well! I'm sorry about Bevan, I'm sorry for my spying, I'm sorry I've been so arrogant, I'm sorry, I'm sorry, I'm sorry!*

For some reason the wrinkled face of the man in the woods came back to her. Delyn was desperately trying to pull her away from the open doorway and into hiding, but she was flailing wildly as she begged the gods of her people.

Let him live! Let my boy live! He can be raised by the Gaians if that's what you want, he can learn from them and make peace with them if that's what he's meant to do, but let him live! Annwn and Belenos, Karanon and Camelas, Mehine and Marna, anyone, please let my son live!

She was still struggling with her blood-soaked clothes when Delyn finally got her into a darkened corner of the barn. She was weeping uncontrollably and he put his arms around her and stroked her hair.

'It's alright Rhia. We won't be seen here, you're safe for now.'

She barely heard him and kept wrestling with her ties. Even had her sight not been blurred it was almost pitch black in the corner she'd been dragged to, and the strings were soaked through to boot. Her head was swimming but still she fought to stay awake, fumbling with her trews and pleading with gods who refused to listen. She felt Delyn's hand on hers and he squeezed as if it might give her some comfort, but comfort could go to the wolves for all she cared. Madlen had never told her what to do if something like this happened but it made sense to get her clothes off first. The *wrongness* in her belly was still there, a horrible, invasive feeling of both pain and emptiness, and she wept even further as her shaking fingers slipped on the strings.

Delyn's hand tried to squeeze hers again and she almost snarled at him but held it back. She managed a mumbled; 'I'm sorry,' before striking on an idea and guiding his hand to the ties of her breeches. Delyn's fingers were not trembling quite as badly as her own and he might help her finally rid herself of the garment. Her fellow tribesman pulled away for a moment.

'What are you doing?'

She realised distantly that he couldn't see in the darkness any better than she could, but speaking was difficult and there was no time for subtlety. She pulled his hand with all the meagre strength she had and put it back on the strings.

'Get these off. Help me.'

He seemed uncertain but a moment later he was working the ties loose and Rhia almost smiled with relief that he understood. And then she remembered that Bevan was dead, Dane was dead, her people were being slaughtered and her son was likely dead or dying inside her. Delyn had managed to get the knots undone and was now easing off her breeches, but Rhia felt herself beginning to black out again. Her head felt heavy and it was difficult to see, but it seemed that for some reason Delyn was now fumbling with his own clothing.

In the time it took her battered brain to realise what was happening, the world was slipping slowly away, and even as it started her eyes rolled back in her skull, and the whole world was swallowed by blackness.

Chapter 13. Negotiations

Near a moon's turn had passed since the Battle of Nantwyn, and still Rhia's emotions alternated between weeping grief and empty numbness. She still recalled little of what had happened after she'd come around in the barn. After Delyn had raped her. According to Meg he'd been in the barn when she and Owain had found her, but he'd disappeared back to Durolwg the next day, and Rhia had said nothing of what had happened. She was too ashamed.

On the long and barely-remembered journey back to Bryngarth she'd re-lived that terrible day over and over in her mind, and had convinced herself it was mostly her own fault. She'd been trying to undress in front of him and had even asked for his help, and it had been too dark for him to see the blood, though he must have noticed it later, after... after it was done. Perhaps he'd thought her mad with grief and had sought to comfort her in some way but then saw what he'd done and had fled in shame? Or perhaps he'd been waiting for such a chance for many years, had let Bevan bleed to death and forced himself upon her when she was weak? She had no way of knowing without asking him herself, and the notion of doing that made her even more ashamed because it frightened her.

The thought of Bevan made her think again of his and Dane's bloody corpses on that nightmare of a day, but she had already wept for most of that morning, and was now in one of her numb phases where nothing in the world seemed to matter a damn. Gwen and Olla had tried to help her as best they could, though they too mourned their brother, and Meghan had taken the loss hard. The once-beautiful redhead now bore a long scar across one cheek and though Rhia thought she still looked pretty, that perfect face had been marred forever. Not that Meg seemed to care overmuch. She took no care of her gorgeous hair any more, and Gwen and Olla practically had to drag her into the longhouse to bathe.

That house was where she stood right now, along with the headmen and their families and the Gadarim of Bryngarth. Many of the Caderyn, under Carradan's orders, had fled and dispersed to the hills with instructions to regroup as best they could, though there was little enough hope for the tribe now. The Gaian army was unbeatable, and now they had no choice but to accept whatever they demanded of them.

She spied Olla across the hall, little Siriol on her lap, and couldn't help but touch her stomach and think of her own child, lost forever. What had she done to make the gods inflict so brutal a punishment on her? What had the Caderyn done that Camelas and all the others had abandoned them in their time of need? She had few answers, beyond her own shameful and foolish actions perhaps, but she could barely care at the moment and simply watched the ritual taking place in the great hall of her people.

Carradan, High Chieftain of the Caderyn, was laying his sword and helm at the feet of a pair of Gaians. Rhia knew she ought to be angry, to be sickened and vengeful that such a thing was going on, but she viewed the whole thing distantly, as if it were happening to some other folk, and not the family and tribe that she had loved her whole life. She watched Ironhorn being surrendered with the same apathy she had felt when she'd watched Dane and Bevan's bodies being buried on the hillside a few days ago. She might weep again later, as she had for her brother and husband, but everything seemed to come in phases at the moment, and right now all she felt was cold indifference.

Standing behind the Gaians were a group of Gorvicae and Rhia tried to summon rage as she saw Gawan, the Leaping Wolf, standing behind his chieftain with a smug look on his black-bearded face. Baercban and his son Sedryn seemed even more pleased with themselves, and Rhia wished she could feel angry when she recognised the younger man as the coward who'd fled from her at Broken Stream. She tried to summon rage or indignation when she saw how the craven now wore Silverbite upon his hip. She tried so hard to feel *something* about this humiliation of her people but nothing seemed to come to her, and she looked on at them, disinterested.

The Gaians were speaking in that strange tongue of theirs, their words translated into Lurian speech by a little man with a strange accent, who seemed to be a tribesman of some sort. Two Gaians stood behind him, both with short greying hair but otherwise looking very different. The one in the armour was tall and lean with a hard face and cold eyes, and was standing straight-backed and silent through all of this. The other was a shorter, round-faced man draped in a cross between a druid's robe and a white cloak, and he spoke on in a droning sort of voice. The interpreter translated.

'And so it is agreed that Chief Carradan may continue to call himself thus, and to be permitted to remain as an advisor to this, the new governor of this territory, the honourable Governor Marcus Portunus Julius. In this your central...' the Gaian looked about uncertainly and the translator had to wait while he paused, '...city, shall be built a centre of local government, with a modest garrison of enforcers to assist in the maintaining of law and order. Taxation of goods and coin shall be levied from all clans within Caderyn territory, to be utilised both here and in the city of Tamora, with a further tribute of one hundred head of cattle each year to the Gorvicae tribe...'

There was a general murmur of disapproval at this announcement but oddly, it was Gawan of the Gorvicae who stepped forward, his voice hot and angry.

'This was not the agreement that we settled! It was agreed that Caderyn territory would be handed over to us and that their tribute would be made to you. No mention was made of Gaians taking control this land, nor of...'

But Baercban cut him off.

'Hold your tongue, Gawan! This is good enough.'

The Gadarim looked as if he were about to argue with him, but then he bowed his head a fraction and stepped back behind his chief. Both the robed Gaian and the interpreter looked awkward for a moment before the man who would soon be their ruler continued, and the little tribesman translated his words.

'That this transition of governance be as expedient as possible, and to strengthen the ties between the Empire and the local headmen, marriages between prominent families are to be arranged. As the Caderyn tribe is among the most prestigious in all the west, you will be honoured to marry your daughters to some of our highest-ranking young men.'

Once again there were mumblings among the Caderyn but Rhia knew that none would dare to speak up against the arrangement. The tribe had been brought to its knees by these Gaians and the terms that they gave could have been worse, she supposed. Doubtless she and Gwen would be the daughters referred to, and again she tried to find her anger, or indeed any emotion beyond shame. *You've let yourself be raped by one man already, what difference if a Gaian man does the same? You killed the husband that you were in love with after all, you should be grateful to have another chance at motherhood.*

She hated herself for the sickeningly timid reaction but try as she might, she could not summon any other. Her father was looking on with as blank an expression as he could manage, though it was obvious to all the tribe that his great heart was breaking. Yet what choice did he have? If these terms were refused the Gaians would destroy the tribe completely, and he had a duty to his people as much as to his family. The robed Gaian continued to speak, while the taller man in armour seemed bored by this whole proceeding.

'Two brothers of the most excellent Dessidus family have already been selected by the provincial governor to marry your own unwed daughters, and arrangements have been made for their transportation to Tamora.'

The Gaian looked as if he wanted to make this sound as positive as possible, but Rhia could tell that he knew his audience was not on his side.

'Here they will enjoy all of the luxuries of civilised life, as will their children, brought up in Gaian households. The light shone by the Empire will shine down upon you all and in time, I am certain that you will be glad of the benefits we may reap together.'

From the faces she saw in the longhall Rhia suspected that such gladness would be a *very* long time in coming, but once again she told herself that it could have been worse. According to Reaghan other tribes, less valuable and more troublesome than theirs, had been practically wiped out and the people sold off to wealthy Gaians like so much cattle. Had any other but a druid told her of this she would never have believed such a thing, but Reaghan did not lie and it meant that the treatment they were receiving in defeat could have been far worse than it was.

Rhia found herself missing the wise old man, but tales of the Gaians' persecution of druids had led to Carradan insisting that he make for the hills with the others. Reaghan had left Bael to keep an eye on things here, though he hid his true self by dressing as just another tribesman, and Rhia found it odd to see him out of his white robe.

The Gaian droned on a while longer but his message had been heard. Rhia looked over at Gwen, wondering how a woman who still felt things might be reacting to all of this and, sure enough, it seemed that her sister was fighting back tears. *I wish that I had tears to shed about our fate. At least that would be something.* Both her father and mother were staying plain-faced and resolute as they listened to the terms of their conquest, though she was certain that they too had strong emotions boiling within them.

Rhia stared blankly as her people's future, and hers with it, was decided by a group of men who'd slaughtered the best of their warriors, and felt little but a vague sense of depression. She had killed a man that she loved more than air or sun or stars, lost a child that might have brought them peace if that old man had spoken true, and had allowed a man she'd thought was a decent Caderyn to rape her without even trying to fight him. Whatever fate that awaited her at the city of Tamora, it was surely no more than she had earned.

*

The farewell had been brief. Her parents, along with Olla and Ewan, had held back their tears and wished the two sisters well, even as Gwen had wept into her sleeve. Rhia, having cried herself out already that morning, had nothing but solemn looks and single-word answers for the family she was leaving behind. Half of Bryngarth had turned out to watch them leave and Rhia had wondered briefly if a riot had been brewing. There were rumblings in the crowd and hard faces among the warriors, and perhaps on another day she might have encouraged her people to fight, to cast off their new-tied bonds and rebel. But she just hadn't found it in her to care and had been neither relieved nor disappointed when the train of riders had left the hill undisturbed, and had started out on the long road heading east.

It was now past midday, though grey clouds obscured the sun, and the countryside around her looked grim. She was sure that the open valleys and green forests were beautiful sights, even in dull weather, but Rhia felt nothing as she watched her people's land drift by. This land essentially belonged to the Gaians now, and the conquered Caderyn would be paying tribute to the Gorvicae for gods-only-knew how long. *It's as if Broken Stream never even happened.*

Rhia looked across at Gwen, whose eyes were still red from crying. Her first pang of any emotion other than her crushing, shame-filled grief came to her in the form of pity. Gwen hadn't been there on that glorious sunlit day when Rhianwyn of the Caderyn had taken a sword from the son of a Gorvic chieftain. Gwen's first and only taste of battle had been the day when their world had collapsed in on itself, when the Gaians and the Gorvicae had ground the Caderyn into the dirt. *You may not have much, but at least once, long ago, you tasted victory. Gwen has never, and will never, know anything but defeat.*

Not that her victory had made any difference, she thought. Even her sword was now back with her enemy, and what punishment they'd dealt the Gorvicae had been heaped back on them tenfold. A hundredfold. Rhia looked at her sister and wondered how she must be feeling right now, having lost a true brother in Dane and a law-brother in Bevan, on top of the degradation of her people and, soon, of herself. She wanted to reach across to her, to hold her hand and try to give her some comfort in her despair, but she couldn't. Even had she been able to think of something, her own numbness constricted her like a noose around her neck.

'You should at least give it a *try*, you know.'

Rhia started for a moment at the unasked-for advice, then remembered that the little interpreter had been speaking to her about something else. The diminutive tribesman, Perrin, was riding to her left and had been trying to convince her to learn some of the Gaian tongue. *Vulgare* was what he called the strange language, and he was pestering her in his odd accent to learn a few words of it as they rode. So far, Rhia had merely grunted or given short answers to his questions. She spoke her own language, and even understood one or two words of the Ancient Tongue, and had no desire at all to clutter her head with this Gaian gibberish.

'I am not interested.'

It was one of the longest answers she'd given to the irritating translator, and he clearly thought this meant he was getting through to her.

'Like it or no, the Gaians are the future. Your tribe, like mine, has tried and failed to resist them and now, like us, you must learn to live with them. Those who live in Gaian provinces and do not learn their tongue have no hope of a future in a world ruled by them.' He looked up at her through his brows. 'Now, you can sit here in stubborn ignorance and wish the whole world would change to suit you, or you can work with what you have and try to make something of all this. It is your choice.'

Rhia looked at him and tried to find some anger in her impatience. He was a short man, even shorter than she was, with a wispy brown beard and his hair cut short on his head. On another day Rhia might have listened to his advice or else shouted him down for his timidity, but today she simply ignored him and urged her pony on a little to get away from him. The interpreter frowned but took the hint, and as she rode on Rhia heard him giving the exact same speech to Gwen behind her, though the only response he got from her was more sobbing.

Rhia came alongside a tall man dressed in armour, his helm decorated by a red crest that flowed back from his crown down to his neck. The Gaian gave her a hard look as they rode but Rhia was as much past fear as she was past anger. She vaguely remembered that his name was Cadmus and that the crest marked him as some sort of Gaian Gadarim, though she hadn't seen the tall man fighting in the chaos at Nantwyn. He continued to glare at her and Rhia simply matched his gaze and glared back. Perhaps this Gaian warrior sought to intimidate or scare her, and Rhia wished that she had it in her to spit in his face and pick a fight. At least then she might die in combat with some dignity.

More than once since that day she had considered doing it herself. Taking a dagger to her own heart and ending this awful cycle of shameful grief and cold emptiness. Once or twice she'd even come quite close, holding a long knife's point towards her and willing herself to drive it home. But she hadn't done it. She wished that it was the love for her family that held her back but truthfully, it was only yet more shame. As much as she could find it in her to hate anything, she hated herself for having so let her people down. For letting Bevan down, even beyond having killed him. She had ignored what she was sure had been a warning from the gods. She had spied on rituals she had no business looking on. She had slain her husband and watched as her brother was cut down before her and then, after she ran and hid like a coward from the fight, she had let her child die and allowed Delyn to… to…

Rhia ground her teeth. She didn't want to think about it, no matter how many times the images played across her vision. The important thing was that she had let her family, and her people, down in every conceivable way, and this marriage to a Gaian was the only way she could think of to even begin to make amends. No matter how much she might want to simply die and let it be done, she had a duty to do, and if she could feel nothing else she could still feel shame.

The Gaian's face had twisted into a sneer and Rhia stared at him only long enough to make it clear that she had no fear of him before turning to look back at Perrin. He'd said his tribe were called the Basiae, though Rhia had never heard of them, and that the Gaians had occupied their territory for many winters now. The little man was dressed in green trews and a heavy brown shirt and might have passed for a Caderyn but for his accent. And Rhia hated to admit that his advice was probably sound.

His people had survived under the Gaians for years and he had learned their language to better his and his family's chances of prospering under them. It made sense, if the Caderyn were to survive under the Gaians too, for Rhia and Gwen to do the same. It made sense for them to try to understand the people they were to be enslaved by. It made sense for them to ensure they could communicate with... with their new husbands. For the first time in days Rhia managed to feel an emotion about that, somewhere in the depths of her numbness; disgust. She pictured a man like the sneering Gaian beside her, laying his hands on her, kissing her, using her as Delyn had...

For a blissful moment she almost managed to catch hold of some rage, but it didn't last. The numbness came back in a dull grey wave, killing her anger and smothering it with nothingness. No, not nothingness. Her shame was allowed to stay alive inside the void of feeling. Rhia closed her eyes and wished for some tears but none came. Likely they would come tonight. The gods saw fit to give her some of her feelings back at night so she could stay awake and weep through it, the loss of her child and her husband and her brother ripping at her like knives in an open wound.

But for now she had no tears, and no rage, only emptiness and shame. In that shame she decided that her duty was all that mattered, to do what she could for her people, however soiled it might make her feel. She slowed her pony a little and let the interpreter catch up. She would learn their words. She would understand them as best she could and give her new husband the children they needed to secure their alliance. Maybe, just maybe, she might reconcile herself with Mehine and Taran and the others if she did this service for her tribe.

For a fleeting moment the thought of children threatened to allow her another emotion, and the crippling grief of losing her child almost struck her. But then the grey nothingness reasserted itself, and the tears that stung her eyes never fell. Rhia rode on in silence, watching her taken land roll by, and wondered which was worse, the grief, the shame, or the endless emptiness?

Chapter 14. Tamora

By the time they gained sight of the Gaian city autumn
was truly making its presence felt, and the sky was filled
with threatening grey clouds.   After eighteen days of
Perrin's lessons Rhia had discovered she was by no means
a natural linguist, though Gwen had taken to it reasonably
well. Her sister was weeping less frequently now, though
how she'd fare once she was married was another thing
entirely. Today she was riding between Rhia and Perrin,
her face screwed up in concentration as she tried to
converse with him in Vulgare. All Rhia could manage was
to pick out odd words here and there, and she gathered that
Perrin was describing the great city or recounting its
history. Their road was leading them out from the hills
and down towards the Gaian settlement and even Rhia had
to admit, it was an impressive sight.

Tamora was settled in a little valley beside a river and
was by far the largest town she had ever seen, the
countless buildings penned in by a massive wall of stone.
All of the homes in Bryngarth could have fit inside it
twenty times over, though the houses here were packed in
so much closer to each other that Rhia couldn't even guess
how many souls might live in the city. The buildings were
all made of pale grey stone and seemed to tower up higher
than the wall in some places, standing like giants looking
out over the valley. It was still too far away to make out
many details but she was certain she saw *actual* giants
there as well, standing motionless on stone columns with
their great arms pointing or waving at them, some of them
bearing swords or spears in their hands.

Rhia continued to stare as the troop of riders plodded
onwards, ignoring the strange chatter of her sister and the
Basian. As they rode closer she realised that the giants
must be stones carved to look like men, though larger and

more intricate than any carving she'd ever imagined. They had faces, and hair, and clothes, their bodies slim like runners' but with muscle heaped onto them as well. How long must it have taken to create just one such carving? And the city was dotted with scores of them. *These must be their gods*, she thought as they rode closer. She might have thought them strange, even laughable on another day – to build carvings of the gods was a fairly pointless exercise, since even a man who saw one would not be able to do it justice. Yet the gods of these Gaians had shown them victory after victory, and it seemed Camelas and Taran had been pushed aside in their favour.

The city drew nearer and Rhia frowned as she thought on it, confused and a little frightened as she looked at the Gaian gods. Did the Gaians' string of victories mean that carved gods had more power than those who were left unseen? Would Taran be made happier or more powerful if the Caderyn made images of him? It didn't seem to make sense, since surely he might be offended if they tried to carve an image of him and got it wrong? Had the Lurian gods been vanquished by their stone-made counterparts, or had they simply abandoned the Caderyn for some reason or another, and might still defeat the Gaian deities if they saw fit?

Rhia shut her eyes. Her confusion about something she knew she'd never understand was letting fear seep through her habitual numbness. She supposed she ought to be grateful to be feeling anything at all, but fear was not a welcome companion to a Caderyn, and she looked away from the stone city and its intimidating deities.

Further up the long column of riders she saw the Gaians in the crested helms, and saw that the one called Cadmus had turned in his saddle to look at her. His face was as full of contempt as ever, and Rhia suspected he had sensed her fear on sighting his great city and was enjoying feeling grand and superior to her and her sister. But then, most of these Gaians seemed to enjoy feeling superior, muttering to each other in their strange language all the time and assuming she was too stupid to understand tone. Their oldest headman, the one called Lepidus, seemed to understand a little of the Lurian Tongue and had explained, in a painfully patronising way, that the Gaian civilization was the greatest in the world, and that she and Gwen were fortunate to be on their way to become a part of it. If she'd had any anger in her she might have cracked his jaw for him but instead she'd simply nodded dumbly whenever he spoke to her, and eventually he'd given up on trying. It had clearly been a hollow gesture anyway. His task in bringing them here was to make gifts of them to the sons of his city's headmen, and it would make him look better in their eyes if the brides seemed keen on the idea.

At first Rhia welcomed the sense of irritation that brought, feeling with it the first tiny red flickers of precious anger, but then she stamped them away as quickly as they came. For one thing, she knew the emotion would never last anyway, and for another, she had a duty to perform here whether she willed it or not. She kept her face expressionless and Cadmus, doubtless having hoped to see some sign of fear or despair, turned back to the road, disappointed.

Gwen and Perrin were still chattering away in the strange language and Rhia tried to concentrate and follow the conversation, but it was no good. They were speaking too quickly for her to keep up and the best she managed was to pick out the odd 'wall', or 'horses', or 'years'. She turned instead to look back up at the city. They were nearing the open gates and two stone gods stood either side of them, short swords held out to cross each other over the arched opening. Soon they would be riding beneath those crossed swords, and then there would be no going back; she would truly be in an enemy land.

*

The over-sweet smell of sweat, both human and animal, was finally starting to fade away as the party rode into the richer part of town. Most of the soldiers in their escort, including the sour-faced Cadmus, had left them near the gate and only a dozen men now followed them, with Lepidus and another crested leader riding ahead. Rhia was grateful that she could finally move freely once again, and that the air seemed breathable, even pleasant at last.

Her first impression of the city had been one of a crowded and smelly pen, with towering grey buildings and arrogant stone gods looming menacingly over them as they crawled their way through streets that were packed solid with townspeople. Mostly they'd seemed to be tribesmen of some kind, maybe Averyn or Duronii, dressed in bright tunics and trousers but with little jewellery evident, and many wearing the strange strappy footwear that the Gaians favoured. Short hair was a common sight in the milling crowds and more than half of the grown men seemed to be beardless. *Maybe they do it to copy their gods?* She mused.

In the poorer part of the town the carved gods had been plentiful but here, where the richer men lived in their broad houses, it seemed that a giant stood on every street corner, and nearly all of the men had faces scraped clean. Rhia and Gwen both stared at them when they passed, marvelling at the craftsmanship as well as the sheer oddness of it all. Many of the male gods were carved wearing armour while others, both male and female, wore either long robes or nothing at all. Their bodies looked strange, even vaguely appealing in an alien sort of way, with lines of muscle carved into the stone making them look strong and healthy, though they carried little fat. Many of the stone gods had been painted in bright colours and Rhia hated to admit that she found their eyes disturbing. They looked somehow both alive and dead at the same time, staring out at nothing and yet seeming to glare at her as well. A moon ago she might have glared back at them as she passed, but her heart just wasn't in it and she avoided looking at their faces.

Beside the looming gods, the stone-built street was flanked by carefully pruned fruit trees and by ever more elaborate houses. Unlike the tall and narrow buildings of the lower city, here the homes were broad and sprawling, their walls painted with pictures of running men or animals or of strange-looking beasts. Rhia was just trying to work out what manner of creature was on the wall beside her, some demon with a man's torso and the legs of a goat, when Lepidus raised his hand and the riding party halted before the largest and grandest of the houses she'd seen so far.

It was easily twice the size of her father's longhall, though much more evenly-shaped, the outer wall painted a pale yellow colour. There were several short stone gods beside the entrance and Rhia watched, curious despite herself, as the young man beside Lepidus dismounted, removed his crested helmet, and then kissed his hand before touching it to the heads of the carved gods. He then hammered his fist on the wood of the door and spoke a few words of Vulgare. Whatever he said it seemed to work because the doors opened immediately, and two strong-looking men stepped outside to flank the entrance while a third beckoned the company inside. He bowed his head repeatedly, first at the young man, then at Lepidus, and then back again.

Perrin gestured to the sisters that they should dismount and Rhia slid from her saddle, her legs and rear aching from the long days of riding. She stretched a little as she walked towards the house, trying not to let her discomfort show. She felt hot and sweaty, and would have liked to take a bath and change into a fresh dress before meeting whoever it was she was supposed to meet here. The Gaians already thought little enough of her people, she knew that much, and she had no wish to give fuel to their assumptions by appearing unwashed and dishevelled when meeting, presumably, somebody of import.

But there was little she could do about that now, though beside her she saw Gwen fussing anxiously with her hair, trying to make herself at least a little more presentable. Rhia was oddly nervous herself, though she managed to crush it with her habitual indifference. These Gaians wanted her and Gwen to marry their sons, a little sweat from the road wouldn't change that. She reached out and gave Gwen's hand what she hoped was a reassuring squeeze, then strode towards the doors with her chin thrust out, prepared to meet whoever this was with her head held high at least. Lepidus had already entered the house and Rhia followed close on his heels, with Gwen and Perrin following behind her. What greeted her inside was like nothing she'd ever seen.

The door opened straight into a cavernous chamber, lit mainly by tiny fires that hovered over the noses of strange, elongated pots. Rhia stared and fought to keep her jaw from dropping as she saw the... she couldn't think of a word for them, the... bronze candles, burning. By their flickering light she saw that the room's walls had been painted like the walls outside, with brightly-coloured figures dashing to and fro all around them. The floor beneath her feet was made of smooth stones, expertly cut to shape and forming patterns underneath them. Columns of stone held up the roof, with little plants hanging from baskets on chains all around them, and in the middle of the roof there was an opening of some sort, showing them a little rectangle of grey-blue sky.

Though her eyes kept being drawn to the bronze candles, Rhia also noticed that the room contained only a few chairs, and was filled instead with short benches, barely large enough for two people to sit on, all padded and covered with bright fabrics. The carving work on the benches, and on the many tiny tables, was exquisite, and Rhia doubted if Jeston had ever dreamed of such fine work.

She was still staring at the magic candles when a group of men and women, in what looked like expensive clothing, approached the newcomers with their arms spread out in greeting. One of them, a man a little older than her father, began speaking to the group in Vulgare. He was fairly unremarkable to look at, being of medium height and build with a plain but honest-looking face and short once-black hair that was losing the battle to grey. He was dressed in a long cream tunic that reached all the way to his feet, held in at the waist by a leather belt. His voice was deep and flowing, and Perrin translated the words.

'Gallant soldiers and honoured allies, welcome to my home. May the justice of Father Gron, the wisdom of Mother Cassio, the courage of Brother Vulco and the purity of Sister Sulis be with you all, now and forever.'

Rhia had no idea what he was talking about but it was presumably a blessing of some kind, because Perrin and the Gaians all kissed their foreknuckles and mumbled something in response. The young soldier who had knocked on the door stepped forward from the group and embraced the old man, who kissed him on the cheek before they parted. The young man moved on to embrace the others of that group while the grey-haired man smiled and looked at Rhia and Gwen. Gwen gave an awkward-looking bow to him but Rhia simply nodded her head. Their host bowed low to them both and, to their surprise, spoke haltingly in the Lurian Tongue.

'Welcome. My name is Lucius Dessidus Glaucus. This is my home.'

He gestured behind him.

'This is my family.'

He spoke very slowly, and with an accent even stranger than Perrin's, but the words came out clearly enough. Rhia nodded again, this time with a modicum of meaning in the gesture, and the old man smiled as he presented a handsome woman.

'This is my wife, Hilaria Dessidus Junia.'

She bowed her head a fraction to them both. She was tall for a woman, and the pile of brown curls on her head made her seem taller than her husband. She wore a long dress of summery yellow decorated with shining beads, and her face seemed to have been decorated with some kind of white powder. It made her look pale and distant, even through the polite smile, and Rhia nodded back as the man spoke again.

'My daughter, Drusia Duronius Livilla.'

A young woman who seemed the living image of her mother stepped forward and bowed her head. She was attractive in a sharp-faced sort of way and wore a similar long dress to the mother, though the younger woman's garment left her pale arms bare, showing several golden bracelets on her wrists. Rhia noticed that the women of the household seemed to enjoy plenty of jewellery, but that the men wore at most a heavy ring or two on their fingers.

The man called Lucius Dessidus Glaucus, Rhia had no idea why they gave themselves so many names, ushered forward the young soldier who had knocked on the door, along with a man who looked so much like him that it was plain before he spoke that they were brothers.

'My old son, Marius Dessidus Antonius.'

The soldier bowed his head.

'My young son, Occidus Dessidus Tullius.'

The brother bowed as well. Rhia assumed that Dessidus must be some reference to their family, presumably it was the name of the older man's father and they used it in his honour. It was strange, but then what wasn't strange in this place?

The youngest man, Occidus, wore a long tunic of deep blue, and was either of naturally skinny build or else the flowing garment made him look that way. There was something of the father in his nose and grey eyes but the sharp bones of his cheek and jaw, as well as his height, were clearly the gifts of his mother. The older one, the soldier, had a slightly broader look to him, though that might have been a deception of his armour. He too had the black hair and grey eyes of the father and the almost harsh-looking facial bones of the mother. Rhia remembered she had heard the name of this family before. *One of these men will be your husband,* she thought, trying to find some emotional reaction, but she was disappointed as all she managed was a vague sense of depression.

She tried to keep her face impassive and focused on her duty as the old man spoke once more.

'Forgive me. This is all that I speak. Welcome again. May I?'

He tilted his head and Rhia was confused until Perrin whispered behind her.

'He's asking permission to embrace you. It's how patricians greet each other.'

Rhia had no idea what a patrician was but she nodded along, and the old man stepped forward to wrap his arms briefly around first Rhia and then Gwen. Rhia tried to be polite and touched his shoulders for a moment but it was just too strange a feeling and they parted quickly. Their host seemed not to take any offence and smiled pleasantly again before speaking once more in Vulgare, this time addressing Lepidus, who had stood around looking bored through this encounter. Perrin translated for the two Caderyn.

'General, you and yours are most welcome to join us for our supper here, I shall want to know all about how my son saw his first action.'

The soldier smiled politely.

'My thanks, councillor. Though I should like to bathe and change if I am to dine in decent company.'

His eyes barely flickered towards them but Rhia could tell that his definition of *decent company* did not extend to her and Gwen. Their host threw up his hands a little.

'But where are my manners? You must all be parched and dusty from the road, please…'

He snapped his fingers, and a gaggle of women in plain yellow dresses with leather collars on their necks appeared as if from nowhere to swarm the group of guests. A pair of them approached Gwen and Rhia and she assumed that they were about to take them somewhere to wash but the young soldier, Marius, said something to his father before they could. The older man nodded.

'Very well.'

He turned to the room.

'While the rest of us better prepare ourselves for civilised dining, my son suggests that he and his brother become acquainted with their brides-to-be. If you would be so kind as to leave your interpreter here?'

He looked expectantly at Lepidus, who nodded.

'Certainly. Perrin, stay here until they're done with you.'

The Basian bowed his head and their host gestured to the group.

'My thanks. Shall we adjourn to the bathing chamber then? I am sure Junia and Livilla can help direct the ladies once they are done here.'

The mother and daughter both nodded and wandered over to one of the padded benches while the rest of them were herded out by the women in the collars, their host following on after them. Before long only the interpreter, the two brothers, Junia, Livilla, Rhia and Gwen were left in the huge room, and the place seemed truly massive now that it was so empty. Perrin attempted to make another introduction between Gwen and Occidus, but was apparently made redundant when Gwen, clearly nervous, began speaking to him herself in halting Vulgare. Rhia had no idea at all what she was saying but the young man smiled at her and spoke slowly in response.

Perrin turned to Rhia and did not even give her a chance to speak first. He knew full well the limits of her language. He said something in Vulgare to the older brother, and he addressed Rhia through him with an awkward expression.

'You will need to learn our language at some point if we are to wed. There is no hurry though and I am sure you will learn quickly.'

Rhia tried not to scowl. It was true she was no linguist but there was no need to be patronising. She spoke to him through Perrin.

'I will indeed learn quickly. Assuming that you will learn the Lurian Tongue as well?'

The interpreter seemed surprised but he passed on her words. The sharp-faced Gaian also seemed a little taken aback but he answered quickly enough.

'I am willing to learn, of course. No alliance is made without compromise and my noble father has taken care to learn some of the language of your people.'

Rhia nodded, glad that her point had been made but still feeling unsatisfied and irritable. Inconvenient though that might be she felt glad to have *some* kind of emotion to feel, and she embraced it as she spoke again.

'And naturally, when we have sons they too will learn the language of my people.'

Again the young soldier seemed taken aback by her forwardness and Rhia felt a tiny flicker of her pride returning to her. She was Caderyn, and this Gaian would listen to what she had to say. On the other side of the room, nervous but genuine-sounding laughter from Gwen and the other brother showed that their conversation, whatever it was, was apparently going slightly better.

Marius spoke through Perrin once again.

'I have no objection. Though Vulgare must be the first language our children learn.'

Rhia nodded and decided that she ought to say something polite. It was in the interests of her people that this alliance went well after all.

'Thank you, Marius.'

Perrin translated and then made as if to speak to her, but the Gaian started speaking first and he translated for him instead.

'My given name is Antonius.'

Rhia frowned.

'Your father said it was Marius. Then those other two names. Why do you do that anyway?'

She was feeling strangely bold given her recent malaise, and had spoken rather shortly without realising it. The Gaian responded calmly.

'High-ranking patricians first have an ancient name, then the family name, then their given name. Marius is the name of a hero from our distant past.'

Rhia shrugged and spoke without really thinking.

'Then why not use his name? Are you afraid you won't live up to it?'

The Gaian reddened a little.

'I shall make my family and my ancestors proud by my actions.'

He hadn't raised his voice but he was obviously annoyed by her. Rhia found she couldn't help herself, for the first time in days she felt almost like her old self again.

'I take it that's a no?'

The sitting ladies seemed shocked and Perrin was clearly reluctant to translate, but presumably he did so. Marius scowled a little.

'No man could match the deeds of Marius, no matter what feats he achieved.'

Rhia found herself squaring up to him, her eyes locked on his.

'You could start by fighting in battles. I didn't see you at Nantwyn.'

The light conversation between Gwen and Occidus stopped abruptly and a hush fell over the room. Marius, or Antonius, met her gaze and looked ready to snap something back, but then seemed to remember where they were and why. He took a deep breath and spoke calmly.

'I saw that battle. The Caderyn fought well.'

Rhia felt a tiny spark of anger rise in her and, ignoring her better judgement, tried to coax it into a flame.

'We *died* well. My husband and my brother died well.'

The silence in the beautiful room was almost painful. She stayed looking into Marius' eyes and for a heartbeat she thought the Gaian might try to strike her, then his eyes softened and she thought he might try to comfort her. But he did neither of those things. Once again he took a deep breath and spoke into the awkward pause.

'I will not debate warfare with my future wife. We shall speak no more of this.'

Rhia wanted to say something, to embrace this foolish anger before it died again, but her husband-to-be cut her off.

'You shall spend the next few days with my mother and sister. They will teach you how a Gaian wife is expected to behave and instruct you in the running of a household. I suggest that you learn a few of our words.'

He nodded to Perrin and Rhia wanted to tell him what he could do with his words, but her good sense was coming back into control. Neither she nor the Caderyn would gain anything from antagonising these people, and her shame at once again letting them down came to the fore. *What if your damned snapping at him made him want to call all of this off? What would Carradan or the others think if the Gaians went to war again because you couldn't hold your tongue?*

She looked across to Gwen. The younger girl still looked afraid but she at least had made an effort to get along with her future husband. *It should be* you *showing* her *how to survive, how to do the right thing, not her showing you! Damn you, your wilfulness has already offended the gods and cost us our freedom, must you always be trying to make things worse?*

She lowered her eyes and spoke more softly.

'I shall. I am sorry, Marius. I meant no offence.'

The young man seemed surprised by her sudden change of tone.

'It's Antoni…never mind. Thank you.'

There was another awkward silence and then the mother stood from her seat and clapped her hands, her smile clearly forced as she tried to break the tension.

'That will do for now. Time that you bathed and changed, I am sure.'

Rhia felt strangely grateful to her, and yet sad that the exchange was over. It had felt good to feel emotion inside her again, even if it had been the worst kind, and at the worst possible time. The two brothers nodded, and Livilla approached the Caderyn sisters as more collared women came to take them wherever it was one washed in this place. As they left Rhia felt the numbness washing over her once more, dulling everything as all feeling inside her died away again. Though she was confident at least that she'd be weeping tonight. When night fell and the grief and shame came to her once more, she'd have this mess to feel guilty about on top of everything else.

Chapter 15. Preparation

One thing you couldn't fault these Gaians for – when they were after something, they did not waste time. It was only her fourth day in the city of Tamora and already the morning of her wedding had arrived. Rhia had no idea what kind of omens the Gaians consulted before they wed, but either they'd been good from the outset or they paid less attention to them than Lurians did. *Not that Reaghan's omens did your first wedding any good.* Rhia ground her teeth and bit back a tear. *It was your actions that were at fault, not his omens. If you hadn't spied on the Gadarim's rituals maybe…*

But more tears threatened at that and she forced them away and tried to focus. She stared intently at her own eyes in the blurry reflection she saw in the polished brass plate. It was nowhere near as distinct as it might have been in a clear pool, but then clear pools were a lot harder to mount on walls, she supposed. She stared into herself and tried to ignore the shame and self-hatred she saw there. It was difficult. The only other feeling able to penetrate the numbness was fear of what this day would entail, and this only fed into her shame. She shoved her chin forwards and thought of duty; to her people, and to Gwen. She might have no strength for herself, but she could at least show some for their sake.

The Basian handmaids fussed around her, seemingly oblivious to her inner turmoil, and chattered amongst themselves in their strange language. It sounded like a mixture of the Lurian and Gaian tongues and Rhia could just about manage to follow what they were saying, though none of it was of any interest to her. They spoke of what perfumes or oils should be used on her hair, what powders should be applied to her face, and whether malachite or azurite would be better to bring out some colour in her eyes. The only times when they stopped wittering on about various cosmetics were when they prattled about how rich and handsome her husband-to-be was, and how fortunate this *barbarian* girl was to be marrying him.

Rhia had never heard this term before but had come to understand it was a generalised, and not especially flattering, term for anything or anyone that was not Gaian. Given that the women tending to her were Basian slaves, people owned by Gaians as though they were cattle, Rhia wondered if they knew just how foolish they sounded in using it to describe her. More than once she'd wanted to shout at them, to clench her fists and batter them away as they fussed and fiddled with her face and hair, but she couldn't find it in herself to do it, and once more felt a surge of self-loathing for the weakling creature she had become. That she'd allowed herself to become.

She frowned as the women curled her hair around the little rollers and used tiny brushes to paint her nails in bright colours, and tried to see something positive in all of this nonsense, just for something to take her mind away from herself. She was at least learning a little more Vulgare thanks to these people. On the few occasions she could bring herself to talk to them she was able to communicate reasonably well, and had found that conversing with the slave-women was a much better learning method than Perrin with all his damned *clauses* and *imperatives*. Why did these Gaians need to have rules for their language anyway? Everyone else just spoke and they were contented. Yet Rhia was beginning to suspect that the Gaians liked to have rules for everything, and the more absurd the reasoning, the better they liked their rules.

It pained her to think on it, but she remembered how she and Bevan had planned their wedding, with all of their families helping each other and enjoying the preparation as much as the day itself. The community had bonded through the hard work and excitement of a great wedding to come, and for all the sweat and toil it had taken, everyone had been together and happy because of it. Rhia almost bit her lip as grief threatened to invade her usual grey apathy, and forced herself to keep thinking about the Gaians and their foolish rules.

Here she had not seen Marius since the day they had met, and had done no work at all in preparation for this wedding. She had been shut up in the house of another long-named fool, apparently somebody quite important, with little but Perrin, the handmaids, and Marius' mother and sister for company. She had seen Gwen a little, as apparently she too had to learn how to be a good Gaian wife, but most of her time had been spent with Marius' kinswomen, who she'd been told she may address as Junia and Livilla. With Perrin translating, they had spent the last four days explaining to Rhia what was expected of her. If the fire in her spirit hadn't been smothered by numbness and guilt, Rhia was certain she would have struck at least one of them by now. *Probably Livilla*, she thought.

Both women had been telling her how she must learn how to run a household, including learning to draw words and improving her skills with numbers, neither of which seemed exactly appealing, but both of which seemed doable at least. Rhia could already sew and knit and though the Gaian methods of doing so were different, she was confident she might learn the subtleties of them in time. Cookery was not going to be an issue for her as, barring special occasions, she would not be expected to do much of that herself.

In all, the practical side of being a Gaian wife did not seem to present any problems – though Rhia still dreaded having to let a man touch her again. No, it was in her general behaviour that the ladies seemed to despair, and Livilla was by far the worst of the two for voicing it.

Perrin had explained that patricians, the rich Gaians, were expected to behave in a certain way, the women in particular, and she had been lectured at tedious length over all the things she must not do. On no account was she to disagree with her husband or his family in public, and she was to be respectful in their discussions in private. She was never to raise her voice or utter any word that might be considered offensive. She was never to discuss her husband's sexual habits or preferences with anyone, not that the women put it in so many words, and she was to always make the utmost effort to appear beautiful for him, and to convey an image of modesty and dignity at all times to all people.

Junia gave out this advice in a manner that suggested she was trying to be helpful but didn't really think it would do any good, while Livilla seemed to delight in correcting everything Rhia did, and seemed to always be waiting for her to make another mistake. Frequent reference was made to her grandmother Livia, Junia's deceased mother, and how the stern old woman would have despaired at having to teach the subtleties of Gaian manners to a barbarian. When not lamenting about how her grandmother might view all of this, Livilla would be thanking all of their strange gods for her own husband, Rabanus, and wondering at how awful it might have been had the situation been reversed and she'd been forced to wed a Lurian.

Rhia had been tempted, many times, to snap at her for being a hateful bitch and suggest that a good Caderyn shaft in her might do her the world of good. But that part of her was buried deep under the mound of guilt and shame, and so she contented herself with the odd glare or scowl when her sister-to-be was critical of her.

Rhia found she was scowling at her own reflection even now and tried to keep her expression neutral as white powder was applied to her skin. The slave-women had already made a complete mask of her face and then removed it again, and were now dabbing and painting and brushing with infinite care. For all her impatience with them she tried her best to keep still as they worked.

She hoped quietly that Gwen wouldn't have to endure such a torment, either from the handmaids or from their future mother and sister in law. Given that Rhia was to be married first, with Gwen and Tullius marrying six days later, she had been given priority in terms of Gaian education, while Gwen had been allowed to keep to herself most of the time. *She has all of this yet to look forward to.* But Gwen had picked up their language well if nothing else, and would hopefully be spared at least some of Livilla's disdain at the prospect of her marrying into their family.

After what seemed like a moon's turn of fussing, the Basian girls told her they were done and she might stand to be dressed. Rhia rose without speaking and padded in bare feet to stand on a little wooden stool. Given her lack of height it barely put her head above those of the collared women but apparently it would make it easier for them to dress her from there. She'd worn a simple sleeveless grey garment while they worked on her face and hair, but one of them unfastened a tie at her shoulder and it crumpled to the floor in a heap.

Rhia had to admit she felt exposed, standing naked on the stool. She tried to tell herself it was because of how scrubbed and scoured she was after the slave-women's earlier treatments. After a long bath that she might have enjoyed under different circumstances, all of her body hair had been shaven off and a variety of perfumed oils and lotions rubbed into her skin that seemed both to soothe it and even out its colour, and it left her whole body almost shining in the light of the bronze candles. In some ways she felt clean and fresh, yet in others she felt foolish and vulnerable, and she tried to convince herself this was why she suddenly felt self-conscious and exposed in her nakedness. She failed.

The truth, and it was a truth that only added to her sense of shame, was that she'd have felt this way regardless of what the Basian women did. In her nakedness she almost felt Delyn's hands on her again, and it was all that she could do not to tremble. She felt an almost crippling fear at the concept of a man, any man, touching her bare flesh again, and at the same time felt overcome with shame at her own body. It was a body that had tempted a man she'd thought was good and noble into becoming something base and terrible, and she felt her fists closing as she looked down at herself. Her skin looked smooth and soft, and she felt a sudden urge to tear her nails across it and see red lines ripping through her flesh. She wanted to rend it, to spoil it, to ruin it. She wanted her body to never again tempt a man to touch it, and she felt tears well up as she realised that even her memories of Bevan were becoming tainted. She tried to think of the joy they had felt in one another's embrace, but each time she tried the thought of Delyn came back to her and the image was gone, or worse; it was soiled into something foul.

Despite herself she felt her body convulse in a sob and the nearest slave-woman started saying something comforting, but Rhia didn't listen to the words. The women muttered a few more words and gave her sympathetic looks now and then, but for the most part left her in silence when they realised she had no wish to talk. Rhia clenched her jaw hard and forced herself to regain some control. She had no right to weep, even if she still did so every night. She had brought this on herself. She had spied on sacred rituals, killed her own husband, allowed her child to die and let a man rape her without any attempt to stop him. She had sown poor seed and now she had to reap it. For Gwen's sake, and for her people, she had to pull herself together.

Two women lifted her white dress into place and began tying it at her shoulders while others fiddled with various rings and bracelets. Rhia couldn't help but think of herself and Meghan preparing each other's battlemarks, long ago when there'd been hope in the world. The dress was beautiful, light and delicate, and the priceless jewellery shone in the candlelight, but she'd have tossed them all into the nearest river in a heartbeat to be back with her friends and wearing woad once again. *But that time is gone, and you have lost your right to wear the blue. Your duty is here now.*

She wondered whether she ought to feel upset or relieved that Carradan wouldn't be there today. His duty was at Bryngarth, just as hers was now here, and General Lepidus would be standing in for him at the ceremony. Apparently he was some type of patrician, just not as important a type as Marius' family, and since Marcus Portunus Julius had stayed in Bryngarth, Lepidus was the only Gaian of sufficient rank and age who had met her father and could thus be permitted to act on his behalf. Rhia decided that despite her dislike of Lepidus it was better that it was this way. She had no wish for her father to see her sold off to this Gaian family, to be a slave to them in all but name. Besides, Carradan had given her to Bevan. If he was not here to give her to Marius then some small part of her could still believe she was Bevan's wife. *You might still have been, had you not killed him.* Her own voice was harsh and bitter and Rhia tried to argue back. *I don't know for sure that what I did killed him, and I never meant to hurt him. I would never...* but her first voice cut her off. *He is dead because of you! We have lost everything because of you! Now be a good little slut and prepare to spread your legs for Marius! It's the least you can do!*

Rhia wanted to weep but she held it back, almost missing her numbness in the face of her fear and shame. The women brought over another reflector, this one long and silvery, far better made than the little one at the table. An unrecognisable but undoubtedly beautiful woman looked back at Rhia from the polished surface. The women fawned and flattered terribly, commenting on how expensive the dress and jewels were and how fortunate Rhia was that the groom's family were paying for all of this. She did not feel fortunate. She felt alone and scared and soiled in this wondrous finery.

One of the collared women tried to joke that the goddesses would be made jealous of her beauty, but Rhia's glare soon stopped anyone from laughing. She wondered what Mehine would think of all this and decided she would probably look down on her for it, but she would at least approve that she did it for her people. Another of the Basian girls tried lightening the mood by saying how fortunate Marius, or Master Antonius as they called him, was. Rhia tried to smile as she nodded but the mere absence of scowling from her seemed enough to keep them happy. In truth she didn't know what was worse, the notion of his seeing her and being haughtily distant as before, or the notion of his seeing her and calling her beautiful. She imagined the young Gaian with lust in his eyes and was ashamed at the fear that struck her as she did.

She stepped from the stool and pretended to admire her reflection from different angles. Her hair had been curled and her skin shone, and it was entirely believable that she was captivated by her own beauty. It meant the collared women didn't see her palm a tiny knife from the dressing table and secrete it in her delicate blue sash. It was barely large enough to cut a single lank of hair, but a cowardly instinct had made her grab for it and now that it was taken she daren't put it back. And she hated herself that she didn't want to.

I'll just keep it as an emergency. I probably won't use it. But if... if it is all too much, if his touch is beyond what I can bear, I can die and be with Bevan again. But I can wait until after the wedding is done. Her scornful voice came back to her again. *What manner of coward are you? Your bridge will be narrow indeed if you abandon your people now. You have no right to end your life, not after all you have done.* She held back another sob and felt the outline of the blade through the cloth but did nothing more. It was true, she had no right, but she couldn't bring herself to abandon the tiny comfort that having the knife there gave her, no matter how her own voice berated her for it.

She wished more than she had ever wished for anything that she was back at home, at her first wedding, the one she'd longed for and worked hard for and which had ended with a bliss she'd never imagined was even possible. She wished that she could feel just one tiny droplet of that feeling again, even if it meant that she would die a heartbeat later. Then she wished that she had died in that dreadful battle at Nantwyn, and that she and Bevan might have crossed the Bridge of Souls together and now both be in the Otherworld, and at peace. *If nothing else, I wish the reason I took this knife was to stab out at my enemies, not to end my own life in craven fear. But there are no woodland dryads or forest sprites here to ask my wishes of, and if there were, Mehine would forbid them to me. As so she should.*

Rhia took one final look at the Gaian woman in the mirror. This was no time for tears or wishes or regrets. She had a duty. It might not be the duty she wanted, to be the warrior that she once was and to fight for her people, but it was the duty she had. Gwen would be looking to her today, and her people's future was in her hands. No time for wishes. It was time to be wed again.

Chapter 16. A Gaian Wedding

Belenos was clear and bright despite the clouds, though the weather was on the turn and the wind had a sharp chill to it. Dressed in her delicate gown, Rhia felt the bite of it the moment she emerged from the house, but she took care not to shiver in the cold. A crowd of people in bright-coloured clothes were lining the stone-paved street and she hated to think of them assuming she was afraid. Even if she was. They might be strangers, a motley mix of Gaians, Basiae, Averyn, Duronii and whatever other peoples lived in or around the great city, but all the same she was determined to hide her fear from them.

Unwillingly, she found herself thinking of her first wedding, her true wedding, when friends and family had walked with her and Bevan from Bryngarth to the Ring of Stones, happy for all the solemnity of the event. She remembered holding back grins through her nervousness as she walked to kiss palms with the man she loved. Even the tramp up the hill and the ache in her freezing feet had been a sort of joy in themselves, a hardship without being a hardship. She remembered feeling the presence of the gods as they'd stood in that glade before the Great Oak, and how the fear she'd felt had been mixed in with a sort of wonder. She ran a finger along the tiny scar below her thumb. *Bevan...* Rhia snapped herself out of it. That was then, and it was done.

Today would be nothing like that, she thought emptily as she began the slow walk to Marius' house. No long trek into the woods for her in a gaggle of well-wishing friends: A short stroll across the town in a procession of chanting strangers, all speaking in a language that she didn't understand as they took her to a ritual she understood even less. Junia had told her a little about it but not much had really sunk in and what had done made no sense to the bride-to-be. She tried to run through the process of it in her head, just to give herself something to think about, but her mind felt like it was trying to catch sand, and the details kept slipping through her fingers.

She then tried to distract herself by looking around at the grand buildings, but this provided little relief either. True, there were many wonders of the stoneworkers' art to look upon; great decorated columns were everywhere, and even the flat stones of the road were well-shaped and precisely fitted, but their greatest achievements were filling her with dread. The countless carved gods seemed to stare both at her and *through* her with their sightless, painted eyes and Rhia was ashamed of herself when she avoided their gaze.

She knew that these were Gaian gods and that she ought not to be concerned, but she couldn't help herself from seeing her own gods in their faces. As far as she knew, the only depictions the Caderyn had ever made of their gods were the ancient cave paintings that had been old when Reaghan was young. Rhia had seen them once and they had looked nothing like these carved wonders, but nonetheless she found herself seeing them here. A female holding out a branch of some sort suddenly became Mehine, staring down at Rhia in disapproval. Another holding a babe became Marna, judging her in silence for the child she'd allowed to die. She saw a rare bearded male and thought of Taran, the god she'd betrayed by spying on Gadarim rituals, or Karanon, Lord of the Mountains, or Camelas himself, the Father of All. A grim-looking couple made her think of Annwn and Damara, King and Queen of the Otherworld, and she almost whispered a prayer to them to send her love to Bevan and Dane, but then their hard, glaring faces made her flinch away from them, and she carried on walking, drenched in her misery.

She was oddly grateful when the walk was over and she finally reached the house, though the short gods beside the door seemed to stare at her just as the others had, and she kept her eyes forward as the Gaians kissed their hands to touch them. The heavy doors were shut and Rhia forced herself not to fidget as they waited. Her fingers longed to twitch or to close into fists, and her toes clenched nervously in the strappy footwear she'd been given. She stared at the doors and tried to keep still. She wanted to run. More than anything at that moment she wanted to turn and sprint away as fast as she could, and she didn't even care where she'd be running to. *I can't do this. I don't want to re-marry, I don't want to be a Gaian, I don't want that man to own me, to have me, to… to touch me, I can't, I can't!* Rhia pressed her lips together hard and felt her legs begin to shake. *I'm sorry! I'm sorry, I love Bevan and I can't go through with this, I can't do it, not even for all my people, I can't do it, I can't!*

She balled her fists closed and her lip began to tremble, and she was midway through turning around, her right foot coming up onto the ball ready to sprint, when the heavy doors swung open and two slaves appeared either side. Rhia panicked and the Basian girl beside her cocked her head as if to ask her what was wrong. Rhia wondered if she had it in her to fight her way free, to take the tiny knife in her sash and escape this dreadful place? She doubted it, her spirit had been crushed by the weight of grief and shame, but maybe her fear might fuel her enough to at least get clear of the crowd? Then she might hide somewhere or crawl away to die, anything but continue along this path!

Her eyes darted back to the doorway and she was wondering if she could slam the doors shut before she fled when a sight from inside caused her to pause. What she could see of the main room looked crowded with people, all clustered either side of a long aisle that led from the door. From where she was she couldn't really make out a great deal, but one face seemed to leap out at her from the crowd; Gwen's.

Like her sister, Gwen had been dressed and painted and fussed over until she was almost unrecognisable but Rhia would have known her sweet face anywhere. She was standing at the far end of the room, looking beautiful in a long gown of pale blue. Rhia couldn't quite see, but she thought she saw Livilla and Junia standing nearby her, and one thing was unmistakable, even from a distance; her little sister was terribly afraid. A casual observer might not have seen it, but Rhia could still remember Gwen pretending she didn't care when the other children had been diving into the river near Bryngarth. At five years old Gwen had worn that same expression when trying to hide just how afraid she was of something, and Rhia felt a tear threaten to spill onto her cheek.

Can you really leave her to face all this alone? Is your own fear so great that you'd abandon her? Rhia bit her lip hard and felt her fingers flexing despite themselves. She was terrified. She was so afraid of what would happen when she was given to this man, this man who would touch her and take her and force a child of his blood into her body. A shiver ran across her skin that had nothing to do with cold, and her hands felt horribly damp and clammy as she clenched and unclenched her fists. She didn't want to do this. She just wanted to run and hide away and let the whole bloody world be damned!

But Gwen was still looking at her. Still sweet, still beautiful. Still afraid. Rhia licked her lips and shuffled on the spot, squaring up to the open doorway as if it were one of the giants at Nantwyn about to take her head. She didn't want to do this. But she had no choice. And so, partly because she had let her people down, partly because of her sense of shame and guilt, but mostly for that sweet, frightened face, Rhia clenched her jaw and jutted her chin forwards, and, feeling as if she were about to plunge into cold water, slowly stepped across the house's threshold.

*

Far from feeling the refreshing chill of diving into water, the moment Rhia walked in she felt stifled by the heat of so many bodies pressed in together, and it was an effort not to start gasping for breath. It was hard not to shake as she walked but Rhia kept her eyes on her sister's face, barely glancing at the crowd or the decorated room. Long banners had been strung up from the ceiling above and glimpses of red, white, blue, green, yellow, pink and purple kept flitting past in her peripheral vision, though whether this was from the banners or the brightly-dressed guests, Rhia couldn't have said.

Gwen was standing near the end of the aisle and Rhia saw that Tullius stood beside her, along with Livilla and the rest of the family. It seemed that Gaian women liked their finery more than the men did, for though Livilla and her mother were dressed in lavish-looking dresses, neither Tullius nor the other men seemed ostentatious in their wardrobe. Their long tunics were clearly of good quality, but they were nothing to the gaudiness of the women's clothing. Even their host, who she was pretty sure was an important man, wore only a long tunic of white with a robe-like garment over one shoulder, the only decoration evident being a thick red stripe running down it.

Standing beside a table at the end of the aisle, all dressed in flowing robes, stood two men and two women, each one remarkably different from the next. Near the centre of them, and clearly in charge of proceedings, was a stocky-looking man of some sixty winters in an elaborate robe of reddish brown trimmed with gold and, unusually, sporting a long white beard. His face was solemn but there were definite laugh lines at his eyes, and Rhia was reminded just a little bit of Reaghan.

Beside him was a younger man in a bright crimson garment that came across one shoulder to fall down into a robe, leaving half his torso naked to the eye. His body was broad and muscular, similar to those of the carved gods who'd glared at her outside and, like the carved gods, his chest hair had been shaved away. Next to this man was a woman of around her mothers' years, with greying hair mostly hidden beneath a hood. Her robes were all of white and silver-grey with only a subtle lining of sky blue at hem and cuff.

Lastly was a woman who might have been Rhia's own age, or even younger, though her eyes betrayed a wisdom many years beyond her looks. She was fresh-faced and beautiful, with thick brown hair that fell in little ringlets to her shoulders. Her robe was a strange mixture of sea green and deep blue and was cut in a manner that clung to her body more than the others' did, and the lines and curves it showed revealed a figure both slender and feminine. Rhia had a moment to deduce that these must be the Gaians' equivalents to druids and herbwives before she found herself standing only a few paces in front of them.

She glanced across at Gwen and tried to look encouraging. Her sister was clearly still afraid but Rhia saw Tullius mutter something to her under his breath, and the younger Caderyn managed a nervous smile. Rhia almost approved. For all her own problems she'd been so worried that after their terrible defeat, and then their promising to these Gaians, her little sister's spirit had been broken. But this Tullius did not seem a bad sort, in a skinny way, and Rhia hoped more than anything else that he would make Gwen a good husband. She turned from them to look to her right, where her own Gaian husband was waiting.

Marius was dressed in a similar tunic to his father, though without the shoulder-robe, and he wore a thick leather swordbelt around his waist. He was looking at her with an expression of surprise, and though he covered it up quickly, Rhia was sure she saw a flash of lust behind his eyes. She refused to shudder. The image of Delyn in the barn came back to her but she shoved it away with a grimace. Gwen was still watching. She could not afford to seem afraid.

Marius looked confused for a moment but if he'd planned on saying anything he never got the chance. The older Gaian druid had started speaking in a loud voice, though Rhia only understood a fraction of what he said. He seemed to be calling on their gods for something, and then the other druid and the herbwives stepped forward. They all waved their arms around and chanted prayers, but what few words Rhia picked out made little sense and she assumed that they were doing the same thing as the older man. *Perhaps they have different druids for different gods here, and that's why they need four of them for a marriage ritual?* She didn't let her curiosity wander too far in that direction as it brought images to her of her first wedding, and instead she simply stared forwards and embraced the numbness as best she could.

The ceremony seemed to take a very long time and Rhia barely understood a word. When they seemed to be asking anything of her she simply nodded. At some point in the proceedings more people in robes appeared and placed garlands of red flowers on hers and Marius' heads. At another, the carcass of a bird was cut open by the older herbwife and its innards held up to the light and marvelled at by the others. Later on Rhia was handed one of the magical bronze candles by one of them, and was encouraged to pass it to Marius, who then passed it to his father, the old man then producing another of these devices and passing it to Marius, who passed it to Rhia, who was then prompted to pass it to Lepidus, standing behind her.

The general was dressed in the same white tunic and shoulder-robe as Marius' father, though his had no red stripe and the soldier still wore his swordbelt. About midway through the ceremony he was called forward and from what Rhia understood he gave her away to her new husband in the name of her absent father. Marius' father stepped forward to say something similar, or to accept the offer, she couldn't really tell, and the brightly-dressed druids all blessed them several times.

More questions were directed at her and at Marius, and eventually Perrin was ushered forward to translate, after it seemed that Rhia had nodded her head to a question she ought to have answered 'no' to. The little interpreter didn't make the questions that much less confusing, though Rhia did sneer a little when they asked if she was a virgin. She muttered to Perrin in her own language.

'What kind of question is that? Lepidus knows I've been wed before.'

The Basian tried to keep smiling as he spoke.

'A different tax is due when widows wed as opposed to maidens. Just nod your head.'

Rhia kept her voice low.

'It isn't true.'

Perrin struggled to keep calm as he hissed back.

'You're just agreeing that you've never lain with a man as an unwed woman, nor are you married already. By Gaian law only their marriages are legal anyway so it's all as true as they need it to be.'

Rhia ground her teeth but nodded. It was disrespect to the gods as much as anything that had brought her to this point, and while these gods might be Gaian gods, it still seemed wrong to lie in front of them. Whenever the druids stepped aside she could see tiny carved gods on the table, and those horrible, sightless eyes might see through her deception. She tried to see it as Perrin did; that as far as they were concerned she'd never been married before, but it did little to assuage her guilt and if anything just made her feel worse, as if she were betraying Bevan even further by denying him. She pushed away such thoughts before the tears could pierce the numbness. She had her duty to do.

A few more senseless words were chanted by the druids and before long Rhia and Marius were beckoned towards the table. Rhia refused to look at him as the couple approached, and stood stone-faced as blessings were made over them by each of the holy men and women in turn. This done, they were invited to step closer still, to where paper and ink had been placed on the table, ready. Five days ago Rhia wouldn't have known what a pen *was*, let alone understood the concept of a *contract*. She had only a vague idea now, despite Junia's patient lecturing. It seemed it was not enough for Gaian families that promises were made in the sight of the gods and of witnesses; apparently they had to record it on a type of flimsy tree-bark so that if an argument happened later, the families could wave this *paper* about as if that somehow made a thing more true. Rhia had not even pretended to understand, but Junia had said it was part of the ritual and for Gwen's sake she was determined to see it through.

The paper was covered in markings of the ink, and though Perrin had assured her she would grow to understand their meanings, today they were just a jumble of purple-black lines. She recognised a portion near the bottom, if only because Junia had shown it to her before, and knew it was the sound of her Gaian name written in letters.

Beside her, her new husband had taken the feather pen from the ink and was presumably writing his own name beside it. Junia had assured her that the signing of the document had been taken care of in advance by herself and Lepidus, and that all Rhia need do was mark the paper in some way when and where indicated. She had to admit that for all the ridiculousness of the ritual she felt foolish scrawling two simple lines beside Marius' carefully printed name. She was sure that her new husband was smirking inwardly at her ineptitude, and she was about to scowl at him when something happened that she could not have imagined. The situation suddenly got worse.

As she'd leaned forward to make her mark the blue sash of her dress had shifted around her waist. It wasn't much, but it was enough to dislodge the knife Rhia had completely forgotten was there. In her focus on Gwen the little talisman that had seemed so important back at the house had completely slipped her mind, and by the time she felt it move it was too late to do anything about it. The tiny weapon slipped from her sash and clattered on the stone floor, and in the silence of the chamber it seemed more deafening than Taran's thunder.

A hundred guests craned forward to see what had happened and those nearby drew in sharp breaths of surprise and alarm. Rhia made to pick it up but the younger druid was quicker than she was, and he swept the little weapon up in an eyeblink. The Gaian studied it for a moment before sharing a glance with his fellow holy man. Words of Vulgare were uttered and Rhia didn't need to speak the language to know they were not friendly. Perrin, his voice a little higher than usual, whispered the gist of it to her.

'You have brought a weapon before the sacred priests, only soldiers of Holy Vulco may bear arms in such presence!'

Rhia was not much enlightened by the explanation but she tried her best, forcing herself to appear calm. *This has to go well! Think of the Caderyn. Think of Gwen.* Her sister was looking on, scared and confused, and Rhia spoke as calmly as she could to the interpreter.

'Tell him it's a mistake. Tell him I thought I was meant to wear it because Lepidus and Marius have weapons.'

She hated herself for the lie, especially since she'd been so reluctant to lie before these gods only moments ago, but she had precious few options available. The Gaians around her looked disapproving at best, and downright angry at worst. Perrin rushed out his explanation as best he could and translated the old druid's reply.

'He says you have caused great affront to the gods by this, and…'

But he was forced to stop as Glaucus Dessida spoke up, and he translated his words instead.

'Your father-in-law is telling them that it must be a tradition of your tribe.'

The druids still seemed unimpressed and Glaucus turned to Lepidus and spoke again, apparently seeking some agreement or support. The grey-haired general was clearly not pleased at having been pulled into this, and he gave Rhia an angry look before he spoke. Again, Perrin hissed in her ear.

'The general has concurred that it is common practice for Lurian women to be armed as well as their men.'

This news started a murmuring of conversation among the guests and Rhia wished she had enough spirit to be enraged at them, to tell them where they could stick their bloody judgemental opinions, but still she found it impossible to reach her anger through the emptiness, and instead felt only embarrassment and shame. It made things ten times worse when she saw Gwen trying to hide her face away.

The druid seemed to be arguing back and it looked like this whole thing might be about to come crashing down when her new husband stepped forward and spoke loudly but respectfully to all of them. The chatter died away as all eyes turned to him and he reached out a hand towards the druid. Perrin whispered his words at her, his nervous little voice at stark odds with the Gaian's even tone.

'May I see this knife?'

The muscular druid flicked his gaze to Glaucus for a heartbeat before handing the blade over to his son. Marius Dessida turned it over in his hands before approaching Rhia and holding it out to her.

'Hold this a moment.'

His simple words were commanding, and even through her embarrassment Rhia felt irritated at his tone. She was highly tempted to refuse him but then remembered where she was and meekly took the blade back. Marius paused a moment before speaking again.

'Now give it to me.'

Once again his tone was aggravatingly demanding, and a tiny spark of real anger threatened to reach the surface of Rhia's mind before her good sense overruled her. Her betrothed nodded, and then addressed the room in general, his voice sounding loud and clear.

'My bride, who was once a warrior, has given me this weapon of hers. As my wife, and as ally to the Most Glorious Gaian Empire, she no longer has need to bear arms of war.'

He turned back to her and nodded his head.

'Thank you, my wife.'

Rhia felt the spark of anger start to smoulder and her eyes widened as Perrin translated. She started to forget her duty, her fear, even the dreaded numbness that had so plagued her since Nantwyn. She was a daughter of Carradan, who was this Gaian to take her weapon from her? Despite her best efforts she found herself glaring at this impudent man, and either he felt the heat from her gaze or else this Dessida was better at dealing with these situations than she was.

'Nonetheless, I shall not always be at my wife's side. The calls of duty may require me to be away from my home and I shall feel better knowing that our children will be always protected, whichever parent is with them.'

He reversed his grip on the tiny knife and offered it handle-first back to Rhia.

'The Caderyn were fine warriors, and with such blood mixed in with that of my own noble ancestors, our children shall indeed grow to be strong.'

Rhia was genuinely unsure whether she should laugh at this man, thank him, or stab him. In the end she chose the second option and bowed her head a little as she took the knife back from him. The room seemed still to be frozen in a state of shock, and before the spell could be broken by arguments, Glaucus Dessida spoke again.

'My son has given his bride a gift. Surely no man can deny that a bride may hold a gift from her husband on her wedding day?'

He spread his hands as if inviting an objection from the crowd and though the druids still looked surly, no voice was raised. The guests either avoided his gaze or smiled as if some great joke had been told, and even Marius managed a relieved-looking smile to his father. Rhia still felt angry with him, despite her own relief at the situation having been settled. She resented the fact that she'd needed this Gaian to step in and fix a problem of her doing, and she tried to fuel the anger that had been building in her since he first spoke.

But it was no good. The moment had passed and guilt and shame came back to her as she realised how close she'd come to letting everyone down yet again. The heat of her rage was smothered once again and for what was left of the ceremony Rhia looked blankly on, her powdered face an inscrutable mask. It soon ended, and the only emotion she managed to will to the fore was fear, as the four priests announced the names of the newly-wed couple.

Marius Dessidus Antonius looked briefly at his new wife and Rhia saw no lust in his eyes, though she was sure it would be back there later on. Later tonight he would come to her and she would have to let him take her. Without a child this wedding might as well not have happened and if she was to serve her people, and Gwen above all, she would have to let this Gaian, this enemy, touch her as Bevan once had. As Delyn had. Rhia struggled to hold back her shivers and tears yet again as the priests announced her new name to the smiling Gaian crowd. Carradus Dessidus Rhianna.

*

Rhia spent most of the feast trying not to think about the mess she'd almost caused, and determinedly not thinking about her first wedding. Her true wedding. She tried to block out the memories of the long, cold walk from the Ring of Stones, surrounded by her family and friends. She tried to forget her mother gently teasing her about her parent's wedding antics. Rhia sat on a padded bench beside a table of delicacies and firmly ignored all the happy memories of that time. Once or twice she glanced down at the tiny cut on the pad below her thumb and felt tears threaten her eyes as she thought of the same cut on Bevan's hand. But one by one she forced these thoughts away. She was married to Marius now, even if the ceremony had been bizarre to the point of ridiculous. For the good of her people she was now his wife, and dwelling on the past would serve no good.

On a bench nearby she saw Gwen nibbling nervously at a bird of some kind and she did her best to smile encouragingly at her sister. She had no idea whether it worked or not but Gwen managed an awkward smile back, and Rhia resolved she must make do with that. She tried another sip of the watered red wine. She had only ever tasted wine on a handful of occasions and always it had been stronger than whatever this stuff was, but the flavour of the Gaian red was fruity and light, and on another day Rhia might well have enjoyed it. It was better than the food anyway.

Half of what was offered looked either unrecognisable or inedible, and on the few occasions she'd tried something it had been over-rich and sickly. Even the pleasant honeyed meat she'd tried when they had first sat down had been ruined for her when Perrin, who'd kept close-by to translate, had explained to her that she was eating mouse! In all she had settled for sips of wine, the odd piece of bread, and the occasional slice of fruit that was brought past by the slaves. The rest of the guests were happily indulging in all sorts of things and though the smells were sometimes intriguing, Rhia just couldn't bring herself to try anything.

Not that eating seemed to rank particularly high in a Gaian bride's priorities. The moment she and Marius had sat down a parade of guests had approached them to touch their hands and offer blessings. Rhia might not have minded so much had they been friends or family of hers, but almost every face here was a stranger, and she felt awkward and foolish just sitting and nodding to the endless line of well-wishers. It was so bad that she actually welcomed the faces of General Lepidus and the hard-eyed Tribune Cadmus, simply because they at least were familiar to her from the ride.

Besides them, and Marius' immediate family of course, the parade of strangers simply blended into one blurry mess of polite smiles and waved blessings. She was introduced to Livilla's husband, Duronius Rabanus, to another legion general named Galerius Gregorius, to several ladies in fabulous dresses who were apparently related to Junia in some way, and to countless old men in shoulder-robes like the one Glaucus wore, all keen to touch her hand and wish her well. But she had no memory for the strange barrage of names that Perrin spoke to her. Names like Horatius, Contis, Laberius, Drusus, Scribonius, Urgulanius, Virius, Coruncanius, Didius and Athenadorus all washed over her in a tide of nonsensical gibberish.

Some of them seemed like they were trying to be friendly. Most simply smiled at Marius and then looked at her as though she was some strangely-shaped shell they had picked up on a beach; curious but far from valuable. A couple gave their blessings with badly masked disapproval, and one or two had to struggle to cover up sneers. Once again Rhia wished she could will her anger back into being but she just couldn't manage it, and she kept her face a neutral mask as she nodded to them.

The day wore slowly on into the evening and Rhia wondered if she ought to try drinking a little more heavily. It might make things easier later on when... when it had to happen. She looked over at her new husband as she sipped at the Gaian wine. Marius had barely glanced at her since the incident with the knife and was currently speaking quietly with one of the men in shoulder-robes. Rhia wasn't sure if he was purposefully ignoring her for some reason, or whether it was just that he was busy dealing with all their many guests. Either way she wasn't sure if she felt more offended by his rudeness or relieved that she didn't have to interact with him. *Yet.*

Gwen at least seemed less nervous than she had been. Rhia had only been able to snatch a few words of conversation with her, but it seemed Livilla approved of her sister more than she did of Rhia and had been keeping her company and helping her to chat with the guests, aided by Gwen's soon-to-be husband, Tullius. Rhia felt annoyed at herself for not having made more effort with the language as Gwen had, but it was just one more thing on a long list of reasons to hate herself today, and it hardly managed to worsen her awful mood.

The evening plodded by and slowly the guests began to leave, lining up once again before the bride and groom to say their various farewells. It seemed to Rhia like the number of people had doubled since the last round of pleasantries she had exchanged, but at least the time spent nodding politely was delaying the time when she and Marius would be alone. She began hoping quietly that the night would wear on too long, or that her new husband would drink too much, and that come the time to consummate this marriage he would be too tired to do anything but sleep. Rhia cursed herself for so unworthy a thought but nonetheless she clung on to that hope. Fear was fast conquering her ever-present sense of emptiness, and when the last of the long line of guests said his farewells she almost wished she spoke more Vulgare, that she might call him back into the house.

But that didn't happen. Soon only the members of her new family remained and each of these began retiring politely to their rooms. Apparently she and Marius were to have a house of their own to live in as man and wife, but for tonight they would be staying at the family home. Rhia drained yet another unsatisfactorily weak cup of wine and noticed that the Basian women who'd dressed her were all loitering nearby, and that both Junia and Livilla were giving her significant glances. Once again she felt that urge to run, to leap up from the padded bench and sprint for the nearest door, but she knew that was no longer an option. If it ever had been one. She was married now, and foreign or not it was in the sight of gods. She felt her fingers tighten involuntarily on the metal cup, but she managed to give a nod to the waiting slave-girls.

Slowly, reluctantly, she rose from the bench onto her feet. She was not nearly so drunk as she had hoped to be before this happened but that couldn't be helped at this point. She spoke a few polite words to Perrin, telling him he could be gone for the night, and asked him to convey something suitable to her new family. The little Basian spoke some words in Vulgare and Glaucus, Tullius and Junia all smiled and bowed their heads, with even Livilla condescending enough to nod. Marius had neither said nor done anything as he sat beside her, and Rhia muttered to Perrin to tell him that she would see him in their room. Even saying the words made her want to shudder a little but she forced herself to remain outwardly calm. Marius simply nodded to the interpreter and Rhia clenched her jaw before making her way across the chamber to her slave-women. Halfway there Gwen approached her and squeezed her hand, but neither sister could think of anything comforting to say, and Rhia walked from the room in silence.

The collared women knew the way and soon led her to a large and spacious chamber dominated by a bed that could easily sleep four, the big room lit only sparingly by a pair of those bronze candles. Here they started to undress her, taking the pins out of her hair and folding her dress carefully, and setting aside the tiny knife that had almost ruined everything. Unlike their task that morning there was no chattering between them now. The women seemed excited and nervous, as though this was *their* wedding night and not hers, and Rhia wished under her breath that one of them might go through this instead of her. Perhaps Marius was drunker than he looked, and might not recognise who the girl was in the dark? A drunken man's plough might care little for what furrow it found, and if it bought her one more night of freedom then surely it was worth it? Rhia banished those thoughts from her mind. She might hate this, even as she hated the fear she knew would only worsen, but it had to be done.

By the time she was fully naked most of the slave women had bowed out, with only two of them remaining, standing dutifully in the shadows. *Are they going to be here the whole time?* Rhia considered signalling for them to leave but realised with a tiny jolt that she dreaded to be alone. She was more afraid of this single room than she had been at either of the bloody battles in which she'd fought. She was wondering whether she might try to start a conversation with them, they understood her far better than the Gaians did at least, but then the chamber door opened once more, and her new husband walked in.

He did not sway as he walked and even in the dim light his grey eyes looked clear. He stared at Rhia for a few moments and she wanted desperately to cover up, but she forced herself to stand upright, feigning a pride she did not feel, and she let him look her body up and down. She felt horribly exposed and was glad when he finally looked away once again, signalling for his own slaves to undress him. Marius was attended by two young-looking boys and though they both snuck odd glances at her, Rhia managed not to react to their gaze. They weren't the ones she was afraid of.

Not waiting for any indication from him, she made her way to the bed and lay down on it. The night wasn't really cold but nonetheless she wished hopelessly that she might crawl under the covers, but that was not an option for her tonight. *He'll want to see what he's taking, no doubt. I'm something new for him to try.* Images of Delyn flashed in front of Rhia's eyes and she ground her teeth together and forced them back with all her might. *This man is not him. If you relax it might be over before you know it. Just do your duty.*

She had almost convinced herself to just lie back and let it happen when Marius fully disrobed and padded naked towards the bed. Panic rushed through her and her eyes went wide and frightened. The Gaian looked confused and Rhia tried to cover her reaction by gesturing to his slaves. Marius turned to look at them before nodding in understanding, and at a flick of his wrist the two boys left the room. Rhia's hands shook as she feared he might dismiss her women as well and leave them alone in here, but either her new husband had decided to let them stay or else it just didn't occur to him.

He reached the bed and by the dim light Rhia saw his body was muscular and shaved clean like the Gaian's carved gods, though there was still some dark hair visible about his legs and manhood. It was also clear that her new husband was... ready for her, and Rhia tried to hold at bay the shame and fear that threatened to drown her. Her husband crawled slowly onto the bed and Rhia felt his hand reach for her face. He spoke a few words that she didn't understand and then kissed her mouth, first softly, and then with firmness.

His hands began exploring her and it was all that she could do not to start screaming and scratching and biting at the man. He was trying to be gentle, she was sure he was, but all she felt as his skin touched hers was a mix of revulsion and shameful terror, though she determinedly kept anything from showing. She wanted to cry but she held it back. *This must be done. He is your husband now and you have your duty. For Gwen, for your people, and for all your damned mistakes you must endure this.*

Marius was kissing her neck now and his one hand was slowly reaching up her thigh, and for all her efforts Rhia started shaking. Her new husband was not rough with her, not rough at all, but nonetheless as she felt him enter her Rhia wanted nothing more than to weep, and as he began to thrust and groan as he took his husband's right of her, she screwed shut her eyes as tight as she could and forbade the tears to fall. She kept her eyes closed.

Forgive me Bevan.

Chapter 17. A Gaian Marriage

Even after thirty days of living in Tamora the carved gods, the *statues*, still made Rhia nervous when she looked at their eyes. To be so staring and yet so obviously blind seemed horrifically unnatural to her, and each time she caught herself looking at one she was sure it was looking back; right through her flesh and into her weakened soul. She passed the huge one of the man with the giant hammer and was grateful that it meant she was almost home.

Home. It was strange to hear the word used here, even in her own head. On their first day of married life she and Marius had moved into what his father had called a modest townhouse, and what any Caderyn would have called a chieftain's hall. It was perhaps a little smaller than Glaucus' home, but the mansion was still easily large enough to dwarf Carradan's longhouse at Bryngarth. Rhia wondered when it was that she'd started referring to it as *home*. It wasn't home, she decided firmly, Bryngarth was home, the longhall was home, her little house she'd shared with Bevan was home. Yet this house was the closest thing she had to a place of safety in this bewildering city.

She avoided the hammerer's painted eyes and walked on through the chilly streets, one slave walking beside her, the other one a step or two behind. The one next to her was Drenn, a large and intimidating-looking tribesman from a province called Greutunnica. The bodyguard kept his eyes sharp as he watched the streets for any trouble, not that Rhia expected there to be any. The Dessida family were extremely well-respected and this was a very safe part of town. Besides, Drenn was a great deterrent to any would-be thief. He was a head taller than most tall men with a torso that was heavy with muscle, and the tattoos along his shaven scalp gave his whole face a menacing aspect. In truth he was a pleasant enough man, from what Rhia

229

understood of his speech, and he reminded her of men like Madoc and Owain in his manner – tough without feeling the need to prove it to anyone.

The slave behind her was a Basian woman named Enora and Rhia wondered how she would have coped for this last moon without her. She'd not known her name at the time, but Enora had been one of the women who'd prepared her for her wedding, and she had been at Rhia's side almost constantly since that dreadful day. It was mainly thanks to her that Rhia's grasp on Vulgare had become, slightly, firmer and the young slave had been both kind and understanding to her without ever making it seem like she was being pitied. She glanced back at her and they shared a brief smile before Rhia turned her attention back to the road.

Before long they would be back at the house and she could relax for a while before Marius came home, having just managed to excuse herself from yet another tedious midday meal with Junia and their extended family. The Gaian women were, for the most part, kindly enough in their own way, but their talk was unbelievably dull and Rhia still had to stop and ask people to repeat themselves quite a lot. Junia was patient with her, and even Livilla had warmed to her a little, but most of the high-born women were clearly growing tired of it.

It was not helped by the fact that Gwen was apparently a natural linguist and had picked up Vulgare like most people picked up walking. She was now able to chat quite easily with the Gaian women, hardly ever needing to pause for clarification. Rhia would have been irritated were she not so relieved. Gwen was clearly still afraid deep down, and the fact that the women at least were *beginning* to accept her made Rhia not mind so much when they looked down on her for her lack of linguistic gift.

In all, she thought, things could have gone far worse for Gwen. Her wedding to Tullius had gone smoothly, and though Gwen had seemed nervous, she'd been nowhere near as terrified as Rhia had feared she'd be. At the ceremony Tullius had copied Marius' little ritual with the knife, a clever gesture that made the Gaians assume it had all been a part of a Caderyn tradition and not an embarrassing mistake that might have ruined everything. Rhia even managed to smile about it with Gwen afterwards, and a tiny bit of her guilt at the mess of her own wedding had eased away.

A chilly wind whipped up from a side street and Rhia drew her shawl tighter about herself. She was just about getting used to these Gaian dresses and shoes, though with winter here she was missing her thick woollen skirts and leggings. Apparently decent Gaian women did not wear trousers of any kind and stayed indoors when the weather was too cold for a dress. Rhia was beginning to regret turning down Junia's offer of a litter to travel home in, but those ridiculous boxes always made her feel ill, and since it was a feigned stomach upset that had let her escape early anyway, it would hardly have looked good for her to have taken one.

Rhia wondered if she ought to feel bad for her deception of the ladies, but she rationalised that it was better this way. There was always a greater risk of her saying or doing something inappropriate if she became too painfully bored in their company, and it was surely less rude to abandon them early than cause some social upset by staying and doing something wrong? Perhaps.

She smiled sadly as she thought of the reactions of Junia and Livilla, and even Gwen, when she'd mentioned a stomach upset to them. All three had instantly assumed that she was pregnant and had given subtle little hints as to what she ought to do to keep 'everything healthy'. Rhia closed her eyes a moment. The thought of carrying a child again was one of the few things that let true emotion break through her habitual numbness. As a rule only harrowing grief and the occasional all-too-brief flash of anger were able to penetrate the dull, dead feeling inside her, and grief was by far the most easily reached emotion. That and shame.

She had not shared her husband's bed since the first night of their marriage, and she hated herself that she was too afraid to do her duty as a wife. She hated the idea of his touching her, but she berated herself for not letting him. This marriage was for nothing if no children came from it and she owed it to her father and her people to provide a child both Gaian and Caderyn, something solid and tangible to show that they were truly allies. A tiny part of her even felt sympathy for Marius, who had ceased to even try to couple with her after he'd seen how much it upset her. He had expected to have a wife and soon afterwards, a family, and instead he had a woman who could barely stand to share a room with him.

She sighed as she walked. Hopefully Marius would still be at the barracks, doing whatever it was he did there, and she might have the house to herself. Rhia pursed her lips together. People kept telling her she ought to call him Antonius like everyone else, but she'd got into the habit of thinking of him as Marius and even he had stopped correcting her by now. Perhaps he liked the thought of his wife knowing him by his heroic name. Or maybe he'd simply not wanted an argument. Probably the latter.

Her husband had made some effort with the Lurian Tongue and what with Rhia's slowly increasing grasp of Vulgare, they were just about able to communicate. And had discovered they had nothing at all to say to each other. They had no common ground about which they could speak, no common friends to talk about, and little enough patience with one another when things became awkward. They slept in separate rooms, ate in separate rooms and, like today, spent their time with different people. Rhia almost wished that he was more of a bastard. If he behaved badly then she might feel better about being such a distant and disappointing wife to him, but he was neither kind nor cruel to his Caderyn bride. While clearly not content with the situation he seemed willing to let her carry on about her own life, and Rhia hated his indifference almost as much as she hated herself.

Just put up with it. Give him and your people a son and you can work the rest out later. You owe it as a wife, and as a daughter. Just get it done. But the thought of a man's hands on her again made her break into a sweat despite the cold, and she was grateful to the weather for an excuse to be seen shivering. Rhia clenched her fists hard and set her jaw. *He is your husband. You can do this.* She really wasn't sure if that was true but perhaps if she said it to herself often enough it would become so. Despite her attempted determination she was still glad that Marius wouldn't be there when she got home, and she might have a little time of relative peace before she had to face up to this.

Before long they reached the house, which from the outside was almost a copy of her father-in-law's home, just shrunk down to a slightly smaller size. The only real difference was that the door to this house had been painted a deep red, one of the few things that Rhia really liked about the place. Junia had told her that the decorating of a house was almost solely the province of that house's mistress, though Rhia's only contribution so far had been the painting of the door. She had hardly been an enthusiastic decorator but she liked the idea of showing Caderyn colours about the place, and she hoped the red door would make the place feel a little more like a home to her. It hadn't worked that well so far, but she had to hope.

She reached the red door and Drenn opened it for her, stepping aside to allow her to enter first. Most Gaians would kiss their hands and place them on the heads of the little carved gods before entering a house, but Rhia still couldn't quite bring herself to do it and was relieved that Drenn didn't seem to see the need to either. Behind them, she knew that Enora would be trying to ask a blessing as subtly as possible, knowing how her mistress was made uncomfortable by the statues. Rhia couldn't help but love her a little for that and made a point of not turning around to watch her.

Once in the main chamber of the house she waved Drenn away and he bowed before wandering off to the slave quarters. Enora stayed with her in the spacious room and Rhia addressed her in her slightly faltering Vulgare.

'Enora, I will rest in my room now. You will come for me before my husband is back?'

The handmaid bowed her head.

'Of course, mistress. Rest well.'

Rhia nodded back.

'Thank you Enora.'

The Basian girl bowed again and withdrew with a smile. Rhia knew that either Enora or one of the other girls would be within earshot if needed. Right now she just wanted to lie down. A part of her wanted to sit and cry a while but Rhia fought it back. Crying would do her no good, she just needed to try to relax. She would send for some wine later on and see if she could build up the courage to talk to Marius tonight. He was not a bad man, she thought, not really, and her Vulgare was getting better. They could maybe come to some agreement that would make this marriage something bearable for them both. The concept was a frightening one but if this was her fate she had to try to make the best of it. With a child they might even find something close to happiness in their lives.

As she walked the unpleasant voice came back to her head, the one that had been scourging her at intervals ever since Nantwyn. *Do you, who killed your husband and child, let another man inside you, betrayed your gods and ruined your people, deserve to know any happiness? Misery is what you have earned you traitorous slut!* Rhia almost faltered but kept walking and thrust out her chin, attempting a little defiance to herself. *I am not the worthless wretch you think I am. I am sorry for Bevan and the child, and for my spying and for Delyn and everything, but I can do something for my people here, and a little gem of happiness in that is no more than I deserve.* She did not find herself to be that convincing and the vicious voice in her head almost cackled. *You deserve* nothing! *You are worth* nothing! *You are a stupid little slut who has earned her fate.*

Rhia tried to block it out and summon up some pride, but it was difficult. The guilt and shame were so heavy on her back they felt like she was carrying a sack of stones wherever she went. She walked on towards her chamber and felt the weight of it start to settle on her heart, and prepared herself for an afternoon of self-hating tears. But when she passed the door to Marius' room she found it was half-open, and the sight beyond it drove all of that from her mind.

Lying on the bed, his head back on the pillows, was her husband. His eyes were closed in relaxation and so he didn't react to the sudden appearance of his wife in the doorway. But the naked slave-girl with her mouth around his manhood noticed her straight away, and her eyes flew wide with sudden panic. She stopped what she was doing and backed away quickly, stumbling a little as she did.

Marius opened his eyes in irritation but then stared across at Rhia in alarm.

Rhia felt anger swell inside her. She might not be sharing his bed but this was her husband! It might have been an arrangement made by others, but even had she not so feared the touch of man, Rhia would not have *dreamed* of being unfaithful to Marius in such a way. They had made a promise in the sight of his gods – did that mean nothing to these people?

She stormed into the room and despite her height was at the bed in four long strides. The slave began to stand but Rhia's left fist caught her jaw while she was still rising, and the naked girl crumpled to the floor without a sound. Marius' eyes widened with anger and he leaped from the bed, his breeches still around his lower legs. His voice was sharp with rebuke.

'How dare…'

But that was as far as he got before Rhia's right hammered into his chin. He spun and collapsed backwards onto the bed and lay there unmoving, a tiny speck of blood on his lip.

Rhia was breathing hard, her fists still clenched, ready to deal out some more punishment if needed, but the room's two original occupants now appeared to be sleeping peacefully. Her eyes were wide and eager and she realised with a start that she ought to feel ashamed and guilty about this. But she didn't! Tentatively, she tried reaching for the numbness inside her, or for the horrid voice that had been berating her earlier, and found that they were not there! Or rather, they weren't *gone* exactly, but the pure heat of her rage had banished them to somewhere else, somewhere dark and deep in her mind where it seemed they could do her no harm. She felt fire and spirit and pride well up inside her, and had to stop herself from screaming out the name of the War God.

She was a warrior of the Caderyn, not a slut, not a slave, and she deserved the respect of her husband. She was about to shove him awake and start shouting at him about this when she noticed that he had fallen in a way that meant both his sleeping face and his naked buttocks were plainly visible, and before she even knew what was happening Rhia found that she was laughing. She was actually *laughing* for the first time in moons and once she started, it was difficult to stop. Enora appeared behind her at some point and delicately closed the chamber door. The Basian girl sounded concerned.

'What happened here, mistress?'

Rhia controlled herself long enough to get out a few words and Enora clearly worked out the rest from context. She whispered urgently to her.

'Madam, it is common practice for married men to couple with their slaves! It is no adultery to take a lover of lower rank than your spouse, especially if…'

But she stopped herself, embarrassed. Rhia knew what she meant though and her laughter faded away. *Especially if his wife will not share his bed.* A tiny flicker of guilt hit her, and though she found she could endure it without feeling crushed by it, nonetheless she sighed quietly. Whatever their customs she could not justify what Marius had done, yet she could sympathise with him at least. She turned to Enora.

'Has he done this before?'

The slave shook her head slowly.

'Never that I know of, and I speak often with all the girls.'

Rhia nodded. Marius had not been bedding his slaves out of habit then. He had done so when his wife had refused to sleep with him. He was still in the wrong, she had no doubt about it, but she had to accept at least a little of the blame for this herself. He had expected, if not a loving then at least a *willing* wife, and she had given him nothing but coldness and distance.

She looked down at Marius' sleeping face and wondered if she might make a little effort with him in future. She felt her anger start to die down but was shocked and delighted to find her pride was still there. Somehow she knew that the tears and shame and emptiness would all come back again, but equally she knew that now she could at least *begin* to fight them off. In some small way she felt herself again, and she found that she was grinning despite herself. Even Enora was fighting back a smile. Rhia looked at her unconscious husband, with blood on his lip and his bare arse on show, and started chuckling again. This marriage was going to take some work.

Chapter 18. City Life

Five years ago, Rhianna Dessida might have felt lost among the mighty buildings and towering columns of Tamora. She remembered her early days in the city, when the statues of the gods had unnerved her with their staring eyes and she had looked away in discomfort whenever she passed one. Not so now. Today she walked along Via Aellius with long, confident strides and was content to look around her and admire the Gaian architecture. Decorated pediments and friezes of every description were scattered around the mighty city, and even here in the Southern Quarter the buildings were impressive to behold.

Rhia swished along in her light yellow dress and was glad to feel the warmth of early spring in the afternoon air. The winter had not been particularly hard but all the same it was pleasant to be able to walk the streets in comfortable clothing, and she made a mental note to make a prayer of thanks to Vulco Belenos when she got back. At first it had struck her as strange when the Gaian priests had made that statement; that the gods worshipped around the world were for the most part the same entities, and that only their names and the stories around them were different in every culture. Apparently there were exceptions, and localised gods were common, but it made a curious form of sense to her that the great gods would be the same wherever you went. These days she often wondered why nobody at home seemed to have seen it that way.

Rhia walked along pondering these deep religious thoughts, but then got distracted by a fruit seller and stopped to pick up some blood oranges. They were expensive, as ever, but she had developed a weakness for the dark-fleshed fruit, after a distinctly uncertain introduction, and she now spent Marius' silver quite freely whenever traders came from Caspea or Votumia. It wasn't as if her husband didn't enjoy the fruit as well, but if Rhia was allowed anywhere near them the odds of him getting any were slim. She gave most of the fruit to Drenn to carry, but handed two of them to Enora to start peeling for them.

By the time the stubborn fruit was freed from its casing and the women had started on the brighter red flesh, Drenn was not keen on fruits, they had almost reached their destination, and before she'd finished her last morsel Rhia was at the barrack gates. The home of the Tenth Legion was surrounded by a long rectangular wall, its corners slightly rounded and with sentries posted at each one. Inside she knew there would be row after row of narrow buildings in which the three cohorts could sleep, though only the very ends of the barracks were in sight from where she was.

Through the open gates most of the view was of the broad and dusty parade ground, where even now a troop of men were being put through their paces by their centurion. Rhia recognised the senior soldier as Centurion Lothar, and the stocky, red-faced man was bellowing at his men in language he would certainly not have used had he known she was there. Not that Rhia minded in the least. She'd used fouler words herself on more than one occasion, and had learned some of the choicer Vulgare curses through overhearing men like Lothar.

She approached the gate and the sentries either side snapped to attention. Rhia remembered her first time coming here, when the soldiers had been wary of letting her near there, concerned that she was spying on their tactics. And so, to be fair, she had been; not out of any real intention of trying to fight these Gaians again, it was far too late for that, but out of curiosity as to how it was they had defeated the mighty Caderyn. She had learned much, and had considered sending word of what she'd learned back to Madoc, but she'd then remembered that he had gone into hiding with many other Gadarim, in what she now saw was a foolish attempt to plan a resistance to their occupiers.

Rhia sighed as she passed the sentries with a nod. It was indeed a foolish plan, assuming it had not been abandoned by now. For all that she was proud to be Caderyn, it had become increasingly clear over the last five years that the Gaians were the future and that was all there was to it, and either a people could try to work with them or they could be crushed and overrun by them. The thought had depressed her when first she had accepted it but these days it didn't bother her so much. Her people were safe, and apparently prosperous, and her father still ruled the Caderyn for the most part. It was folly to try to fight on for mere stubborn pride.

She walked through the arched entry with its carved lion statues and read the inscription before she passed beneath it: *Legio X Etrucia – Justly Proud.* Rhia was a little proud herself that she could read it. She now spoke Vulgare reasonably well, though her friends still teased her for her accent, but learning to decipher their damned symbols had been a nightmare, and once again she had fallen far behind Gwen in her studies.

Rhia frowned, her good mood threatening to fade. She had grown worried for her sister in the last year or so, becoming ever more wary of her brother-in-law, Tullius. Though he was attentive enough to his Caderyn wife in public, Rhia had often seen her shy away from his gaze if he stared at her, and once she'd seen her flinch when he had touched her arm from behind. It might well be nothing, Gwen was a shy girl by nature after all and had been through a lot, but nonetheless it caused Rhia to worry sometimes. But she put it from her mind for the time being. There was nothing to be done about it right now.

The men under Centurion Lothar were now moving and wheeling in formation, each man's long red shield locked tight together with that of his neighbour. Having faced such a formation herself Rhia was well aware of how effective it could be, but since watching it from a distance she had noted it did have certain weaknesses; the formation struggled to move quickly and was not as adaptable as a single warrior, and an attack to the flanks or the rear of the column would cause it serious disruption and prevent the circulation of fresh troops. Rhia pondered briefly on how this might be taken advantage of but then banished those thoughts from her mind as well. Old habits might die hard but there was no purpose in observing such things now.

Rhia was wondering how long the poor sweating men had been at it when a figure emerged from around the corner of a building and she saw her husband, looking impressive in his leather breastplate and shining mail. His crested helm was beneath his arm and she saw sweat bead on his brow, and his dark hair looked plastered to his head. He smiled as he saw her and started striding towards the gate, and Rhia smiled back at him with a wave. After five years of marriage she still could not say that she *loved* Marius, but what they had was probably the closest thing to it that she would experience again, and they had managed to make things work out far better than she'd expected.

She smiled wider as she remembered the night she had knocked her husband out cold, and the blazing row that had threatened to follow which had eventually turned into laughter. A few nights after that encounter she had plucked up the courage to share his bed again, though flashes of Delyn had come to her and she had burst into embarrassed tears. Marius had been patient and simply talked with her a while, and a few nights later they had tried again. Then again a few nights after that. It had taken time, a long time, before Rhia could relax when they were coupling, but eventually she had managed to overcome most of her fear, and had recently reached a point where she could enjoy it. Sometimes she still wanted to cry, either in grief for Bevan or in shame from Delyn, but for the most part she was able to lie with her husband as wives were supposed to, and eventually of course it had led to…

'Mama!'

Rhia's smile became a grin as from behind her husband, running gracelessly along on his little legs, their beloved son came pelting towards her, his sandals flapping clumsily on his feet.

'Lucan!'

Rhia sank down to her haunches as the little man ran up to her, then enveloped him in a hug and lifted him into the air. The child squeaked with delight and Rhia spun him about and lifted him high again. The soldiers nearby were holding back smiles as the boy giggled again, his blue eyes shining with childish joy.

Rhia noticed once again how heavy he was these days. Carradus Dessidus Lucianus was past his third winter and his mother had no idea where the time had gone. It seemed like only days ago that she was groaning to bring him into this world and now he was growing into a boisterous young lad, and it seemed he'd been playing legionary again.

He was wearing a tiny version of the crimson tunic worn by the men, with a grey woollen vest worn over it to represent a shirt of iron rings. His little belt was studded and had a wooden scabbard on it and his father, walking behind him, had his wooden sword and shield held in one hand. Rhia put him down and put on her best centurion voice.

'Attention soldier!'

Lucan snapped his heels together in their oversized legion sandals, and banged his fist onto his chest before throwing his arm out in front of him.

'Yes sir!'

His voice was high and brimming over with enthusiasm, and Rhia felt her heart melt as she saw him trying to emulate his father. The sentry nearby could not hold back his smile any longer, and Rhia smiled back at him and nodded, recognising Legionary Porcius. The soldier held his spear up straight and then leaned it forward, feet spaced at shoulder width.

'At ease!'

The boy copied his movement exactly and grinned up at the veteran soldier. Lucan was the darling and unofficial mascot of the Second Cohort, and there were few men among its soldiery who hadn't dandled him on their knee. Porcius nodded his head.

'Good form soldier. Dismissed.'

Little Lucan grinned and moved to hug his mother again, then remembered he'd forgotten to salute and slammed his fist so hard on his chest that Rhia had a flash of worry that he might bruise. She wrapped him up in a cuddle before nodding to Drenn. The bodyguard hoisted the boy up and set him on his massive shoulders, and Lucan was soon giggling again. Marius approached them and Rhia gently touched her husband's arm.

'Did he get in the way?'

Marius grinned.

'Oh, absolutely. But the general isn't here yet so nobody cared.' He nodded to Porcius. 'The men not on duty have been schooling him in swordsmanship.'

Lucan started nodding vigorously.

'They said I'm really good!'

Porcius nodded.

'Indeed he is, madam. He'll be beating us all down before long.'

Lucan grinned at that and made clashing sounds as he began slashing the air around Drenn's head with an imaginary sword. Rhia looked at him lovingly for a moment before turning to her husband.

'Will you be long here? We've so much to plan for tonight and I need all the help I can get.'

Marius shrugged.

'Once the general gets here we should be done in an hour or two.'

Rhia frowned.

'Lepidus works you too hard. Brictus doesn't have his officers doing this sort of thing every day, nor did Gregor come to that.'

Marius half-smiled.

'That's why the Tenth is the best and the First and Fourteenth aren't.'

Porcius banged his spear-holding hand against his shield in agreement. Rhia kept up her scowl.

'I'm all for hard training for fighters but this is ridiculous. He knows you have a supper tonight, gods we've even had to *invite* him, you'd think he would let you leave early to prepare.'

Her husband raised an eyebrow.

'General Lepidus doesn't put as much stock into social events as some people.'

Rhia put her hands on her hips in a somewhat un-Gaian gesture for a woman but she didn't care.

'If he wants to get anywhere with the Daerian Senate he would be wise to keep in your father's good graces.'

Rhia didn't exactly approve of that situation but the point had to be made. Marius shrugged again.

'I'm sure he knows that. And I'm just as sure that he hates it.'

Rhia half-nodded, reluctantly sympathising with the man. General Lepidus, as well as commanding the Tenth Legion, was also a councillor of the senate in Tamora, the body which governed all Gaian territory in Daeria. Apparently there was a larger one in Gaivia for governing the whole Gaian world, and Marius' father had the right to stand in it, but he had instead chosen to come here. Rhia could understand that; she had little enough patience with the *local* version of this council. Unlike a Lurian chieftain, who would listen to his advisors but then make his own decision, the Gaians insisted on their most prominent people all agreeing to something before any actions were taken. It was a nice idea in theory she supposed, but in reality it meant that they debated and flattered and plotted endlessly amongst themselves in an effort to get their own way, or to gain greater influence.

Given what Rhia had heard of their *politics*, it had initially amazed her that anything at all got done, much less that the Gaians had somehow built an empire despite this foolishness. Then Marius had pointed out that in Gaivia there was a man named Mallea Tiberian who stepped in and forced them to a decision if it looked like something was taking too long. It was a pity there was no *emperor* to do something like that in Tamora. It might make the whole process of governing an awful lot simpler.

For all of Rhia's general dislike of Lepidus, he at least seemed to share her sense of impatience with the senate, and stalwartly refused to flatter people to get on their good side. It meant he likely wouldn't get very far there, but at least it meant he was respected for his integrity. Rhia gave her husband's arm a gentle stroke.

'A pity he doesn't do well at those games they play. He might retire and then I could be married to a general.'

Marius looked at her through his brows.

'Cadmus is First Tribune, not me, and my only combat experience is a few scraps with the Rydicae, it hardly makes me a grizzled veteran. Besides, Lepidus is of middling birth and his knowledge of subtle politics could be carved onto a pebble.' He turned to Porcius. 'Not that you heard that, soldier.'

The legionary was stone-faced.

'Wouldn't dream of it, Tribune Dessida.'

Marius nodded to him.

'Good.'

Rhia sighed but did so with a smile.

'A pity. Your current wage and allowance are alright I suppose, but just think what I could buy with a *general's* pay!'

Marius smiled. In truth, Rhia lived in more wealth and luxury than she could ever have imagined, but it was always fun to tease him. He nodded to the bag over Drenn's shoulder.

'Have you been buying oranges again?'

Rhia looked up at him demurely. She'd seen Livilla do this with Rabanus a hundred times and it made Gaian men do anything you wanted.

'Maybe.'

Marius sounded resigned.

'And is there any chance of my getting any?'

Rhia leaned forward on her tiptoes and kissed his cheek.

'We shall see.' He smiled and she stepped back again. 'Meanwhile I have a celebratory evening to arrange on my own until your precious general lets you go.'

Marius leaned forward and put a quick kiss of his own on Rhia's cheek. She smiled. She couldn't call it love, not like what she had with Bevan, but she had to admit that she liked Marius a great deal, and it was always nice when he was affectionate.

'Very well, my dear. I shall see you later.'

Rhia nodded, first to him and then to Porcius, then motioned to Drenn and Enora that they were going. Lucan waved furiously hard at his father and the legionary, and both men raised their hands back to him. Rhia smiled as she looked up at her son, sitting high as a giant on her bodyguard's shoulders. She reached up to squeeze his hand for a moment before letting him go back to swinging his imaginary sword, his toys having been handed to Enora.

All in all Rhia found she was surprisingly contented as she wandered back to the house. Over the last few years her dreaded numbness had disappeared, and even her fears and shames were only a shadow of what they'd once been. She missed her home, and she missed her family, and she still had mixed feelings about the fate of the Caderyn, but for the most part she was as happy as she felt she was capable of being. Rhia walked along the stone-paved streets of the mighty Gaian city in relative peace and contentment, and wondered what sort of wine they should serve tonight.

*

In the end, Rhia settled for a mixture of white grape and green apple wines for the majority of the meal, with the more robust red saved for later on. Marius would have argued that the reds would complement the beef better, but since they were mostly serving poultry dishes Rhia had decided the red could wait. *Besides, if he wanted his opinion heard, he should have come home in time to be of use.*

Rhia let her hand hover for just a second before helping herself to another bit of goose wing from the nearest platter. She had to admit that she had a weakness for the rich flavour of goose meat, and she strongly suspected her dresses were getting tighter as a result. She adjusted the hem of her current, and gorgeous, crimson gown and cast her eyes around the room as she chewed.

Over the last five years she'd made her mark on their comfortable home, and the red and blue of the Caderyn was visible on everything from tablecloths to curtains to carpeting. The coverings of the couch cushions had been embroidered with azure whorls and swirls, and more than one of Rhia's friends had spoken admiringly of her work. Beside the door and on one or two of the little tables were the modest statues commissioned by Marius in the second year of their marriage, both as a gift and as a gesture to his Caderyn wife.

From where she was she could see two of her favourite examples of them; Vulco Taranis and Sulis Mehine. The War God was depicted in a subtly different way to most Gaian statues, being both bearded and with long hair that reached past his broad shoulders, though the sword in his right hand was of Gaian style. The Lady of the Woods was depicted as a beautiful young woman, as Gaian goddesses tended to be, but wearing the Lurian deity's trademark cloak of evergreen leaves and a garland of tiny flowers around her head.

It was strange. Rhia had always felt uncomfortable being looked at by the carved gods, and she still sometimes felt a little self-conscious in front of them, but there was something comforting about these ones, as if the gods of her people could still be with her. She sometimes felt they were judging her for living here instead of at Bryngarth, but Rhia hoped they understood that what she did she did for her people, and she was certain they would approve of her décor. A little part of the Caderyn was alive and well, even in the heart of a Gaian city.

That thought made her think of little Lucan, long sent to bed, and the life he was fated to lead. She was determined that he would learn the Lurian Tongue as well as their customs, and Marius had agreed that they would all visit Bryngarth together before the boy reached ten. It would be lovely to see her family again, and for Carradan to meet the grandson who might pave the way for a solid future for their people. Rhia risked drifting off into fantasies about her homecoming, and she dragged her mind back to the present and her duty to her guests.

Conversation was flowing nicely between the dozen or so people sat around the little fire pit. Weaving in and out of the various couches, the kitchen slaves carried platters of food or jugs of wine, and Rhia gestured for her cup to be refilled as she listened to the chatter. The evening had begun with much praise and congratulation to her father-in-law, Glaucus Dessida. He had recently been appointed as Governor of Daeria, the closest thing the area had to an overall ruler, and most agreed he was by far the best man for the job. He was wise and educated, kindly without being weak, and had made an effort to learn something about the tribes he was to rule, unlike many of his fellow councillors who saw him as something of a maverick for his study of barbarian tongues and customs. Rhia had found that she liked him, and he had been a good friend to her and to Gwen.

After a great deal of embracing and congratulating about that, the conversation had now turned to the politics of ruling, and Rhia half-listened as the men there debated theories. Lepidus, now sporting a narrow red stripe on his shoulder-robe, was leaning forward on his couch, gesturing with his right hand while his left held a cup of wine.

'I still say that Cornelius Felix was correct in his original methodology; it is only through direct control that any real progress can be made in government. This is particularly true in the case of provincial government.'

His First Tribune, Cadmus, nodded beside him. Though Rhia was hardly fond of Lepidus, she certainly preferred him to his subordinate. The first officer of the legion still looked down on her and her sister, though he was careful not to do so too overtly. He was a good soldier but his family was not a prominent one, and offending the Dessida clan was not a wise social move for anyone.

Glaucus argued back in a calm voice, though it was clear he believed strongly in what he was saying.

'And after Felix seized power and had made his many reforms, he stood down from his position and handed power back to the senate and people.'

Next to him his friend and student, Drusus Duronia, chipped in.

'He is even quoted as stating that he regretted the necessity of such actions.'

Lepidus leaped on his words.

'Yet still it was a *necessity*. Republican ideals are all very well, but in the real world they are impractical to the point of being actively damaging to a people.'

Marius had been chatting quietly with Narbo Galerian, Gregor's brother, but now decided to weigh in with his opinion.

'Damaging, sir? I can see how a direct form of ruling is beneficial by virtue of its simplicity, but I have always been raised on republican ideals and I cannot see how such things could actively *damage* a society?'

Rhia smiled quietly to herself. Marius might know it was unwise to argue politics with his commander but nonetheless he felt his beliefs ought to be voiced, albeit in respectful tones. He was clever but still kept hold of his integrity. She had to respect him for that. Lepidus turned to his host.

'Antonius, true republicanism means ensuring that every citizen's voice is heard in the formation of government, correct?'

Marius nodded.

'Correct.'

The general nodded back.

'Therefore to follow its codes to the letter, the man who leads the nation should be one chosen by an election of the *entire* citizen populace, rather than selected by a small group from the existing senior senators, correct?'

Marius gave a look that said he knew this was a trap but nonetheless he nodded politely, unable to fault his commander's logic.

'I suppose one could argue so.'

Lepidus spread his arms.

'Then surely the man who is elected need only be popular with the people in order to govern? He need have no official standing or service to the state, nor any real evidence that he is qualified to govern, merely the ability to appeal to the majority of the citizens, most of whom are too stupid to know what is good for them anyway. How could such a system of leadership *not* damage the society it governs?'

Narbo answered before Marius could.

'But surely the military dictatorships were based on the popularity of the generals who took control?'

Glaucus chipped in on his side.

'Think of Cornelius Felix. It was his popularity with his troops and with the mob that allowed him to become a dictator.'

Cadmus spoke in support of his superior officer, his voice dry and gravelly as usual.

'From what I recall, General Felix was elected as consul not once but twice before he became dictator. Is that not a fair enough measure of his fitness to rule?'

Drusus turned to the veteran soldier.

'Then why not be contented to use his powers within the structure of the senate? It had been working well enough before, why not again?'

Lepidus answered that one.

'Because during his life the territory of Gaivia had increased, and with provinces in Caspea to command, a more direct form of rule was required. With the Empire only increasing ever further, we are wise to adopt a similar policy now. Look at the damage that is done to productivity by the rebellions of the Rydicae? And the Gorvicae have been making rumblings that make me suspect they are heading down the same road.'

Rhia listened a little closer on hearing the name of her rival tribe. For all their agreements with the Gaians after Nantwyn, more and more the Gaians had been imposing themselves on Gorvicae territory, and Rhia was always glad to hear of their troubles. The dreadful defeat at Nantwyn had been of their doing after all, and it amused her that their allies were now turning on them.

Lepidus continued, and gave a semi-polite nod to Rhia and Gwen.

'At least the Caderyn have had the good sense to behave responsibly, but even in their lands there are rumours of dissent. A firm hand and a strong ruler could solve so many of the problems that are facing western Daeria,' he turned to Glaucus, 'and it is you who has the chance to be that man, governor.'

Glaucus made a dismissive gesture.

'I have no intention of acting with weakness, general, yet still if we are to build an ideal world then our actions must first be governed by our principles, even at the expense of an easier practicality.'

Lepidus shook his head.

'A noble sentiment sir, yet as you yourself say; impractical. Look at the troubles we had with the tribes of Avidia?' He nodded to Cadmus. 'It took us years to subdue those savages and even now they must be ruled with an iron hand. I do not argue for complete dictatorship, merely that we better emulate the Emperor's example when ruling the provinces; a single voice and strong leadership taking precedence over endless debate.'

Glaucus once again spoke calmly, his voice soft and genuine.

'You bring in your examples of troubled territories Severus, yet look at the successes we have had on this little continent? Look back on the successes of our ancestors' conquest of our fellow tribes of Sedalia? They are as integrated into civilised culture as any could hope to be, and I have great hope of the same for the tribes here.'

He smiled at Rhia again. It seemed that Cadmus was about to disagree with him on some point, but before the tribune could say anything another voice spoke into the pause.

'Gentlemen, I do believe these fine ladies will drop to sleep if this conversation continues.'

The voice had come from another veteran soldier; the grizzled commander of the Fourteenth Legion, General Brictus Balius. The debating men looked around at the womenfolk and with the exception of Rhia, who was quite enjoying the topic, they did indeed look like people trying politely to hide their boredom. Gwen, Livilla, and Rhia's friends Vorena and Lelia, all sat or leaned up a little straighter on their couches, but it was the regal voice of Dessidus Junia who spoke for them.

'Dearest sirs the subject is, I am certain, a most worthy and fascinating one. Alas that we were unable to contribute much to the discussion.'

General Balius smiled at her.

'Then let us change it to a subject in which we may all participate.'

Junia smiled back.

'As you say, Brictus.'

Rhia, though she'd been interested, joined the other ladies in smiling politely at the general. Rhia had found that she liked Brictus Balius. Like Lepidus he was a career soldier of middling birth who had reached high rank by hard work and personal merit. Unlike Lepidus however, he had shown no interest in following this with a political career. He was perhaps a decade older than the commander of the Tenth Legion, being close to his sixtieth winter and thus well past an acceptable age to step down from military service. Yet he had made no plans to enter the senate, either here or back in Gaivia, and had once told Rhia that he looked forward to enjoying a quiet life of horse-breeding from his villa outside Corinia.

Vorena started them on a new topic by giving a scathing review of the performance of Madam Pelegia, who had sung 'The Verses of Octavius' a few nights ago at the theatre. Rhia had never heard the apparently famous poem before, but according to both Vorena and Lelia it had been a truly dire sampling for her, since though they both conceded that Pelegia's voice was good, she had absolutely no stage presence. Livilla answered by singing the praises of a certain Madam Carova who she had once heard recite it in Gaivia, and conversation turned to matters theatrical for a while.

Rhia and Marius both enjoyed the theatre but she did not contribute much to the chatter, and for the most part sat and listened as she picked at a tray of pheasant wings. She noticed, as she had done many times, that Gwen spoke little despite her excellent grasp of the language, and mostly sat down quietly sipping meekly at her wine. Beside her, Tullius was laughing as he recounted the time he'd seen Posthumus Morien playing Gluteanus in 'Solstice Eve', and Rhia worried again about their home life.

Gwen had miscarried twice and her only living child had died after less than two moons. Rhia had tried to be there for her each time, though it had brought back some painful memories, but for all her efforts Gwen had shrunk back into herself a great deal, the shy girl becoming ever more so, and it seemed her husband had done little enough to help. Rhia couldn't be certain, her sister was so close about things these days, but she was fairly sure that Tullius blamed his wife for their lack of children, and had likely made her feel far worse when he ought to have been giving his every support. She'd never seen any bruising, and Gwen had not once spoken of it, but Rhia harboured a suspicion that he had beaten her at least once, though she had no proof of anything and was not certain enough to confront him.

She watched him tell his tale, his wife nodding along quietly at his side, and wondered what went on behind closed doors. She looked hard at his face, so disturbingly like Marius' and yet not so at the same time. *If ever I discover that you have hurt my sister, I shall make you regret raising your hand to my blood.* She glared at him a moment longer and then tried to think of something more positive. For all that she knew, Gwen was merely upset and feeling guilty about her lost children, something Rhia could certainly sympathise with, and she was misjudging her brother-in-law terribly by her suspicions.

The conversation started flowing away from theatre to gossip, and Rhia tried to switch her mind off to it. She worried sometimes at how keen she was to discover the latest scandalous secrets of some gentleman or lady of their acquaintance. She liked to think herself above it, but she couldn't help but take an interest if so-and-so had been discovered meeting in secret with his ex-wife, or when such-and-such had happened at a house considered too reputable for that sort of behaviour.

Marius arched an eyebrow at her and she resisted the temptation to stick out her tongue at him. Annoyingly, her husband actually *was* above this sort of chatter, or at the very least he just didn't care about it, and Rhia noticed the soldiers of the party were giving up on even pretending to listen. Narbo was lapping it up, and even Glaucus and Drusus chuckled a little as they enjoyed the guilty pleasure of gossip, but for the most part it was the women who did the talking.

Marius rolled his eyes at her and Rhia found herself wishing the night was over, and the guests sent home. She looked forward to a night in the arms of her husband where, after a long time of feeling frightened or uncomfortable there, she now finally managed to feel warm and secure. Sometimes she even enjoyed their lovemaking, and wondered if the mood might take her Marius tonight. *Who knows, you might even conceive again soon?* After nearly five years of marriage Rhia suspected she was not especially fertile, but the single child she'd borne was growing up to be hale and strong, and she was confident that if she carried again, his little brother or sister would turn out just as robust.

She looked again at Gwen and Tullius and felt sorry for them both. Their marriage was clearly strained, but surely a child might do something to better that? It might give them both something to love, and that love might bring them closer. It had worked with her and Marius after all. Rhia decided she would make sacrifices to Sulis Mehine and Cassio Marna. She was reasonably familiar with all the rituals and if it helped them to conceive it would be worth it. She started running through her head what sort of things she would be needing, and said a quiet prayer that her sweet sister might soon know the same happiness that she did.

Chapter 19. Sarriban's Cup

Severus did not like Praecus. He didn't like his greasy black hair, or the un-soldierly slouch of his round shoulders. He didn't like the way his hands were always half-closed and fidgeting, and how his little eyes would rarely meet those of the person he spoke to, although when they *did* his gaze was unsettlingly intense. Most of all he didn't like that he was becoming reliant upon him, though he comforted himself that the little magicker needed him more than he needed the magicker. Unfortunately, as with many people he did not like, the general was still frequently obliged to work with him.

Right now, the greasy-haired man was placing a large silver bowl on an altar table, having filled it with whatever sacred liquid it was he'd prepared. They were standing in the cavern-like chamber below the Aboran barracks, the giant warriors waiting patiently in line before the table. The housing area for the auxiliaries had been constructed on the site of the old Atrian Theatre, and the numerous rooms below it had proved useful to Severus. It had given Praecus somewhere where he could practice his strange arts undisturbed, away from the prying eyes and wagging tongues of a city where a secret was a difficult thing to keep.

Severus watched as the big tribesmen were beckoned forward, and one at a time they drank from the bowl. The Aborans, like the Gaians, the Etrucans and the Golessians, were a tribe of Sedalia, the warm land on the far coast of Caspea where the great city of Gaivia stood. Like the Gaians, and the Etrucans and Golessians, the Aborans claimed descent from the long lost island of Attia, and as such were a somewhat more civilised tribe than most that the Empire had conquered. Though still, they had their oddities.

He watched as they took their turns to drink, bowing before the table where a strange-looking statue had been placed. It was of a god, presumably one of their native pantheon, with almost grotesquely muscled arms, and eyes that bulged far too large for its head. Its mouth was open in a scream and its face distorted in what looked like some strange mix of black rage and wild ecstasy. Praecus, having started the ritual and muttered whatever prayers he had to mutter, now stepped away from the altar and approached Severus and Cadmus, who'd been watching from the wings. The short man looked up at him with a smile.

'You shall not be displeased with the results, I can guarantee.'

Severus hid his disdain well.

'Perhaps. You are certain of your improved concoctions?'

The little magicker smiled again.

'When combined with the correct rituals,' he gestured to the table, 'the new elixir's potency is guaranteed.'

There was a time when Severus might have snorted at that. He'd encountered enough would-be sorcerers and soothsayers in his day to know how full the world was of frauds and liars. But he had seen with his own eyes what the Destroyers could do, and had noticed that when their elixir was taken without the accompanying rituals, the results were never quite as impressive. *There is something in what he does here.* He looked again at the screaming statue. *Though what it is I do not think I want to know.* Severus liked to be in control but some questions were best left unanswered.

'It will not be long before the Destroyers are deployed in the field again. How go your other... experiments?'

He wasn't sure if he could take another of the magicker's sickly smiles but he kept his face a mask of courtesy as Praecus answered again.

'It is certainly true that the Aborans are the men most suited to this treatment, though I have found several others with great potential for enhancement. In theory the power of the robus can be given to any man, though its effectiveness might not be so great.'

Severus furrowed his brow.

'How so?'

Praecus shrugged.

'I can offer only theories general, but my best estimation is that the Aborans have in their blood a greater affinity for the magic of the robus. The power may be tapped into by any who utilise the correct methods, but some men are more in tune to it than others.'

Severus nodded, barely understanding but understanding enough.

'And when such men breed amongst themselves, this aptitude for... magic remains strong amongst their tribe?'

The sorcerer bowed his head.

'Indeed, general.'

Beside him, Severus heard the gravelly voice of Cadmus, who'd stayed silent until now.

'Then how is it that the Gaians, who were the mightiest tribe of all, do not have this aptitude?'

The question was clearly challenging but Praecus' answer came out smoothly.

'Many Gaians do, and somewhat more commonly than most tribes of Caspea, though as I say it is in the Aborans that the robus flows most strongly.'

Severus watched his auxiliaries as they sipped at the strange elixir and made their obeisance to the altar. He had been the first general in years to use such troops as a standard fixture of his legion, rather than as a temporary measure. Along with his Nomad cavalry, this unconventional approach to warfare had helped the Tenth to a string of victories across the Empire. Severus hated to admit it, but a part of the credit for that had to go to Praecus. Because of him, the grinding machine of the legion shieldwall could now spit forth shock troops in the form of the Aboran Destroyers, and an already great army had become undefeatable. Cadmus spoke again.

'Perhaps. But it is the Gaians who should be gaining from this knowledge directly, not via some lesser tribe's efforts.'

Severus turned back to the conversation, where Praecus was speaking reassuringly to his first officer.

'And you shall, my good tribune.' He turned to face the general. 'I recall your insistence that your own men not be utilised in my initial experiments?'

Severus did not nod and he kept his face stern.

'The soldiers of the Tenth are not your playthings to be meddled with. When I am assured of the safety and effectiveness of your methods, then and *only* then will I subject my men to them.'

Severus hated the fact that the little sorcerer had essentially just been insulted and yet continued to hold his cupped hands together before him, fawning like a common slave before his patron.

'But of course. As such I have been in contact with Tribune Abellan of the Fourteenth. He is discreet and has permitted me to administer some blessings on his cohort, and to give them a taste of Sarriban's sacred wine.'

Severus nodded grimly. He did not like the idea of tricking soldiers into becoming test-creatures for this strange magician, but better it be done to General Balius' men than to his own legionaries. Doubtless the old man would have approved of it even less than Severus, but fortunately Tribune Abellan was an ambitious and unsatisfied young man and, invaluably, he knew how to keep his mouth shut.

'And it has been effective?'

Praecus tilted his head a fraction.

'It is only a mild version of the elixir, general. The Aborans have had generations to accustom themselves to its properties, and their bodies and minds can cope with large doses of Sarriban's wine. A normal man must be weaned slowly onto the potion or he risks the power of the robus quite literally tearing him apart.' Praecus' smile widened. 'I recall this one slave that I tried this on in Basia, who just...'

But a glance at the two soldiers showed the sorcerer they were in no mood for an anecdote. He bowed his head again.

'From what little I can tell at this point, yes. But it is only in combat, when the blood pumps hard through the veins, that the effect of the blessings and elixir can be truly seen.'

Severus nodded slowly, thinking. If the Tenth were ever to benefit from this *robus*, then he must see it tested thoroughly first. Blind optimists might see it otherwise, but the truth was the tribes of this continent were like a case of sawdust waiting for a spark. So many of them resented the Gaian presence in their lands and without more men, or *better* men, the legions would be hard pressed to keep order. His petition to recruit an extra cohort into each legion had already been turned down twice by Daeria's senate. Something had to be done.

He treated himself to a vision of his frequent fantasy. The one where he had subdued all of Daeria under his hand, and the might of Gaivia was unquestioned from the City to the Western Sea. The one where he was hailed as a conqueror and a hero, and all the soft-handed patricians who'd looked down on him for so long would be forced to pay him the respect that he deserved. *With a Gaian army who could match the raw power of the Destroyers, even the Emperor himself would learn to fear me!*

The rebellious thought came unbidden to his mind and he pushed it away, though it did not disappear. *Later. First the horse and* then *the cart!* His first officer spoke from beside him.

'There are always squabblings going on with the Rydicae and the Bearnicans. It should be easy enough to arrange for the Fourteenth's Second Cohort to be sent to deal with one.'

Severus nodded again, focusing on the task at hand.

'True. But I would want to see the results of this elixir with my own eyes before I allow my own men to be thus... used.'

He was sure there was a better word for it but for the moment it was the best he could come up with. Cadmus stated the obvious problem.

'What reason could you have for wanting to accompany them? What excuse could we use?'

Severus pondered even as the tribune spoke. It would be difficult. The Fourteenth's officers were all competent enough not to need anyone's assistance in the field, and he and Cadmus were far too experienced to be going along simply to observe. And ideally, Severus would want to be commanding the men himself, to ensure that they maintained discipline in the face of their new strength. A somewhat unworthy thought struck him then, but it was Praecus who voiced it.

'General Balius is fast becoming an old man. A sudden illness might allow you to take a temporary command of his legion? His tribunes are experienced but they would need supervision if it came to large-scale combat.'

Severus frowned, though his interest was piqued. The Fourteenth's First Cohort was in Glevia to take part in the

First Landing celebrations, while their Third Cohort were on active duty north of the Albia Mountains. A large enough problem in the north or the west might necessitate taking the Second Cohort to support them, along with a detachment of the Tenth. It would make sense; taking the men's comrades along to help them but bringing reinforcements from Severus' own legion. The only other active legion in Daeria was the First, and they were stationed at Corinia and could not be expected to assist. *Yes... a serious enough incident could justify it.*

Even as he mused on this, the magicker spoke again, his voice soft.

'The Gorvicae might be encouraged to cause the necessary trouble, and I could supply you with a draught that would incapacitate General Balius for a moon's turn. Should you wish it of course, general.'

Cadmus answered before Severus could.

'How certain can you be that none of this could be traced back to you, and so to us?'

Praecus gave another of his unsettling smiles.

'I am a cautious man. The tonic I could supply you with would make his sickness appear perfectly natural for a man of his years. As to the... trouble, the right word to the right tribesman, and perhaps a little gold, and these savages would be delighted for an excuse to kill some Gaians.'

Severus nodded slowly as he pondered. So many of the tribesmen of this land harboured resentment, even among those that ought to be well-integrated by now. Praecus seemed to read his thoughts.

'These tribes will always be a nuisance to you unless a strong hand is used on them. I hear that their strange priests still preach to them of independence, and that many chiefs are powerless to stop their influence. A new and decisive military victory would work wonders, and if their priesthood could then be suppressed...?'

Severus nodded again. He too had heard that the druids, and of course the warrior elite, were the ones most responsible for rebellion amongst the tribes. Another victory over the warriors would undermine their credibility, but the druids were the real problem.

'I could not actively suppress their religion without the approval of the Senate, and Glaucus Dessida is an idealistic fool. I cannot see myself convincing him to allow their persecution.'

Praecus shrugged.

'He is not so much younger than General Balius. Perhaps he too might fall ill?'

Severus gave him a hard look. He was uncomfortable enough with all this as it was.

'Even if he did fall ill, it would only elongate the political problem, not simplify it.'

The magicker kept his voice even.

'But if, during a state of military emergency such as the one that may soon come, he were to succumb to a more serious illness...'

Severus cut him off.

'No. I am no murderer, Praecus.'

He clenched and unclenched his fists irritably, then gave the sorcerer a significant look as an idea struck him.

'If we found evidence of human sacrifice among the druids it would be sufficient grounds to make their cult illegal within the Empire, and the governor would be forced to suppress them. Could such evidence be found?'

Praecus frowned a little.

'I have heard of such practice among the Dariniae and the Seiriae, but that was long ago.'

Severus did not change his tone.

'Could such evidence be found?'

Praecus pressed his lips together. He clearly preferred the idea of simply removing Glaucus as an obstacle but he bowed his head after a few seconds.

'I could investigate it. But it will be difficult.'

Severus nodded.

'All that is worthwhile is difficult.'

He looked again at the massive Aborans as they drank from their silver bowl. The old soldier did not like these clandestine methods any more than Praecus liked hard work over simple murder, but it had to be done. The Empire's presence in Daeria might seem strong but it was brittle as well, and the right strike in the right place could shatter it beyond repair. With a legion of Gaian men like this he would be unstoppable, and whatever it took to reach that goal it would be worth it.

Lepidus gave a last nod to the sorcerer and turned to leave, motioning Cadmus to join him. The tribune gave Praecus a final glare before following his commander. Praecus bowed of course but neither one of them acknowledged it. They had crossed the dim chamber and were at the bottom of the staircase before Severus turned back to face the magicker.

'Praecus, I admire your work and you are of great value to me. But I will have no more talk of murder in my hearing. Understood?'

The little man did not speak but gave another of his cringing bows and Severus spun on his heel and started walking again, glad that his point had been made. His work was important, but so was sacred Gaian blood, and the sorcerer needed to be told there was a line. *And yet,* an unwelcome voice spoke in his head, *think what you might do with two legions of Destroyers, or three, or four? Think what you could do for the Empire if you could but fight through the bureaucracy? And how better to fight than with men filled with this robus, fresh from the destruction of the rebel tribes of Daeria? If only men like Glaucus were not in the way...*

The general continued to climb the stone steps, his mind taking him places he was not sure he wished to go, and yet he followed along willingly all the same.

Chapter 20. A Day of News

Their bath had only been brief, but nonetheless Rhia felt wonderfully refreshed. She'd not had the chance for bathing the day before, there was so much planning to do for the Salissa Festival, and she'd felt positively ripe when she'd walked into the Novilis Bathhouse. But despite only having time for a quick scrape down and a short soak, she felt clean and somehow lighter, and she knew she would feel better still after a massage.

Rhia, Vorena and Gwen allowed the attendants to dry them off before padding from the bathing chamber into the massage area of the bathhouse. Like the other rooms of the complex, this chamber was beautifully but simply decorated with multiple sculpted columns and light curtains of pale blue, and marble statues to Lady Sulis were liberally scattered about the place. Here the tiles of the floor matched the blue of the curtains, and the white walls were painted with frescos of graceful ships and seabirds, with mermaids and dolphins leaping between the waves. From behind a thicker veil the music of a harpist could be heard, not playing any single tune but simply plucking away at notes in a smooth and even manner, all adding to the air of relaxation that the room was to provide. Rhia and the others chatted only a little as they approached the tables, and they lay down on their fronts while slaves approached with towels and oil.

'It is just such a shame,' Vorena was saying, 'it was only what, three days ago that we were dining with him? To think he should be taken from us just like that.'

She snapped her fingers to illustrate her point as she adjusted her breasts to lie down comfortably. Even after becoming a mother Rhia's own bosom required only a little adjustment, though even the curvy Gaian would have seemed flat-chested stood next to Meghan. Rhia felt sad for a moment, missing her old friend, and then continued to feel sad as she missed a new one.

General Balius, who had seemed in perfect health only days ago, had succumbed to an infection of the stomach and had died the day before. He had reminded her of Carradan in a strange sort of way. In his manner there was little enough similarity but the general had always had the same *feel* about him, if that made any sense; a warrior who was tough and strong but had a big heart underneath it that he was not afraid to let the world see. Rhia frowned as she answered.

'I have grieved for him. He was a good friend to us.'

She nodded to Gwen, who nodded back.

'Yes. I remember him coming riding with us once, years ago, and telling me all the Vulgare names for the trees and plants we saw. He must have named a hundred of them for me.'

Rhia smiled a little, remembering it.

'He was always so good with Lucan as well. He didn't spoil him the way so many do and Lucan loved him all the more because of it.'

Gwen looked away a moment and Rhia cursed herself for her thoughtlessness. Gwen loved Lucan and spent all the time with him she could, but talk of him so often reminded her of her own child, poor little Danis, who had not seen a third moon before he'd died. Vorena broke the silence as the slaves walked in.

'We must pay a visit to Caria in the next few days. With her sons away and all she must be very lonely.'

Rhia nodded, glad that she hadn't had to think of something to say. She waved to Fabia, unquestionably the best masseuse in the Novilis Baths, before either of the others could grab her. She spoke up again as the slave began oiling her hands.

'I should probably write to Livilla about it, though whether she'll return before the funeral I've no idea.'

The others nodded. Livilla, along with her husband and children, were away at their villa in Verrisi at the moment and Rhia doubted if her brother-in-law would want to return any sooner than he had to. Rabanus was not fond of city life. Though by his name it was clear that Marcus Duronius Rabanus had been born into a very elite family, Rhia suspected he'd have been happier as a common farmer somewhere, and he clearly hated the high society of Tamora. Almost as much as Livilla loved it.

There were a pair of nods from the others at this but then conversation ceased for a while as the masseuses began their work. The massages at the Novilis Baths always began the same way; a brief rubbing down to get the back relaxed, and then a deep driving into the flesh that was almost painful to experience. They all knew that this was a much more effective way of loosening up their muscles and that the relaxing part afterwards would be that much more glorious as a result, but it made the process no less uncomfortable, and trying to chat while it happened was somewhat challenging.

Fabia had hands that were somehow both soft and amazingly strong, and Rhia felt her muscles begin protesting as she dug into them. In the silence of this torment, apart from the gentle harping in the background, Rhia pondered how her attitude to slaves had changed since coming here. She remembered the time when the concept of people as property had been horrifying, and how she had considered asking Marius to get rid of their own slaves. But since then her view had changed considerably.

Fabia, who she had chatted to many times, seemed quite contented with her life as a slave here and was living far more comfortably in Tamora than she might have done in

Udergosc where she'd been born. The same thing was true of Enora, who'd been owned by the Dessidas for years. Rhia wondered how she would have coped through her early days in the city, not to mention her pregnancy and early motherhood, without her loyal personal slave to help her through it. Enora had been something far closer to a friend than a servant and though she might be property as far as the law was concerned, to Rhia and to Marius she was practically family.

Rhia frowned a little as Fabia started using her elbows to drive into the muscles of her back, and she tried not to grunt under the pounding. *But is it as simple as this everywhere, I wonder? We might treat our slaves well but there must be masters who treat theirs cruelly.* She doubted if men like Cadmus had many qualms about whipping their slaves for every minor offence. And there were worse men than him around, she was sure.

Vorena's voice broke through her thoughts.

'A pity Junia is not about, she knew Caria better than anyone.'

Rhia wanted to nod but daren't move while Fabia was still pummelling.

'Glaucus has visited her, and he and Brictus were always close.'

Vorena grunted, either in acknowledgement of the remark or in discomfort at Carlene's elbows. The Greutun slave might not be the expert that Fabia was, but she made up for this minor shortfall with enthusiasm and raw power.

'I'm sure she is glad of it, but Junia and Caria have been friends since before the flood. She'd have been such a comfort to her.'

Again Rhia refrained from nodding, though she agreed with the sentiment. Marius' mother had known Caria Balius since they were young girls, but Junia had left for Gaivia only two days before. Rhia would have to send a letter to the house in Glevia, and hope Junia would wait there long enough to receive it before taking ship.

The three ladies lay in silence a little while as the massage, at last, moved from the deep, probing kind to the more gentle, relaxing kind. Rhia simply breathed deeply and listened to the trilling of the harp as Fabia's hands eased the tension from her back, her neck and her shoulders. She could still feel that the slave's hands and thumbs were incredibly strong, but the hard part was now over and Rhia could quite happily have dropped off to sleep. By the time Fabia had finished her calves she was on the verge of dozing, but she came to herself a little as the slave spoke.

'All is done now, madam. Would you like anything further attended to?'

Rhia had learned that in a less reputable bathhouse that might have meant all *sorts* of things, but the Novilis Baths was a decent establishment and Fabia merely meant to ask if anything still felt tense. Rhia, as ever, shook her head. The Basian masseuse's skills were still unmatched and for all the pain of the first part of it, Rhia was so relaxed she felt ready to melt.

'Thank you Fabia; that will be all.'

The auburn-haired slave bowed and made her way quietly from the room, her colleagues joining her after asking similar questions of the others. They would remain in easy earshot, and the sound of the harpist's music still drifted through the veil, but otherwise the three patricians were left alone for a few minutes. Rhia generally took this time to close her eyes and let her mind drift, but today she had decided to try to coax Gwen into talking to her. They so rarely had the chance to speak in anything like real privacy and she had wanted to voice her worries for some time. She did her best to sound casual.

'So Gwen, how are things with you? It seems an age since the last time we really chatted?'

Her sister blinked a few times and wet her lips before she spoke.

'I am well, I suppose. That tapestry I've been working on is more than half done now. Junia thinks it'll look lovely opposite the south window in the reception room, in the gap between the lamp tables.'

That wasn't quite what she had meant and she was sure her sister knew it. Rhia tried a different tack.

'I couldn't agree more, dear. But how are *you*? And how is Tullius? He seemed a little distracted the other day.'

He had in fact seemed no such thing but Rhia wanted to see her reaction. Gwen hid it well, but her eyes had fluttered for just a second at the sound of her husband's name.

'He is well. All these drills that Lepidus has been putting the legion through lately... but I don't need to tell you about them. No doubt Antonius is feeling the strain too?'

The deflection was not as smoothly done as it might have been, and Rhia decided to press her further.

'He manages well enough, but then he's used to it. But you two must have a difficult time of it, Tullius being the junior tribune and all and so getting all the work kicked down to him. He must be under a great deal of stress and that is bound to upset you as well.'

Gwen opened her mouth as if to say something but then stopped herself before speaking again.

'I try to keep him happy.'

Rhia frowned and there was an awkward pause but Vorena, perceptive as ever, came up with a suggestion.

'You know, I never tire of hearing your delightful accents, my dears. You seem to add an almost lyrical touch to your words. Tell me, would you mind speaking a little in your own tongue for me? Just so I can hear what it sounds like?'

She had spoken casually and carelessly but Rhia could have kissed her at that moment. Speaking in the Lurian Tongue unprompted would not just be rude but it would imply that there was something confidential to talk about, which might make Gwen close herself off. But having been invited to, the sisters might speak in relative secrecy without Gwen becoming scared that she was being pressured to talk.

Rhia smiled at her friend, grateful for the idea.

'If you insist.'

She turned back to Gwen and kept her face pleasant as she switched to her native language.

'I am worried for you, sister. You seem so nervous lately, though you try to hide it. Are you unhappy?'

Gwen looked furtive. She must have known that only Vorena, the harpist and perhaps a nearby slave or two could hear them, and that even the Basian slaves spoke only a dialect of their tongue, but even so she seemed wary of someone eavesdropping on them. She stammered over her first words.

'I... I am contented with my lot.'

Rhia frowned at her, then controlled her expression again. Vorena almost certainly knew what they were talking about, but for Gwen's sake she tried to maintain the façade of privacy.

'That is not what I asked. Are you unhappy?'

Gwen licked her lips again and Rhia felt pity mix in with her love for her. Rhia knew what it was to feel weak or without worth, gods knew she still struggled with it now, and she saw the signs of something similar in Gwen; of something that made her miserable and yet too filled with shame and self-hate to realise she did not deserve to feel so. In truth, there were still days when Rhia felt ashamed for what had happened with Delyn, and for Bevan and his child that she'd let die. There were nights when she still felt hot tears of shame at her behaviour, but over time those dreaded nights had grown few and far between. In Gwen, she saw a fear and shame that followed her day after day.

'Are you unhappy with… your husband?'

She had to stop herself from using Tullius' name, since it would be obvious to anyone listening what they were talking about. Vorena might know anyway but any slaves listening in would not, and besides, she had to make Gwen feel she was safe. Her sister was silent for a while and when she spoke she didn't look her in the eye.

'Sometimes. Sometimes when he's angry…' but she stopped herself and started speaking very quickly, 'but I've been such a disappointment to him, really. I've given him no children and I can be *such* a trial to live with. He's patient with me really, and he's so sweet sometimes. Most Gaian men would have asked for a divorce from me by now but he's willing to stay with me because he loves me so much, he really does, and I mean, that's the important part, isn't it?'

Normally such a question would be rhetorical but Rhia saw the querying look in her sister's eyes. There was fear in there as well, and just a tiny hint of appeal. *She wants to ask for help, she just doesn't know how, or doesn't think that she deserves it.* She sighed. Rhia knew the only reason she herself was no longer so lost was a combination of an understanding husband in Marius, and her own will and pride as a Caderyn warrior. The struggle might be far from over but she had come forward in leaps and bounds thanks primarily to those two factors in her life. Factors that were absent in Gwen's. Gwen had seen only one battle in her life, and Nantwyn had been the worst defeat her people had ever known. And as for her husband…

'Gwen listen to me, if your husband is…'

But at that moment a pair of slaves came in with trays of wine-cups and Rhia saw her sister almost physically recoil from her. The rare moment of private intimacy was shattered, and whatever she might have coaxed from her was now buried again. Rhia wanted to curse but held it back and Vorena spoke politely to them both, though her face was clearly concerned about what had just happened. *She might not speak the language but she knows Gwen enough to be worried for her.*

'Ladies, that was delightful. So much nicer than some of the guttural languages one hears in Caspea.'

She checked around to make sure that Carlene was not in earshot but the Greutun masseuse had not come back into the room. Rhia smiled to be polite but said nothing as another slave started towelling the oil from her back. Behind the smile Rhia was frowning at herself, frustrated that they'd been interrupted before they'd managed to find anything out. She suspected more than ever that something was going on with Tullius, but it could still be something as minor as his having raised his voice to her. Whether he'd raised his *hand* to her or not, she still had no idea, though her suspicions about that were beginning to deepen.

I must find an excuse to speak with her in our own tongue again. If she feels safe enough she might just open up. Rhia furrowed her brows as the slave dried her off, praying quietly that her sister would be willing to talk. And praying harder that her dark suspicions were all for nothing.

*

Rhia pondered about Gwen and Tullius for much of the walk back to the house, though when she got there all

277

worries were banished from her mind when she found Lucan, resplendent in his miniature legion uniform, galloping about the reception chamber on his little wooden horse, his shield-arm holding the stick-mount between his legs while his sword-arm waved around with boundless enthusiasm. A smile spread across her face and she made to step towards him, but as she did something small flew past her head and she flinched back, her arms coming up reflexively.

'Beware arrows!'

She turned to see her white-haired father-in-law sitting comfortably on one of the couches, a basket of kindling beside him and a smile to match her own on his face. Lucan squealed happily as he swiped at the thrown stick and then reared his mount as his tiny sword cut through it.

'Look mama, look!'

He gestured wildly at the broken 'arrow' and Rhia nodded her head.

'Good work there, soldier!'

Lucan beamed at her and started galloping back the way he'd come, only for his grandfather to hurl another stick at him. This one he caught on his little wooden shield and Glaucus wasted no time in throwing another one. Rhia approached him with a smile.

'Enjoying yourself, father?'

The governor feigned a serious look.

'These soldiers seem younger every day, it seems. I must be getting old.'

Rhia chuckled a little and touched his arm as she sank into the next couch.

'You are not getting old, my son is a prodigy that's all.'

Glaucus sighed but he was smiling as he did it.

'He has energy enough for it, that I'll grant. He has been repelling Avidian archers since mid-morning. Before that he was busy slaying a Grenn warrior that Ermingild was obliged to impersonate.'

Rhia's face became concerned.

'I do hope he's not been tiring you out?'

The old man waved a casual hand.

'Nonsense, my dear. With Livilla and her brood out in the country I've no other grandchildren to distract me from all my noble toil.'

He threw another stick and Lucan's tiny sword made short work of it. Rhia glanced at the silver-topped cane resting against the table.

'All the same, with your leg and all…'

Again the old man brushed away her concerns.

'My leg will mend just as well playing with my grandson as it will sitting at a desk of papers. And I know which type of mending I prefer.'

He reached into the basket and hurled another piece of kindling. Rhia frowned. Her father-in-law had broken his leg badly in a fall from a horse and had only been back walking for a few days. His physician had instructed him to walk daily but only sparingly, and to rest as much as possible until it was healed. Glaucus did not enjoy a litter any more than Rhia did and that meant he'd either ridden over here, and thus risked another fall, or else the old man had walked on his damaged leg across almost a mile's worth of streets.

The governor seemed to see her thoughts.

'I was assisted into my saddle and had Ermingild ride beside me the whole way.' His frown deepened. 'Like I was some form of cripple.'

Rhia touched his arm again and tried to sound both soothing and firm.

'You will heal in good time father, just be patient. And you are staying here for supper by the way, you can go home in the morning.'

Glaucus sat up a little straighter to object.

'It is barely after noon and I have…'

But Rhia cut him off.

'Is the Senate in session today?'

'Well no, but…'

She folded her arms.

'And is Ermingild incapable of fetching Myron or your papers if anything urgent is needed?'

'He is quite capable, but…'

Rhia glared at her father-in-law through her brows.

'And do you intend to pass up on the chance for Abia's pheasant in applewine sauce, which I have especially requested that she cook for us this evening?'

Glaucus fought back a smile and threw up his hands theatrically.

'What manner of husband has my son been to you that you rule his house like such a dictator?'

Rhia didn't miss a beat.

'The kind that enjoys the quiet life that giving me my own way tends to lead to.'

The white-haired man chuckled despite himself.

'Well then, who am I to deny the valiant Tribune Dessida from a quiet life when he gets home?' He bowed his head a little. 'You are too kind.'

Rhia smiled at the old man.

'We are glad to have you here.'

Lucan had realised that the arrows were no longer flying and hurried over to latch onto his mother's leg.

'Did you see me cut the arrows mama?'

Rhia ruffled his hair, which was thick and dark like his father's, and looked down at him with a smile.

'I did indeed, little soldier.' She gave his shoulder a quick squeeze. 'And it was so impressive, I think I shall ask Abia to make you some milkbread for tonight.'

Lucan clapped his hands in delight but Glaucus raised an eyebrow at his hostess, his kind voice thick with irony.

'Of course, you only serve it for the youngsters.'

Rhia thought it would set a bad example to stick her tongue out at him in front of Lucan and so settled for a raised eyebrow of her own. It was true, she had a fondness for the children's treat herself, but there was no need to admit that out loud to anyone. She was trying to think of something suitably witty to say when she heard heavy footfalls at the doorway, and moments later saw Marius striding in with General Lepidus a pace behind him. Both men wore the tunics and breastplates of the legion, and both of their faces were serious. Marius' features softened for a heartbeat on seeing his wife and son, but his commander spoke to Glaucus before any greeting could be made.

'Forgive the intrusion governor, but your steward informed us you would be here and the news that I have is pressing.'

Glaucus began rising to his feet and Rhia hurried to pass him his cane. He had to lean a little awkwardly but he managed it under his own power. He nodded only briefly to his son before he spoke.

'What news do you have to report, General Lepidus?'

Lepidus gave a slightly disapproving glance towards Rhia but seemed to realise there was no point in asking her for privacy.

'Sir, we have a full-scale revolt upon our hands. The Gorvicae have gathered their warriors and have killed a party of inspectors sent to survey their land. They have murdered Councillor Falconius and attacked the Fourteenth's Third Cohort. Tribune Pallona reports that their numbers are in the thousands and he requests urgent reinforcement.'

Rhia's eyes darted around for someone to hand Lucan to. She wanted to hear this but equally didn't want to distress her child. Mercifully, Enora appeared at the doorway and Rhia placed his tiny hand in hers. Lucan looked a little confused at suddenly being sent away for no reason, but Rhia did her best to sound unconcerned.

'You go with Enora for a moment now, my love. We've some boring household talk to get done at the moment. I'll be with you soon.'

How much he believed her she didn't know, but he went along willingly enough and Lepidus spoke again before Glaucus could comment on his report.

'Sir, with General Balius gone, I recommend that I take their Second Cohort along with my own First Cohort, and go to relieve these men. It is best they be reinforced by their fellows and Tribune Abellan is a fine officer, but if the numbers are as great as Pallona reports...?'

He left that hanging in the air for a moment to give Glaucus the time to envisage the situation. It also gave Rhia a chance to think. The Gorvicae were not technically overruled by the Gaians, though they might as well have been for all the taxation that was levied on their trade, and how much interference the Gaians made into their business. From what she'd heard there was resentment among them, as there was in many tribes, but it made so much less sense for the Gorvicae to cause trouble for the Gaians than it did for any of the others to. The Caderyn or the Rydicae could be said to be conquered peoples who might fight for their freedom, but Baercban had arguably made the best deal one could make with these people. *Though*, Rhia thought, *none of* his *family have wed into Gaian nobility. They are distant partners to the Empire at best. Perhaps they have grown to resent it?* If they had, and this was their solution to it, then the Gorvicae were even more stupid than she had thought.

Mixed in with her confusion was a tiny gem of glee at the thought of her old enemies facing the might of the Gaian military, especially since her husband was a part of it. Her own people had suffered so terribly at Nantwyn and that war had been the making of Baercban and his craven son, and that smug-faced bastard Gawan. Rhia disliked the thought of any tribesmen being slaughtered as the Caderyn had been, but if it had to happen to anyone, she was glad it was to them.

Glaucus' face looked grim and Rhia saw that he seemed to have aged in the space between sitting and standing up.

'Can some agreement not be made by negotiation? I have no wish to court war with these tribes and undo all the hard work that we have done.'

Lepidus spoke calmly.

'They are out for blood, governor. Your intentions are admirable but negotiation will have to wait until later.' His voice became stern. 'Right now our troops are pinned down and outnumbered and I cannot permit their lives to be risked for the sake of mere idealism. We must retaliate, and demonstrate to them what happens when they resort to violence against us. After that is done and the immediate threat is nullified, *then* the negotiators may come and do what it is they do.'

Glaucus did not look pleased by this ultimatum but neither did he argue against its logic. He drummed his fingers on the polished head of his cane.

'If Gaian lives are at risk then that must be our priority. You say that the rebel warriors number in their thousands?'

Lepidus nodded, seeming relieved that he didn't have to argue any further. Rhia was still wondering at why Baercban had done something so foolish but she had the sense not to interrupt their conversation. It would hardly be constructive.

'Indeed so, governor. Tribune Pallona reported at least three thousand and probably more.'

Rhia frowned, running the numbers through her mind. A modern legion consisted of barely half that, and a single cohort could boast at best five hundred infantrymen. Gaian legions might be killing machines but she herself had observed that they had weaknesses, and she'd no idea if Pallona's cohort had Destroyers or horsemen to support them. Glaucus seemed to be thinking along similar lines.

'Severus, in your professional opinion is there any current threat to the security of this city?'

Lepidus furrowed his brows at the change of tack but then shook his head.

'None at all, sir. This revolt is more than fifteen days' march away and the Rydicae have been behaving themselves for the most part. Even if they were to stir up again their rebels have not half the numbers required to realistically threaten Tamora.'

Glaucus nodded very slowly and Rhia started worrying that he was still sharing her thoughts. Marius had not long ago been made Full Tribune after Tribune Clavius had been promoted to Chief of Staff, and her husband was now commanding officer of the Tenth Legion's Second Cohort. She swallowed anxiously as her father-in-law spoke the exact words she'd feared he would say.

'Then I think it would be prudent to take two of your own cohorts along with Tribune Abellan's company. If battle must be joined it must be swift and decisive and I would have this matter dealt with as expediently as possible.'

He crossed the room, leaning on his cane, and placed a hand on Marius' shoulder.

'My son Antonius would be fortunate to see his first major action as a commander with his mentor still at his side.' He turned and nodded to Lepidus. 'You will take both your First and Second Cohorts with you general, and let the Gorvicae face the might of a full legion when you arrive.'

The general frowned for a second but then seemed to approve of the idea. Doubtless he would have preferred to take his Third Cohort with its more experienced tribune, but he knew better than to argue when he'd been given more than he'd first asked for. Rhia simply stared at her husband and tried to keep the worry from surfacing. Visions of Bevan fighting the Gorvicae flashed across her eyes for an instant, as did an image of Marius balked in blood, but she shoved them away with a firm effort of will. *Marius will not die. The legions are unstoppable. Remain calm.*

She took a slow breath and kept her composure, thinking cynically that Livilla would be proud of her for maintaining a patrician's proper façade. Lepidus was nodding his head.

'As you say, sir. I have already sent instructions for Abellan's men to assemble. With your permission I shall muster this force and leave the city with all possible speed.'

Glaucus nodded back, his face still grim.

'By all means, general. Your orders are to engage the enemy and to put a definitive end to this revolt, though I stipulate that casualties among non-combatants are to be minimised, and all efforts made to make a peaceful resolution should the enemy attempt to seek terms.'

Lepidus seemed far from enthusiastic about that but he bobbed his head all the same.

'Should they seek to surrender we shall show mercy.'

Glaucus nodded his approval and then spoke again, his voice calm but still commanding.

'If you can spare him a moment, general, I would give my blessings to my son before he leaves?'

Lepidus turned to Marius.

'I shall expect you at the barracks within the hour, Tribune Dessida.'

Rhia's husband snapped his heels together and threw out a salute from his chest.

'Understood, sir.'

Lepidus returned the gesture and then repeated it towards the governor.

'I shall be about my duty sir. Hail Tiberian!'

Glaucus' face remained stern as he saluted back.

'Hail Gaivia.'

If Lepidus disapproved of the more old-fashioned term he did not show it, and he spun on his heel and left without further comment.

The moment he was gone Rhia abandoned all pretence and rushed forwards to hug her husband. Marius put his arms around her and she felt his strength as he squeezed her close to him.

'Have no fear. I will be alright.'

His voice rumbled in his chest beneath her head and the words sounded comforting and confident. But then Bevan had been confident. Rhia shook away that thought and nodded. She leaned back a little, breaking the embrace, though she took hold of both of his hands.

'Of course you will. I'll not have you leaving me to run this place all by myself!'

He smiled at her and held her hands tighter in his. Rhia looked up into his eyes. She didn't love him. She couldn't. What they had together was nothing like what she'd had with Bevan years ago. But she cared for him, and had cared for him even more since their son had been born to them. She thought of Lucan growing up without his father to smile down at him and a tear threatened to fall but she held it back.

Glaucus stepped in before she could get upset.

'You have nothing to fear, my dear. Antonius knows his trade, as does Severus for that matter. This revolt will be put down in a month and they will be back here and bragging about it a month later.'

Rhia managed a smile and stepped back a little more to let the father give his blessings. She was close enough to hear them but her mind was far away. She was thinking of Marius fighting Gorvicae warriors, and was praying quietly to Vulco Taranis that he keep her husband safe. A part of her, that part that she kept hidden away except at times when she needed to draw strength from it, wished that she could be going along with him. She yearned to see Baercban and Sedryn punished for what they'd done, and the warrior deep inside her itched to grasp a sword again, and wondered if that coward still had Silverbite.

But the rest of her was arguing down that part. The Caderyn warrior in her gave her pride and strength as needed, but the time for that woman to actually fight in combat was long over. She was a wife now and a mother, and besides, the Gaian legions could manage perfectly well without her. A little, unwelcome voice in her head also reminded her of what had happened the last time she fought beside a husband in battle, but she latched on to the pride of her warrior self, infused it with the quiet strength borne only by those who know motherhood, and forced the bitter voice to keep its peace. She had not meant to harm Bevan. She had a duty here and now. She was a good wife and a good mother, and there was honour enough in those things.

Glaucus and Marius were still exchanging words as Rhia said more quiet prayers in her head, making a mental note to make sacrifices to the right temples once Marius left. *I must make sure he wears his Vulco amulet too. It was blessed only three days ago and should still have power enough so long as he keeps it on.* She shook away her worries and said her silent prayers as the father blessed his son.

Hear me, I am Carradus Dessidus Rhianna. Gods of the wood, gods of the sky and gods of the Underworld, keep this man safe as he rides away to war. Let the Gorvicae be punished for the bloodshed they create. Let them bleed as the Caderyn bled on the red field of Nantwyn. Let the legions of Gaivia crush the rebels without loss. And may Marius Dessidus Antonius come home safely to his family. Gods of the wood, gods of the sky and gods of the Underworld, bring us victory, bring us peace. And bring him home.

Chapter 21. Gadarim

Rhia prayed and fretted and even worried herself to tears some nights but as it happened, it all transpired as Glaucus predicted. Within a moon's turn the uprising of the Gorvicae had been crushed, and the ringleaders taken, killed or scattered to the winds. Baercban had apparently survived the conflict, as had his cowardly son, but his greatest warriors were either slain or dispersed, and the territory of the Gorvicae had now been fully absorbed into the Gaian Empire. Unlike the Caderyn, whose numbers and resources had led to a fairly cordial negotiation after Nantwyn, the subjugation of the Gorvicae was apparently a more ruthless affair, and Baercban had been fortunate to keep his life. *But then*, Rhia supposed, *you can't have everything.*

She smiled to herself as she took another sip of wine. They were just enjoying a selection of cheeses to round off a midday meal and the golden wine was sweet and delightfully peachy. For the most part, Rhia was in good spirits. Her enemies were defeated, her husband was home safe, and her son was finally getting to grips with his letters. Like his mother, Lucan had struggled terribly with his reading at first, but his tutor had told her yesterday that he was making remarkable progress, and Rhia could not have been more proud.

She looked across to where he sat beside his grandfather, speaking earnestly about something that she couldn't quite hear, but that Glaucus was demonstrating the most rapt attention to. Rhia smiled at the old man. He was still wearing a beard in mourning for his two friends, General Balius and Councillor Falconius, the former of whom had been practically family to him. *At least he seems happy with Lucan. And his leg is growing stronger every day.*

Beside the governor, Marius was sitting quietly and picking at the cheese without much interest. Rhia felt a little pang of compassion for her husband. His company had been in the thick of the fighting and from what little he'd said, it had been an ugly affair. Rhia had no idea what a battle looked like from the perspective of a legion, but if it in any way resembled what it looked like from the other side, then it was a messy, glory-less affair and she sympathised with his lack of enthusiasm. Apparently the Gorvicae had fought hard, and with greater numbers than anticipated, but the iron discipline of the three cohorts had driven them back and scattered them.

Unusually for a man of the Tenth, Marius had spoken most highly of his rivals in the Fourteenth. Normally, as Rhia had discovered early on, it was traditional for every Gaian legion to assume it was immensely superior to every *other* Gaian legion, and particularly so when it came to legions who were stationed together. While the soldiers rarely went so far as to fight in earnest about it, friendly jibes were commonplace, and the occasional drunken brawl was considered natural.

However, Marius had described the fighting of the Fourteenth who'd been sent with him as incredibly ferocious, almost to the extent of it affecting their hard-drilled discipline. He'd spoken of Tribune Abellan's cohort charging screaming into the fray, outstripping both companies of men from the Tenth and battering through the Gorvicae like a ram smashing a door. Rhia supposed it made sense, given that it was their own comrades they were on their way to help. Gaian soldiers were fanatically devoted to their own legion, and apparently the cohort who'd been under pressure had suffered heavily, the Gorvicae going so far as to impale the heads of two centurions on spears beside the road. *It must have driven even these cold warriors wild*, she thought, and tried not to think how she would feel to see Madoc's head stuck on a pole.

She looked again at her husband, and hoped he might at least find some distraction with Lucan later on. Before he'd left Rhia had called Marius to their rooms and they'd made love with a passion she was rarely able to feel, and she had hoped for more of the same on his return. But his face had seemed so drawn, his eyes so grim and distant, that she'd known without a word that he would be in no mood to couple.

Tullius, having stayed in the city with the Third Cohort, was still pressing him for details about the campaign, oblivious to the fact that his brother clearly did not want to talk about it.

'But I thought they simply came on in a horde?'

Marius wasn't looking at him as he replied.

'Yes and no. They have perhaps realised that fighting as lone warriors is ill-suited to battling a shieldwall, yet they have not the training for much else.'

Tullius looked confused and Rhia hoped he would just drop the subject. Gwen, sat beside him, looked as uncomfortable as Marius, though she was wearing so much cosmetic today it was difficult to tell. *Why such heavy pallor for a midday meal? Is she trying to impress him or something?*

'So what did you mean when you said, *together* then?'

Marius sighed a little.

'I mean they tried to *stick* together when they charged, watch one another's backs, that sort of thing. It wasn't a shieldwall or anything, it was just a more cautious way of fighting. It made it that much harder to push through them.'

Tullius nodded slowly and seemed about to speak again, but Glaucus got there ahead of him.

'Leave your brother to his food awhile, Tullius. You have hurled questions at him ever since he returned.'

The slender man shrugged.

'It is not just for my curiosity, Father. General Lepidus thinks I have a gift for working in intelligence. Only yesterday he...' But Tullius stopped mid-speech and a look of mild alarm spread across his face. 'Blast it! I'd forgotten.'

Rhia noticed her sister's eyes flutter nervously as he spoke but she covered it up quickly. Rhia found herself worrying for her again but was distracted when Tullius put down his cup and turned to address her directly.

'Rhianna, would you be able to come with me to the barracks this afternoon?'

Rhia was slightly taken aback. She was on cordial enough terms with her brother-in-law but they never went out anywhere together unless it was part of a larger family group. She failed to keep the surprise from her voice.

'The barracks?'

Tullius waved a hand impatiently.

'Not the legion barracks, the auxiliary one, the general and Praecus wanted to speak to you about the Gorvicae.'

If anything this confused her even further and Tullius elaborated without needing prompting.

'I mentioned to Praecus, he's one of the general's advisors, that you had fought the Gorvicae several times yourself and that the Caderyn and the Gorvicae had been both friends and enemies in their time. Did I do wrong?'

Rhia shook her head, still a little uncertain.

'No, that is true, for the most part. We have both fought with them and traded with them in equal measure over the years, though I am far from an expert on their tribe.'

Tullius looked relieved that he hadn't been misleading his superiors and waved his hand again, dismissively.

'That needn't matter. You will be more familiar with them than anyone else in the city, I suspect. Would you mind terribly coming with me and answering a few questions? It should not take too long.'

His tone was polite enough, though Rhia guessed she was being used as a method for Tullius to curry favour with his superior officers. He had a slightly too-eager look in his eyes, and she suspected he had already told his commander that she would be coming with him, and was now terrified she would say no. Her eyes flicked back and forth between him and his wife.

Gwen seemed, if anything, more nervous than her husband at the prospect of her refusing him, and Rhia wondered if this slender, eager-eyed young man would take it out on her sister if she made him look foolish in front of Lepidus. *But how?* She kept her face even as she pondered. *Would he berate her? Belittle her? Beat her?* That last dark thought made Rhia want to clench her fists and she had to remind herself that she had no proof of her suspicions. Gwen might flinch around him a lot, but she was a nervous girl by nature and Enora, who had known the family for years, had been convinced that Tullius could never raise his hand to a woman. *But then what about that day at the bathhouse?* Gwen had come so close to confessing something to her, but alas, Rhia had not had another chance to question her.

Tullius was perching on the edge of his seat, eager for her response, and Rhia decided to put him from his misery.

'Of course I can come along. Anything to keep those damned Gorvicae in their place.'

Tullius breathed a sigh of relief, though Marius looked a little pained. Rhia remembered that they had planned to take a walk around the fountains with Lucan this evening. She reached over and patted his arm.

'I'm sure it won't take me too long my dear, and if I miss you at the fountains then when I get back *you* can complain at *me* for a change.'

Marius took her hand in his and managed a little smile. He'd not done that much since this last mission and Rhia made sure he saw her smiling back.

'Very well, my dear. But I shall hold you to that.'

Rhia gave his hand an encouraging squeeze before turning back to face his brother.

'It shouldn't take too long, should it?'

Tullius was too busy feeling pleased that he was about to look good in front of his superiors to even pretend to hide his satisfaction.

'Oh no, I'm sure it won't.'

*

The sky outside was overcast with grey, making even the spring afternoon seem dark, but the temperature was mild and the rain kept off them for the walk. It wasn't all that far to where the auxiliaries were billeted and Rhia had seen no need to bring Drenn or Enora along with her. Along the way she had tried to marshal her thoughts a little regarding the Gorvicae, in the hopes of keeping this meeting as brief as possible. It wasn't as if she knew all that much about them anyhow; she knew the names of several prominent warriors and from what towns or clans they hailed from, she knew roughly how many fighters the Gorvicae could realistically field, and where a couple of their defensible locations would be. That was more or less it. She knew some of the traditions of the Gadarim of course, but she had decided early on that she would be frugal in what she shared about them. Much of what she knew of them she had no right to know, and a Gaian would have even less right to know.

Marshalling her thoughts was not easy however, since Tullius had spent most of the journey harping on about his hoped-for position.

'If all of this goes well the general might allow me onto the legion staff, you know. I'd be sorry to leave my cohort of course but for a junior tribune to be allowed onto the advisory staff is a rare opportunity for anyone.'

Rhia nodded along, trying to hide her boredom at his chatter. It was painfully clear that Tullius wanted to advance in his legion's hierarchy, and that doing it the way his brother was – by patience and dedicated service – was not quick enough for him. He wanted advancement *now*, and according to Marius he'd been dogging the general's footsteps for months on end.

Rhia had no interest at all in hearing about her brother-in-law's ambitions but since they had some walking to do yet and he seemed in a talkative mood, she wondered if she might try to question him about his life at home.

'Rare indeed. Gwen must be delighted that you are being shown such favour?'

Tullius paused for a second, clearly surprised that his audience had actually been listening to him.

'She seems to be, though she keeps her thoughts to herself for the most part.'

There was another little pause and Rhia leaped into it before he could change the subject back again.

'She always was a quiet girl, but I don't doubt that she is happy for your success?'

It was a broad term for a man being permitted to run errands for his superiors and to fawn at others' feet, but if it flattered Tullius' ego enough for him to drop his guard then it was worth it. The slim man stuck out his chest for a moment but then cast his eyes down to the stone-paved street.

'I think she is. To be honest Rhianna, we don't really talk all that much.'

Rhia wondered how hard she ought to push him to get more but he carried on without her help, speaking half to himself.

'I think it's because of the child. As you say she is a delicate flower but we were getting along well enough before that. After Danis died she sort of wilted, and I don't think I helped her all that much.'

Rhia wasn't sure if he was genuinely sorry or just putting on the gloomy voice for her, but she decided to give him the benefit of the doubt and tried to sound consoling. They were walking arm in arm, and she placed her free hand on his elbow for a moment.

'It cannot have been easy for either of you. I myself once lost a child and it is no ordeal to recover from lightly.'

Tullius nodded slowly, walked in silence a few paces, and then blurted out.

'I shouted at her a few times you know, after it happened. I get short with her sometimes even now, sometimes for no reason. It's not as if I *mean* to, it's just... sometimes I look at her and I think of the babe and I...'

Rhia supplied the answer, understanding taking the edge away from her anger.

'And you are sad to have lost him and so you blame her for it.'

Tullius looked embarrassed.

'I don't mean to, I really don't. I just can't help sometimes thinking if I'd married... you know, someone *else*, then maybe it might be different.'

Rhia frowned. The implication that he might have been better off with a decent Gaian girl was hardly a welcome sound when he was married to her sister. A part of her wanted to snap something harsh at him, but then her sympathy came back into control and she kept her voice soft and calm.

'You cannot know what might have been. What you *can* know, is that the wife you have is both loving and devoted.'

Once again Tullius nodded and Rhia thought she saw a tear shine in his eye. Rhia's worries that he'd had been abusing his wife were slowly melting in the face of his contrition. *If this is an act then he belongs at the theatre. Perhaps this is all there is to it after all. Perhaps there is hope for them both.* She favoured him with a friendly pat on his shoulder but they spoke no more words and walked the remainder of the way in silence.

It wasn't long before they arrived at the auxiliary barracks, a large circular building quite unlike the standardised camp of a legion. Even in the dim light of the overcast day it was clear that most of the structure was rebuilt masonry on a ruined foundation, and Rhia suspected the original building had been something quite spectacular. The bases of moulded columns were evident every few paces, and the stonework was worn but skilfully decorated. The work done on top of this was of a plain and practical sort, with simple grey walls and an ugly-looking gate.

Tullius led her through it, having given the watchword to an Aboran guard, and led her through a short corridor that led out into an open space. Rhia saw the beginnings of tiered seating opposite her and guessed that this must have been a theatre long ago. Though Gaians were fond of some spectacles that Rhia found somewhat unsettling, for the most part she had enjoyed the fact that the Dessidas were patrons of theatres, and she had watched countless plays, musicians, swordfights and races at the other grand theatres in Tamora. From the rusted cages she saw attached to one wall, she suspected that this place had been used for some of the more savage games one often saw, and she tried not to think of all the poor beasts who had been slaughtered here. For all their civilised affectations Gaians were awfully fond of blood, and Rhia avoided visiting theatres where such sports were commonplace.

Tullius, rather than leading her into the open space, turned left and beckoned her to follow, leading her along another corridor and then down a flight of steps. What little light came in through the windows was dull and grey, and Rhia watched her step as she descended. At the bottom was another corridor, this one lit by wall-mounted lamps, and Tullius knocked politely on the first door to their left. A short, dark-haired man stepped out into the corridor to greet them.

'Ah, thank you, tribune.' He cocked his head at Rhia. 'Rhianna Dessida, I presume?'

His voice was polite enough but Rhia hoped he did not plan to embrace her. His hair was greasy and his smile just a little unsettling. She nodded to him.

'You presume correctly.'

Thankfully, the dark-haired man simply bowed his head in response.

'Glad to meet you. My name is Praecus, I serve as an advisor to General Lepidus.'

Rhia nodded again and decided to get straight down to business.

'I understand you wish to speak to me about the Gorvicae? My knowledge is limited but I will tell what I can.'

Praecus smiled, not seeming discouraged. Rhia expected him to ask her into his office but instead he waved a hand along the corridor.

'I am sure your contribution will be invaluable. Shall we?'

Rhia shrugged and started walking in the direction indicated, and Tullius fell into step behind them. Praecus spoke casually as they progressed.

'I am sure there is much about their people that you know, but my principle concern at present is about their warrior caste, these *Gadarim*.'

Rhia instantly felt herself tensing at the word and resolved to tell this man only the bare basics. He forestalled some of that however.

'I am aware that they whiten their hair or beards with lime, that they fight at the forefront of their armies, and that they enjoy a certain status among their people. I have seen similar things before but I am always keen to learn what I can about any new foe.'

Rhia nodded quietly for a moment and tried to match the casual air of Praecus' tone.

'There is little more that I can tell you that you do not already know. Each tribe's Gadarim are different and yet some traditions exist among all of them. When they become Gadarim they take a warrior name; names like Smiling Fox, Charging Bull or,' she resisted spitting at the name, 'Leaping Wolf. It gives them an identity beyond that which they were born with, and it binds them to the land, and to their own fate as warriors.'

Praecus nodded along quietly as they walked but said nothing and Rhia continued, determining to only tell a little more to this strange Gaian.

'To become Gadarim a fighter must pass several tests of his merit, such as courage, strength and will. They test themselves against pain and fear and swear oaths to live lives of honour in the eyes of the War Gods.'

The little advisor scratched his chin for a moment.

'And how are these tests administered?'

He turned to look Rhia directly in the eyes and she had a horrible suspicion that he was seeing her thoughts. She shoved away the shameful memory of when she'd spied on Ossian's initiation, and focused on the greasy hair of her interrogator.

'I am afraid only a Gadarim could tell you that. Their rituals are secret to most. All I know is that the tests are hard and that not all would pass them.'

Praecus stared at her for only a moment longer before looking away and continuing his steady pace. At the end of the passageway a man walked through a heavy door and Rhia recognised him as Tribune Abellan, the officer of the Fourteenth whose ferocity Marius had so praised. Rhia had only met him once or twice at social functions but they exchanged polite nods all the same. She might have said something but he seemed to be in a hurry, heading towards them with long strides. It looked like the legion officer was drying his hands on a cloth, though it was difficult to see much in the corridor's dim light. His face was blank and when Praecus gave him a querying look, Abellan just shook his head.

The soldier passed them in silence and Praecus apparently didn't see a need to comment on it. He continued his questioning.

'But those who *do* pass these tests are presumably well-prepared for pain and fear before they even reach the battlefield? These men would be the bravest of the brave?'

Rhia forgot about Abellan as she felt a little flicker of pride amidst her discomfort, though she tried to keep the smile reaching her face.

'Of course. Even the worst man of the Gadarim could not be called a coward.'

She thought grudgingly of Gawan and hated to admit that he was at least a brave man, even if he was a bastard. Praecus nodded again thoughtfully and spoke half to himself as they reached the heavy door that the soldier had come through.

'Yes, that would explain a great deal.'

The door opened up onto a warm, cavernous chamber, and Rhia's eyes were greeted by a scene out of a nightmare.

The heat and light came from a brazier in the centre of the room, inside which a crackling fire cast orange light on the stone walls. Besides Rhia, Tullius and Praecus, the chamber had only two other occupants: One was an Aboran, stripped to the waist and sweating, replacing a long-handled poker into the brazier and causing sparks as the wood was disrupted. The other was a naked man chained to the wall by his wrists and ankles, and though the firelight made them seem black instead of blue, Rhia clearly saw his body was decorated with battlemarks. The unfortunate man was drenched in sweat and blood oozed from scores of small wounds, but the battlemarks were un-smeared by the fluids, and Rhia realised at once that they were tattooed onto his skin. The man in the chains was a Gadarim.

Rhia felt the bile rise in her throat. One of the Gadarim's eyes had been gouged out of its socket, and a quick glance at his bound hands showed several fingers either crushed or simply missing. His torso was a mess of shallow cuts and vicious burns and his left leg was bent sideways at an impossible angle, the foot impaled on a spike driving up from the floor. The warrior's head was sagging onto his heaving, bloody chest, and she suspected he was not screaming only because he was too exhausted. Praecus continued speaking as if nothing were out of sorts.

'This one has told us nothing, despite the best efforts of Strabo here, and were it not for all his cursing I'd have thought him simple-minded.'

Rhia coughed, feeling certain she was about to vomit, and her hands began shaking uncontrollably. She clenched them into fists as Praecus spoke again.

'But if they are trained to resist pain then that would make sense. But fear not,' he gave her a tiny smile, 'we only chained him up yesterday, and Strabo always gets them singing in the end.'

Rhia stared at the man, too shocked and horrified to even speak. He tilted his head, seeming confused.

'This man is Gorvicae, my lady. He is your enemy, is he not?'

Rhia's mind was still reeling from the horror of the sight and she found herself nodding without thinking. Praecus nodded back.

'Well then, all is well.'

He was smiling cheerfully, more like a man glad to have avoided a moment of social awkwardness than a man showing a woman the tortured shell of an enemy warrior. Rhia turned to face Tullius and saw that he was staring unblinkingly at the chained Gadarim. Terror, horror and morbid fascination seemed to be warring with each other for what dominated his expression. Rhia tried to pull herself together as Praecus spoke to her once more.

'Is it a mark of this man's status that his warpaint is made permanent? I notice that the marks the other fighters paint onto their bodies are tattooed onto the flesh of the warrior caste.'

He was speaking quite calmly still and Rhia had to fight to keep from retching. She tried to remind herself that the Gorvicae had caused endless harm to her people, but somehow she was finding it hard to be convinced.

'It means that Taran and Mabonac always watch them.' She managed to choke out. 'The gods can always give them strength if they are always watching.'

Praecus nodded very slowly and Rhia tried to clear her head. She tried telling herself that she was glad of this. Ever since her pride had finally come back to her she had wished harm on the Gorvicae for Nantwyn. She had prayed to the gods, both Gaian and Lurian, for ill-fate to dog their footsteps, and she'd cast a score of lead curses on their tribe in Tamora's temples. She risked a look up at the warrior as the Aboran guard stepped close to him, and winced as the huge man kicked the prisoner in the groin. The warrior cried out and spat blood through his cracked lips, and Rhia fought back tears as she looked away. *I didn't mean this! Not like this!*

Shame and fear began to fill her again as Praecus moved up to the guard. He whispered something that Rhia couldn't quite make out but then realised with horror what he must have told him to do. The Aboran smiled coldly and selected a curved blade from a tray beside his captive. Rhia wanted to cry out but no words came to her as the giant auxiliary cut into the tattooed arm of the bound man and then slowly, carefully, began tearing away the skin. The Gorvic screamed.

Rhia's legs turned to water at the sight and she stumbled into Tullius, who just about kept her upright. Praecus was speaking again, though Rhia barely made sense of his words.

'Yes they are most impressive for men who are not enhanced as the Destroyers are.' He spoke almost to himself. 'But then perhaps their own rituals...?'

He turned to Rhia.

'Tell me, do your *Gadarim* partake of any potions or receive the blessings of your priests during their rituals?'

Rhia couldn't speak. She was rooted to the spot with terror and disgust as a brave man was flayed alive before her eyes. Beside her she saw Tullius try to look away a few times but always his gaze kept turning back to the torturer and his victim, as if the fascination was just barely strong enough to overcome his sense of revulsion. The Gorvic warrior screamed again as more flesh was stripped from his body, and for a single terrible moment, his remaining eye locked onto Rhia's. She felt her heart stutter in its beat and her face drained of all blood. She recognised him.

His name was Nuallan. The Running Boar. Her mind was assaulted with a barrage of images, more overwhelming even than the sound of screams or the wriggling in her gut. She remembered seeing him at Broken Stream, fighting with Madoc. She remembered him coming back with them to Bryngarth as a prisoner, and how he and the others had offered Marna's blessings on little Siriol. She remembered him later at Nantwyn, fighting and killing Caderyn warriors. The image came of him plunging his sword into Bel, and then falling back as Dane caught him a glancing blow.

Rhia tried to control herself. Praecus was still watching her patiently, clearly confused that she wasn't revelling in the destruction of her enemy. She looked at Nuallan. *He is* my enemy. *He has killed my friends and helped cause a war that almost destroyed us all. But what kind of monster could do this to another man, no matter how much enmity lay between them?*

Rhia forced herself to keep looking as Nuallan was tortured before her. He was her enemy. He had killed Meghan's brother. But he was Gadarim. No matter what else he might have said or done, he had earned a better fate than this. Brief flashes of Madoc and Owain and Ossian came to her mind and she imagined what any one of them would do in her place. Not one of them would simply stand here, weak-legged and trembling, as a fellow warrior was skinned alive by cowards.

Rhia turned her head to look at Tullius, with his strange fascination, and at Praecus with his casual indifference. The shorter man repeated his simple question but Rhia was no longer listening. *You fool!* These *people are the enemy!* These *people are the ones who slaughtered your tribe and made them into little more than slaves.* These *people are the ones who revel in conquest and in cruelty. And you are raising your son to be one of them!* She felt a dizziness hit her and she steadied herself on a table. *You have been blind Rhianwyn. And willingly so.*

Nuallan let out another terrible scream and Rhia clenched her fists tight and ground her teeth hard against each other. *You must do something.* She straightened herself up and faced Praecus directly, but before she could say anything a cry of alarm came from the Aboran guard. Both Rhia and Praecus snapped their heads around to see that Nuallan had somehow wrenched one chain loose from the wall, and his free hand was now battering down frantically at his tormentor.

The Aboran was strong but he'd been caught off his guard, and he'd now dropped down to one knee with both hands above his head. Rhia glanced sideways at Praecus, who looked irritated but unworried, and saw him bring a hand up in front of him and begin mumbling. Rhia watched as a subtle green light began to play about his fingers, and wondered with horror if this greasy-haired man was some perversion of a druid.

Whatever he was, and whatever he was doing, Rhia had no intention of letting him cast his wicked spells on the bound Gadarim. Her instincts started taking over and a sudden clarity came to her thoughts. She moved even as she was reasoning. *I cannot stop the magicker, and I cannot save Nuallan, not while we are here in this city and surrounded by our enemies. Even if I freed him from the wall we could never escape. I must get away from here alive and tell my people about the sorcery they face. But there is one thing I can do for this brave man who was once my enemy. Just one little thing, but damn it all, it is better than nothing.*

The Aboran had just managed to start fighting back in earnest but Nuallan hammered a fist into his jaw and the bigger man was sent sprawling. Rhia crossed over to him in only four strides and whipped a knife up from the table as she went. The Gadarim either hadn't seen her coming or he was too tired to keep going, because by the time his one eye met hers again and registered what was happening, she had already plunged the blade under his ribs into his heart. A look of shock crossed over his face for a second, and Rhia pressed her face close to his and chanced a whisper as she drove the blade deeper.

'Cross the bridge unharmed, Running Boar.'

She had said it so quietly she wasn't certain even the warrior had heard it, but she hoped that what she saw in his eye was recognition or relief before it rolled back up into his skull. What life had remained in him left his body.

Rhia sagged for a moment but then drew the knife clear and, resisting the urge to vomit or to shake in voice or movement, she replaced it on the table and looked back to where Praecus stood, the light around his hand now gone.

'You're welcome, sir.'

Tullius was staring at her in disbelief but Praecus' face was as calm as ever, if slightly quizzical in its expression. Rhia fought to keep her tone even and not let grief and shame overwhelm her.

'As you say, he was my enemy. And *someone* had to control him.'

She raised an eyebrow in what she hoped would be seen as a mocking gesture, and Praecus smiled his sickening smile and bowed his head ever so slightly.

'Many thanks, my lady. We shall all of us know better than to become *your* enemies, I hope?'

Rhia wanted to retch, wanted to cry, wanted to hurl herself at this twisted magicker and open up his throat. But she forced herself to stay calm. *You have Lucan to consider, remember. Get back to him.* She tried to say something suitably witty in response, but though she felt her lips form the words and heard the sound coming out, she had no idea what exactly it was she said.

Whatever it was it caused the two men to bow again and before she knew it she was walking back through the doors and into the corridor. She was sure she felt the cold eyes of the magicker on her back but she fought back the urge to turn and simply kept walking, swift but calm. She barely got past the main gate of the barracks before she finally doubled over and vomited, but there was no time to stand there shaking, or to indulge herself in crying. Tullius would doubtless be following her up and she had to get home straight away.

Rhia forced herself to stand up straight, took a deep breath of clear afternoon air, and fled from the old theatre as fast as she could, hot tears of shame and rage blurring her vision.

*

By the time she eventually got back to the house, night had fallen and the streets were pitch dark. Rhia had no idea what sort of roundabout route she had taken to get there. After her initial sprint from the barracks she had begun walking in a daze, and though she was sure she hadn't taken all that long to get back home, a worried-looking Enora told her that she'd been gone for several hours, and that Master Glaucus had gone home and Master Antonius with him, the latter intending to come back via the auxiliary barracks in the hopes of finding where his wife had been all this time.

Rhia knew she ought to feel annoyed that Glaucus had insisted on going out again with his bad leg, and that she ought to feel guilty for being gone so long as to cause

Marius worry, but she was still too shocked and frightened and angry to say anything to Enora. She managed to get out that she was tired and was going to her room, and simply waved away the concerned looks of her trusted slave. *Slave. When did I become so comfortable with that word?*

She wandered to her room in silence, entered, and then shut the door tight behind her. A part of her wanted to see Lucan, to hold him and squeeze him and make sure he was alright, but she daren't be around him just yet, not with her mind like this. A similar part of her wished for Marius, with his strong arms and gentle words, but again, she was mostly glad he was not here. He would only add more confusion to her mind. There was a little jug of wine and a beaker left on her dressing table and Rhia poured herself a cup without even realising it. She drank it down in one and then proceeded to pour another, sipping at the second cup as her thoughts raged in her head.

For years now she had convinced herself that the Gaians were their friends, that since they were the only future it was best to simply get along with them, and she had wilfully been blind to the darker side of their society. These were people who liked to watch men die for their entertainment, people who lay on soft couches to gorge themselves on food and wine served up to them by the sweat of others' labour. These were a people who treated anything that was not *them* as something freakish, something wrong, something to be feared and hated and then conquered and absorbed. These were a people who tortured brave warriors of other tribes, for nothing else than to satisfy their twisted curiosity and natural cruelty. *These* people were the barbarians. Rhia took another sip as the fuzz of her dazed walk began to clarify into anger, though it was directed at herself as much as her enemies.

Always you blamed the Gorvicae for what happened to your people, and fooled yourself into believing that these Gaians were not the true enemy. Yet it was the Gaians who slaughtered us at Nantwyn with their wall of shields. It was the Gaians' Destroyers who ripped through our ranks and butchered our fighters even as they ran. It was the Gaians who changed war from something glorious into something foul, from a noble duel between warriors into a soulless machine for stealing land and enslaving people. Rhia sighed as a tear rolled down her cheek. *It is the Gaians who now rule both Caderyn and Gorvicae. They let us kill each other and simply mopped up what was left. We have been fools, and I the worst of us all.*

She felt herself start to weep with despair and reached for her anger to try to fight it. She forgot about men like Marius and Glaucus, and her friends Vorena and Junia. She focused on the monsters; on Praecus and Cadmus, Lepidus and Tullius. She thought of the fascination with which her brother-in-law had watched the torturer today. *Gwen is in danger for as long as she is with that man, I see that now.* Grief and shame welled up in her again but she held on to the anger, the only thing she had to keep herself from collapsing inward and becoming a creature of nothingness once more, a numb and empty husk that was no use to anyone. She had been that once before and she must not be so again. She had to hold on to the anger or the shame would overwhelm her.

Images of Lucan flashed before her eyes. For all her noble thoughts about duty to her people she had raised her only son to be a Gaian. She had dressed him in their clothes and kept his hair cut short, and had let him play at being a soldier, not a warrior. She felt the tears well up anew behind her eyes and looked at the little statue of Sulis Mehine beside her bed. Half-Gaian or not, the eyes of the goddess seemed to bore into her. *You have done so much worse than let yourself be defeated. You have let the enemy change who you are. You have become that which you should be defending your people from.*

Rhia picked up the tiny statue and stared at it for a moment, trying not to let the shame overwhelm her rage. She had intended these things to be made in honour of her gods, and all she'd shown their sightless eyes was a house of blue and red cushions fit for conquerors to sit on while they feasted. She looked up from the little statue and caught sight of the beautiful mirror that Marius had bought for them. The light was dim but it was enough for her to see what was reflected there.

Rhia looked and saw a Gaian woman, dressed in a flowing Gaian gown and holding a carved Gaian god. Her fist clenched hard and first black shame then white rage boiled over in her soul. She drew back her arm and hurled the little statue at the long glass pane, and as it shattered into a thousand pieces, Rhianwyn daughter of Carradan let loose her hatred in one long and terrible scream.

Chapter 22. Through the Veil

At some point in the night Marius had arrived home. Rhia had heard him and Enora muttering to each other outside the door, but he hadn't come in. She'd not heard exactly what was said but she guessed that Enora had told her master that his wife was upset and did not want to be disturbed. He had argued only a little and then his footsteps had faded away, and presumably he'd slept in some other room of the great house. That had been some hours ago now and dawn had crept into the bedchamber, casting a grey light on the smashed mirror and broken statue.

Rhia had barely moved in hours and was sitting perched at the edge of the bed with her head hanging forward, her forearms resting limply on her thighs. She stared blankly at the polished tiles of the floor, and the tiny fragments of her mirror that were dotted about the place. Since before midnight she had sat there and stared at the same spot, her eyes not registering the image as her mind whirred with activity. At first she had simply been filled with rage and hate, mixed in with liberal amounts of shame and fear, and she had paced the room incessantly, clenching and unclenching her hands and alternately weeping and growling through her teeth. Eventually this had simmered into something she could focus as she forced herself to start planning what she must do to escape this.

She had to leave Tamora, and Lucan had to come with her. That had to be her first priority. What happened after that, she wasn't sure. How welcome would she be back home, having lived for half a decade with what she now knew were the enemy? What kind of horrors might the Gaians have inflicted on her people while she sat comfortably in their city debating what wine she should serve? Rhia shook her head a little. *This isn't helping. Think practically, as a warrior should.*

Rhia tried to view the situation as a whole and did her best to keep her emotions under control. *What are the facts?* Firstly, Praecus and his kind had shown the true nature of the Gaians and she must escape them and tell her people of the threat they truly faced. From what the magicker had said it seemed he was able to make the Destroyers into what they were by sorcery, and Reaghan and the druids must be warned in case he unleashed something worse. So far, so simple.

Secondly, although she and Gwen were essentially prisoners she had already made an agreement to travel with Marius and Lucan to Bryngarth before long so that Lucan could meet her family. All it need take was a little persuasion and she might be able to move that trip forward, and with good fortune they might even be able to get Gwen to come along too.

Unfortunately, that was where the many, many problems with this plan started. For one thing, Gwen lived in obvious fear of her husband, and Tullius had seen Rhia flee the Aboran barracks last night. If her brother-in-law suspected that she had become disillusioned, he would hardly be likely to allow his wife to leave the city with her. Not only that, but there was Marius to consider. Should he come with them, and how might the Caderyn react to his presence if he did? When they heard of Nuallan's fate would they blame her husband for the crimes of his people? *Will they blame me?* The Caderyn were not a cruel people by any means, but the truth she had to tell about Praecus and his actions would stir an anger in them that might all too easily boil into violence.

Rhia pressed her lips together. It was a risk she had to take, but what of her husband? Marius was a good man, and an active man. Should she tell him everything and let him make his own decision? But how would he react to the news of what she'd seen? Rhia had no doubt he was in ignorance of what was happening, but the fact was he was a Gaian, and an important one at that. His place was with his people and he would know that all too well. Would this one account of hers be enough to make him abandon them? And if not, how was she to escape this city with their child?

Rhia put her fingers to her temples and pressed them in hard, but even as she tormented herself with questions, her stomach gurgled. A voice in her head spoke quietly. *You'll not be carrying Lucan anywhere without some food inside you. Eat something, feed your body, and then you can make all the plans you like.* Rhia had no appetite but the voice was speaking sense. Her legs and back ached as she eased herself upright and she was glad she'd kept her shoes on when she felt glass crunch beneath her feet. She took a last look at the ruined mirror and wondered briefly what it must have cost to create such a marvel; a marvel she had destroyed in half a heartbeat. She stared at the tiny pieces and was almost entranced by the little pinpricks of reflected morning sunlight, but then her stomach growled angrily from beneath her wrinkled dress, and she resolved to go and get something to calm it down.

As she walked from her room to the main chamber of the house, she wondered how she might somehow get Gwen to come home with them. She thought of the fascination on Tullius' face as he watched the tormentor last night, and shuddered. Whatever else might be happening in their marriage, she couldn't leave her sister with this man. Though how she was to get Gwen out was another matter entirely. It might look suspicious to the Gaians if *both* of their Caderyn hostages were suddenly homesick.

She was so preoccupied with these thoughts of escape that she didn't notice Glaucus until she was only a few feet from him. He was chewing on some fruit from a platter in front of him, and waited to swallow before he spoke to her in greeting.

'Good morning Rhianna, I do hope you are well?'

A surge of contradictory feelings came over her as Rhia did her best to smile pleasantly. Glaucus was a good man, a kind man, there was no denying that. He, like Marius, was living proof that there was such a thing as a decent Gaian, though she knew they were in a definite minority. Her confusion irritated her as it took away some of her precious rage, but that didn't change the fact that *this* enemy was a good person.

'I am well, father,' she began, and then, suspecting he might have heard something from Marius or the slaves, added, 'I was a little unwell last night but I think I am past it.'

The old man nodded and poured a cup of watered wine for her, and Rhia took a sip before sitting down. She helped herself to some flat cakes as her mind continued to whirr. Perhaps she could tell Glaucus of what she'd seen? He was noble and powerful and would certainly not approve, perhaps he might be able to put a stop to this? There was a chance, but a voice in her head driven mostly by fear quickly struck down that thought. *Even if he believed you about what you've seen, Praecus didn't seem the type to give up on his work easily. And besides – he is Lepidus' creature.* Rhia's understanding of Gaian politics might not be comprehensive, but one did not spend five years as the daughter-in-law of a councillor, and later governor, without learning a thing or two about how things worked.

Glaucus had more political power than any other man of the Daerian Senate, but he was personally against using it too directly. Lepidus on the other hand, though only a councillor, held the respect and loyalty of the army, and not just of his own legion either. The presence of Tribune Abellan last night was a worrying indication that at least *some* of the Fourteenth men were deep in his pocket. The general had also made it perfectly clear in word and deed that he was in favour of political dictatorship. If Rhia pushed Glaucus into opposing him on something he was set on, and she suspected that Praecus' work was of *great* interest to him, Lepidus might respond by seizing power militarily, and that could put Glaucus and his family in danger. She couldn't believe Lepidus would go so far as to actually *kill* him over it, but he had men like Cadmus and Praecus who she doubted were above murder, and either one might take such action and be forgiven after the deed.

Rhia realised that he was looking at her and that she had been silent for some time. She scrabbled in her brain for something to say.

'I am told you did not stay the night?'

She put as much playful disapproval into her voice as she could manage and Glaucus gave a guilty smile in return.

'I had an appointment I had forgotten about. Besides, Antonius was worried for you. Tullius said you left the barracks alone and you were out for quite some time.'

Rhia brushed it off as best she could.

'I had felt a little faint during my interviewing, it was very warm and stuffy down there. I needed a walk to clear my head.'

Glaucus seemed about to comment but she evaded, gesturing to the couch.

'You did not bring your cane today?'

The governor shrugged.

'It is not so far to walk and I wish to strengthen the leg. My physician informed me that a gentle exercise is good for it.'

Rhia frowned in concern but didn't chide him as much as she normally would have.

'It is far enough.'

Glaucus shrugged again.

'In all honesty I had only meant to walk as far as Drusus' house but then I thought I ought to drop in and check that all was well with you.'

Rhia at first wondered why he'd come at so early an hour, but then remembered he'd once told her that he needed little sleep these days, and that the volume of work he had often required early mornings. She tried for another smile.

'Thank you father, but I am well.'

Still calling him that? But then he deserves it, I suppose. Glaucus patted her arm affectionately and was telling her he was glad of it when the sound of footsteps caused them both to turn around, and Marius appeared from the hall. He was concealing it well but Rhia could tell he was upset, and his father rose from his seat with a subtle grunt.

'Good morning Antonius.'

He looked briefly between Rhia and her husband and a blind man might have seen the tension between them.

'I am afraid I must be on my way now. I must speak to young Drusus and I have much work at home, shall I see you both for supper at my house this evening?'

It was clearly an excuse to let them talk in private, and because he didn't want to be caught up in an argument, but Rhia didn't mind that he was leaving them alone. She had to talk to Marius. Her husband nodded to his father.

'Of course we shall.' He walked up and embraced him briefly. 'I shall see you later, Father.'

Glaucus nodded his head and then turned to Rhia. She stood up and let the old man embrace her too, and surprised herself by how much she both enjoyed and was frightened by the hug. This was a man who cared about her, a good man who loved his grandson, and this might well be the last time she would see him. Without thinking she planted a quick kiss on his cheek and when she spoke she had to fight to keep her voice calm.

'Thank you for coming here, father.'

The old man seemed surprised but pleased at her affection and nodded once again to them both before he left. As the door closed Rhia made a motion of her hand, and those slaves who were in attendance took the hint and vanished from sight. Marius looked her directly in the eyes and his voice was strained with the emotion he held back.

'What happened with you last night? I was worried.'

Rhia looked back into his clear grey eyes and for a moment considered lying to him, but she dismissed the idea in a heartbeat. He might be a Gaian but he was a Gaian like Glaucus, and he had been a good husband and father. He was not Bevan, he never could be Bevan, but he was someone that she cared for and respected, and he deserved to hear the truth about those men that he served with, and why his wife must flee his city and his people. And why she wanted him and their son to come with her.

And so Rhia kept her eyes on his as she asked him to sit down, took a tiny sip of wine and a very deep breath, and told him everything.

*

With slaves coming in and out every now and then, and with Rhia having to keep stopping and starting again, the story took much longer than she'd thought it would. Despite this Marius sat listening in silence, barely moving from his seat with his eyes fixed on her. He didn't speak for a long time but when he did, his voice was strained.

'I know that you are not a liar. All the same, this is not easy to believe.'

He rose and paced for a moment and paused with his back to her. He spoke without turning around.

'You say my brother did not speak, but merely watched all of this.' He took in a deep breath. 'Do you think he was complicit in any of it?'

Rhia shook her head, and then remembered he wasn't looking and so spoke.

'I can't be sure but I don't think so. He seemed to have no objection to what was going on but I do not think he knew much of it beforehand.'

She saw some of the tension ease from Marius' shoulders but there was little relief evident in his voice.

'All the same, he is close to Lepidus and Praecus both and has been trying to get closer for months, if not years now. With no real combat experience he's had no opportunity for promotion and he sees this... work as an alternative method of advancement.'

Rhia nodded. Tullius ranked just below Marius in the legion and so far had only sat and watched in one engagement with the Rydicae. Unlike Lepidus, the Dessida brothers were of sufficient status that either man might qualify to be a Grand Marshal someday, and Tullius had spoken of his ambitions in that direction before. He clearly saw this as his way in.

Marius was obviously finding it hard to condemn his brother and Rhia tried to give him a little solace.

'But as I say he was not involved in it. He may see what is happening and decide to distance himself from it?'

They both knew the odds of that were highly unlikely but it seemed Marius appreciated the gesture, and he turned back to face her with a nod.

'Perhaps. For now we must decide what to do next. The torture of prisoners is hardly pleasant but it does happen when intelligence is needed. It is your mention of sorcery that has me worried, and I have heard a little about this Praecus before now.'

Unexpectedly, he took a step forward and briefly took Rhia in his arms.

'I am glad you are safe.'

Rhia frowned a little in both confusion and in worry. Her determination to leave had been partly motivated by fear, but she had not felt in any *personal* danger in the barracks last night. She squeezed back a little before withdrawing, and Marius continued.

'As far back as Nantwyn I was concerned about the influence he seemed to have over the general, and so a few years ago I made some inquiries. There were rumours that he was once a member of a banned cult, one that was suspected of practicing sorcery, though no proof was ever presented. With no evidence I had to leave it at that. But if Praecus is indeed using forbidden practices on our soldiers then both our people and yours will be in danger. Both he and Lepidus have spoken out against our policy of working with the tribes and would not hesitate to stamp them out given the chance. Lepidus adheres to the old idea of Gaian superiority.'

Rhia frowned a little.

'And yet your father, who is of your ancient nobility, believes otherwise?'

Marius nodded.

'There are some exceptions to this rule; but true nobility rarely see the need to prove it to anyone. My father could be a senator in Gaivia if he wanted but he brought our family out here instead. He has always said it is our duty to spread civilisation to other peoples, for their benefit as much as ours.'

Rhia saw the idea forming in her husband's mind and leaped in before he could speak it.

'We cannot simply go to him and expect him to fix all of this.'

She was going to give her reasons for it but she saw that he was already working it out for himself. If anything, his understanding of it would be better than her own and he seemed to reach a similar conclusion.

'He is sometimes too principled for his own good. He would confront Lepidus about his use of sorcery and Lepidus would declare the Gorvicae revolt as a military state of emergency. He could seize power and have my father arrested for attempting to disrupt the war effort.'

Rhia's brow furrowed.

'But you said that the revolt had been crushed?'

Marius threw up his hands, clearly struggling to contain his frustration.

'Then he would claim it had sprung up again, or use the Rydicae or the Caderyn as an excuse.'

Once again Rhia was confused.

'The Caderyn? But surely my people are on good terms with the Gaians? No-one would believe him if he said we were a threat.'

Marius looked uncomfortable for a moment before he spoke.

'You are honest with me, it is only right that I am honest with you. There have been reports of insurrections, nothing large-scale or even that serious, but rumblings nonetheless in your tribe's territory. Some of your druids and warriors have been causing trouble for their local governor, and some of my fellow officers think that something bigger is afoot.'

Rhia stared at him for a moment and spoke quietly.

'Have there been any deaths?'

Again Marius looked awkward but he answered promptly.

'Some. A few of our enforcers and a handful of Caderyn, I do not know the numbers but they are small.'

Rhia felt anger start to seep into her voice.

'And when exactly were you going to tell me that our people were killing each other? Were you waiting to casually mention it in bed one night?'

She glared up at her Gaian husband but he refused to be cowed.

'I knew of no details and had no wish to upset you. I had hoped that all would be contained and that nothing would come of it.'

Rhia was not assuaged and jabbed a finger at his chest.

'And when we made our visit to Bryngarth you think nobody would have told me? You think the *small number* of those killed had no families or friends?'

Marius had the decency to look guilty for a moment but then swiped his hand sideways in a negative gesture.

'This is not the time to argue about this. We must act on what you have discovered.' He paused for half a second to think. 'We could make for the villa in Verrisi. Take Father along with us. Once there we can tell him everything and plan how best to tackle Lepidus and Praecus.'

It was not a bad plan. Livilla and Rabanus were already there and with Junia on route to Glevia there were no other close family members for Lepidus to threaten if Glaucus moved against him. And with Glaucus in a position to oppose Lepidus in safety, the evil of Praecus might be brought under control by legal means. But Rhia was still angry at Marius' lying, or at least lying by omission, and the answer she gave was harsh.

'It may be well for you to run away to your country estate, but I have my people to think of and it is they who will face the onslaught of this sorcery. If they haven't already felt it at your legions' hands.'

Even as she said it she felt a stab of guilt at the barb. Marius was proud to be a soldier of the Tenth and he must already be upset that such a thing was happening among them. He fumed and seemed about to speak but Rhia carried on before he could.

'And what about Gwen? I'll not trust her one more day in the company of your brother and no doubt you would be taking him with you on this jaunt out to the countryside?'

Marius butted in before she could stop him, his voice raising.

'He is no demigod but he is my brother, and your sister's lawful husband! Besides which, if left here he might be used to pressure my father. Whatever foolish arrangement he's made with Lepidus or this sorcerer I will talk him out of it and bring him with us.'

Rhia found her own voice rising as well.

'Even if you did I wouldn't trust him. I've seen the way Gwen flinches when he comes too close to her. She is afraid of him Marius, you must see that?'

Her husband's short answer made her fairly sure that she was not alone in her suspicions.

'He is my brother.'

Rhia had no intention of letting him escape from this argument so easily. It did him credit to stick by his family but he was still in the wrong.

'I will not run away and hide while my people die fighting off yours. Send your father away to do his fighting and I will go home to do mine.'

Marius' answer was sharp. She had pushed him hard enough already with talk of his brother and his legion.

'Your people are best served by your maintaining our alliance! You will stay with me and my father and we will resolve this thing together.'

Rhia's voice rose further as she stepped even closer to him.

'I *will*? You do *not* command me, Tribune Dessida!'

Marius took in a breath, clearly preparing to fight back, but then something behind Rhia caught his eye and he let it out silently, and his expression turned to one of shock and guilt. Rhia turned around to look and saw a man in the doorway that she recognised as one of Glaucus' slaves, though it wasn't him that made her suck in a breath. Lucan, his little face screwed up as he fought back tears, was standing with him, having clearly thought that he was helping by showing the man into the main room. *He must have felt so grown-up to do that*, she thought. *He will have been so polite, I'm sure. He would have come in expecting us to be proud.*

All anger at Marius left her and she rushed forwards to embrace him, but the little man backed off a pace and then fled towards his room. Rhia called out to him but he ignored her. She started to head after him but the man he'd led in raised his hand.

'Your pardon, Lady Dessida, but I think you ought to wait here a moment.'

Rhia very nearly told him what he could do with his opinion but his face was so grave, and his words so insistent, that despite her urgent need to go and comfort her child she found herself hesitating. The slave looked to Marius and bowed his head low.

'Master Antonius, I am not sure how to say this.'

He fidgeted with his hands as Marius approached him, and Rhia noticed that her husband too seemed to have lost his anger. The sight of little Lucan so upset by their quarrel had taken the fight out of him as much as it had taken it from her. He brought his features under control quickly however, and faced the messenger with classic patrician calm.

'Then say it as simply as it can be said, my man.'

The slave fidgeted a second longer and then seemed to gain some boldness.

'As you say, master. Then forgive me for being the bearer of such news, but I must tell you that Master Glaucus, my master and your own most noble father, is dead.'

Chapter 23. A Death in the Family

Glaucus Dessida had not been tall in life, but in death he seemed to Rhia to look so very small, so fragile. His body had been lain out on one of the beds at his house, still dressed in the clothes she had seen him wearing earlier. Before they'd arrived someone had clearly done their best to clean up some of the blood on his head, but little specks of red still showed amidst the grey and white of his hair. He was facing up, his eyes and mouth mercifully closed. The dreadful wound to the back of his skull could not be seen but all the same, the sight was not a peaceful one.

Rhia reached for her husband's hand and gave it a little squeeze. Marius kept staring at his dead father's face but he squeezed her fingers back all the same. His face was a mask, a carefully built disguise for what she knew must be a whirlpool of emotions beneath. Rhia herself grieved for a good man's death, and was afraid at what this meant for their plans to expose Lepidus. She felt lost and frightened and sad at the sight, and she had only known her father-in-law five years. *For Marius, it must be as if half his world has been ripped away, yet for all the sign of it on his face he might be staring at a statue.* But Rhia was his wife, and she had long learned to see through him.

Had they been there alone she might have tried to talk to him, but sharing the room with them were Ermingild, Glaucus' Greutun guard, an elderly physician and a stocky watchman. The men had been silent for some time but now the watchman broke the silence with a cough.

'My condolences, sir. I can assure you I have men scouring the area for the thieves. They'll have Dis himself to pay for this when we track them down sir, never fear.'

Marius was silent for a moment, still staring at the shell that had been his father, but when he replied his voice was even and strong.

'Thieves?'

The watchman nodded.

'We believe so, sir. We've found no witnesses as yet but his purse was missing when we found him.'

Marius nodded very slowly, his eyes still on the body, and Rhia tried to help by taking over the questioning. She spoke very quietly.

'Where was this, exactly?'

The stocky watchman lowered his voice appropriately.

'In a side street not far from the house of Councillor Duronius Drusus, barely an hour ago. A decent enough part of town but these criminals grow bolder every day.'

He looked ready to embark on the traditional watchman's rant about how the whole city was going to the wolves, and she decided it was not something Marius needed to hear right now.

'Indeed so, sir. I wonder, would you mind giving my husband and I a little time alone with our grief?'

He nodded dutifully but Marius spoke before he could move.

'It is alright. Let us get whatever questions that need asking out of the way.'

Rhia hesitated a moment but nodded her head and gestured for the watchman to speak. He cleared his throat again.

'There is little enough to cover from here, I think,' he turned to Ermingild, 'though I should like to know where the gentleman's bodyguard was when all this happened?'

The Greutun slave towered over the watchman but the shorter man looked in no way intimidated. Rhia saw shame in the big man's eyes and he hung his head a little as he spoke, his words brief and his accent thick.

'I should have been there. Master said he was only walking to his friend's house and no worry. Daylight, safe, open streets all the way. Should have come anyway.'

The watchman nodded slowly and Rhia tried to sound comforting.

'He took a detour he'd not planned in order to visit us, you could not have known.'

Ermingild moved his shoulders in a barely perceptible shrug.

'Should have been there.'

Rhia patted the big man's arm in sympathy but couldn't think of anything better to say to him. Marius spoke from behind her, his voice flat and monotone.

'It is not your fault, Ermingild.' He sighed a little. 'I must write to my mother, I suppose.'

Rhia stepped away from the slave and moved to stand closer to Marius. She placed a hand on his shoulder and spoke softly.

'I will write to Junia and Livilla.'

Marius nodded slowly as Rhia tried to think what she should say. It would be hard enough telling them that their beloved husband or father was dead, especially for Junia, who would only just have heard about her friend Brictus' demise. But she also had to warn them to stay away, that their family was in danger from Lepidus and his sorcerer. Not for a moment did Rhia think Glaucus' death was by mere robbery, and now she thought on it, the death of the old general now seemed suspiciously convenient.

Marius spoke again in his emotionless voice.

'We should find Tullius as well, he must be told.'

The mention of his name made Rhia nervous, though she stroked her husband's shoulder all the same. She was saved from having to comment by Ermingild's thick voice.

'Master Tullius was at house earlier. Him and other officer. Not sure where they go.'

Marius half-turned.

'What other officer?'

Ermingild thought for a second.

'First Tribune.'

Marius turned fully to face him, a flicker of curiosity showing through his blank mask.

'Tribune Cadmus?'

The slave nodded and Marius covered his frown quickly, turning to the watchman and speaking smoothly.

'Well, I shall speak to them as soon as possible. Meanwhile, if you do not mind, my family would like some privacy.'

Both the watchman and the physician bowed their heads respectfully and Ermingild escorted them to the door without a word. Marius remained with his father but Rhia did the polite thing and walked their guests towards the doors. They were halfway across the reception room when Rhia noticed something lying on a table and voiced her confusion about it, mostly to herself.

'He never said it was broken.'

The watchman turned around and saw what she'd been looking at.

'No madam, it was not. Until some coward broke the thing across his head. We found it thrown away not far from the gentleman's body, bloodstained and clumsily hidden.'

Rhia looked at him and struggled to keep her own mask in place, then looked back at the two pieces of wood. The watchman shook his head in disapproval.

'What manner of craven attacks a man of his years with his own walking stick? I tell you, this city will boil over with crime if we do not stop it.'

Rhia held up a hand before he began his inevitable rant.

'Indeed so, sir. Many thanks again for your labours. May Father Gron lead you to justice.'

The blessing was an obvious dismissal of the man and he bowed his head once again before walking through the open door, the grey-haired physician leaving with him.

Ermingild closed it behind them, and Rhia spoke to him quietly as he came back.

'Stay here a moment, I shall have work for you.'

The big slave bowed to her and Rhia made for the table, picked up the pieces of Glaucus' broken cane, and hurried back into the bedchamber to Marius. Her husband had not moved much and was back to staring at the body of his father, but he turned around as Rhia closed the door. He opened his mouth to speak but she interrupted.

'Marius, he was killed with this.'

She held up the pieces of wood and for a moment he seemed confused, then his eyes widened a fraction as his mind raced.

'He didn't have it with him. He said he wanted to try walking a stretch without it.'

Rhia finished the thought for him.

'He hadn't the time to go back and get it, not if he was found an hour ago. Someone who was at the house took it and then killed him with it, thinking it might look natural. It was clumsy so he then hid it, but it must have seemed the best way at the time.'

Marius frowned and nodded slowly, his voice filled with suppressed hatred.

'Cadmus.'

Rhia nodded back, relieved that he hadn't mentioned his brother. Tullius was not the man Marius was and he was certainly a danger to them, but she doubted he was capable of murdering his own father. Cadmus on the other hand was a heartless bastard and a dog to Lepidus. She'd once heard him say that a good soldier put his legion before anything else on earth, before country, before family and before gods. *Yes, if Lepidus convinced him it was for the good of the Tenth, that man would smother babies in their cribs.*

329

Marius's face was grim and Rhia saw the resolution outweigh his grief.

'He will pay for this. But we can prove nothing, not yet anyway.' His eyes started darting from side to side as he thought aloud. 'I will write a message to Drusus to investigate as best he can but for now, we must be gone. Lepidus wanted my father out of the way and even without this matter of Praecus, if we start asking questions Lepidus may get rid of us too.'

He began pacing back and forth as the ideas sprang from his mind.

'Lepidus will declare a state of emergency and seize power. From there he will consolidate his popularity with a military victory over the Gorvicae or the Caderyn, and with the general's warmongering unchecked who knows what that sorcerer will get up to.' He looked at his wife. 'You especially are not safe. Nor is your sister and nor is Lucan. Lepidus sees no need for such alliances with the tribes and you might become a symbol through which Gaians or Caderyn might form a peace. And he has no love of that.'

Rhia touched his arm and spoke softly.

'We will go to Bryngarth, it is as safe a place as any and my people will protect us.' A mix of hope and fear tinged her voice. 'Will you come with us?'

Marius was still thinking aloud.

'The villa at Verrisi is not safe for you, perhaps not for my family either. I shall send word to Livilla and Rabanus to make for Glevia straight away. Mother should still be there and they can find some place of safety, maybe contact Gregor Galerian at Corinia. I can send Ermingild with the message, he is loyal to our family unto death.'

Rhia nodded but then repeated herself.

'Yes. But what of you? Will you come with us?'

Marius touched her hand and looked her in the eyes.

'Bryngarth will be the safest place for my wife and son.' He held her hand a little tighter. 'Where else should I be?'

Rhia threw her arms around him and felt him squeeze her back. She'd been more afraid than she'd admit that he might say no. She tried to tell herself it was because he would be useful to protect and guide them along the road but she soon gave up on that. Lucan needed his father with him. And Gaian though he was, Rhia needed her husband too. She felt tears threaten her eyes but she held them back and composed herself.

'We can take Drenn and Enora with us, they may be questioned. And we must get to Gwen.'

Marius frowned a little.

'A large party is more easily tracked... but so long as we have no more all should be well. I can have horses ready outside the city before dusk. Meanwhile I shall find Tullius and speak with him.'

Rhia worried what exactly he might say or do regarding Tullius. He might be Marius' brother but she did not trust him. She opened her mouth to say something but Marius cut her off, his eyes on hers.

'I know he is loyal to the legion. Damn it all, so am I. But family must come before all.' His eyes started moving as he began planning again. 'I will go to the barracks and tell Lepidus I wish for time to mourn my father and that I'm going to stay with Livilla in Verrisi. Hopefully he won't object to my staying out of his way. While I'm there I can maybe speak to Lothar. There are plenty of legion men who trust me as I trust them, perhaps I can let him know to keep his eyes open.'

Rhia wanted to object but she knew it would do no good. Marius would be cautious, his son's life was at stake after all, and Centurion Lothar was a good man. Rhia remembered the bond that was formed when warriors fought side by side and she could hardly blame her husband for wanting to warn his men of their danger. Because whatever Lepidus might think, with a sorcerer practicing his skills on the soldiers, danger was exactly what they were in. Marius continued.

'Hopefully I can find Tullius there, and I pray Vulco I do not bump into Cadmus.'

His voice had become hard and Rhia took his meaning at once. He was afraid, genuinely afraid, that if he saw the man that they suspected had murdered Glaucus in cold blood he would forget the wider view of their predicament and simply kill him there and then. Marius Dessida was not a man prone to bouts of temper, but Rhia knew him well enough to know the passion that lay beneath the calm façade. He loved his family more than anything in this world and if he saw his father's murderer he would not be able to stop himself, and at best he would find himself arrested and condemned. She nodded her head.

'Very well. What will you tell Tullius?'

Marius was clearly still working that part out and waved his hand irritably as he spoke.

'I will tell him Father was murdered and that we are all in danger. I can leave the details out of it until we are clear.'

Rhia felt bad for saying it but someone had to bring this up.

'And if he decides he is more loyal to Lepidus and to the legion than to you?'

Marius' voice grew cold.

'He won't.'

Rhia hated to do it but Lucan was at risk. She pushed.

'I pray not, but what if…'

He interrupted impatiently.

'I will leave speaking with him until last, and if I suspect he might betray us I will deal with it, alright?'

Rhia nodded quietly. He clearly didn't want to think about this and she had no wish to antagonise him further.

They were about to have a very long ride together. Marius looked back at his father but kept talking, half to himself.

'I'll have Drusus arrange the funeral. We will have to leave tonight, under cover of darkness. If you, me, Gwen and Tullius all leave at once the very day my father was murdered it will cause gossip straight away. If we tell everyone we are closeted in mourning and then slip out quietly, we can be well away before Lepidus knows we're gone.'

Rhia stroked his shoulder again and felt another pang of sympathy for her husband. Only an hour ago he'd been told his father had been killed and now he stood here in his presence, talking of how to use their grief as a cloak to escape from his murderers. Her brave husband kept on planning, his eyes still on his father.

'We can use a wagon to get through the gates at dusk when the traders are leaving the city. I'll send fast horses out early with a slave I can trust on the pretext of giving them exercise. We could meet him at the pine grove by the lake, you know the place?'

Rhia nodded.

'Yes. But if you're seeing Tullius last of all we'd best meet near the city walls, it would take you too long to meet us back here.'

Her husband bobbed his head a little, still looking at the body.

'I'll have a wagon and supplies ready before I go there. Where shall we meet?'

Rhia pondered a moment before answering.

'I'll send Enora to get Gwen and we can meet you near the left tower of the north gate, there's an open space beside a tanner's where we can wait.'

Marius finally dragged his eyes from Glaucus and faced Rhia squarely again.

'I will meet you there half an hour before dusk. Make sure you wear something plain.'

Rhia nodded. They stood in silence for a moment and Rhia thought of the house she was about to go back to for Lucan. She thought of the red and blue cushions, the tapestries, and the little statues of the gods her husband had given her. Thanks to Marius and Lucan, over five long years of living there the place had finally felt like it was a home. And now she was leaving it forever. She felt sadness mix in with her fear at their predicament but she forced these thoughts away and tried to focus. *Right now we must escape, you can mourn this half-life you've lived here later on. And mourn for Glaucus Dessida.*

Rhia looked at the body of the kindly old man and sent a silent prayer for him to Camelas, the ancient god of fathers. *May he cross the bridge unharmed.* The Lurian god, or the Lurian face of the god or whatever he was, would take good care of a man like this, no matter what crimes his people might have been guilty of.

Once again she felt tears wanting to fall but she pulled herself together and faced her husband.

'Very well. I'll make a start.'

There was another moment's silence and then Marius leaned down to kiss her. It wasn't a passionate kiss exactly, nor a disinterested kiss either, but rather a kiss that conveyed his care for her, hard and strong and powerful. He nodded his head.

'Very well.'

Rhia wasn't sure exactly what she ought to say. The sudden kiss had unbalanced her a little, given the situation they were in. She settled for a nod and then made for the door, though his voice came from behind her before it opened.

'Make sure Lucan has his sword, he'll not go anywhere without it.'

He attempted an easy smile but it was a struggle, and Rhia knew it. She tried to smile back, hoping her own was more convincing.

'I will. I know our boy.'

She'd half turned back to the door again when Marius spoke to her once more, and this time his face was grave and marked with worry.

'And make sure Drenn carries his.'

Chapter 24. The Escape

By the time she'd packed some things, changed into nondescript clothing and gathered the others for their journey, dusk was already dangerously close. Rhia walked briskly through Tamora's stone-paved streets, her brown cloak whipping about her ankles. Every now and then a gust of chilly wind would catch it and she'd find herself having to adjust it again, doing her best to look casual without *looking* like she was trying to look casual. The road at this time wasn't busy but there were enough people and carts about to let them blend in to the crowd. And to keep Rhia's eyes darting nervously about.

The breeze made even the spring evening feel cold, though the chills down her spine had little to do with the weather. She was afraid. Her anger at the Gaians, as well as at herself, was being smothered by her terror of what might go wrong tonight. If Lepidus, or worse still Praecus, suspected that she and hers might cause trouble for them... she flicked a glance over her shoulder, as she did about every ten paces, just to check that Gwen and Lucan were in fact still there behind her, and drove a knuckle into her palm out of habit.

Her sister, dressed plainly as she was, strode along beside Enora with worry etched on her sweet face. According to the slave Gwen had taken some persuading to leave her house at all, and still she seemed uncertain of what they were doing. It was understandable since she clearly lived in terror of displeasing her husband, but all the same Rhia found she felt more irritation than pity. She felt sorry for her sister for whatever it was Tullius had done to her, but right now speed was everything, and Gwen's hesitations had already cost them precious time.

Lucan, mercifully, seemed to have dozed off again over Drenn's huge shoulder. When they had first fled the house her little man had been scared and confused, and still upset after having seen his parents fighting earlier, but the big Greutun slave had been a blessing to them all and had managed to make their daring escape seem more like a game to the youngster. Rhia had been worried that his excitement might draw attention to them, but Drenn had been wiser than she'd known and had exhausted the boy with playing while she and Enora rushed about the house, preparing. It meant that her son was now sleeping peacefully in his arms as his mother fled their home with her heart in her throat.

Rhia nodded to the big man before turning back around, still trying to look casual as she hurried to their destination. They were running late. Marius was to meet them by the tanner's place half an hour before dusk and though the sky above was overcast with heavy, smoke-grey clouds, Rhia could tell from a glance that the light of day would soon be fading. She shrugged her shoulder to adjust her canvas bag and picked up her pace a little, still trying to seem nonchalant. Even were there not the danger of pursuit by Lepidus' soldiers, a conspicuously nervous walker would draw the eyes of every cutpurse in the street, and Rhia's simple-looking sack contained more wealth than most of them could even imagine.

Apart from knowing it was a long way west and around the Canwyn Range, Rhia had little memory of how far it was to her home, or how long it would take them to get there. Her humble canvas bag contained a change of clothes, a woollen blanket, and every coin, jewel and golden cup that she could scavenge from her former home. Marius should be bringing along some supplies as well but food could spoil; gold would keep.

It seemed to take them an age but eventually she caught sight of the tanner's shop below the gate-tower. Just around the corner was an open space hidden from easy view, and she ushered the little group that way. They must have made better time than she'd thought because Marius wasn't there yet, and they huddled together beside the near wall, out of easy sight of the street. Lucan was still snoozing on Drenn's great shoulder and Rhia held back the urge to touch him for fear of waking him up. She nodded to the big slave and indicated Enora, and with great care he passed the sleeping infant into her hands. Lucan was too big for the Basian slave to easily carry any more, but Enora found an empty crate and manoeuvred the boy into sitting on her lap. He didn't stir. Rhia looked at them. *I remember when Enora could hold him in one arm, he was so small.* Drenn moved quietly to the wall and put his back to it. His long cloak concealed a wide-bladed sword and he rested his hand near to it, relaxed but ready.

Rhia watched from the building's shadow as pedestrians passed on the road, seeming oblivious to the group as they plodded out of the city. Outside the walls there was a small town of poorer homes and many traders would be on their way back there after a day of work. With a little good fortune, they would blend in amongst them, unnoticed.

Rhia almost jumped when she felt a hand touching her shoulder and whirled around to see that Gwen was still looking nervous. She spoke in a whisper.

'I still don't understand, are you sure we need to do this?'

Rhia answered with a hard look but Gwen carried on.

'Why would anyone want to murder Glaucus anyway? And even if they did, what danger is that to us?'

Rhia frowned. She felt guilty for not telling her sister the whole truth, but it had seemed simpler just to tell her they were in danger and must run. She heard the fear in Gwen's voice as she carried on, her fingers fidgeting anxiously.

'I left so much in disorder in the house, you know. I'll have a nightmare of a time when we get back.'

Rhia had avoided telling her that in all likelihood they would never see this place again, and was beginning to regret it. *But then if you'd told her everything she'd have even more to doubts and worries than she does now.* Gwen had been speaking in Vulgare out of habit and Rhia answered in Lurian, trying to keep the edge from her voice.

'This isn't the time to worry about that.'

Gwen started to reply in Vulgare but then caught herself and switched to their native language.

'I… it isn't that simple, you know.' Her hand fidgeted frantically. 'I sent out invitations this morning for a supper in two days' time, all to very prominent people. Enora gave me no time to send out any cancellations and even if she had, what could I say? And what will T-Tullius say?'

Rhia did her best not to scowl at her sister. She didn't know if it made things better or worse that she'd told her that Tullius would be meeting them. *Might* be meeting them was the word she had used, of course. She had no confidence at all that he would choose his brother over his general. Rhia looked at Gwen again, practically shaking with nerves as she panicked about invitations and embarrassment. She was ever a shy girl but what had happened to the would-be warrior who had marched with then to Nantwyn? *She found defeat and degradation, much as you did. But she had no loving child or caring husband or warrior's pride to pull her free of it.*

Rhia gently touched her arm.

'All will be well, try not to think on it.'

Gwen shook her head, whispering harshly.

'You don't understand! If Tullius…'

But Rhia interrupted her with a hiss, her patience snapping.

'Enough! Tullius can live with it or the skinny git can go bugger himself!'

Gwen looked horrified.

'You mustn't say that! He's a good husband to me, and I've been so...'

But again Rhia cut in before she finished.

'I said enough! You have done nothing to wrong him and he treats you worse than a slave, I'll not have you defend his attitude any longer!'

She saw tears appear in Gwen's eyes and her lower lip started shaking.

'But all he wants is a son, like his brother has, and I've let him down so badly, and I've...'

Rhia took her by the shoulders and shook her, hard.

'Say nothing bad! You are worth the world and you deserve better than that man. Not all things are within your control and what has happened, happened *to* you, not *because* of you.' She stared in her eyes and spoke slowly. 'You are *not* to blame!'

The tears began to fall down Gwen's chalk-pale cheeks, leaving little trails in the cosmetics as they ran towards her chin. Even as she stared at her, Rhia realised with a jolt that what she'd said was as true of herself as it was of Gwen, it had just taken a great deal of time and some good people to make her realise it. She too had value and deserved happiness in life. What happened at Nantwyn had not been her fault. What happened to Bevan had not been her fault. What happened with Delyn had not been her fault. She had made mistakes, and sometimes her mistakes had led to consequences, and she would do all in her power to make amends for what she'd done. But she had never done anything with evil intent and the wretched tragedies that had befallen her and her tribe were *not* her fault. She was not to blame. *I am not to blame.*

A sudden lightness and freedom seemed to fill her for a moment, and her spirit soared even further as Gwen enveloped her in a hug. Rhia hugged her back and felt her sister convulse in a sob. They stayed there for a while as the light faded from the sky, until Gwen leaned back a little and whispered through her tears.

'T-Tullius, he…'

But once again she was interrupted, not by Rhia this time but by Drenn. The big slave had given them a sharp hiss and then a nod, but then his posture seemed to relax and his hand released his sword's leather grip. Rhia and Gwen looked at him oddly but then a heartbeat later Marius came around the corner. He was dressed in a similar dark cloak to Rhia's own, though she could just about see the outline of a sword belted beneath it. Over each shoulder he'd slung a heavy-looking sack and it took Rhia a moment to realise why she felt unnerved; he was on foot.

He exchanged nods with Drenn and then hurried over to her, wasting no time.

'I've had to leave the cart, the gates are closed.'

Rhia's heart started to hammer and she saw Gwen's hand fly to her mouth, but she kept her voice steady as she answered.

'Do you think Lepidus suspects something?'

Marius shrugged.

'I don't know, but I doubt it. I'm here later than I thought and they may have simply shut them early.'

Rhia nodded, her heart slowing a little but still pounding. However banal the reason for it, the fact was they were still trapped. She glanced over his shoulder.

'Is Tullius with you?'

She saw Gwen struggling to look calm and then fail to hide her relief as Marius answered.

'No. That's why I'm late, I couldn't find him. He was not at the barracks or at his house. I left a message for him at Father's house with instructions to seek refuge with Livilla and Rabanus.'

Rhia probably did a poor job of hiding her own relief but she did her best. He was Marius' brother after all.

'Then you have done all you can. But what now? Can you order the gates opened?'

He shook his head.

'I could, but when the guard is changed they'll mention it to their watch-officer as a matter of course, and by morning Lepidus will know that we have gone.'

Rhia nodded grimly. They could not afford to lose their head-start. She saw only one alternative and it wasn't one she liked.

'Over the wall?'

Marius nodded quietly and she saw Gwen was looking panicky again. Drenn seemed indifferent as to what was going on but Enora, still with Lucan on her lap, looked pale in the fading light. Marius did his best to rally them.

'At least that way we will only leave a sign that *somebody* has left the city in secret, not who. I came prepared for this. I have strong rope in my satchel long enough to get us down.' He looked at them all in turn. 'But we must go now. The guard will change soon and we'll have an easier time evading bored men than we will evading fresh ones.'

Rhia looked around the group and saw fear in all but Drenn. In Marius and, she hoped, in herself it was well-concealed and sensible fear. In Enora and in Gwen especially, it seemed the type that might easily turn to panic, and she decided not to let them think too long.

'You heard him – grab your things and let's be gone!'

Both the women seemed more than wary but they obeyed her all the same, Enora passing Lucan on to Drenn without a word. They gathered up their supplies and Marius took out the rope from his satchel, looping the coil of it over one arm to be sure his sword-hand remained free. Whether he'd be prepared to actually *kill* a fellow soldier if it came down to it, Rhia had no idea. She set her jaw and looked at her Gaian husband. *I doubt if he knows if he would either.*

*

Rhia didn't know exactly how high the city wall was, just that it seemed a great deal higher when standing at the top and looking down than it did when standing at the bottom looking up. The walkway was broad and on the outer side a battlement rose up with merlons that were taller than her head, but on the inner side of the wall there was no barrier to a drop that suddenly seemed a very long one indeed. Marius had been wise in his timing, and the only sentries they'd seen had been bored-looking and tired. They had snuck past one already near the base of the steps and the only other one nearby was the sentinel on the gate tower above them. The light was fading ever faster and a combination of dull grey walls, dull brown cloaks, and a sentry whose job it was to look *out* rather than in, meant they had so far remained unobserved.

Marius had already un-shouldered his rope and packs, and Rhia was busy tying two of those packs together while her husband removed his swordbelt and then made the rope fast to a merlon. Gwen and Enora both huddled as best they could into the battlement's shadow, the slave keeping the now half-awake Lucan close to her. Both women looked scared but were trying to hide it from the boy, who'd been told to keep very quiet for this part of their 'game'. Drenn, his hand near his sword again, stood silent watch over the escapees.

Rhia was glad that for all her fears her hands were mostly steady, and in a few minutes all had been made secure. Marius and Drenn exchanged a few nods and gestures and it seemed that her husband would be going down first to make sure all was clear, with the big slave providing the rearguard. Rhia stepped up but he anticipated her and swept Lucan into his arms. The boy barely made a sound as rope was made secure around him. Marius made several loops from the length to form straps for his feet and then fastened himself to the boy. It took some doing, but he managed to get them both secured and over the battlement, and Rhia watched in well-hidden terror as Drenn slowly lowered her husband and child down the wall. He played the rope out slowly, and every second Rhia felt certain that it would break or his strength give out, or that some soldier would appear and cut the rope and send them plummeting to their deaths, and it was all she could do to make herself breathe steadily.

But eventually, after what seemed like an age, the big slave stopped playing it out and she saw the dim shape at the base of the wall start moving about as he unfastened the straps. She saw the rope jerk as Marius gave it two hard tugs and Drenn began hauling it up again. Next, and quickly, came the packs that contained Marius' sword, and another nightmare came to Rhia's mind, this time of his being attacked down at the wall's base and unable to defend himself, but once again it all went well, and the packs were lowered down and the rope soon brought back up.

Gwen was to be next, and Rhia started coaxing her to her feet. She was nervous, and the absence of Lucan now made her more willing to show it, but eventually she got her up and Drenn started helping her into the straps. It was because their guardian was distracted that none of them saw the man approaching until he was only a few paces away. His voice made them all jump, though Drenn and Rhia both dropped into crouches straight away, ready to fight.

'What is all this?'

The light was dim, and it took Rhia a second to recognise the slender man. She felt wary, but there was no time for subtlety now. She hissed a whisper at her confused-looking brother-in-law.

'Keep your voice down! How did... never mind. We are all in danger here and we have to go.'

Gwen's eyes had widened with fright but Rhia signalled Drenn to keep helping her with the straps. Tullius' expression became even more confused and he stepped closer, eyes scanning around the little group.

'What are you doing here?'

Rhia leaned around the big slave and whispered again.

'I don't have time to explain. Either come with us now or get to Livilla as soon as possible. Marius has sent her a letter explaining everything, meanwhile we *have* to keep moving.'

Given his likely divided loyalties, Rhia hoped fervently that he would take the second option and let them be. Unfortunately he stepped closer still and spoke in an urgent whisper, and she saw a mixture of fear and excitement behind his eyes.

'You're fleeing the city?'

Rhia felt Gwen shaking beside her and prayed that he didn't intend to come along with them. No matter what else he was mixed up in Gwen was afraid of him, and Rhia had no wish to have him around. She nodded.

'Yes.'

Tullius blinked and licked his lips nervously before looking to Gwen. She was having trouble getting her feet securely into the straps as she kept shaking and losing her balance. She met her husband's eyes and then looked away quickly, stumbling some more. Drenn dropped to a knee to try to help and Tullius stepped towards the pair and leaned down. None of them saw the blade until it was too late.

The short legionary sword swept silently from its scabbard and plunged into Drenn's broad back, the tip emerging just below his chest. Even in the dim light Rhia saw the bright red of her bodyguard's blood on it. His plain, honest face convulsed with pain for a second and his eyes flew wide, then with a grunt that spat fresh drops of blood from his mouth, the big man toppled sideways and collapsed to the hard stone floor. Gwen let out a tiny cry and toppled backwards onto the battlement, while Enora simply huddled beside the wall, frozen in place.

Rhia made a sound that was half grunt and half scream and leaped towards the murderer, but Tullius quickly swept the blade clear and levelled it at her face. She pulled herself up short, so close she could smell the fresh blood on the iron. Her eyes darted to Drenn's sheathed sword but Tullius followed her gaze and shook his head, his voice dripping with scorn.

'Now, now. Let's not be having any unladylike thoughts.'

Rhia's thoughts were filled with visions of blood and violence, and it must have shown in her expression because the young man checked himself a second before he started speaking again, and she could tell his attempt at confidence was forced.

'Gods but you've led me a merry chase tonight, and my own wife a part of it to boot. Come here, woman!'

He barked the last words out as a man might call his dog and pointed to a spot on the wall to his left. In the corner of her eye Rhia saw Gwen leaning against the battlement, terror evident in her eyes. She tried to stand her ground and even started to say something.

'I don't...'

But Tullius cut her off.

'Here!'

He pointed again and the defiance left Gwen's face. Rhia wanted to stop her as she meekly approached her husband, but the blade was still held close to her and she knew Tullius would not hesitate to kill. Her mind raced, trying to make some kind of plan. Marius was too far off to help, even assuming he had heard what was happening up here. Drenn was dead and his sword out of reach and Enora was just watching them, wide-eyed. Drenn's dagger was a little closer to her, sheathed at the other side of his belt, but Tullius would surely cut her throat the second she tried to reach for it.

Gwen approached her husband and, in an almost casual gesture, he fetched her a backhanded slap across the face. Rhia tensed to leap at him, her blood boiling, but he pressed the blade closer to her throat, forcing her to stop. He spoke to his wife in a voice that sounded sickeningly reasonable.

'You see what you drive me to? You think I *want* to hurt you?'

Gwen was backing away and shaking her head, not daring to meet her husband's eyes. She stammered out a response.

'N-no.'

Tullius nodded, his words still a hideous parody of caring.

'Of course I don't. But you have to learn how to behave properly, you know that?'

She nodded, still shaking uncontrollably.

'Y-yes.'

Rhia saw a horrid smile appear on his face.

'You can make up for it later tonight, can't you? We can think of something special for you to do for me.'

Her sister didn't seem to have it in her to speak, but she nodded again, fear and panic plain on her sweet face. Rhia felt her limbs shaking with rage but she somehow managed to hold it back. She wanted to scream but wrestled it down to a growl.

'How? How did you know we were here, Tullius?'

That sickening smile turned on Rhia and even as he answered she felt a blow hit the side of her face. The punch had neither strength nor technique but it caught her by surprise and Rhia staggered and dropped to one knee, leaning on Drenn's still-warm body for support.

'I have friends.'

Rhia looked up from where she lay to see Enora, her personal slave and trusted friend, standing over her, shaking her hand as though she'd hurt it. A detached part of Rhia's brain told her the Basian slave must not have struck her properly and had likely sprained her wrist when she'd punched. Most of her was filling with even more anger and a physical sense of nausea as she thought of how many times she'd left Lucan with this woman, how many secrets they'd shared, how many private moments. She watched as Enora moved to Tullius' side and draped an arm casually over his shoulder, slipping into place there with an easy familiarity. The young man smirked as she kissed his cheek.

'Enora has been mine since we were little more than children.' He gave her rump a hard slap and the slave smiled mischievously. 'She was my first, and though Father saw fit to send her to Antonius' house, she will always be mine in her heart.'

His free hand stroked her cheek. Rhia felt as though her whole world had just been thrown into a tumble, careening uncontrollably like a barrel down a hillside. *I trusted you, Enora.* Behind Tullius Gwen was still shrinking away, and Rhia gathered from her look that she hadn't known of this, but that it came as no great surprise either. Rhia remembered the time she'd found Marius with a slave girl and how jealous she'd been, and that was back when she had barely known him. Gwen it seemed had grown used to her husband bedding slaves. Tullius started talking again, half to Rhia and half to himself.

'It'll be nice to have Enora more often, now I don't need her to keep an eye on you anymore. And now that Father isn't around to object.'

Rhia saw him smile and realised the full horror of what this man was. Her only hope for reasoning with him had been to tell him about Cadmus' killing of his father. It seemed that was no longer an option. The slender man sighed.

'You've no idea, Rhianna, how good it felt to snap that cane over his thick head after all these years. After two decades of hearing about the wondrous Antonius and the beautiful Livilla, and how proud they were making him every day. After six long years separated from my favourite toy.' He stroked Enora's cheek again. 'And five long years of a forced marriage to a barren, barbarian whore.'

Rhia felt her hands start to shake but she controlled herself. She had to think. Her fall had placed her within reach of Drenn's knife and if she was quick enough, she might get a chance to use it on this odious man. This man who had murdered his own father; a good and kind old man who'd been dedicated to his family and his people. Tullius was smirking as he spoke, enjoying his position of power over her.

'Oh, you can glare all you like, Rhianna. Glare and spit at me as much as you want, it will do you no good. Praecus wants to question you but he can wait a little while, he told me. He won't mind if I keep you and break a little of your defiance before he questions you.' He jerked his head towards where Gwen leaned against the wall, still terrified. 'Your sister had a little of that in her when I started but it died out pretty fast. Something tells me I'll have a harder time of it with you, but Enora and I do enjoy a challenge.'

He turned and kissed the slave and Rhia edged her hand down to where she knew the knife to be. It nestled just behind her left hip and the movement she needed was subtle. She felt the wood of the handle beneath her palm but stopped shy of drawing as Tullius looked back at her, eyeing her up and down like he was purchasing a horse.

'Yes, a challenge. I think the first thing to do will be to knock a few teeth out, I'll have a use for your mouth that you just might object to.'

Rhia felt suddenly cold as flashes of Delyn and the barn came back to her. That feeling of helplessness, and the endless shame that had followed her for so long afterwards. For a moment she felt very scared and alone and her fingers started twitching uncontrollably. But then Enora, her dear Enora, made the mistake of chiming in.

'You'll let me indulge myself a little too, I hope? There are all sorts of things I'd like to try with her...'

But the Basian slave got no further than that. Her words, her smile, her confirmation that this trusted friend was as much a monster as her master, was all the fuel Rhia needed to let her rage burn away her fear. In a single, smooth motion, the daughter of Carradan drew the knife, sprang to her feet, and rammed the dagger's point into her former handmaid's throat. The iron ripped through flesh like it was butter and when Rhia sliced the blade free, bright blood sprayed onto Tullius' face.

The slender man blinked and stumbled back but Enora's falling body got in Rhia's way as she tried to follow, and by the time the path was clear he had the sword up and ready again. His bloodstained face was a twisted mask of pure hatred and his voice had changed from mocking to a guttural-sounding snarl.

'I will rip you in half for that! Once I'm done with you, you will be *begging* me to end it!'

Beside him, Rhia saw Gwen rise to her feet and make towards him.

'Tullius, you...'

But another slap from him, much harder this time, sent her crumpling to the ground where she lay still.

'Shut up, whore!'

If Gwen heard him she gave no sign of it. She simply lay still. Rhia darted forwards but Tullius' blade had the reach on her and she was forced to keep her distance again. The young man bared his teeth.

'Oh no you don't!'

Rhia kept her grip firm and stared him in the eyes, her words slow and deliberate.

'You will not do that again.'

Tullius smiled at her and started walking forwards, forcing her back and hiding Gwen from her sight. Rhia wanted to look around him to make sure she was still breathing but she forced herself to focus on her enemy. He was still moving forwards, a wicked gleam in his eye.

'Will I not? And who will stop me when you are bound up in my cellar, with a line of giant slaves waiting to plough you one after the other? How will you keep me from disciplining my own wife when you're bleeding and crying and begging me to kill you? Who will stand to defend your useless slut sister when I have you pinned to my wall and you're weeping as you choke?'

Rhia felt her fear begin to creep up again as the blade flicked closer to her face. Tullius was mad, she saw that now, and mad in the most dreadful and perverse of ways. He would do everything he threatened and more if he took her alive. *He will not take me alive*, she decided calmly.

Marius and Lucan have already escaped. He cares for me but he cares more for our son, he will get him to safety. She ground her teeth. *And even to wound this monster will be worth it. At least Taran will think me a little redeemed.*

Rhia glared up at the soldier and braced herself to spring. He would lunge forwards first and then cut to the side if she dodged, and she would have only one chance to stab at him before the iron bit into her body. She wondered how much it would hurt to die, but then remembered she didn't care. She would not be made the plaything of this sickening man who had tormented her sister. She would die as she wished she had lived – as a Caderyn.

She tightened her grip on the blade and Tullius' eyes widened as he read her intent but he never had the chance to lunge forwards. From behind him, silent as a shadow, Gwendolyn daughter of Carradan crashed into her husband's midriff and drove him three paces sideways, and then out into empty air. She did not let go as he struggled, nor had she intended to, and husband and wife plummeted into the night, still locked in their final embrace.

'Gwen!'

Rhia's cry came out shrill and harsh as she leaped forwards to try to save her. It was drowned out by the panicked scream of Tullius as he hurtled to the ground, and almost instantly cries of alarm went up along the wall. A dull thud came from somewhere below her and Rhia felt her sorrow crash over her like a wave, and for a second felt as though she might actually drown in it. She staggered, righted herself, and then staggered again, leaning hard against the merlon to which the rope was tied. Emotions raged behind her eyes but a distant voice somehow made itself heard over the commotion.

'Rhia?'

It was coming from below her and, though he was barely a grey outline in the night, she recognised it. It was the voice of her husband. *He is waiting for you with Lucan. With Lucan! You have to go, Rhia, and you have to go now!* She looked back at the bodies of Drenn and Enora, and thought of the other two that would now be lying at the base of the wall. Rage fled in the face of grief but she forced herself to listen to her fears. *If you do not move now you will never see him again. You can mourn for the others later but now you have to go. Move!*

Fear for her son galvanised her into action and without a backwards glance Rhia caught hold of the rope and swung herself over the wall. The climb down must not have been easy, and she was sure that more than once she almost fell, but at no point in the journey did Rhia really know what she was doing. Her thoughts were all for her sweet sister, and she prayed for her as she descended.

Gwendolyn, daughter of Carradan, lived in fear but died with courage. May she cross the bridge unharmed. Taran, Mabonac, Camelas and Annwn, Gron, Vulco, Cassio and Sulis, may her killer know only endless torment as he falls and climbs and falls again. May his eyes never see the green fields of the Otherworld. She squeezed out tears of grief and told herself they were all of rage. *May Dis and every god who values justice unleash eternal holy vengeance on Occidus Dessidus Tullius!*

Chapter 25. The Sorcerer

Cadmus felt his knee begin to throb as he made his way
down the steps. It usually only played up in cold or damp
weather but for some reason today it had decided that
stairs were the enemy. The tribune kept up his pace and
resisted the urge to grimace. Cadmus had been a soldier
for more than twenty years and little things like aches and
pains were beneath his giving them notice. *Though they
are getting more numerous and more common these days,
old man. Your fortieth winter has been and gone and your
body reminds you of it every morning.* He shook it off
irritably. He might be getting older but there was no point
in harping on about it. Besides, he had other things to
focus on.

He reached the base of the steps and continued along the
corridor, eyes keen even in the half light. The little
magicker was probably with his pet Aborans in their
chamber and he strode on towards the door at the end of
the passage. The general was not happy with his strange
advisor, and Cadmus was there to make that clear to him.
In truth the veteran soldier was fairly sure that the general
was glad enough to have his enemies out of the way, but
he disapproved of bare-faced murder, and he disapproved
of deception from his subordinates even less. As far as
Cadmus was concerned, so long as the legion was kept out
of it, these soft-hearted old soldiers and whining
politicians could all go to the wolves together, but General
Lepidus was a man of principle, and so this little magicker
needed a talking-to.

An Aboran Destroyer stood guard beside the door to the
ritual chamber, and Cadmus locked eyes with the giant
without fear. He might have envied their immense
strength, especially as he suspected his own would soon be
leaving him, but they were still inferior to the legions, and

it was important that they understood this. All the magic potions and chanted prayers in the world were no substitute for iron discipline, and in that the Tenth Legion was mightier than a Titan. Without even realising it he stuck his chest out a little, the better to show this auxiliary the gold lion on his crimson tunic. The Aboran came to attention and gave what presumably passed for a salute among these people. Cadmus nodded his head a tiny fraction in response and marched through the doorway without a word.

Sure enough, in the spacious chamber he saw a handful of the Destroyers receiving blessings and elixir from the greasy-haired magician. The tribune approached him confidently, despite his knee, and found himself comparing the man to the general he'd followed since Avidia; the comparison was not a favourable one. Where Lepidus was tall and lean, Praecus was short and slight, but with enough bulge showing at his belly to betray his weakness for soft living. Where the general was stern and upright, the sorcerer was round-shouldered and cringing. And where Severus Lepidus was a soldier in the best sense of the word, Contis Praecus was... he didn't even know *what* he was.

Cadmus wasted no time and addressed the sorcerer with a voice that might have been born for the parade-ground.

'Advisor Praecus, the general is displeased with your latest antics.'

The little man turned to face him with a sickeningly servile smile, and Cadmus felt contempt well up inside him.

'My dear Tribune Cadmus, you must know that I have done the general nothing but good by my actions, and what your own officers choose to do is beyond my control.'

There was truth in that of course, but Tullius would never have acted so boldly without the magicker's encouragement. Besides, it set a bad precedent to let Praecus act too much on his own initiative.

'That is by the by. We are here to obey orders.'

The little man nodded slowly and said something to the nearest auxiliary, who grunted in understanding. He turned to his fellows and they bowed away from the sorcerer, moving over to another part of the room where they sat on the stone floor, quiet as a pack of children awaiting their tutor. Praecus turned his attention back to the soldier.

'Our orders are to assist the general in the subduing of the tribes, an action far more important than even he knows. I did just that.'

Cadmus studied the man for a moment. He had clearly meant to arouse his curiosity by his remarks, yet for all the obviousness of the ploy the old soldier couldn't help himself.

'What do you mean?'

The little man smiled again.

'I am glad that you asked. You seem a solid man, Cadmus. I like the general but he is sometimes too much an idealist whereas you... you strike me as a man who gets done what needs doing.'

What that said about how his morality came across, Cadmus wasn't quite sure. He liked to think he had his own code, but it was true enough that he was no weakling, and that sometimes bad things needed to be done for the greater good of the Empire. And Cadmus was proud to be a man who would serve his Empire and legion in such a way. He responded to the half-compliment with a simple nod and the sorcerer continued, his voice conspiratorial but still sensibly shy of friendly.

'It is their druids. They must be removed, and quickly.'

Cadmus furrowed his brow. While leaders like these druids were often the focal points for rebellion, in the end they accepted the truth the same as anyone else; the Gaians are the future, you can work with them, or you can be destroyed.

'We keep a watch on any troublemakers, don't you worry.'

Praecus shook his head and his voice became more earnest.

'It is more than that. Daeria is one of the few remaining places where such druids still practice their lore openly, and our armies will soon drive the last of them into the sea.' He lowered his voice and leaned in closer to the soldier. 'But it is in these last days that they will be at their most dangerous. They have power tribune, power beyond anything even they can fully comprehend, and if pushed to desperation they may call upon that power. To the ruin of us all.'

Cadmus tried not to recoil from him. The little man made him uneasy despite himself, and all this talk of magic was beyond him.

'This is hardly my area. I merely came here to tell you of the general's orders; you are to obtain his approval, either directly or through myself, before undertaking any more such *assistance* as you have done. You take great risks and he will not have you jeopardise his plans.'

The sorcerer shrugged his shoulders.

'The risks I take are minimal but I will adhere to his wishes. We want the same thing after all.'

Cadmus sneered a little. He was far from convinced of that second part, and pretty unsure of the first part come to that.

'It was a risk bringing Dessidus Rhianna down here. Tullius told me you almost performed your... craft in front of her.'

Praecus shrugged again, unconcerned.

'I was reacting instinctively to a potential escapee. Besides she has likely seen some form of robus used before, to say nothing of the fact that the prisoner was a Gorvic and her enemy. She killed him herself out of panic and rage, I felt it. And the hatred flowing through her,' he shivered a little, 'it was intense. Likely she'd have welcomed watching me set light to the man.'

Cadmus wasn't sure what unsettled him more, the man's apparent ability to sense people's emotions, or the blind arrogance that seemed to come with it. He had felt hate and fear and rage alright, he'd just assumed it was directed at the captive. The soldier put scorn into his voice and tried his best to think blank thoughts.

'Unfortunately we are in no position to ask her. She and Tribune Dessida fled the city tonight, along with their boy. It looks like his brother tried to stop them and both he and his barbarian wife fell to their deaths. Our best guess is they are heading west, back to her homeland.'

Praecus' look of confusion quickly became one of alarm.

'But she hated him, she… they must be stopped!'

His eyes were wide and Cadmus enjoyed seeing the clever bastard on edge. All this talk of magic and druids and *robus* made him uneasy and it was good to be able to speak of something that he understood. He put on his best 'patronising civilians' voice.

'Don't you worry yourself, our scouts were after them within an hour of the alarm and Flavian knows his trade well. Besides, the legions will be moving west as well soon enough, just as soon as the general can wangle it.'

For all that it was distasteful, the killings arranged by Praecus had paved a smoother way for Lepidus to seize power, and Cadmus would be glad to be on the march again. *Not that your knee will thank you for it.* He ignored the pessimism in his head and focused instead on capturing young Antonius. He had shown a certain promise in a naïve sort of way, but that he would betray the Tenth like this was beyond despicable. Cadmus would enjoy taking his head for it.

Praecus had crossed to a low table nearby and was swigging back a cupful of wine. He did not offer Cadmus a drink and carried on speaking once he'd swallowed.

'If they reach the Caderyn and she tells… our plans must be expedited. The legions must be augmented as soon as possible.'

Cadmus frowned, disapproving of this panicky reaction.

'You've nothing to concern yourself about, these precious druids…'

But the little man interrupted him and began pacing nervously back and forth, speaking half to himself, half to the officer.

'The Fourteenth have reached the first stage with few enough problems, they can be moved forwards. The Tenth must begin their augmentation straight away.'

Cadmus was not so sure about that. He'd seen what Abellan and the Fourteenth boys were capable of, but the vital discipline of the legion had clearly been compromised by their new strength. The Tenth were the best because they trained to be the best, and he had definite scruples about putting his men through whatever this magicker had in mind for them. He knew the general did as well. Praecus seemed to, or perhaps *did*, read his thoughts and spoke offhandedly, as if annoyed that his own stream of thoughts had been interrupted by the soldier's.

'The dosage for non-Aborans has been fully tested now, Tribune Cadmus. Your men will receive only the very best and I shall manage their robus with care, I can assure you.'

Cadmus was unnerved by this sudden perceptiveness and tried to mask his thoughts as he replied.

'Maybe.'

The magicker gave an exasperated shake of his head and took a few quick steps towards the soldier. Cadmus was surprised by how nervous that made him. He was no hero but he was a bold enough man and twice the size of this greasy little fellow. But he was a greasy little fellow with powers that the veteran had no way of understanding and, more than that, he moved with a confidence that made it clear he was not in the least bit intimidated by him.

Without a second's hesitation he seized Cadmus' hand in both of his and muttered a word or two with half-closed eyes. The tribune jerked his hand away in a heartbeat, but not before he'd felt a warmth pulse through his skin and seep into his bones. The magicker stepped back and simply watched him for a moment, looking impatient.

It was strange, yet not unpleasant, and Cadmus felt the warmth pass up his arm and pause at his shoulder, where long ago the muscle had torn when his shield had been ripped from his arm. The warmth lingered there for a moment and then continued on its way, but not before the dull ache, the one he barely registered any more it was so familiar, vanished from his body without a trace. The old soldier blinked and looked down at the arm, and rolled the shoulder a few times as the warmth spread to his chest. The joint felt strong, with no grinding or clicking as he moved it, and by the time the warmth had reached his waist, his back, which he hadn't realised had been tense, suddenly relaxed as if he sat in a warm bath.

He looked at the sorcerer in fear and wonder as the warmth paused at his knee and the pain from that disappeared as well. The little man smiled a narrow smile, clearly feeling he had better things to do with his time.

'This is but a taste, without any of my elixir or my rituals. The strength and power that I can give you is beyond anything you can imagine, Cadmus. Through me, you and all the Tenth could become the greatest warriors that the Empire has ever seen.'

His voice became smoother as the warm feeling faded away, though Cadmus' aches and pains did not come back.

'With the robus that I can give you no enemy could stop you, and no amount of bitter winters could dull your strength. Imagine the life you might lead, the victories you might enjoy? Tell the general what you have experienced. He has seen what my elixir can do but he trusts you more than any living man. Tell him what you feel right now, and you and your legion can fulfil your full potential. Yours will become the greatest military unit that has ever fought a battle.'

'We already are.'

Cadmus' answer came out automatically but he was still reeling from the sensation of the magic. It was as if twenty years' worth of scars had been lifted from him, leaving behind only the lessons he had learned from them, secure in a body that felt young and strong again. Somehow he knew that what he felt now would only be temporary, and he found himself fantasising about what he might become with more of this. Cadmus was a strong and fearsome man, the finest soldier in a legion of fine soldiers. What might he become if he took in more of this magic, this *robus*? Seeing it in others was one thing but *feeling* it was something else entirely. He felt his natural distrust of the sorcerer start to lose the battle to curiosity and need.

Praecus was still looking at him and Cadmus forced himself to calm down.

'I shall think on it. Meanwhile magicker, I have work to do. I trust you understand my message from the general?'

Cadmus fought back his fantasising and kept his face as stern as possible, though he strongly suspected that Praecus was not fooled by the façade. The little man bowed his head, hands held close in supplication, and gave yet another of his sickening smiles.

'Of course, tribune. Of course.'

Chapter 26. The Mountain

The mighty Canwyn Mountains were wreathed in fine mist as the fugitives trundled past their bases. For the first time in six days they were risking travelling by road, though the path they were on was not the stone-paved highway of the Gaians that ran north of them, but a simple dirt-track that clung closer to the towering mountains. The older road ran perilously close to the domain of the Carrocks but so far they had not seen any, or not for certain anyway. Rhia had heard some worrying tales of the diminutive mountain folk, but she comforted herself in thinking that the Carrocks weren't actively *looking* for them. The same could not be said for her husband's former comrades.

Rhia leaned forward in her saddle, weary and afraid all at once, and took another backwards glance towards the east. They had lost sight of Tamora before dawn on their first day, and now all she saw behind them was more and more patchy woodland, not a creature in sight larger than a sparrow. She turned back to face west and prayed quietly that it would stay that way. For their first three days the pursuit had been hot over open ground, and the sight of Gaian soldiers had been a constant fear for them. Once or twice they had come so close she'd seen sunlight glinting from their helmets, and had been certain that they would be overtaken.

But whether by the grace of the gods or the speed of their mounts they had reached a swollen river late on the fourth day, and had just barely managed to ford it. Lucan had been terrified and even Rhia had feared they would be swept away by the rushing water, but they'd made it to the west bank in safety and then taken good care of their tracks. Splashing upstream for what felt far longer than necessary, they came out of the chilly water on a rocky patch of ground and led the horses carefully onto the road.

Since then, with minimal tracks and no scent to follow, they had dared to stay on this simple dirt path, clinging closely to the mountains where the trees would keep them hidden. *Of course, it would keep any pursuers hidden too, but best not to think about that. It won't do you any good.*

Rhia looked across to her husband. Marius was looking grim, his eyes focused straight ahead of him. It was currently his turn to share his horse with Lucan, and their son was keeping unhappily quiet in the face of his father's mood. Rhia herself had hardly been merry on their journey, which the boy had learned by now was not just a complex game, but at least she'd tried to smile at him now and then. Marius on the other hand had worn the same perpetual scowl for six long days and nights, communicating in short, concise sentences, and then only sparingly. Rhia worried that Lucan thought he might have done something wrong and resolved to speak with him quietly once night fell and they made camp. There was no point at all in speaking to Marius.

She hadn't been able to bring herself to lie to him when she'd reached the base of the wall that night, though she liked to think she had been kind in sparing him the details. She had told him that Enora had betrayed them to Lepidus, and that Tullius had been sent to bring them back to him. She said that they had quarrelled and that Tullius had grown angry, killing Drenn and threatening both Gwen and herself, and that in a struggle with his wife he had stumbled and both had fallen to their deaths. It was mostly the truth after all, and to tell him more would only have hurt him. *And he is hurt enough. The Tullius I knew may have been a monster but Marius knew him since they were children, and no child is born evil.*

Rhia looked again at her own boy, a child whose father's army had conquered her people and killed her first husband, and knew she could never hate him for it. Even when he misbehaved he was so innocent, and she loved him as dearly as if he were Bevan's child. And for all his sullen silence she knew that Marius loved him too. She considered striking up a conversation with him but she knew it would do her no good, and the awkwardness might further upset Lucan. *I will speak to him tonight perhaps, after Lucan is asleep.* It was a long way from here to Caderyn lands, through all the territory of the Bearnicans and skirting close to the lands of both the Gorvicae and the Carrocks. Even discounting Lepidus' pursuit or any hostile locals, the road they took might harbour bandits around any turn of it, and she'd heard tales that kellas cats still prowled in the mountains' shadow. A long and dangerous way for a family to travel in awkward silence.

They plodded along through the evergreens and Rhia wondered why she wasn't as crushed by Gwen's death as Marius was by Tullius'. Perhaps it was because she was accustomed to grief and had learned to live with it the hard way after losing so much already? Perhaps it was because the Gwen she'd grown up with and loved had been fading into nothingness for years, and to see her die with pride and heroism was… not a relief exactly, nor even really a comfort, but something somehow similar to both. Rhia had cried more than once for her sweet sister, but she was not so helpless in her grief as she had been before.

Marius on the other hand had taken his loss hard, and since it came so soon after his father's death, it was perhaps not so surprising. Rhia had of course kept secret Tullius' confession to the murder, but even discounting that Marius was now, perhaps for the first time in his life, lost and alone. He had no family to turn to, no general to report to, no Empire to serve. He was just a man on the run with his wife and child, running towards a people who might kill him as much as welcome him. All in all, she thought, he could be doing worse than riding in silence.

Rhia ignored her earlier advice to herself and urged her mount closer to his. Her husband didn't react but little Lucan risked a smile and Rhia smiled back as best she could. Marius kept his eyes forwards and didn't look as Rhia touched his arm. She wasn't really sure what to say, she couldn't say much in front of Lucan anyhow, but she felt that she had to say *something*. He was in such pain, that was obvious, and she was his wife after all, in spite of everything. She started speaking without any real idea of what came out.

'Marius, we…'

But his hand quickly went to his mouth and he turned his face towards her. His grey eyes were flat and hard and he'd not shaved since they had left, giving his solid jaw a ragged dressing of stubble. He looked tired and stern. And wary.

'Not so loud.' He whispered and flicked his eyes towards the mountains. 'Watchers.'

He had spoken in Lurian, which Lucan understood less well than Vulgare, and Rhia had the sense not to move straight away. As casually as she could she turned her face in the direction he had indicated, and at first she saw nothing untoward. The mountain slope was still bathed in mist but beyond grass, trees and rocks there was nothing to be seen. Then a tiny movement caught her eye and it was an effort not to reach for her knife. Beside one of the boulders, indistinct but definitely there, crouched what looked like a very short, very stocky man, his grey-brown cloak making him almost invisible against his surroundings. It was only his movement that had let her see him at all and even now he was difficult to focus on. Marius spoke quietly once more, again in the Lurian Tongue.

'They've been watching since last night. Archers. If they wanted us dead then we would be already but all the same don't stare. Just keep moving. Not a word in Vulgare.'

Rhia nodded her head a little. From what little she knew of Carrocks they were not an aggressive people exactly, but they kept themselves to themselves and were very jealous of their territory. And they had no great love for the Gaians. Rhia glanced down at the Gaian dress she wore and was glad her simple cloak mostly covered it. She looked across to Marius and tried to comfort herself that the only overtly Gaian thing he carried was his sword. Beyond that, and their bulging packs, they seemed relatively inconspicuous and she prayed quietly to Karanon, the Lord of the Mountains, that these Carrocks would know them as friends. Or at least, not as obvious enemies.

She glanced back to where she'd seen the grey-clad archer by the rocks but he had disappeared from sight, either fled or gone to ground. Rhia took a deep breath and unconsciously placed herself between his last position and where Lucan sat, the boy still looking confused. She doubted they would let fly at an infant, but after the losses she had suffered in the last few days, Rhia was leaving nothing to chance.

*

Night was falling fast when they finally halted for the day. Lucan had become tired and cross as well as afraid but Rhia had calmed him down and he now lay with them at the foot of a tall pine, wrapped in a blanket and snoring softly. As escapes went, she thought, they had at least picked a good time of year for it. Though there was still a thin mist about the mountain there was no rain and the ground was dry. Despite not having seen anyone following them since the river, both she and Marius had agreed to light no fires at night, relying instead on their thick blankets and one another's heat for warmth. They sat like that now, huddled close together beside their son, and Rhia whispered gently to her husband.

'I've not seen any more since that one at the boulder. You?'

She felt him shake his head beside her.

'I thought I did as I was tying up the horses but I might have been imagining it.'

Rhia nodded.

'I know what you mean. I've been jumping at every shadow all day.'

Marius grunted quietly but said nothing and the pair lapsed into silence. Rhia wondered if this was a good time to try to talk to him about his grief. He wouldn't want to, but it might do him good to air his feelings a little.

'Marius, I know you're in pain. If you think it might help to talk about it…'

She tailed off, not really sure what she should say next. For a while there was silence between them again, but just as she thought she ought to try something else, Marius let out a sigh.

'I keep expecting to wake up and find this is all some terrible dream. It's as if… as if everything I thought I knew, everything that was solid and stable in my life… it's just gone.'

Rhia knew it hadn't been easy for him to say that and she rummaged in the blankets until she found his hand. She squeezed it encouragingly.

'Believe it or not, I know exactly how you feel. It is hard. Very hard. But you will overcome it in time.' She nodded to the sleeping child beside them, nestled between their packs and his father's leg. 'And you have him at least.'

Marius sighed again as he looked down at Lucan. He managed a smile.

'I do. I suppose if my world had to be turned upside down I was blessed to keep him with me through it all.' He gave her hand a squeeze of his own. 'And I'm glad to have you with me, and not just because you're his mother.'

He leaned over and planted a gentle kiss on her forehead and Rhia felt a little warmth inside her at the touch. Complex as the situation was, it was nice to have somebody here who cared for her, and she nuzzled in a little closer to him.

'I'm glad to have you with me too. And not just because you're his father.'

Marius shuffled a little, taking care not to disturb the sleeping Lucan, and put an arm around her shoulders. It was strange. They were husband and wife after all, they had coupled together more times than she could count, and Rhia was fully prepared to admit that she would like them to again. Yet somehow here, huddled together beneath a tree, she felt closer and more intimate with him than she ever had in their bed.

Rhia closed her eyes. On the first few nights of their escape they had set a watch, sleeping only half a night each, but there seemed little point to that here. They'd seen no pursuit since the river, and the Carrocks that Rhia was certain were still watching them would have attacked by now if they meant them harm. Besides, all three were exhausted and needed the rest.

She was just getting drowsy when she heard it; a shuffling in the undergrowth that seemed louder than the usual background noise of the wood. Her eyes snapped open and she felt Marius' body tense beside her. He'd heard it too. They both stayed as still as they could and began scanning the trees for the source of the sound. The horses were asleep, tethered a few paces away, but otherwise she could see nothing but the trees. The sky was already black and the half-moon cast only a faint grey light. Rhia saw no movement, but she did hear the sound again, accompanied by something that made her blood run icy cold; voices.

They were faint, the men were only whispering to each other in the dark, but the indistinct words sounded frighteningly like Vulgare. Marius started moving very slowly, wary of making the least noise. He carefully wrapped Lucan up in his blanket and gently held him out to Rhia. Rhia slowly adjusted herself so that one satchel was on her shoulder before accepting the child and holding him close to her. He was a lot bigger than he used to be but she could still manage him, just about. Her heart was hammering in her chest but she fought to remain calm. They'd not been sighted yet, and they might easily slip away quietly without incident. She held Lucan close to her and prayed to Karanon than his mountains would keep them hidden.

Marius rolled up their blanket and gathered their things, making sure that his sword was still within easy reach. He was moving with what seemed like an agonising slowness, but Rhia knew that it was necessary if they were to minimise their noise. The shuffling in the undergrowth seemed to be coming closer, though whatever the men were talking about, it seemed it had been resolved. Marius gave her a nod and jerked his head roughly southwest towards the slope. It took them further from the road but the rockier ground would be harder to track, and hopefully they could find a spot to observe anyone coming up at them. Rhia wanted to kick herself for not suggesting they had gone there in the first place before they slept, but she had never been tracked across a country for days on end before and neither, it seemed, had her husband.

He seemed to be doing a competent job of it however and from the frustration on his face had clearly thought the same thing she had. With her pack on her back and Lucan in her arms her shrug was only a subtle one, but it looked like he understood and he came close to an ironic smile. They would have to leave the horses, waking them would cause too much noise, and reluctantly the two began walking, with frequent looks behind them in the direction of the sound. It was faint, but still there, and Rhia felt as if every brush of a leaf on her cloak or swish of grass beneath her feet was now something deafeningly loud.

They managed to get quite far from where they'd started, and Rhia had high hopes as they reached a little crop of boulders with a good view down the steady slope. They were almost relaxing as they slipped around out of easy sight, and Marius even let out a tiny sigh of relief. And then Lucan woke up.

He wasn't really all that loud, no more than conversational, but in the deadly silence that they had so carefully been keeping, his voice might as well have been the roaring of a lion.

'What's happening mama?'

The words seemed to echo around the woodland like a warcry and Rhia's heart leaped to her throat. Away down the slope she heard the voices again, speaking louder now, and this time she definitely recognised Vulgare.

'It came from that way!'

Rhia frantically shushed the child and looked at Marius, who was hiding his fear well. It was there, just as hers was, but he made his face a mask and kept his voice low and calm.

'Well, not much use hiding now.' He shucked off his pack and removed his cloak. 'They'll find the horses soon enough. Try to get further up the slope and then cut across west again, they might struggle to track you.'

Rhia stared at him as he fumbled in one of the packs.

'What do you mean?'

He drew out a short-sleeved shirt of mail and quickly threw it over his head.

'They know we're here now and we can't outrun them with Lucan. I'll keep them occupied while the two of you head further up, with a little help from Fortuna I'll kill a couple then give them the slip. Keep going and I'll meet you both at Nantwyn.'

He started buckling his belt on over the mail and Rhia saw shapes moving further down the slope. Their horses were stirring and she heard a male voice say something calming to them. She put a confused and upset-looking Lucan down for a moment and took her husband by the arm. Her voice hissed in a whisper.

'These are trained scouts, you won't *give them the slip* if you stay here to engage them.'

Marius shrugged stoically.

'I can try. And we've few other options.'

Rhia glared at him.

'I can fight too, you know. Probably better than you can somewhere like this.'

She'd not said it harshly and Marius nodded that she was probably right. His experience of warfare was all of fighting in formation, or of charges on horseback to break an enemy line. Fighting alone was something Gaian soldiers liked to avoid, and his skill at this type of combat was middling at best.

'Probably. But one of us has to get Lucan away and your people will trust you a lot more than they will me. We've no proof that he's anything but the son of a Gaian without you around to speak on his behalf.'

Rhia opened her mouth and then shut it again. He was right. She hated it but he was. Unless someone stayed to slow them down there was no way to get Lucan out of here, and if Marius turned up alone at Bryngarth with a boy that no man there had seen, who would believe him if he claimed he was Carradan's grandson? Rhia balled her fists.

'I don't want to leave you.'

Marius forced a half-smile.

'I don't want to be left. But that is no longer our choice to make.'

Rhia felt the threat of tears begin behind her eyes but she held them back with an effort and threw her arms around her husband. He wasn't Bevan. He could never be Bevan. *But damn it all he... he's cared for me. He's Lucan's father. And he's willing to die for our son without a thought.* Rhia squeezed him tighter and felt the coldness of the mail on her neck and hands, and the tears came to her eyes despite all of her efforts.

Marius hugged back but soon broke off the embrace and kissed her gently on the mouth before turning to their son. Lucan was standing very quietly and awkwardly, clearly knowing that he had done something wrong but not understanding what it was. Marius didn't waste words.

'Be good to your mother. Take care of her. Make us proud, my boy.'

He leaned down and kissed his son on the forehead before straightening and nodding to Rhia.

'Get going.'

His words were brief and croaked a little as they came out, but Marius kept his mask on and turned to face down the slope. Rhia could see men moving up it by now, legionaries in dark tunics with their short swords in their hands. Marius drew his own sword without a sound and crouched down beside a boulder, watching the soldiers as they approached. Rhia just stood there, unable to move. She didn't want to leave. She wanted to stay here and fight. She was born to be a warrior and these men were her enemies. And they were about to kill her husband.

Marius cocked his head and then looked behind him.

'Go, will you!'

Rhia glanced at him briefly and then looked back down the slope. More and more men were coming through the trees, twenty at least though it was hard to tell in the silver light. Marius glared at her but made an effort to keep his voice down.

'You're wasting time – go now!'

Rhia set her jaw. She could hear the fear in his voice, both for them and for himself, and she nodded grimly and took Lucan by the hand. He looked frightened but he knew that his talking had been a bad thing and so kept silent as Rhia lifted him up, tears welling in his eyes. Rhia hoisted him into position and took a last look at her husband, crouching by the boulder, waiting to die. The soldiers were closing in on them and if she didn't move now then his sacrifice would be for nothing. She looked at the father of her only child and whispered to both her gods and his. *May he cross the bridge unharmed.* She tore her eyes away and started running up the slope.

But then, before she could get a good start, she heard the shouts of warcries and then a gurgle behind her, and she spun around on the spot. Rhia cursed herself. Her delaying had cost more time than she had realised. It was too late to run. The first man had already reached the boulders, and Marius had taken his throat before the soldier had registered where he was. Another three were now rushing towards him and Rhia knew she was about to see him die. For a mad moment she was frozen, able neither to run towards the battle or away from it, but then she forced herself to act. *You cannot run now, and they won't let you live.*

She knew it was a foolish plan but she had no other choice. She set Lucan down and spoke quickly.

'Hide!'

The child looked scared and confused but he nodded obediently and ducked behind a tree. Rhia drew the knife from her belt. They were all doomed now, she knew it, but the least that she could do was to die fighting and hope Lucan went unnoticed. She planted herself before the tree, feet spread and knees bent, and hoped that Marius might take a few of them down with him as he died. Though there was little hope in her, Rhia said a silent prayer to Taran that her husband at least would not suffer. But apparently, the War God was a true friend to them tonight.

As the men charged towards him black arrows seemed to sprout out of their chests. The shafts were thick and heavy, and the power of the shots punched the soldiers from their feet. Rhia saw Marius' head whip around and she too began searching for the shooters. She heard the thrum of a bowstring from disturbingly close but no amount of squinting showed her anything but shadows.

Below her more Gaians had appeared around the boulders, and Marius was backing up as another volley of heavy arrows thudded into them. One legionary was only staggered and aimed a clumsy swing at him, but he parried it away and cracked the man's skull with a swift counter-cut. Arrows were flying all around them and Marius spun on the spot to look up the slope, dashing up it as soon as he spotted Rhia. Soldiers tried to follow him but they were shot down as they tried, heavy shafts thumping dully into chests and heads.

Rhia was still searching for the archers and saw a few blurry grey shapes off to her right but that was it. It had to be the Carrocks, she was certain of that, but they clearly knew their country well and were practically invisible.

And it seems they do not like Gaian legionaries on their land.

Marius panted up to them, his head ducked low against the storm of arrows hammering into the men below. The Carrocks might be aiming principally for the soldiers but the air was thick with whizzing shafts, and Rhia too had dropped into a crouch. There was no more sense in whispering but she kept her voice as low as she could.

'I don't know about you, but I think this might be a sign that we should stick together!'

Marius broke into the first genuine smile she'd seen in days and for a second she almost forgot the terrible danger they were still in.

'Perhaps you're right. Is Lucan safe?'

Rhia turned to the tree and panicked for a moment to see that he was gone, but he had only moved around to the other side of the trunk, and was now holding a stick in both hands, feet braced against the ground, ready to fight. Her heart swelled as she saw determination on the little warrior's face and she took him gently by the hand.

'We have to go now, my love.'

The boy looked from one parent to the other, confused.

'Father said look after you?'

Rhia nodded.

'And you have, and I feel much safer now, but we need to run again I'm afraid.'

Lucan looked down at the chaos on the slope, where those unfortunate enough not to have been killed outright were crying out as arrows pierced their limbs and bellies. His tiny hands fidgeted nervously on the stick but he managed to nod as he stared.

'Alright. We can go.'

Rhia nodded back and grunted as she swept him up into her arms. She turned to Marius.

'Do you think we can creep back to the horses once this is over?'

Her husband shook his head.

'I doubt it. It's slaughter down there right now but that looked like half a century of men at least, and they won't *all* be killed.'

Rhia nodded. Even a legion would break after enough casualties and those who ran would doubtless take the horses. She cursed quietly. They had some gold, and in a town they could buy new mounts, but right now they were stuck in a wood beneath a mountain, and their gold was as much use as a sword made of cheese. She sighed.

'On foot it is then. Grab my bag.'

Marius complied and hoisted her satchel onto his shoulder. They'd probably have to abandon some of their heavier things before long, but for now best not to leave a trail for any survivors to follow. She looked down at the soldiers, now taking cover behind the rocks and trying desperately to identify their attackers. *Not that there'll be many survivors of this.*

She tried to take a satisfaction from that but fear and weariness were forefront in her mind. Even without pursuit they still had more than half of their journey ahead of them. Once past the Canwyns they'd have a long walk through the Caderyn lands, and they'd have to skirt any large settlements for fear of Gaian occupiers. There might not be a legion stationed there but the governor would certainly have military enforcers, and they had to remain hidden until they reached her father's house. *And then what?*

Rhia tried not to think about that as she started to walk, moving as quickly as she could from the slaughter by the rocks. Marius walked behind her and she heard him turning every few paces, making sure that no-one followed them from the one-sided battle below. Rhia doubted anyone would. Or perhaps she just hoped it. So far Taran or Karanon or Mehine or whoever it was had been good to them as they fled back to her homeland. Rhia sighed and took a weary step, her body shaking slightly now the immediate danger was past. *Let's just hope the gods choose to remain on our side.*

Chapter 27. Homecoming

It took them twelve days to reach the western end of the Canwyn Range. Once or twice they'd caught a fleeting glimpse of a grey-clad archer but otherwise the walk was uneventful. On the thirteenth day, having already dumped their bulkier valuables in a cave, they risked visiting a settlement, and paid twenty silver coins for two horses and some fresh supplies. It had been well over the odds of course, but they were paying for an absence of questioning, and they knew it.

Eventually they entered Caderyn territory, using roads only where they had to and using the sun and stars the rest of the time to keep their course roughly westward. By the time they caught sight of Nantwyn in the distance, Rhia was in country she knew well enough that they managed to keep off the roads altogether, though they had to travel a very long way around to get anywhere. She was keen to avoid not only large settlements but also the dark memories she had of Glyscoed Wood. *Though whoever that stargazer was, he was right about the Gaians' victory.*

Eventually, after another eight days of roundabout riding, Rhia saw her old home for the first time in five long years. She tried to keep Lucan, who was sharing her new mount, as dry as she could as she looked towards Bryngarth through the steady spring drizzle. It was that constant, powdery sort of rain that soaked a person without their really noticing until it was too late, and Rhia did her best to keep him out of it. He'd been good on the journey so far, despite its hardships. He'd been cold, hungry, tired and scared and yet had cried only a little, and had always done as he was told. Rhia suspected he was putting on a brave face for his mother and she felt both great love and great sadness that her boy was doing so. She adjusted the hood of his new cloak and gave him a quick squeeze as she looked ahead.

The hill looked much as it always had in her memories; long and low and solid, though the drizzling rain made the whole scene somewhat hazy. Rhia wondered why it was she didn't feel some great surge of relief, some great swelling in her chest that she was seeing home again. There was definitely *some* sense of relief in her, and a little touch of happiness at the prospect of seeing her parents, but no overwhelming wave of emotion. She looked at the land that had been home most of her life and found her fears and worries weren't at all diminished, and what sense of pride she felt was overruled by a sense of dread, the fear that what she might find at Bryngarth would not be her home after all.

Rhia glanced over to Marius and pointed, though she'd no doubt at all that he'd seen it. He nodded, sending droplets of rain falling from his hood, but otherwise made no comment. His already quiet nature had been made worse since he'd killed that soldier. He'd later mentioned that he'd recognised the group as the scout company of the Fourteenth Legion, and that the man he'd killed had been their commander, a certain Centurion Flavian. Rhia was sure she'd heard the name before and had probably met the man, but the face hadn't been a familiar one. For the most part she was just grateful it had been a Fourteenth company and not one of the Tenth. Marius was taking it hard enough already and if it had been his old comrades who'd come upon them, she'd no idea how he would have reacted. She frowned. *He'd still have stood up to protect our boy. He'd just be hating himself a lot more right now had it been them.*

Rhia could sympathise, and returned the nod quietly as they rode across the squelching grass. The Gaian soldiers were people he had trusted implicitly, and he'd been forced to abandon that trust in the blink of an eye. Rhia looked at the scattered farms and little settlements of the smaller clans. There had been a time when she'd have trusted any house there to give her shelter, trusting blindly in the general goodness of the Caderyn. But Delyn had shown her quite clearly that there were Caderyn without honour and that what you saw was not necessarily what you got. The farmers on this plain might wish her no harm at all, but living in Tamora had made her wary of gossipers, and she knew that Lepidus had informers among the Rydicae and Bearnicans. It made sense that he might have some among the Caderyn.

She furrowed her brow as they made their cautious way forward, aiming to skirt the farmstead ahead and approach Bryngarth from the south. There was no legion stationed here, but the enforcers of the tribal governor would be everywhere. From what Marius had said they would be mostly ex-legion men or mercenaries, sent here to keep the peace rather than as a real military presence. They would need to be dealt with somehow, as would this local governor, Portunus, but that was far easier said than it was done. Even were they not a group of well-trained, well-armed men, they had all of them had five years to form relationships with the locals. Even among enforced military garrisons there was trading, odd friendships and forbidden love affairs. Without knowing more about what was going on here they couldn't possibly begin to form a plan. And to know more, they had to get inside.

The best plan she had come up with was to make for Peira's house in secret and have her smuggle them into the longhall. Once with her father they could start working out exactly what it was they had to do to get these Gaian enforcers gone, and begin preparing themselves for Lepidus and the inevitable invasion of their lands. It wouldn't be easy. A dozen horrifying scenarios crossed her mind involving her father or mother or Peira having died, and her and Marius being captured and detained. She pictured Lepidus arriving in triumph with his army, his sorcerer at his side as he sat down in her father's chair. She pictured the grey-haired general having Marius nailed to a cross as a deserter, and then making her watch as little Lucan was put to the sword. She clenched her jaw and gripped the sopping reins tight in her hand. *Do not think such things! First things first, we must get to the hill. We find Peira and Barden and we work it out from there.*

The thought of her child in danger was still enough to make her shake, and she tried to take her mind from it by whispering in his ear.

'You see this land, all around us right now?'

The boy was soaked and probably very miserable but he replied dutifully enough.

'Yes mama?'

Rhia held him a little tighter to her.

'This is the land of my father, and his father, and all of your ancestors right back to the beginning.'

Lucan pondered that for a moment before he spoke.

'Is your father here?'

Rhia tried to hide her fear that she had no way of knowing, and that he might well not be. The last message she'd had from home had been almost a year ago.

'I think so.'

Lucan again took his time in answering.

'Is he like my other grandfather?'

Rhia couldn't help but smile as she tried to picture two men who would have looked more dissimilar, but then, in their hearts, they were indeed very much alike. *They probably would have liked each other.* It was both a happy and a sad thing for her to realise.

'He has a big beard but otherwise yes, he is very like your other grandfather.'

Little Lucan nodded his hooded head again and water dripped onto her hands. His happy response was simple but Rhia found herself oddly moved and was glad of the constant rain as an excuse for her to sniff.

'Good. I think I'll like him.'

*

They managed to cross the plain without incident and sold their horses to a farmer not far from Bryngarth's base. Marius had done the talking, for fear of anyone recognising Rhia, and had once again come off worse in a deal for the sake of quiet expediency. His dark beard was now full and his grasp of the Lurian Tongue was good, but still he sounded very much like a foreigner, and his story of being a Rydicae on his way to visit relatives was a flimsy one at best. The middle-aged farmer might have asked some awkward questions had Marius not been willing to sell the horses for only two-thirds what they were worth. Horses were awkward things to take up the hillside, especially when said hillside was thick with mud and besides, riding into town might draw unwanted attention.

And so, now on foot, the little family made their careful way up the slope towards the town. Rhia couldn't help but think of all the times she'd walked up this hill, from her first tentative climb as a child to her return in shame after Nantwyn. She remembered climbing up after their triumph at Broken Stream, and the joyful walk with Bevan on her wedding night. She had climbed this little hill in every type of weather from pouring rain to bright sunshine, from thick grey fog to white blankets of snow, and each climb had been different, sometimes happy, sometimes sad, and sometimes simply bored as she plodded her way back home.

Today's walk up the hill was by far the strangest she'd ever had. Today she walked up through the steady drizzle with a Gaian husband and a half-Gaian child, and for the first time in her life felt like an outsider. Despite the countless other times when she had walked this same path, today it didn't truly feel like home. *But then where is home? Tamora wasn't home, the road wasn't home, and now this place, that was always home, isn't home anymore either. Do I even have a home anymore?* Rhia held onto Lucan's hand a little more tightly, the skin soaking wet in the rain. *If I have a home at all it's where he is. Anything else I can work out later on.*

It took longer than she remembered for them to finally reach the top, though Lucan did his best on his tiny legs. Rhia shifted the strap on the canvas bag over her shoulder and looked around the flat top of the hill. There might have been one or two new buildings since the last time she was here, but otherwise the settlement looked much the same as it ever had, though admittedly it was hard to tell in this weather. The rain had turned from light and powdery into something more substantial and the heavy clouds above them blocked off Belenos' light. Rhia hunched her shoulders against the wet and made sure she had a good grip on Lucan's hand. A lesser boy might have been crying by now in hunger or fatigue or in misery, but he was holding it back admirably, scrunching his face up against the tears. Rhia did her best to smile at him and strode onwards with her head down.

They entered the streets with Marius close behind them, and Rhia started making towards Peira's house. An upside of the weather was that Barden might not be out hunting in this and quite possibly they would both be at home working on the pelts. Rhia avoided the street of shops, though business was hardly likely to be thriving today, and wove between buildings with an old familiarity, noting again that barely anything had changed in her absence. *Yet still it feels strangely different here.*

The rain was getting heavier and she kept her head down low. So low that she didn't see the old woman until it was too late, and the two collided with a simultaneous yelp. Rhia felt Marius tense behind her and she flustered a little as she spoke.

'Forgive me, I didn't see you.'

At the same moment the old woman bowed her head.

'I'm sorry about that.'

The voice sounded familiar and Rhia peered hard through the rain. The woman was scruffily dressed in a tattered brown dress with a grey shawl that came over her head. Like Rhia she'd been walking bent forward and she remained that way now, looking up at her. What hair showed from under the shawl looked dirty and unkempt, with several long strands of grey running through what was otherwise a vibrant red. A familiar red. Rhia looked harder at the woman's face then almost leaped back in shock. It was Meghan.

Her scars had healed well and she was still beautiful, though her face seemed hardened somehow, suspicious and uncertain. Meg squinted through the downpour and took a few heartbeats to speak.

'Rhia?'

Rhia felt a lump start to rise in her throat and she nodded, not trusting herself to speak. The sound of her friend's voice had somehow struck her harder than a blow. Meg's eyes quickly took in the man and child who were standing with her and she took hold of Rhia's hand with one of her own. The grip was strong.

'You need to... I should...' she began but then shook her head and nodded along the street. 'Come with me. We need to get you indoors and dried out. I've much to tell you.'

*

The stew was plain indeed compared to the delicacies of Tamora, but after nearly a moon's turn of fleeing through woods and mountains, the simple hot meal was a welcome thing. They'd rarely dared to risk stopping to buy decent food and Rhia had to admit, she was not much of a hunter. Her city-born husband had been even worse. It had taken a great deal of willpower not to simply devour the food straight away and to take the time to make sure Lucan ate properly. His chin was dripping with the liquid within moments of starting and he was making a fine state of his clothes. Meghan had insisted that they change out of their wet things and Rhia felt guilty that he was staining the fresh shirt he'd been given. Meg hadn't had any children's clothing to offer and so he wore a man's green shirt like a smock, the sleeves rolled up many times.

Rhia felt almost as foolish-looking, Meg's dresses having clearly been made for someone more feminine of figure. *Not that she's looking too sultry at the moment.* Meghan's face hadn't really been damaged from the fight at Nantwyn, but when the scarring was combined with the haggard expression that she wore, and the early strands of grey in her red hair, she seemed a far cry from the vision she had once been. The dress she wore looked old and shapeless, and Rhia suspected it had not been washed or mended in some time. Her hostess sat across the fire from her, sipping her own soup with her arm held awkwardly, and Rhia felt a surge of pity for her old friend. She remembered how she'd seemed to just give up on things after Nantwyn, where Bel and Dane had both met their ends. Somehow, she'd hoped that time would have helped Meg heal as it had helped her. *But Meghan has no Marius, and no Lucan.* Rhia felt a surge of anger that her

386

friends would let her sink to such a state. Meghan seemed to read her mind, or at least read her expression.

'I'm not so broken as that, you know.'

Rhia blinked and her friend smiled and spoke again before she could apologise.

'You've not changed all that much, Rhia. You're looking at me like I've been abandoned and you're angry with Olla and Peira for not sticking by me.'

Rhia looked down a little guiltily.

'Well, yes.'

Meghan shrugged.

'It's true that I still grieve, even after all this time, but this,' she gestured to herself, 'is mostly for show. It pays not to look too pretty these days.'

Rhia's eyes snapped back up to look at her, and beside her Marius had stopped eating. Once again Meg shrugged disinterestedly.

'In all fairness old Portly tends to keep his men controlled. Many of them are decent enough and just want a quiet life here with a bit of fun now and then, and a few have even talked about *marrying* local lovers. Others of them... they want what isn't theirs to take. Portly had one of them lashed only last moon for forcing himself on a Bryngarth girl, but that's only because the damned fool got caught. Plenty of them don't.'

Rhia's mouth gaped open, not so much at the revelation of what was happening, but at her friend's casual tone. She held Lucan a little closer, trying to shield his ears, but he was distracted by the warm soup and wasn't paying attention. Rhia kept her voice down nonetheless.

'Meg, have you been...'

She didn't want to say it aloud and was glad that her friend shook her head before she had to.

'No. Garius tried once or twice when they first came here but I gave him a sore groin for it, and he took his shaft elsewhere. Since then I've made sure not to look my best, just in case.'

Rhia couldn't help herself from putting a hand on her arm. Meg smiled again, but there was sadness behind the expression.

'It's not so bad, you know. Owain sometimes comes and stays with me and I make a decent living working with Peira, making cloaks. The Gaians take a portion of it all but they're alright for the most part. You just have to know who to avoid.'

Rhia stayed silent for a while and Meg looked like she was preparing herself to say something unwelcome when Marius surprised them both by speaking.

'The men who enforce Gaian law, they are soldiers?'

Meghan eyed him uncertainly for a moment before answering. Rhia knew that Marius would be thinking disapprovingly of whoever commanded them and was probably hoping that if they lacked discipline in their comportment, they might also lack it in their training.

'They wear mail and swords, yes.'

Marius nodded.

'How many are there?'

She shrugged.

'I don't know, they keep coming and going to different parts of the territory.' She paused a moment and looked to Rhia and then back at him. 'Who are you?'

Husband and wife shared a glance and Rhia gave Marius a tiny nod. He took a deep breath.

'My name is Antonius Dessida, I was an officer of the Tenth Legion. And I am Rhia's husband.'

Meg's eyebrows went up and she looked at Lucan, still slurping happily at his stew.

'And this is…?'

Rhia stroked her boy's hair without thinking.

'This is Lucan, our son.'

Meghan's eyes went from the child to Marius and back to Rhia again.

'There is much you need to hear Rhia but I think your story will be longer than mine. Tell me everything.'

Rhia put down her bowl and took a little draught of water, and told her friend nearly all that had happened to her. She left out the part with Delyn, she had no desire to repeat that, and kept things vague about Tullius' betrayal, but otherwise the story was true and complete. When she reached the part about Praecus, Meg licked her finger and drew a circle in the air to ward off his evil. *Strange that you've forgotten that ritual in your time living with the Gaians, but then sorcery was never something you really had to worry about, not with Reaghan around to protect us.*

Rhia managed to stay dry-eyed throughout the telling, even when Meg had wept for Gwen, and by the time she reached the end she felt exhausted more than anything. For a little while the only sounds were the gentle snores of Lucan, now curled up under some furs, and the crackling of the yellow fire that lit the darkening house.

Meghan shuffled around the fire to sit next to her friend and took both of Rhia's hands in hers.

'I am so sorry for Gwen. She was a sister to me as well.' She looked down for a moment and took a deep breath. 'And I am sorry that I must give you more bad news.'

Rhia's heart began to skip but she kept her face as calm as possible as Meg continued.

'As I say it is sometimes bad here. Portly is not a wicked man but his soldiers can cause trouble and claim they do it in his name. Mostly people put up with it, we all saw what happened when we tried to fight the Gaians.'

She gave Marius a sideways look but he neither looked away nor tried to stare her down. He simply kept his face neutral and Meg kept going after a moment.

'Less than a moon ago one of the soldiers, Nerus, pushed his chances too far. He'd taken a fancy to Olla the first time he'd seen her, but she's off living with Eogan's family for most of the year so nobody thought anything of it. But she came here on a visit not so long ago and he clearly felt like trying things again.'

Rhia gripped her friend's hand tighter. *Not Olla too. Not both my sisters.* Meg squeezed her hand back.

'She wasn't harmed Rhia but... but...' tears appeared on her scarred face and she forced herself to continue. 'He was there with another man, presumably to keep watch, and Eogan and your brother came upon them when Olla cried out. Eogan knocked Nerus down but the second man faced Ewan and he...'

The redhead squeezed out another tear and Rhia forced herself to keep her voice calm.

'Dead?'

The simple nod that Meghan gave made Rhia feel like screaming and crying all at once. Before she could say another word Marius was at her side, his arms wrapped around her and pulling her close to him. For a heartbeat Rhia considered resisting the pull. He was a Gaian and an enemy, and the Gaians had killed her brother and sister. But the warmth and comfort of his embrace was too tempting to refuse and she could almost feel his concern for her as he held her tight to his chest.

Rhia couldn't think of what to say. She'd had nightmares of coming back to find only misery and corpses, and a part of that had come horribly true. *Ewan.* Her big brother. The one who'd always been there to watch over them, whether they wanted him to or not. Of course he'd met his end in defence of the last sister he had. Given the choice, Rhia doubted he would have wished another way.

She let herself cry only a little as she thought of him. She had things that needed doing and there would be time later to mourn. *For him and for Gwen, assuming I'm alive to do it.* Rhia straightened up a little but kept close to her husband.

'What happened to the man who killed him?'

Meghan's eyes were still watery but she looked eager as she spoke.

'That's just the thing. Ewan fetched him a wound but soldiers appeared and dragged him off before Eogan could finish him. They have him now at the governor's house and no punishment has been given. Portly says he's going to lash him but he doesn't dare bring him outside for fear of us rioting to kill him.'

Rhia found herself leaning forward, despite her grief. Her old friend, anger, was being fuelled by a wild hope.

'You think our people would?'

Meg nodded slowly.

'Owain disappeared the day after it happened, as did Barden and a couple of others. The word is that people have been gathering in the hills and that plans are already being made.'

Marius chipped in before Rhia could, his curiosity just as aroused.

'What manner of plans?'

Meg shrugged at them both.

'I don't know. But I hear there are other Gadarim with them and they intend to force old Portly to hand him over, and who knows what might come after that? If you told them what you've seen about the Gaians using sorcery...'

Rhia felt her heart beat faster. The horror of her grief was being slowly burned away as her greatest fear gave way to her greatest hope. She'd been so afraid of finding her people and her family dead or worse; turned into broken slaves. Now Ewan, dear Ewan, was dead but from his death they might kindle a flame of rebellion in the hearts of the Caderyn. Her people were ready to be freed, they just needed a nudge. She looked Meg in the eye.

'Has Reaghan been seen with these men in the hills?'

Meg shook her head.

'No, but if he was with them he'd be keeping his head down for now. Most of the druids are doing that at the moment, we've heard stories of bad things happening elsewhere.'

Rhia nodded. Likely Praecus had been encouraging the Gaians to kill or persecute them. But it would take more than some greasy-haired magicker to get the better of Reaghan.

'Is Bael still here?'

Meg nodded.

'Yes. He poses as your father's bastard son by an old lover; does a good job of lounging about the place looking useless and pretending he drinks too much.'

Rhia smiled a little, imagining the serious young man impersonating a drunkard.

'We need to get to him then, he can get the message to Reaghan, and we need to contact Owain and whatever fighters are with him.'

Rhia gently eased herself to her feet, taking care not to wake Lucan from his contented fireside doze.

'But before anything else, I have to see my father.'

Chapter 28. A New Plan

The longhall of her father looked much the same as it ever had, though like everything else it was grey and grim-looking in the rain. Not far from it, across an empty patch of grass, she could make out the new Gaian-style house built for Portunus and his family. Clearly intended to look very grand and superior, the great rectangle mostly appeared merely odd and out of place, like a seashell in the middle of a wheatfield; neither especially greater nor lesser than what was around it, but definitely different and alien. Through the haze of drizzle Rhia saw that armed men patrolled around it with more stationed at the doors, and felt glad that the governor had not seen fit to do the same thing here.

The longhall was unguarded, and the yellow light that peeked out from within looked warm and welcoming in the rain. Rhia hurried up to one of the side doors near the rear. Meghan had already come here to find Bael and had then returned to the house, and was now keeping an eye on Lucan while Rhia and Marius made for the hall. Meg had said that the young druid would meet them in the rear chambers but that a council was in session and that they may have to wait for him. A part of the character he had invented as Carradan's bastard son had been a sense of undeserving entitlement, which meant he always attended when the governor met the chieftain. Rhia and Marius had agreed to wait for him in the back rooms and they reached the closed door together. Rhia leaned her ear against the soaking wood for a moment, her cheek was already damp anyway, and after a cautious few seconds she eased the door open.

Inside it felt strange, as if Rhia was a stranger in her own home. She led Marius into the open space behind the hall and saw the doorways that led to the sleeping chambers, where she and Gwen and Olla had lived together through their childhood. She saw the huge bathing tub, empty of water and leaning against the wall, with towels hanging neatly on their pegs next to it. The battered old chest full of spare bedding was still there, and as she looked she saw that every little nick and mark was exactly as she remembered it. Nothing had changed. And yet everything had changed.

Now Gwen was dead, along with both of their brothers, and Olla had been forced to walk carefully in her own town for fear of rape. No longer did Meghan and Peira come here to bathe. No longer was this a place of laughter and safety among friends and family. Rhia remembered the wild joy she had felt here on that day when her father had told her she had his leave to marry Bevan. Now she crept about here with her Gaian husband, trying to find a way to defend what was left of her people from his.

Rhia glanced back at Marius as he closed the door behind them. He probably thought of this place as just another plain-looking room, if he was even thinking of it at all. He didn't know, couldn't know, what this simple place meant to his wife. He gave her a concerned look and Rhia snapped herself out of it. *No use dwelling on the past. Marius is a good man and with a little help from Fortuna there is hope for your people. Stay focused.*

She nodded to her husband and made for the door to the main hall. From the other side she heard voices and though she struggled to make out the words, it sounded like they were speaking in Vulgare. Meg had mentioned that most townspeople spoke at least a little of the language to communicate with the enforcers and administrators. Few of them spoke it fluently but apparently it was understood well enough to be the chosen language at council. More than one voice was speaking in that tongue, and by the lilting accent of one or two of the speakers, Rhia deduced they were native Lurians.

She stayed there and strained her ears for only a few minutes before a slurring voice sounded quite close to her.

'I need to piss. Back in a moment.'

Rhia heard a footfall near the door and stepped back quickly as it opened, hiding herself in the shadows behind it. Marius flattened himself to the wall and a slightly swaying figure appeared in the frame before shutting the door again as he walked in. Rhia was midway through springing for him when she realised that it was Bael. Even forewarned by Meghan it had been hard to recognise him beneath his persona.

The young druid was dressed in a red tunic that stank of sweat and beer, and his dark hair hung lank about his shoulders. His posture, always sure-footed and upright as befit one of his calling, was now slouched and clumsy, and his honest face that was so often sombre or wise now wore a lopsided and mean-looking expression, like a man certain that he had the world fooled about how crooked and cunning he was. The irony was that even Rhia, who had known what to expect, *had* been fooled by him completely, and it was only at the last second that she realised who he was. Bael turned to where she'd stopped mid-leap without the least hint of uneasiness in his bearing.

'Rhianwyn, so good to see you.'

His calm voice was a far cry from the vulgar slurring from a few seconds ago and even as she watched, his back straightened up and his bloodshot eyes cleared to their old crisp and piercing blue. *So like Reaghan's.* Rhia knew there must be magic in how he changed their look so quickly, but unlike the sorcery of Praecus she felt no horror or dread at seeing it. This was the magic of the druids, the pure and holy magic of earth and air and water.

For a second she felt humbled in the presence of the man, but then fought herself back into control, hope fighting off her nerves. *Bael can perform his magics with ease and he is but an apprentice to Reaghan. If he comes to our side and is willing to use it...* She whispered hurriedly.

'Bael, I've no time to explain, a Gaian army is coming and we have to make ready, they...'

The young druid interrupted her, but managed to still seem polite.

'They have a sorcerer, yes, Meghan told me. You were quite right to come to me, though we shall need to speak to Reaghan before moving further. Already there is talk of unrest among the Caderyn and this new information could be the pebble to start the avalanche.'

Rhia nodded vigorously.

'Exactly! Meg told me there are warriors gathering in the hills. Are we enough left here to drive out the governor's men?'

Bael looked briefly to Marius and then back to Rhia.

'Probably, but not without much loss on our part, and I would avoid bloodshed if at all possible.'

Rhia was a little taken aback but the druid explained before she could object.

'I have seen the hearts of these Gaians and there are good men amongst the bad. I should prefer that they surrender to us peacefully or else leave without need for battle.'

Marius did his best not to snort at that but something gave him away, and Rhia nodded in agreement as she whispered to Bael.

'We have no time for such sentiment!'

Bael barely raised an eyebrow but there was power in his words.

'Reaghan would speak as I have. You know this.'

Rhia looked into those clear blue eyes and saw a shadow of the older druid there. Bael was right of course, it was exactly what Reaghan would counsel. *Let us hope he is more willing to join the fight once he hears about Praecus and his Destroyers.* Rhia shook her head in resignation.

'What do you suggest then?'

The young druid looked thoughtful.

'Presumably whatever this General Lepidus is doing, he does it without the blessing of his superiors?'

Rhia nodded.

'Yes.'

Marius elaborated a little.

'Sorcery is dimly viewed by decent Gaians as a thing not to be trusted. However, if he wins himself sufficient fame in war and downplays the role played by Praecus, he will likely be forgiven his dabbling.'

Bael nodded slowly.

'Hmmm, perhaps we might use that to our advantage here. If the Gaians here could be...'

But before he could continue a scrabbling at the door behind him caused all of them to turn. Rhia saw the druid hurriedly change his eyes back to their bloodshot state and fall back into his former slouch. Both Rhia and Marius backed away a step or two and a second later the door opened and Rhia almost burst into tears.

Bragger had been standing on his hind legs, pushing the door, and as it came open he let out a bark of joy, his tail wagging madly behind him as he leaped up at Rhia. Marius tensed a moment but Rhia couldn't help but smile as the loving hound reared up and started licking at her face. She put her arms around him and crouched down a little, her voice far more emotional than it had any right to be. He was just a dog after all, just an animal, but seeing him and smelling him made her feel at home for the first time since her arrival, and she rubbed at his ears affectionately.

'Good boy, good boy!'

She was so engrossed that for a moment she forgot where she was and it took her a second to realise that people were staring at her from the hall. Bael and Marius had both had the sense to fall back into the shadows but it was too late for Rhia to back off now and she straightened up, her face serious again. A quick and subtle shake of her head told Marius to stay where he was and she strode confidently into her father's great hall, as if she had every right to have just appeared there. *As do I.*

The longhall was much as it had been before and was currently filled with bearded Caderyn men, most of whom she recognised as the headmen of various clans. They were all staring at her open-mouthed but she looked away from them and up to the high table of her father. He was sitting in his chair, his jaw hanging down in shock, and Rhia couldn't help but notice the new grey streaks in his hair and beard. *So many.* Beside him had been set another chair, this one carved ornately from dark-stained wood, and in this chair sat the man she had seen only once, more than five years ago.

Julius Portunus was a short, round-faced man with silver hair and an encroaching paunch. In age he seemed to be somewhere around his fiftieth winter and he wore a grey tunic and a white shoulder-robe like those worn by Tamora's councillors. He was staring at her like the others, though she saw no recognition there, and when he spoke his voice was droning, as if even in rebuking he was bored.

'What is the meaning of this?'

The two men in mail who were standing behind him kept their hands near their swords but did not draw them. Carradan stood up from his chair but the governor turned to face him with a frown.

'Chief Carradus, our council is still in session, be so kind as to take your seat.'

Rhia's father glared at him and stayed standing, though he didn't speak back to him either. The governor continued, a touch of nervousness entering his dull voice.

'Please, we are in the midst of an important discussion. This unrest is most difficult for all of us and we have yet to reach an amicable solution, now I like to think I have built up a good relationship with your people, but if you recall the terms of the treaty set by myself and General Lepidus...'

But he got no further than that as two things happened at once. Carradan ignored the seated man and began walking around the table towards his daughter, and Rhia spoke up in interruption.

'General Lepidus is a man without honour, sir. He has ordered the murder of both the noble General Brictus Balius and of my own beloved father-in-law, Governor Lucius Dessidus Glaucus.'

There was a moment of silence and Portunus and his men all looked at her in obvious shock. Whether it was from the news or because a tribeswoman had just spoken in such eloquent Vulgare she couldn't be certain, but her observation was interrupted by her father's crushing embrace. The feeling of his arms around her countered her nervousness wonderfully, and the sound of his voice made her fears all but vanish.

'My daughter. Welcome home.' He squeezed a little tighter and Rhia squeezed back before he broke off the embrace to look at her. 'What has happened to you?'

His eyes were full of concern but Rhia held up a hand and spoke quietly.

'Later.'

Her joy at seeing him was punctured by the knowledge that she'd have to tell him about Gwen, but that could wait. Her father took hold of Bragger, still eagerly wagging his tail, and stepped away a little from his daughter.   Portunus was sputtering out something unintelligible and Rhia tried to keep the initiative.

'All that I say is true, and more. I am Carradus Dessidus Rhianna and I swear it by Father Gron, the Lord of Justice.'

Governor Portunus was clearly a nervous man and the best reply that he could manage was:

'But General Lepidus, he…'

But the Gaian tailed off uncertainly. Rhia noted that his voice was still droning, even when anxious, and she realised that this was simply the way he spoke. She decided to keep up the pressure.

'If my word for it is not enough governor, then I present to you my husband, the noble Marius Dessidus Antonius, Second Tribune of the glorious Tenth Legion.'

Hearing his cue, Marius stepped out from the shadows, his bearing erect and confident. For a second it looked as if the Gaians didn't believe it was him, he was after all simply dressed, scruffy-haired and bearded, but his expression and sheer presence marked him out as a patrician, and even the Caderyn headmen seemed impressed with the young man. He spoke clearly, his voice polite but firm.

'I concur fully with the testimony of my wife. General Lepidus, my former commander, is guilty by association of the murders of these two men and the situation, alas, is dire indeed.' He paused for effect, locking eyes with the governor. 'His advisor, a man named Praecus, has been shown to be a practitioner of sorceries and has practiced his foul art both on his Aboran auxiliaries and on the loyal men of the Fourteenth Legion. I believe that General Lepidus plans to use them on my own comrades of the Tenth Legion as well, demonstrating beyond a doubt that he is no soldier, no true man of the legion, and no true Gaian.'

Yet again the longhall was filled with a shocked silence and, like Rhia before him, Marius kept the initiative while he could.

'His madness for power has driven him to murder, and to further sate this lust he intends to wage unsanctioned warfare against the tribes of the west to test his sorcerer's powers.'

Rhia joined in at the last.

'And we must stop him.'

Portunus was still staring open-mouthed at the newcomers, and Rhia saw that he was not alone in his speechlessness. Her father was simply looking at the two of them wide-eyed, and the assembled headmen were doing likewise. Portunus seemed to find his voice at last and addressed Marius with a bow of his head.

'Tribune Dessida, I grieve with you for the death of your noble father. He was a fine man.'

Marius nodded back.

'That he was, and a loyal servant to the Empire all his life.'

The governor bobbed his head, his expression still nervous and his hands fidgety.

'I do not doubt your word sir, but I find such accusations hard to believe. Are you quite certain of your information?'

Marius' eyes never left the man.

'Beyond any doubt. I have seen the effects of Praecus' sorcery at first hand and it is disturbingly powerful. If General Lepidus continues to utilise it I have no doubt that his ambitions will stretch to beyond Daeria. Many times have I heard him extol the virtues of military dictatorship. Should he continue to grow in power, it is my belief that he will seek to challenge the Emperor himself.'

Portunus spluttered even further at this and his men looked awkwardly at each other, unsure of what to do.

'That may be so. Nevertheless… I myself am uncertain… such a singular affair…'

Rhia frowned at the man who'd justly earned the nickname 'Portly'. He was clearly an indecisive and nervous politician who probably hadn't asked to be posted here, and certainly wasn't keen to become involved in a major crisis. Fortunately, Carradan stepped forward and interrupted him.

'Well I am *not* uncertain. My daughter does not lie. And if she says that this Gaian does not lie then neither does he.' He nodded to Marius who bowed back to him. 'This threat may be hard to believe but it is real if they say it is. And we must prepare ourselves to face the storm.'

A murmur of agreement rippled through the assembled men and Portunus looked around the room uneasily. Rhia wasn't sure what he was more afraid of; the concept of Lepidus' sorcery or the threat of the Caderyn defying his rule. He must have known they were on the brink of rebellion and it would take only a nudge to tip them over. Behind him his men tensed and one of them put a hand to his sword. Rhia leaped in before anyone went too far. A part of her wanted nothing more than to let these enforcers try something only to die in the attempt. It would serve many of them right from what Meghan had told her. But there were half-a-dozen of them in the longhall alone and good Caderyn men would die if it came to a fight. *Besides*, she thought irritably, *Bael was right, Reaghan wouldn't approve.*

She addressed the nervous-looking governor.

'Of course sir, should the Senate or the Emperor be informed of this in good time, a great deal of strife might be avoided.'

She paused significantly to let the Gaians work out the rest for themselves. *And the men who so inform him will doubtless be rewarded.* Portunus shifted in his seat.

'Well, I mean… I suppose…'

Marius saw the plan at once and interjected smoothly.

'It would come best from a gentleman like yourself, governor. Were you to make for Glevia you could speak to my noble mother before continuing? I have detailed all of this in a letter to her. I would also advise that word be sent to Corinia to inform General Galerius of the First – it may be that this could all be resolved locally and the Emperor merely hear about the success of it from you?'

That thought seemed to appeal to the governor a lot more and he nodded his head slowly, as if considering.

'I suppose I could go, though the road is long.'

Rhia tried not to sound over-eager.

'True, but you will have your guard with you, and none would dare attack a man of such prestige.'

That was mostly a bare-faced lie, but it was true that many people would hesitate to attack a local governor, it might come back to haunt them were they identified, and with a little good fortune he could be away before Lepidus was marching his legions the other way. The nervous man nodded again.

'True, though I would need to keep a presence here, of course.'

Carradan nodded his head.

'I agree, governor, I shall need some assistance to continue running the province in your absence. I suggest that your administrative staff remain at your house.'

Portunus looked uncertain at that but the sea of approving Caderyn faces made up his mind for him. He wanted to leave and get credit for warning the Emperor, and only minutes ago he had been speaking highly of his relationship with this tribe. *And he might be a worrier but I don't think he's a fool. He knows there's trouble coming and he'll see this escape for what it is.*

'Very well Chief Carradus, I shall entrust the continued running of this province to your care. The Emperor must be informed of this and it is my duty to inform him.' He eased himself up out of the chair and motioned to the men behind him. 'I shall be away to my house to prepare.'

There was a chorus of polite agreement from the headmen, all of them bright enough to know not to look too pleased. The moment they had gone the room was a buzz of conversation, and several men approached to welcome Rhia with smiles and hugs. Rhia hugged them back, though in her relief she now remembered how tired she ought to be. Carradan smiled only briefly before he raised his voice to the crowd.

'Men of the Caderyn, tonight we have had good news but disaster snaps at its heels.'

He strode to a spot behind the high table where Rhia saw a pair of little hooks had been driven into the wall at head height. They had certainly not been there when she had lived here, but had apparently been there long enough for spots of rust to have appeared on them. *They must have put it up almost as soon as I left.* The Chieftain of the Caderyn reached up and lifted the sword that had hung from it, a little cloud of dust puffing into the air as he did. Carradan's face was unreadable as he felt Ironhorn in his hands again, but Rhia could almost *feel* his pride as he spoke on.

'We must gather the clans and assemble the Gadarim, and Reaghan must be found. Once again, I fear, the Caderyn must go to war!'

Far from being greeted with dread, his words caused a cheer to erupt from the headmen. They soon began talking amongst themselves, sending the tribesmen who'd been attending them hurrying from the hall to send out messages. Carradan spoke a few words to Merwyn, the headman of Broken Stream, and then turned to face Rhia with a beam.

'You have done well today, Rhianwyn. I know your time has been hard and I will want to hear all. But before anything else, Olla told me some time ago that you sent word to her of a son? Did you bring him with you?'

Rhia nodded.

'I did.'

Carradan looked from her to Marius as though one of them might produce him from their cloaks.

'Well, where is he, child? Where is my grandson?'

Her father was wearing a broad smile and Rhia hated herself that she must break it, but better that the news came to him now than later. She placed a hand on his arm and looked into his face, keeping her voice as gentle as she could.

'I will take you to him soon Father, I promise. But first things must come first. I have some terrible news.'

Chapter 29. A Council is Called

Carradan had wept for the death of his daughter, but had managed a smile when he saw his grandson. For her father's sake Rhia had taken him to Meghan's house to see Lucan and to give him some privacy to grieve for Gwen. Not that he'd had much time to spare. Within an hour of their leaving it the longhouse had been packed with people coming from all over Bryngarth, and all of them had wanted to speak to him.

The chieftain had been patient, despite the burden on his heart, and had returned to the hall to deal with them, telling them all he could and assuring them that all was in hand. Portunus had not even waited for morning before leaving Bryngarth, Rhia suspected so that he could take Ewan's killer away without incident. That had angered more than a few of the Caderyn, herself included, but there was little to be done about it now. Once they were gone, the administrators had been told gently but firmly that they were to mind their own business for a while, and the Gaians had complied without a fuss. Overnight, Carradan and the headmen had sent gallopers across the territory, summoning all warriors to Bryngarth at once, their leaders to attend a council at sundown two days later. Rhia had smiled at that. Rebellion must have been in the air for some time – it took more than two days to cross the Caderyn lands.

When that day came the town had been filled to bursting point and every house and barn in Bryngarth wound up taking in lodgers, and still more men were coming from all over. Warriors and Gadarim, along with druids who'd been in hiding, came to the town in droves and at sundown that night the hall was packed with bodies, the benches overflowing and scores of tribesmen forced to stand.

Rhia and Marius sat at the high table with Carradan, Madoc sitting on his other side, a black patch over one eye. Rhia remembered how he had been struck down at Nantwyn and was glad that despite all he seemed to still be strong, if somewhat morose. His son Gwyr had died of his wounds two days after the battle and he and Hefina had not tried for any more children. The First Man of the tribe seemed content merely to guard his lord, though Rhia saw at a glance that he was filled with hidden pain.

She looked about the packed hall and picked out a few faces, though they mostly blended into one in a sea of human flesh. She spotted Owain standing beside Meghan with an arm around her, and for all that she'd loved Dane Rhia hoped the two of them were happy. *Perhaps with Owain back here now they'll decide they want to wed? Five years is long enough for her to grieve.* Rhia felt a little pang for the brothers she'd lost and was reminded that no amount of time was long enough to grieve, but the pain at least got dimmer as years went on. For the most part.

Near the top table were the senior headmen, including Delyn's father Aeron, the headman of Durolwg. From what she'd heard, Delyn had disappeared and most believed him to be somewhere in Niswyn, though what he did there was anybody's guess. Most people viewed his chosen exile as something of a mystery, and assumed he felt ashamed or afraid after the battle. Rhia let them think so, but suspected she knew the truth, at least in part. Though whether it was honour or simple cowardice that had made him leave, she couldn't tell.

Her mother saw her staring blankly and cocked her head in curiosity, but Rhia simply smiled at her and thought of something more pleasant. Olla had not joined them in the hall, having taken Lucan and his cousin Siriol into the quieter back rooms, and apparently the two were getting on well. Rhia was glad. Lucan's only friends of his own age were half a world away, and there was every chance that he would not see them again. It was good that he had someone here to play with. *Especially after what the poor boy has been through. I wish I could just go out and play and not have to worry about this.* The thought was a little unworthy perhaps and she shook it off quickly enough, but the truth was that for all of her desire to seek justice and vengeance, she envied the children their innocence of this.

Before she could become too engrossed with her own feelings her father stood up from his chair, Portunus' one having been removed, and Madoc banged his fist on the table for silence. It took a few moments but conversation soon died out and Carradan addressed the group.

'Comrades, you have all heard of the terrible threat that now marches on our land, and today we shall make our plan for how to best protect our people. Every voice shall be heard.'

There was a brief pause before one of the clan leaders spoke up.

'I am no coward, but I say we make for the hills with all possible speed. We should get our people to safety whilst we are able.'

There were disapproving looks but significantly, no-one shouted him down. Another man spoke up in agreement.

'I say the same. It cuts me to say it but we learned at Nantwyn that Gaian legions cannot be beaten in the field, and if there is sorcery at work,' he licked a finger and drew a circle, many others copying him, 'our chances are even less. Let us save what people we can.'

Murmurs of reluctant agreement filled the hall but Carradan spoke through them.

'Until lately I might have agreed with you Alraig, but what I hear of this sorcerer has changed my view. My daughter and her husband,' he gestured to Rhia and

Marius, 'have told me that this *Praecus* intends not to take our lands but to destroy our people utterly. Running and hiding is no longer an option.'

Many of the men nodded but Alraig pointed at Marius.

'You trust the word of a Gaian, and a Gaian soldier at that?'

Several men grunted in agreement. Rhia inhaled to say something in his defence but Marius spoke for himself, his Lurian simple but understandable.

'I am a Gaian, and I am proud to be a soldier for the Empire. But Lepidus caused the deaths of my father and brother. What Praecus does to men is evil. These men have threatened the lives of my wife and child and they must be stopped. I will help to stop them.'

He spoke his words boldly without sounding like he wanted a fight, and even Alraig seemed taken aback.

'Perhaps so. But forgive me, we have had little enough reason to trust your people.'

Marius nodded.

'I understand. But you can trust me to protect my son. And my son is with your people now. Let us start there.'

Sounds of approval came from some of the Caderyn, though plenty still looked at him sceptically. Carradan took advantage of it.

'My new son has given us good cause to trust him, and it is to him that I would turn for help. He has offered to help train our warriors in ways that will defeat the Gaian legions. He knows their ways better than any of us and he can teach us how to fight them.'

Once again the hall was divided as some men appeared encouraged and others looked distrustful. The man who'd spoken first, Rhia forgot his name, spoke up again.

'I did not see him at Nantwyn. Knowledge or no, how do I know he is fit to teach men to fight?'

Marius did not alter his tone in the slightest.

'You can fight me now if you wish. But it would just mean one less man to fight Lepidus when he comes.'

There was nothing confrontational in his tone but he spoke with an easy confidence that implied to all that *he* would not be the one to die. Rhia had to admit she was impressed. Marius was only a middling swordsman but he carried himself as though he were a champion. The doubtful Caderyn spoke a touch more respectfully.

'There is no need for that. But I have no way of knowing your skills nonetheless.'

The lone Gaian nodded.

'Let me train your men for two days. You will see my worth.'

Once again, Rhia was impressed as the belligerent man nodded quietly. Twice in as many minutes Marius had turned men who were against him into, if not quite supporters, then at least men willing to give him a chance. *One thing I'll say for Gaian patricians; sometimes casual arrogance gets you a long way.*

Some of the tension seemed to leave the hall, though Aeron still seemed uncertain.

'Is there no way we might make peace with these Gaians as we have done before? We have not suffered badly under their rule and their soldiers have at least kept the Dariniae raids under control.'

He seemed about to continue but was interrupted by Merwyn.

'Perhaps so, but the damned Gorvicae took liberties with their tribute, cheating us every damned chance they got.'

Another voice chipped in.

'I hear they have it worse than us these days, mind.'

Merwyn shrugged.

'Serve the bastards right.'

Aeron cleared his throat pointedly and the two men ceased their talk. Aeron continued his address to Carradan.

'Can we not at least *attempt* a peace before we throw men's lives away in war?'

Carradan shook his head.

'I know that you speak out of caution and not fear, my friend. But you heard what has been said; these Gaians come only to kill. My Gaian son tells me he suspects it was this sorcerer's influence that led to the slaughter of Nantwyn's civilians back when all of this began. This Praecus is a man without honour. We shall perish if we run just as easily as we would in battle. And I for one would sooner meet Annwn with a sword in my hand.'

Several voices, including every Gadarim there, rose in an encouraging cheer. Aeron didn't look happy about it but he nodded in resignation. Carradan continued, clearly trying to keep their spirits high.

'But we need not meet him yet if we are cunning. We can raid them on the march and attack their supplies until Marius' men are trained to fight them. Then we can meet them face to face and crush them and their sorcerer into dust!'

Another cheer erupted, this time from more throats, and many men banged their fists on the tables in their enthusiasm. Rhia found herself joining in and such was the noise of it that no-one noticed the big doors opening at the end of the longhall. As such, the group of men walking into the hall got some way into it before they were noticed. They strode into the empty space before the fire pit and the halls' cheers quickly turned into jeers and protests. They were Gorvicae.

Baercban, High Chieftain of his tribe, walked at their head, the heavy furs around his shoulders making him seem broader than he was. His hair and beard were both pale blonde, and the face beneath did not look pleased. To his right walked his coward of a son, Sedryn, and Rhia joined in the protests when she saw Silverbite hanging at his hip. She shouted louder when she noticed Gawan, the Leaping Wolf and the killer of Dane, marching sour-faced on his chieftain's left.

Carradan stepped forward and raised a hand, and Madoc banged the table for silence once more. This time the Caderyn took much longer to settle down and it was only when their chieftain spoke that they finally stopped their protests.

'What are you doing here?'

The challenge was not loud but it was laced with subtle menace, and one couldn't help but notice that though Carradan was shorter, he was clearly built more solidly than his Gorvic counterpart, for all the illusion of his furs. But Baercban refused to be cowed.

'Is that any way to speak to a man you're paying tribute to?'

A number of voices answered that but Rhia made her voice heard above them.

'You can shove your bloody tribute up your scrawny arses!'

Next to her she saw Marius raise his eyebrows and smirk a little, and she remembered with a mixture of amusement and embarrassment that she'd not spoken like this in Tamora. *Clearly the Gorvicae just bring it out in me.* Gawan sneered at her.

'I hate to think what's been done with yours, Wildcat – those Gaians have some funny tastes, I'm told.'

Both Rhia and Marius stood up ready to rush him but Carradan spoke again before they could, his voice heavy with restrained anger.

'You will apologise for that Leaping Wolf, or by Taran's thunder you'll find your head nailed to my door.'

He glared at his fellow Gadarim and a hush fell over the crowd. Baercban was looking at his First Man in disapproval, and after a few heartbeats the warrior answered.

'I meant no offence to you, Charging Bull. I apologise.'

He pointedly kept looking at the chieftain and not at Rhia, and it was obvious he was apologising to him and not to her, but before she could say anything Merwyn was speaking again.

'Why do you come here anyway? You should know that your Gaian masters have left, and your time of crowing over us is over, Baercban.'

There was a chorus of agreement and the Gorvic chief bristled.

'They are no masters of mine!'

Merwyn scoffed at him.

'You might have fooled me. From where I stand it seems you have been their dogs since they came here, and you must be greater fools than any thought to come here now without their protection.'

Gawan took a step towards him and Baercban took in a breath to speak, but before he could another voice came from the doors.

'They are here at my invitation.'

The deep voice was calm and yet powerful nonetheless, and it echoed through the hall far more than any normal man's voice could have done. All eyes turned to the doorway but Rhia knew before she saw him who had spoken in such a way. It was Reaghan.

The druid was exactly as she remembered him, his white robes flowing down to his bare feet and his old and gnarled staff held firmly in one hand. He walked slowly into the centre of the hall, his expression calm but resolute. Behind him came a procession of men, some clearly druids, some with the bearing of chiefs. The white-haired man halted between Carradan and Baercban and spoke again, his voice now merely clear rather than echoing.

'Long have I suspected the presence of sorcery among the Gaians and now the proof of it has been spoken. My brothers and I have met and we are all of us in agreement; our differences must be set aside in the face of this threat.'

The two High Chieftains still glared at each other but the first comment came from Bradan, the headman of Mobryn. Bevan's father.

'What the buggery is that man doing here?'

He was pointing at one of the men who'd followed Reaghan, a tall and dangerous-looking man with long hair and a beard blacker than a crow's feather. His face was long and lean with a thin scar beneath one eye, and creeping up one side of his neck Rhia saw the blue tattoos of a Gadarim. He was dressed in a dark tunic and a wolf-pelt cloak, and seemed more amused than offended by the outburst. Several men in the hall, including some of the Gorvicae, started protesting again, this time aiming their disapproval at the newcomers. Once again, Reaghan raised his voice.

'Chief Ierryn and his people are also here as my guests. This Gaian threat is as real to them as it is to us.'

The silence that followed this was reluctant, and Rhia realised the man must be Ierryn the Black, High Chieftain of the Dariniae. *No wonder Bradan was the first one to object. Mobryn has suffered from their raids for years. So have the coastal Gorvicae, come to that.* She strongly suspected that men would have drawn swords had the druid not stated that he was here as a guest. Enemy or not, some things were just not done. There were still mutterings of dissent from the crowd however and Reaghan spoke again, his voice firm.

'We must put aside our differences if our peoples are to survive. For now I will settle for a lack of open hostility.'

He glared around the room and Rhia noticed that the Gorvicae and Dariniae looked to him first before turning to the druids of their own tribes. The various robed men nodded their heads and a surly silence fell upon the hall. It was strange to hear a druid say something so like a command, but then times were desperate and his wisdom was sorely needed. Carradan was the first of the chiefs to speak.

'If Druid Reaghan says it must be, then it must be. We will gather our warriors together as one.'

Baercban still looked sceptical.

'Assuming we can indeed fight off these Gaians and their sorcerer, what happens when this is done? Lepidus is not the only Gaian out there and we shall have to deal with them, one way or the other. And I shall deal as is best for my tribe.'

Beside Reaghan Rhia saw Ierryn the Black nod in agreement, though he said nothing. He didn't seem the overly talkative type. Carradan looked to the Gorvic chief.

'Lepidus is not all of Gaivia, we may yet find a peace with the Empire once we defeat him. But tomorrow is for tomorrow. We shall talk of this later but for now, unity is all.'

There were sounds of approval from the crowd, though much of it was grudging, and Reaghan bowed his head to his chieftain. Anwen, one of the Caderyn's few female chiefs, spoke respectfully to the druid.

'And what tribe is to take charge of this alliance?'

For a moment it looked as if the hall might erupt again, this time with everyone shouting the virtues of their own people, but Reaghan answered before it could begin.

'No one tribe shall be ruler over another in this. We shall fight as one, as a single tribe of free Lurians.'

There were many mutterings at this but then Marius spoke up to the assembly.

'Forgive me, that *is* wise, but no beast lives with two heads. An army must have one commander. One chief should be placed in charge, in battle at least.'

A few men sneered at a Gaian offering counsel, but it was obvious that he spoke sense and most of them kept their peace. It was Reaghan who spoke once again.

'I agree, son of Dessidus, and I would ask of all you chiefs and headmen, who among you would doubt the prowess or the honour of Charging Bull?'

There were several nods and grunts of approval but Baercban puffed up his chest.

'No Gorvic will bow to a Caderyn!'

Both Gawan and Sedryn voiced agreement but Reaghan turned his piercing eyes on them and the trio fell silent.

'I do not say you must call him your chieftain, nor bow and scrape to any man. I asked a simple question; does any man here doubt his loyalty, his courage, his strength, his focus or his will?'

Rhia had to hold back a smile as the Gadarim's virtues were listed and not a man of the hall dared challenge her father on any of them. Sedryn looked as if he wished to speak but simultaneous glares from Gawan and his father silenced him before he could start. Rhia eyed the chieftain's son with contempt. She knew from Broken Stream that the rat-faced man was nothing but a useless coward and she suspected that Baercban and their First Man knew it as well. He backed down with bad grace, sulkily folding his arms. Ierryn, standing behind him, twitched his mouth up in a tiny smirk but otherwise no-one commented. Reaghan let the pause go on a moment longer before addressing the hall again.

'It is agreed then. We shall act together for the time being, as a single tribe of Luriae against this common threat, and Carradan son of Cadog shall be our elected leader.'

The assembled chiefs murmured their assent with various degrees of enthusiasm and Carradan stepped forward to speak again.

'My thanks to you all – and I swear by all the gods to do all I can to live up to your trust. Let us prepare ourselves.' He turned to where Madoc and Owain stood nearby. 'Send forth messages to the other tribes, to the Orugae, the Bearnicans, and the Rydicae if you can. Have them send any man who would fight this madness to Bryngarth. With sorcery abound in this land they are in as much danger as we are, though they may not know it.'

The two Gadarim nodded and disappeared to find riders. Carradan turned back to the hall, which contained almost every headman of the newly-allied tribes. As he spoke Rhia felt a fluttering in her stomach and resisted the temptation to reach for Marius' hand.

'These Gaians are dangerous, and even more so if they have sold themselves to sorcery. Perhaps we shall all of us be dead soon, and all of this will be for nothing.' He paused a moment and drew Ironhorn, raising his voice. 'But better to die free than live in chains! And with the blessings of the gods and with unity between us, we may yet prevail. Call your warriors. Assemble every fighter in the west to Bryngarth. The Gaians are coming – it is time for war!'

Rhia found herself shouting along with the others as, for a brief moment, differences were lain aside as Caderyn, Dariniae and Gorvicae raised their voices as one, and the longhall rang with the name of the War God.

'Taran!'

Chapter 30. Training

Yet again the shieldwall had collapsed, and yet again Marius was doing an admirable job of keeping his patience. He shouted and blustered at the brawling rabble but just about managed to keep his good humour, despite the obvious frustration he was feeling. It had all been going so well; the tribesmen had kept their formation, more or less, as they marched or wheeled and even as they jogged, and the front rank had kept their shields as close together as they could. Rhia had been proud of what they'd achieved in just a few days and had seen hope on the horizon for their new legion. And then the lines had clashed, and everything had turned to chaos.

The two newly-made cohorts had disintegrated within seconds into two mobs of warriors battering wildly at each other. Rhia was glad that they held only light staves of wood instead of swords but even these were causing damage enough. She waded in with her own baton as Marius called out for the fighters to disengage. Most of them responded to the call but plenty were clearly enjoying the scrap and had to be pulled apart by the Gadarim, who were acting as centurions and optios.

Rhia sighed. She might not have been a soldier but she'd seen the training of the Tenth more times than she could count, and the comparison in her head was not a favourable one. Their smoothly manoeuvring formations of men were a far cry from the rabble that now brawled in the afternoon sun. The weather was warm, and Rhia knew that the fighters would be thirsty and frustrated. She knew equally well that Centurion Lothar would never let his men end an exercise with a failure, and it seemed that Marius was of the same mind. She tried not to think of the legion men that she knew, men that she might end up killing before long.

Instead she focused on trying to get her formation back together, and grabbed Adara by the back of her tunic and dragged her from a Gorvic fighter. She had rushed him to the ground and was now struggling to wrestle his staff from his hands, but Rhia hauled her back and away from him while another Gorvic helped his comrade to his feet. All around them warriors were sneering insults to each other but, mercifully, it seemed no blood had been spilt this time.

Rhia watched as the various fights were broken up and the two cohorts started backing away from each other. It wasn't as if her people were stupid; they understood the need for changing how they fought, and the Gorvicae had even tried it already to an extent, with warriors fighting in small groups as opposed to fighting alone, but the concept of drilling as a unit was completely alien to these people. Even when fighting together, a Lurian's concept of battle revolved solely around proving one's personal courage in the eyes of the tribe and of the gods. Friends might look out for one another and watch the back of a comrade in the throng, but for the most part battles were a simple affair of rushing forwards and getting stuck in to the fighting, and what training took place was a means of honing skills and building strength. *Nothing like this.*

The two bands looked surly as they reformed their lines, and jibes were still being flung back and forth. It probably didn't help that the cohorts were formed from rival tribes, but even Reaghan was not such an optimist as to suggest Caderyn and Gorvicae fight together in one formation. Gawan was bawling angrily for his section to get back in line, and Rhia knew that their frustration was even worse than that of the Caderyn.

Her own tribe had, for the most part, accepted Marius as her new husband and as an expert on Gaian warfare. There were plenty who disapproved of him of course, but by now everyone knew the story of their escape from Tamora and even if they didn't *like* him, they were beginning to respect him. *It probably helps that his hair and beard have grown so much. For all his talk he doesn't look much like a Gaian any more.* Rhia wondered if Livilla or Junia would even recognise him if they saw him now, dressed in a homespun red tunic and baggy green trews, bellowing in Lurian at this unruly mob. His grasp of the language was improving day by day, and Owain and the Gadarim had supplied him with some rather choice curse-words. It was largely a good sign, Rhia thought. It meant they wanted him to be a part of them.

The same could not be said for the Gorvicae. Only a few moons ago the Tenth Legion had been fighting them, and it hadn't taken much questioning to discover that Gawan had been heavily involved. Apparently, though Baercban had been in favour of it, the uprising had largely been the plan of Gawan and Duran. It seemed they'd heard a rumour about the Fourteenth Legion being severely weakened by disease, and as such would be an easy target for attack. This had turned out to be false of course, and the shame of the defeat was still heavy on them. It must have been galling beyond belief for them to stand here and take orders from a man who'd caused the deaths of their friends and comrades.

When he'd first begun this training several Caderyn had asked if Marius had been at Nantwyn. He'd answered honestly that he had been there, but only to observe as he'd been deemed too inexperienced to fight yet, and most people had left it at that. But Nantwyn had been more than five winters ago, and it was less than five moons since the Gorvicae uprising. What little credit he got for being good at what he did was mostly undone by badly-masked resentment. *When they bother to mask it at all.* Gawan and the other Gorvicae Gadarim glared murder at him quite openly, though as yet not one of them had done more than sneer. She wondered if it was more an understanding of his usefulness or the instinctive reaction to obey their druids that kept them from simply attacking him here and now. *Probably a little of both, but I think Reaghan's word can sometimes work miracles.*

The senior druid had been working endlessly to keep the tribes working together, and had gone so far as to give a name to the Lurian alliance; the Caledon. Rhia understood only a little of the Ancient Tongue, mainly from the older place-names in Caderyn territory, but she knew that it was a mix of the words for *hard* and *comrade*. It was a good word, and people liked it. Rhia wondered if it was intended to simply mean a strong alliance, or if the druid had maybe had a little twinkle in his eye when he'd thought of it, and that the *hard* part referred to the hard work it would be to keep them together.

Rhia started getting her own cohort back into line. The Caderyn were, marginally, better behaved about it than the Gorvicae and it didn't take long to get them in some sort of order. They obeyed her without too much grumbling and Rhia was pleased at their response. Against the objections of Gawan and several of his warriors, she was the only Lurian officer of the First Caledon who was not of the Gadarim, her position being at the insistence of Marius, the legion's unofficial commander. Rhia would have been happy simply to fight and to help with the training but her husband had argued, quite correctly, that her familiarity with the Gaian legions was second only to his own, and that he would need her in a position of authority.

The Gorvicae Gadarim hadn't liked it, naturally, but they'd had little choice but to accept it. While Carradan was officially the general of the legion, it was Marius who held it together and his opinion on most things was final.

It had been his idea to give the legion a banner as well, though Rhia had been the one to make it happen. A legion needed a standard, a symbol for the fighters to be united behind, and if any force needed unity, it was this one. Rhia had approached Madoc to ask his permission about the design but the First Man had approved the decision and so even as the warriors sweated out here, back at Bryngarth their new banner was being sewn.

Rhia pressed her lips together at the thought of the Caderyn's First Man. The loss of his son had changed Madoc more than any were willing to admit, though he was still a good man for all his grief. He had gone so far as to apologise for not being able to induct Rhia into the Gadarim of the tribe, and thus spare her this awkward situation. She had, he said, displayed many of the virtues necessary for joining the warrior elite but he feared that if it were put to a gathering of them, which it must be, voices might be raised in objection to her. She was after all a mother, he'd said, and even among the rare female Gadarim, *mothers* who were Gadarim were almost unheard of. He had shown his kindness was still there when he refrained from stating the more obvious reason; she had married a Gaian, and for all that Marius might be helping them now, there was no certainty where his loyalty would lie once all this was over. *I can hardly blame them, I suppose. All most of them have seen of Gaians are their soldiers and tax collectors. And they don't know Marius the way I do.*

Rhia had surprised herself by how little anger she'd felt at that. There had been a time when to be Gadarim was all she could have wanted but now, though that yearning was still there, she had other priorities. Even if she didn't have a war to help win, which she did, her son was now the first thing that she thought of every morning, and the last thing that she pictured before she slept. She was still a fighter, she was proud to be one and she *had* to be one, but now her focus had turned to the reasons *why* she had to fight more than simply how to. The breeze blew a curtain of dark hair across her eyes and she shoved it back behind her ear. *Blonde wouldn't have suited me anyway.*

The lines were more or less ordered again and Rhia looked over at the field beside the woods to where another pair of cohorts were drilling. Madoc's men and the Dariniae cohort were practicing simpler drills than Rhia's and Gawan's, simply advancing and retreating over and over, shoving forwards with their shields and jabbing out with wooden staves. Fewer than half of the warriors had swords of their own, though they weren't using them today, the rest having always used axes or clubs in battle. It meant the metalworkers of Bryngarth were working just as hard as the warriors in an attempt to equip them all before the Gaians came. A minor blessing was that shorter swords were more suited to a legion formation so the blades took less iron and marginally less time to make, and overall Rhia was confident that their army would be fairly well-equipped with them. Shields on the other hand, were another matter.

Caderyn, Gorvicae and Dariniae had been making swords and knives of some kind for untold generations, but shields were a completely new idea. According to Reaghan there had been Lurian tribes who'd used something similar a long time ago, but no-one living in the west had made a shield in centuries, and it was apparently not as simple as it seemed. A Gaian shield was more than half a man's height and made of three sheets of glued wood, bound together in an iron frame. Jenkin and his apprentices, along with every other carpenter that could be found, were working hard to produce as many of these as possible, but it was taking a long time and they were rarely up to legion standard. Rhia looked over at the cohorts drilling near the treeline.

Only the first rank of each formation was equipped with a shield, the Caderyn having daubed them with red and blue paint for their tribe, the Dariniae in plain black. After each exercise the ranks were switched around, the shields being passed between them so that all could practice with them. The process was slow and clumsy and involved no small amount of squabbling, and Rhia wondered what men like Lothar would think of such an affair. *Our warriors might be good at fighting, but at this warfare we are such amateurs!* She envied Elfed and Eogan, training the new bowmen down near the river. They at least were simply perfecting what they already knew how to do, ready to attack the Gaians from ambush or provide support for the legion. *Not like us.*

Marius was now striding in between the two cohorts, his best parade-ground voice booming out equal measures of criticism and praise. Well, almost equal.

'Stop me if I'm wrong, but I think I said "stay in formation", not "stay in formation until it looks like there's fun to be had!"'

Rhia was glad the only objections to that were a few surly grumbles. He continued to pace as he went on, his officers' baton tucked under one arm, his hands clasped casually behind his back. For a moment Rhia smiled and almost laughed out loud as she realised this was the closest thing to comfortable he had been in over a moon's turn. He was in enemy territory, fleeing for his life, the safety of his wife and son a constant worry, and his family either murdered or in hiding. But *this* he was good at. He could train and lead men as well as any man of the Tenth, and everybody knew that the Tenth Legion were the best. Walking slowly between two lines of fighters who were still at least partly his enemies, he seemed relaxed and confident and completely without fear.

'Now your manoeuvring is getting better and your speed of march is good, but it is *vital* that your formation holds on contact with the enemy. I understand you each want to do your best for your tribe, that is natural, but you will not serve them best by getting yourselves killed.'

For the most part the warriors either nodded or said nothing, though a few of them scowled at the Gaian. It was understandable. Even if they didn't hate him personally, which many Gorvicae certainly did, plenty of them would be thinking back to that black day at Nantwyn, and remembering the deadly efficiency of the Gaian legions. Like Rhia they must have realised that the time they had was limited, and that the progress they had made was not impressive. *Lepidus could be here before Leu grows full again. Even if we did nothing but train and sleep every day until then, we still could not hope to match a Gaian legion shield to shield, and they know it.*

Marius continued his mixture of encouragement and critique, and Rhia tried to think on the positive side. They should at least have some superiority in numbers. Already they had four cohorts of nearly five-hundred fighters, making the First Caledon almost as large as a pre-Strife Gaian legion. There had been talk of their splitting the force into several smaller legions but both Reaghan and Carradan had disagreed; the message of unity was the most important thing. If needed, multiple cohorts could be commanded by the senior Gadarim there but for the sake of its identity, the legion should stay as one for now. Rhia had agreed and Marius had come around to it.

With more fighters arriving at Bryngarth every day it was likely the First Caledon Legion would number almost six thousand warriors. The Caderyn would hopefully make up around half of that, assuming that sufficient men were found and trained in time. Baercban had said he could muster some two thousand more Gorvicae to add to the five hundred he had with him, and Ierryn had mentioned a subordinate chief in Niswyn who could gather perhaps a thousand more Dariniae.

Rhia ran through the numbers in her head, and was strangely grateful for all those boring hours of running a household in Tamora. Organising men was a little different to planning the family expenses, but the principles were largely the same and Marius had found her invaluable in the logistical side of things. Already she had been sending out messages to farmers to make sure they all stayed fed at least while their new legion was being formed.

All told, they should number almost seven thousand fighters, most of them trained into the legion with others serving as archers, horsemen and scouts. If the Orugae, Rydicae or Bearnicans sent anyone that would swell their little army even further. To her knowledge, Lepidus would have his two legions, each of around fifteen hundred men, along with some eight hundred Aboran Destroyers and a few wings of Nomad cavalry. In theory, that meant seven thousand Caledon against barely four thousand Gaians. *But the Gaian legions are a damned sight better trained than we are, and it won't just be Aborans enhanced by magics this time...*

Rhia shook her head. Now wasn't the time to think that way. The numbers were on their side and they would be fighting on their own territory, making movement and supply that much easier. Besides, she and Marius had fighters to train and they needed her focus here and now. Even as she thought this, her husband's voice came to her across the field.

'Is your cohort ready, Tribune Dessida?'

Rhia smiled as she gave a last quick check to her line, enjoying their little game.

'Ready and willing, Tribune Dessida!'

Marius gave a smile of his own in response, and Rhia liked that several warriors seemed amused by the married couple. Her husband called across to the Gorvicae section as they formed up behind their green-painted shields.

'Tribune Gawan, is your cohort ready?'

The Gadarim scowled as he replied.

'Let's get on with it!'

Marius nodded his head a fraction and managed a patient smile.

'I shall take that as a yes.'

Rhia wondered what General Lepidus would have said if one of *his* officers had spoken in that tone. Rhia was tempted to shout something offensive to her counterpart in reprisal for his cheek, but she thought better of it. *This isn't a Gaian legion, and this alliance of tribes is a fragile thing. Let's just hope it stays together long enough to see off Lepidus and Praecus.*

Once again negativity threatened to dominate her mood and she dragged her mind back to the matter at hand. The situation might be dire, there was no doubt about that, but the best way to get through it was with bold hearts and well-trained fighters, and that was what they were making now. The two lines faced off against each other again and slowly began to advance. Rhia hefted her clumsy shield and twirled the baton around her wrist. The cohort upped its pace. *And here we go again.*

*

Belenos was red and sinking down to the horizon before Marius finally called a halt. The fighters were exhausted but they had finished on a high point, with both cohorts

427

keeping formation long enough to attack and withdraw effectively. Just. They had a long way to go, and everyone knew it, but they'd made progress today and the tribesmen smiled through their fatigue as they collapsed onto the grass. Buckets of water were carried up from the stream and the fighters gulped at it greedily or else splashed the cooling liquid on their faces. The two cohorts were so tired they barely even had strength to bicker. Not that they didn't try, of course.

Gwydion, one of the Gorvicae's Gadarim, had sunk down near to Rhia.

'He'd have called a stop to this two charges ago if you damned Caderyn could hold your line straight.'

He spoke without any real malice, probably because he was too tired for it, and Rhia idly threw a pebble in his general direction, missing him by a clear foot. She was just as tired as he was.

'And he'd have stopped us two charges before that if you damned Gorvicae could tell your left from right.'

Gwydion blushed a little. On a command to wheel left about a quarter of Gawan's company had faltered in confusion and caused a break in their formation, leading to some over-enthusiastic Caderyn leaping into the breach and laying about them with their staves. Marius had shouted himself hoarse at both cohorts and the fighters responsible had been singled out and made to march and wheel at speed until even watching them felt dizzying. The remaining tribesmen had at least enjoyed a rest because of it, and had all laughed together at the fate of the culprits.

But despite their brief rest Marius had driven them hard afterwards, and Rhia's shoulders burned from the weight of the shield and baton, and her legs felt like they were made of water. Painful, aching, hollow water, which she knew made no sense but at this point, she didn't care.

Gwydion grunted and stretched towards the pebble she had thrown. His arms were covered in tattooed battlemarks, including a flying dragon where his forearm met his wrist. *Presumably that's meant to be Mabonac, though he really should be green instead of blue.* In Tamora, the priests would doubtless have argued endlessly with each other about which was the more holy; the Dragon God's official colour or the sacred blue of the woad in which the Gadarim's tattoos were depicted. Rhia knew priests who could have debated that point for hours and still never have come up with an answer that would satisfy them. She wondered if Reaghan and the druids ever did that, talking endlessly about the nature of the gods. Rhia's understanding had been confused as much as explained by her time in Tamora but then a druid would know so much more than she did. She was pondering whether it was truth or lies what the Gaians had told her about Lurian and Gaian gods being essentially the same, when Gwydion flung the pebble back at her, bringing her back to the present. He missed by a slightly smaller margin than she had.

'No wonder these Gaians are such miserable bastards – if they do this every day they must have no strength left to hump at night.'

She shrugged.

'They're used to it, and some of them are even pretty good at humping afterwards.'

She nodded towards Marius, who was wandering between the sitting warriors giving words of encouragement here and there. Gwydion gave a grudging nod.

'He'd have to be to keep a Lurian girl in his bed, I suppose.'

A young lad came around with bucket and beakers and the two warriors drank in comfortable silence, too weary to do much else. The happy quiet was obviously too good to last however and Rhia frowned as she saw Gawan and Marius approaching, clearly arguing about something. She heard their voices, calm but clearly strained, as they came closer.

'It's important because a breach in the wall weakens everyone in the formation.'

'Your people did it at Nantwyn, *and* at White Ridge – your walls opened and the giants came out to attack.'

'The Aborans came out to exploit an advantage and besides, Gaian legions are trained for that manoeuvre, *we* can barely keep a shieldwall together.'

'Keeping Gadarim in the wall hampers their fighting ability.'

'But the wall *increases* everyone else's.'

Rhia felt her mood darken as they approached, but she was spared from having to join in the argument by the appearance of her father and Reaghan coming towards them. A closer look showed her that Ierryn and Baercban were there too, along with Sedryn the coward and grey-bearded Hywel, the eldest of the Gorvicae's druids. They reached Rhia and Gwydion at almost the same moment as Gawan and Marius, though the two men were so busy arguing they didn't notice them until the last second. Carradan was the first to speak.

'No serious problems, I hope?'

Carradan's voice was friendly enough and though Gawan's lip twitched a little the Gorvic settled for a shrug of his shoulders.

'Nothing to concern chieftains.'

The Caderyn chief gave Marius a questioning look but the Gaian simply nodded along.

'Minor setbacks father, nothing serious.'

Rhia liked that Marius referred to Carradan like that and the chieftain smiled happily in response. Gawan and

Baercban on the other hand were looking on with obvious disapproval but Carradan spoke again before they could comment.

'I am glad, my Gaian son.' He took a deep breath. 'Unfortunately the word I had today *does* concern chieftains, and it will concern the three of you as well.'

He indicated both Rhia and Gawan along with Marius, and Rhia was the first to ask the question.

'What has happened?'

Baercban gave the answer.

'The Gaians are on the move. Word from the north is that the Panther Legion is attacking Gorvicae land, along with their horsemen and giants. They have reached the Silver Lock and have laid waste to several villages.'

Rhia took in a breath as Gawan and Marius spoke at once.

'When?'

The two men eyed at each other for a moment but then turned to face the chieftains and druids. On the ground beside them, Gwydion started clambering to his feet as Hywel answered for his chief.

'This news is already three days old.'

Gawan did not waste a heartbeat. He dragged Gwydion the rest of the way up and spoke directly to Baercban.

'They must suspect what we are doing. I can take our men north tonight, with good weather we could...'

But Marius interrupted him.

'The men are not yet trained, not by a long way. If you take them against a legion now all you will do is get them killed.'

Gawan glared at him and clenched his fists. They were big and heavily scarred.

'If I wanted your opinion, Gaian, I'd have asked for it.'

Marius was no great warrior himself but he looked down at the Gadarim as if completely unimpressed.

'You've just spent all day asking for it, Gorvic. You may know your way around a sword but you know full well what a legion can do, and that's without counting what sorcery Praecus might have worked on them.' He turned to face the chiefs. 'Was there any word of the Te... of the Lion Legion?'

Carradan nodded.

'Their banner was seen near White Ridge but they did not march with the others. Possibly they are coming down here to us?'

Marius pondered for a moment before shaking his head.

'No. They will secure that area until the expedition into Gorvic land is complete, then they will head down here in force to deal with us. Lepidus must know that we would be massing at Bryngarth but he wants to make sure the Gorvicae are cowed into submission before he sets forth.'

Gawan sneered.

'Maybe Gaians would be *cowed* by such an action but my people are bred for war.'

Marius fought to contain his irritation.

'Your people are bred for *fighting* and it is not always the same thing.'

Sedryn foolishly decided to comment on that.

'Spoken like a man who fights his battles from the rear.'

Marius turned to face the blonde man but Rhia couldn't resist speaking first.

'As opposed to one who fights at the front and then runs when a woman raises her voice to him?'

Sedryn bristled but neither his father nor their tribe's First Man spoke up for him. Both Gawan and Baercban looked profoundly uncomfortable and seemed almost grateful when Reaghan moved the talk on.

'I am no warrior, but it seems that the tribune has a point. Both of our peoples have faced the legions and known defeat and, as he says, that was before this sorcerer was given free reign. He is wise who learns from his mistakes.'

No-one dared to argue too forcefully with the druid and Gawan kept his tone respectful.

'Perhaps so, Druid Reaghan. But wise or foolish I am leaving here tonight, and many of my warriors will come with me. Caledon or not, our first duty is to our own tribe.'

Rhia shook her head. She hated the thought of leaving Lurian villages undefended but Marius was right and besides, they needed the men here.

'You won't help your tribe by getting slaughtered.'

She did her best not to sound confrontational but it was difficult with Gawan. He might have good intentions in wishing to defend his people, but there was no escaping the fact that this was the man who'd killed her brother, and Rhia could never forget that. Her tone came across far harsher than she'd intended and the warrior took a breath to spit something back, but Reaghan raised a hand before he could.

'Enough.'

The old man's voice was quiet but the air fairly thrummed with power and the little group fell silent in a heartbeat. Reaghan turned and spoke to the three chieftains.

'It is wise to continue to prepare, yet it would be wrong of us to abandon Baercban's people to their fate.'

Ierryn seemed entirely unconcerned about that but Baercban and Carradan looked seriously at one another. Carradan spoke first, thinking aloud as much as announcing a plan.

'We could send some of our fighters to harry the Gaians a little. We do not need to bring them to battle, merely draw them away from towns and villages.'

Rhia finished the thought.

'Eogan and Elfed could take their archers through the woods? They could attack and withdraw to discourage the legions?'

She thought of her own experience with the Carrocks in the mountains, and remembered the deadly effect of well-concealed archers. Carradan seemed in favour but Marius shook his head.

'They will be expecting that. For such a plan to work we would need a solid infantry force to fall back on, something that could destroy a large scouting section or hold off something stronger still.'

Gawan shrugged.

'Then I will take my company to support them. They are better trained than most and they know the terrain.'

Rhia wanted to argue against his cohort being best-trained but decided now was not the time for pride. Carradan was nodding his agreement.

'If you avoided meeting them head-on you might buy time for your people to flee, and tie up Lepidus and the Panthers whilst we gather and train more warriors.' He looked to Marius. 'Would one cohort be sufficient?'

Rhia's husband shook his head slowly and scratched at his jaw. Rhia knew he still wasn't used to wearing a beard, or to the Caderyn's somewhat rudimentary bathing, and he complained about the itching every night.

'I would want to take two to be on the safe side. Even if they are to avoid pitched battle there is always the danger of being pinned down. Two formations to support your archers would give the commander greater flexibility.'

Gawan nodded.

'Very well then, Madoc's fighters can come with me, if they will.'

Marius shook his head again.

'If we are sending unprepared men we might as well send the *most* prepared of them. Your cohort and the First Cohort are the ones most advanced in their training.'

The Gorvic slashed his hand through the air and spoke at exactly the same moment that Rhia spat out her response.

'I'm not taking *her* with me!'

'I'm not taking orders from *him*!'

They glared daggers at each other for a moment, and Rhia wondered yet again how it would feel to kill this man. She had imagined it long ago when they had argued after Broken Stream, but back then it had simply been blind anger. Since then this man had brought the Gaians into their land, killed Dane before her eyes, and by an extension of his actions caused the deaths of Bevan and Ewan. If ever a man deserved her hatred it was this one, and a glance into his eyes told her the feeling was mutual. *Caledon or not, one day I will kill this man. Or else he will kill me.*

Carradan raised his hands to pacify them.

'That will not be necessary. If these cohorts are to be tested in battle, best it be with a commander experienced in such things. Rhianwyn, would you object to your cohort being led by Marius for this?'

Rhia felt her fists clench involuntarily. She had worked hard to get this troop into shape and they were *her* warriors to lead into battle.

'I can lead my section, Gawan can lead his, and Marius can command overall. That makes sense?'

The Gorvicae seemed unimpressed with that but they said nothing. Marius gave her an apologetic look before speaking to the group.

'It does and it doesn't. I agree that I should command the first action of the legion, I am best suited to it, but if I go we will still need someone here to continue training the other cohorts.' He paused. 'That has to be you.'

Rhia couldn't believe this. Marius had always supported her as his equal and now he was telling her to stay at home and behave herself while the men went off and fought. She locked eyes with him and prepared to say something fierce but a gentle cough from Reaghan caused her to turn. The elder druid was looking quite calmly at her, and she felt embarrassed for the outburst she'd almost made.

'The good tribune is right, Rhianwyn. You know the Gaian legions better than any of us here and we will need your knowledge.'

His words were gentle and seemed to dissolve some of her anger. He was right of course. It made sense to send Marius, who was experienced in the field and had to prove he was on their side, and it made sense to send Gawan, the First Man of the tribe whose land was under threat. It made sense to keep her here to help prepare the rest of the legion. It all made perfect, logical, bloody sense – but that didn't mean she had to like it. She wanted to be fighting Lepidus, to repay him for the deaths of her sister and her father-in-law, and protect her people from the sorcery of Praecus. But one look at Reaghan's piercing eyes told her exactly what he was thinking. *Doing what is right generally means not getting what we want*. She sighed.

'You are right, father. That is how it should be.'

Both Carradan and Marius let out badly-hidden sighs of relief that her anger had not been provoked, but Gawan couldn't resist a smirk as he spoke.

'Well I suppose I'd sooner fight beside a Lion than the Wildcat,' he turned to Marius, 'but don't expect to be telling me what to do, Gaian.'

Rhia fumed but Marius kept his head.

'I'll expect you to follow my orders if we come to battle because that is what our chiefs agreed upon when this legion was formed.'

His voice was perfectly calm but Rhia could sense the tension beneath it. Gawan sneered a little.

'*Our* chiefs now is it?'

Baercban gave him a warning look but it was Carradan who spoke.

'It is indeed. Marius is my son now.'

Like Marius and Reaghan he had not spoken loudly, but the words had been hard as stone. Gawan curled his lip a little more but left it at that, turning to his own chief instead.

'Then we shall be away tonight. I will leave Duran here to act as your guard, the rest of the warriors I will take with me.'

Baercban nodded slowly, though it was clear he was being told a fact, not being asked permission. In war, the First Man of a tribe's Gadarim had far greater power than in times of peace, and few chiefs would disagree with their First Man's decisions in front of anyone. Rhia got the feeling that if anyone was the type of man to take advantage of such a situation, it was Gawan. The Leaping Wolf seemed to have only minimal respect for his chieftain, and none at all for his cowardly heir.

The conversation quickly turned from debating what action to take to how best that action should be arranged, and Rhia found her mind drifting as she started to fret for her husband. She hated the notion of being another housebound mother, sitting at home and worrying for her man when he went to battle, but she couldn't help but feel a stab of fear as well at the thought of his not coming back. At the thought of little Lucan being left fatherless. *And of being widowed twice over in only five years. Admit it girl, you care for him more than you allow him to think. More than you allow yourself to think.*

She shook the thought away and looked down at the tiny scar below her thumb. He was not Bevan. He never would be Bevan. But he *was* Lucan's father. And yet again he was going to war, to fight *her* enemies, and she was not going with him. *And he'll be fighting beside men that he was fighting* against *last time. Men like Gawan, who will kill him if given an excuse.* Rhia spoke a silent prayer while the chiefs and druids talked, and wondered if Reaghan could hear the words in her head, then decided it didn't matter if he could. She prayed to the God of War, to Taran or Vulco or Vulco Taranis or to all three, and asked that her husband be brought back safe to his wife and son. She prayed to the Gaian gods and the Lurian gods that Marius of the Caderyn come home safely from this battle. She prayed that he would make the Gaians bleed for what they'd done to him and for what they had done to her people. And she promised as much as prayed that the next time he went to war, he would go there with his wife at his side.

Chapter 31. The First Test

Antonius Dessida looked down the long dirt road and took the slow, familiar breaths of a soldier calming his nerves. He was afraid, as any sane man was when battle loomed, but years of training and a fair amount of real experience meant the young man was as prepared for it as anyone could be expected to be. He held his fear in check with steady breathing and calm focus, and he watched the forest track with eyes that assessed terrain as a matter of habit.

The beeches and birches stretched close to the road, which curved away to his right towards the southeast. The archers scattered at intervals through them could barely be seen, even in clear daylight, and would hopefully be a hindrance to the Gaian cohort on its way here. There was a slight, very subtle, slope to the ground that would act in their favour when the time came to advance, and the sun, now past its zenith, would prove little hindrance to their own sight and some discomfort to the enemy. His cohort was stretched across the breadth of the road and not far from where he stood, looking ancient and mighty beside its neighbours, a wide-trunked oak stretched its branches to the sky. The oak was a symbol of Father Gron, and the young Gaian whispered a prayer both to him and Vulco Malus that he might be made victorious on this day.

Good plan Marius, offer prayers to Gaian gods as you stand with tribesmen against a Gaian legion! He shook his head. *Gaian gods stand for Gaian virtues, and Gron knows there's more virtue on my side of the field than on Lepidus'!* He felt satisfied at the argument and then had to hold back a smile. Yet again he'd been talking to himself as Marius and not Antonius. That was all Rhia's fault. She'd been calling him that for ages of course, and he had to admit he rather liked it, but she had naturally then introduced him as Marius to everyone here, and it was now used so often to address and refer to him that even in his own head he had begun to adopt it. *You're going native, my boy. They always said your father had too much time for these barbarians and look at you now, changing your name for them.*

He shrugged the thought off. His father had been quite right in observing and learning from the tribes, and he'd met far more savages among the Gaians than he had among the barbarians. Not that he wasn't proud of his own people and their history; the city of Gaivia was the most beautiful in the world and its people shone the light of civilisation wherever they went. Unfortunately, even among the greatest and noblest of peoples, there were always those who brought shame on their ancestors. Marius sighed a little and thought of his old mentor. He'd always known General Lepidus to be a hard and ambitious man but never had he dreamed that he would stoop so low as this. To become involved with sorcery and murder, all in the name of greater power, it was... it was hard to fathom.

Lepidus had been a man he had respected, even admired to a degree, for all their political differences. A self-made man and a legendary soldier, Marius had looked up to him and had learned much as his student. And Tullius... Tullius had worshipped the man. Marius ground his teeth and tried not to think about that. He'd been concerned about his brother long before Rhia had got them caught up in all this, but he had turned a blind eye to it, not wanting to look. Tullius had grown obsessive and furtive, even as his wife had grown more quiet and nervous. *Perhaps if I'd intervened a little earlier...*

Marius clenched his jaw tighter and forced himself to concentrate. He could agonise about Tullius later, right now he had a battle to win. He looked along the line of his cohort. With him, three centuries of Caderyn warriors stood four ranks deep, stretched along a front of less than thirty yards. Behind them a further two centuries stood in reserve, ready to add support where it was needed. They seemed eager but nervous as they waited in the sunshine, and Marius was grateful the young druid had come along. Bael, one of the first Caderyn he'd spoken to, walked up and down the line offering blessings and reassurance, and the warriors seemed comforted by his words. Despite his pleasant nature Marius was unsure of how comfortable he was around him, given that druids were practitioners of magic, but at least he was giving some heart to the men. Apparently Lurian druids did not use their powers directly and were closer to being priests than sorcerers, but nonetheless, Marius was wary. *Though if, gods forbid, we encounter sorcery today, at least we will have someone who might counter it.* Not that they should.

The cohort of the Fourteenth on its way here had doubtless been affected by Praecus' magics, but there was no reason to assume that he would be with them himself. From what Gawan's people had said, most of General Lepidus' force was on its way to the Gorvicae capital, and this cohort was simply coming to secure a riverside village and its bridge. With Fortuna's blessing, they should just have the infantry and a few Nomad outriders to contend with, and Eogan's bowmen would be taking care of them. That just left the legion men. A single cohort of the Fourteenth to contend with twice their numbers attacking from ambush. Simple enough in theory.

He exchanged nods with a few of the men and made sure to look encouraging without overdoing it. *'Good commanders must inspire and lead by example but they must also be something separate from the men. If they see you as just a rich man's son they won't respect you as a soldier; if they see you as simply one of them they won't respect you as a commander. Balance, it is the key to everything'*. Marius grimaced a little as he remembered the lesson. It had come from the general.

He resisted the urge to pluck at his tunic as he felt himself beginning to sweat under the mail. The weather had been damp but it was definitely getting warmer, and so far they'd had no clouds to block the sun. He tried to remember what month it was but it had been a long time since he'd kept close track of the days, and the best that he could manage was that spring was fading and summer was almost upon them.

Bael passed by him with a simple nod of acknowledgement, though if Marius was actually *blessed* by the priest, he didn't notice it. Like the rest of the men he would be fighting on foot, something he'd not done in earnest for three years. In the last fights with the Gorvicae he had commanded from horseback, and his only combat had been a few swings of his sword. He had not fought in a shieldwall since the early fighting against the Rydicae. In a tradition now all-too-often ignored in the legions, General Lepidus still insisted that all junior officers fight in the formation for their first engagement as combatants. The destiny of officers might be to direct things from the rear, but the general preached the message that without experience in the wall a man could never understand it, and not one soldier of the Tenth, from the general down to the clerks, had been excused from locking shields before the enemy.

And now Antonius Dessida stood in the front rank again. The Caderyn had to see that he was a man worth following, and the only way to do that was by fighting alongside them. His swordsmanship might not be the greatest, but in a solid shieldwall it didn't have to be. Guts and discipline were what would win a battle in formation, and both had been hammered into him for years. He looked about him at his fellows in the line. Nearest to him was Hefin, one of the Gadarim centurions, and the two exchanged wordless nods. Like all the warriors here he had daubed his body with blue warpaint, though unlike most of them, the warrior elite had painted them *over* their existing tattoos, as well as bleaching their beards and moustaches with white lime. Marius vaguely recalled Rhia saying something about the woad drawing the attention of the Lurian gods of war. How much truth there was in that he had no idea, but he did suddenly feel self-conscious as being the only one there not sporting blue paint. He almost smiled to himself. *A fine sight of a Gaian soldier* that *would make you!*

Marius scratched at his itching beard to cover the potential smirk. He was generally good at maintaining a blank mask but he could almost smell the battle getting nearer every moment, and emotions were always harder to control at times like that. He found himself thinking of Rhia again. He still felt bad for not having her at his side today but the training had to continue and she was the best person to get it done while he was gone. It was strange. For all their many *many*, problems together he still surprised himself sometimes by how much he cared for his Caderyn wife. His well-controlled fear was born as much of not seeing her and Lucan again as it was of his own death or maiming. And his reasons for staying and fighting with his former enemies were as much about protecting his wife and son as they were about justice or vengeance.

He pictured little Lucan, playing happily with his new family at Bryngarth. He seemed to be adapting well and had made friends with other children, but all the same, the boy must have been so confused. To suddenly go from city life to living among the tribesmen was hard enough for Marius, and *he* knew what was going on. To a child that young it must have seemed like his world had been stood on its end. Then he thought about the ambush of the Carrocks in the woods, and how his son had been so determined to be brave. He let a tiny smile slip through the professional mask. *He'll be a soldier one day, or a warrior, depending on what happens in the next few months. Maybe depending on what happens in the next few hours.*

He rolled his shoulders to loosen them and did his best not to fidget further. Eogan's men should be in sight any moment now and hard on their heels would be the Gaian cohort. Provided the archers had done their work of eliminating the scouts, the Fourteenth should run straight into Marius and his men. Eogan's people could then disperse to the trees and the Caderyn cohort would advance to take them head on. According to the local information there would be no Aborans with them on the march but nonetheless, the odds would not be in the Lurians' favour. The Fourteenth were a trained legion with years of experience, and Marius had seen for himself the effects of Praecus' spells.

He suppressed a shudder. Their best hope would be that, as before, the new ferocity and strength of the legionaries would counteract much of their discipline. If that were the case, the Caderyn cohort should be able to hold them in place long enough for Gawan's men to come from the trees and form their own shieldwall behind the Gaians. With archers peppering their rear ranks and Marius' men holding their front, the Gorvicae cohort should be able to smash through them, and the legionaries would be surrounded and destroyed. So simple. As most plans were until a battle began. Marius remembered a maxim of the great General Felix, who had fought in three civil wars long ago, when legion had battled against legion. *No plan survives contact with the enemy.*

Marius sighed a little. Assuming that all *did* go to plan, and that Gawan didn't let the Caderyn bleed too heavily before intervening, the cohort of the Fourteenth should be devastated with minimal loss to themselves, and General Lepidus would be forced to react and thus give time for more Gorvicae civilians to flee. Whether that meant he would come directly south towards the Caderyn or simply consolidate his position with greater care, Marius couldn't be sure, but he suspected the latter. General Lepidus was many things, but headstrong wasn't one of them.

Marius was just pondering how he'd feel if, or more likely *when*, he had to face the Tenth Legion in battle, when the sound of cries from the road ahead snapped his mind back to attention. The sound was indistinct but he had been prepared for that. Lookouts stationed at the curve of the road were frantically waving red cloths, indicating that the enemy was approaching. A moment later the first of the sprinting archers came into sight on the track, ready to lead the Gaians into the first part of the trap. Marius picked up the wooden whistle from around his neck and blew three blasts on it, two short, one long. The men knew what to do but he shouted the order out anyway – better to be too clear than not clear enough.

'Stand to!'

The line, which had been standing relaxed and bored, formed up at once, the shields of the first two ranks coming together with admirable precision. *Not bad.* Swords were drawn by the front two ranks while the warriors behind stood ready to add their weight to support pushes, or to pull back wounded and slip into their place. Marius exchanged another nod with Hefin beside him, and then gestured to Bael that he should withdraw to the rear. The young druid bowed his head and complied without a word, waving his hands in strange motions as he walked past the men.

Marius kept his eyes on the road and soon dozens of Caderyn archers were sprinting around the corner, skidding as they swerved before pelting up the little incline. He kept his face blank, kept his movements minimal, though within his chest his heart was pounding hard. He resisted the temptation to kiss the amulet around his neck and said the prayer quietly in his head. *Vulco Malus Taranis, God of War, be with us now.* Hot on the heels of the fleeing archers he saw the first gleams of mailed bodies and painted shields and, hanging down above them beneath a shining golden eagle, he saw the panther pennant of the Fourteenth's Third Cohort. Marius drew his sword and leaned into his shield, and watched the Gaian legionaries begin to charge. *And here we go.*

Chapter 32. The Druid

Peira's house was only dimly lit by the orange light of the crackling fire, but it felt homely and comfortable, and Rhia found herself dangerously close to relaxing. The smell of woodsmoke and salted oats filled the air in the humble place, combined with a subtle aroma of damp from the previous night's rain. Peira's cloak was hanging up near the fire to dry it off and the sweet, almost sickly scent of it mixed in with the other smells of the house.

Rhia looked around it and wondered what on earth she had done with all the space she'd had back in Tamora. Peira and Barden's whole house could have been squeezed into just one of the many chambers there, which Rhia had slowly filled with expensive ornaments and hanging fabrics. In truth, a part of her missed the big house with its open space, drinking wine from silver goblets and with slaves to attend to her whims. She was content enough here most of the time but sometimes she caught herself pining for the decadent lifestyle of the Gaians, and had to remind herself of the price of such opulence. The luxury of that life came at the price of others' freedom, and it caused men who might otherwise have been great to become lazy and hedonistic. There were decent types among them of course, dear Glaucus could never be called ignoble, but so many people became so dazzled by their own wealth that they forgot the more important things in life. Rhia frowned. Life among the Caderyn kept one's priorities a little straighter. *Still, it'd be nice to have somebody to cook for me again.*

She continued to stir the pot of porridge one-handed while her other arm was occupied by Peira's youngest child, Brynn. The baby boy was sleeping peacefully as Rhia rocked him back and forth, all the while keeping the spoon going so that the porridge didn't stick to the pot and burn. For all the awkwardness of the double-task Rhia found she didn't really mind helping out, and if she were honest she was glad not to be shouting at warriors for a change. They now had four cohorts training at the Caderyn's capital, and though Third and Fourth were doing well, Fifth and Sixth were still newly-formed and had a *very* long way to go.

The two new companies were of Caderyn fighters, the Gorvicae being mostly held up in their own land and the Dariniae as yet having only enough men to form one. Ierryn had said his subordinate would be here soon but until then only the Third Cohort was made up of the islanders. She began wondering how long it would be before more of the Gorvicae came, but that just led to fretting over what Marius was doing so she pushed the thought aside. No good would come of worrying. He would come back or he wouldn't, and that was all there was to it. At least Lucan had enough family here to raise and love him should his father fall. *Who are you trying to fool? You're terrified that Marius will be hurt or killed out there, and all the uncles in the world cannot replace a boy's father.*

Rhia ignored the criticism in her head and turned to watch the other children playing. Siriol and Eirian, Peira's eldest, were tossing a leather ball between them while Lucan, in the middle, tried to catch it before they could. All three were laughing and Rhia knew she ought to tell them to take the game outside before they broke something but she couldn't make herself do it, it was such a joy to watch. Lucan had been through so much lately, and so young, it was nice to see him smile and play like any other child. Peira was watching them too as she poured milk out for her friend.

'Nice to see, isn't it?'

Rhia nodded, continuing to stir.

'Yes. They seem to be close already.'

Peira smiled and placed a cup on the table before relieving Rhia of little Brynn so that she could drink. A part of her wanted to keep hold of him but mostly she was glad to have her arm back, it had been well on the way to going numb. She nodded her thanks and took a sip of the milk, which was wonderfully fresh and cool.

'It's so strange to see Eirian playing here when the last I saw her she was just a bump.'

Peira laughed a little.

'She was a lot more manageable when she was a bump, not like Brynn here.' She rocked the sleeping babe a little. 'Barely a cry from him since the day he was born, and even then he calms down a lot faster than *she* used to.'

If Eirian heard that she didn't comment, and was clearly busy with her ball-throwing anyhow. Lucan might be shorter than either of the girls but he was both quick and nimble, and had almost caught them out a few times. Rhia and Peira between them hauled the cooking pot from the fire and began ladling the porridge into bowls.

'A pity Meg still has no children. She would make a good mother.'

Rhia half-agreed.

'As she was, she would be. These days I don't know how well she'd cope.'

She felt bad for criticising her friend in such a way but Peira simply shrugged away the comment.

'She took Dane's death hard, Camelas knows we all had reason to grieve, and she's kept her head down while the Gaians have been about, but don't let all that fool you. Meg is still Meg under all that matted hair.' She whispered a little so the children wouldn't hear. 'And I've not heard Owain object!'

Rhia leaned forward despite herself and whispered in reply.

'She did say that he came to her sometimes – are they a serious item then?'

Peira shrugged again, though she was grinning as she did so.

'If you mean will they wed or not I've no idea, but if they keep at it the way they have been they may soon have no choice in the matter.'

Rhia's eyes widened. Gaian women could often be indiscreet in their affairs, but Lurian girls tended to limit what they did outside of marriage. She leaned even closer to her friend.

'You mean they... they do everything?'

She felt like a gossipy girl rather than a mother, a warrior and a leader of men but she just couldn't help herself. Peira nodded.

'Everything and *then* some. Erin told me they sometimes go to Owain's place down the valley and Meg's been visiting Madlen every couple of moons. Why go to see a herbwife so often if not to make sure you're not...?'

She glanced around her to check the children weren't listening but they were far too busy playing, Lucan and Siriol now throwing the ball with Eirian in the middle. Peira turned back and leaned close again.

'And from what Meg has said herself, apparently Owain is a very *blessed* man!'

Rhia fought to hold back a grin, revelling in the simple joy of gossip. For a second she felt sad as she remembered poor Ailin, a man far from blessed and yet he'd had that mysterious charm over women, but she shook the idea away. He'd been dead more than five years now and he hadn't suffered when he went. It was a cleaner fate than many who had fallen at Nantwyn.

She was just leaning forward to whisper another question to Peira when a polite knock on the door caused both women to jump, and a moment later it was opened and

Reaghan stood silhouetted in the opening. Daylight flooded into the house around the druid's darkened frame, and Rhia felt her face grow warm under his gaze. Yet again she felt like she was just a gossipy little girl and beside her she saw Peira looking just as embarrassed. Reaghan could not possibly have heard them from outside the house but he *was* a druid after all, and something in his eyes told her he knew what they'd been doing. He smiled politely and bowed his head.

'Marna's blessings, and forgive the intrusion.'

Peira shook her head and wiped her hands on her apron.

'Nothing to forgive father, please, won't you sit?'

The white-haired man nodded his thanks to her and leaned his staff against the wall before sinking down into a chair.

'You are too kind, my child. I cannot stay long, I merely wished to have a few words with Rhianwyn.' He nodded to Rhia. 'Would you care to come for a walk?'

Peira shook her head again.

'No need for that, father. It may rain again today and you might get caught out in it. I can take the children outside a while and give you space to talk? We'll come back in again if the weather turns too foul.'

Reaghan looked ready to object to the offer but Peira's face was genuine and so he turned back to Rhia.

'I am happy with either, I leave it to you, my child.'

Rhia traded a glance with her friend and decided it would be rude to reject her hospitality.

'We can talk here.'

Peira started ushering the various children from the house, a task made more difficult by having to hold little Brynn in one arm. Reaghan smiled and rose to his feet, taking the babe from her and rocking him gently while Peira herded the others. The baby never stirred and was still sleeping when Peira took him back and smiled her

451

thanks. The old druid smiled back at her, and Peira and the children left the house. Reaghan gently closed the door behind them.

Alone with the druid Rhia suddenly felt anxious, and was at a complete loss as to why. She knew and trusted Reaghan as much as any man alive, why should she suddenly feel nervous about him? The druid sank back down to his seat and looked at Rhia without staring, his voice calm.

'I had thought you might want to speak with me, child. If there is anything you would like to talk about, I am here.'

A dozen different thoughts ran through her head at once. She thought about Bevan, and the omens of their marriage. She thought of her first wedding, and the strange feeling she'd confided only to her mother. She thought about the stargazer in Glyscoed Wood before Nantwyn, and the warning that had proved so close to true. She thought about the battle, and Delyn, something she'd never shared with anyone before. Initially it had been because she'd felt ashamed and frightened, and she told herself she didn't talk of it now because it was all in the past. Yet something in those blue eyes made her look more closely at herself, and she realised that a part of her was still afraid, afraid of reliving that dreadful day even for a moment.

There was so much she wanted to talk to Reaghan about, to hear his voice and take his counsel, and just to get it out of her. She thought of telling him about Gwen and how sorry she was for failing her, or about Glaucus and her confusion about the Gaians. So much to talk about, to unburden herself of to this wise old man. But time was a precious thing and Rhia had her priorities, and so she asked the question that she knew had to be asked, and that only the druid would be able to answer.

'What do you know of the sorcery that will be used against us, and how might we counter its power?'

Reaghan's brow furrowed slightly, though to Rhia it seemed to be in sorrow rather than disapproval. He must have known the weight she carried with her, even if the details of it were vague. Though a man of immense power and wisdom, Rhia had learned over the years that the one thing that defined him was that he was kind. Even in the midst of their peril he'd wanted her to open up and talk to him about her worries rather than talk about war and strategy. But he could see that she had already made up her mind and so took a deep breath and began answering her question.

'The question is not easily answered child, and what I tell you must remain between us. But I will explain what I can. Sorcery is both similar and dissimilar to the magic of the gods that we druids may sometimes use. Like our magics, its power can be drawn from earth and air, from water and fire, and from the human vessel in emotion and will, in breath and in blood.'

Rhia found herself forgetting her regret in having to ask about this instead of unburdening her woes. She had never before dared to ask a druid about the magic of the gods, assuming and accepting that she was not allowed to know. For all their need she had been nervous asking this now, and had been half-convinced that Reaghan would not speak of it. Yet here he was, sombrely telling her the secrets of his sacred order. Rhia leaned forward, fascinated and a little afraid, as the old man continued, his voice low and grave.

'This power, what we of the brotherhood call the ava, exists within all life upon this earth. It is around us in this very room,' he gestured lightly to the dimly-lit house, 'it is within us with every breath we take, and it ebbs and flows through all this land from the soil beneath to the sky above. Because of the great power of the ava, its nature is kept secret from all but a few. But if you could see it child...' his blue eyes seemed to gaze into the open air between them, 'it is beyond merely beautiful. It is... it *is* beauty.'

He was quiet for a moment and Rhia wondered if he was going to continue, but then a hard look came across his face, stern enough to make her want to back away from him.

'When used by the druids it is a thing of subtlety and care, used for the betterment of our people, to help and to heal. For a hundred generations and more the druids have safeguarded the knowledge of the ava and used it only to honour the gods who created and live within it. Yet there are some,' at this his expression twisted into distaste, 'there are some who would use it against the purity of its nature, who would befoul it with blood magic and human sacrifice and use the ava for their own gain and power, forgetting why it is there in the first place.'

Rhia spoke very quietly, almost *feeling* the gentle man's anger, tightly bound in by his iron self-discipline.

'And what is that, father?'

The old druid managed a little half-smile.

'You would need to live a druid's life for many long winters before I answered *that* question, my child. Suffice it to say that those who manipulate the ava for wrongdoing are abominations in the eyes of the gods, and will doom themselves and all the world if they are not stopped.'

Once again Rhia kept her voice quiet, feeling as if she was truly seeing this man for the first time. The passion in his voice, the simmering rage, it was all so unlike the wise old teacher she'd known all her life. Here was a shadow of the figure she had once feared, and Rhia understood better than ever why no man of the tribes would stand against him.

'What Praecus does with his rituals, can he defeat us with them?'

Her opinion was torn between her unqualified confidence in Reaghan and her fear at what she and Marius had seen. Reaghan took his time in answering, and his answer was not as comforting as she had wanted.

'Depending on how much he has learned and how much power he has forced into these men, they may now be something far stronger than any man that we have here. Their use of the ava in such a way will destroy them all eventually, but whether that is before or after they have destroyed us? That even I cannot answer.'

Rhia persisted, trying to keep polite as she questioned him.

'But the druids read signs and omens, can you not see?'

Reaghan clearly knew why this had been her first objection, and this time gave her an answer that contained at least some of what she wanted.

'Omens and sightings are intangible things at best, Rhianwyn. Before you were first wed I saw signs of a hard but happy marriage between west and east. Naturally, I had thought this referred to you and Bevan.' He took a deep breath and sighed. 'I was wrong. And though you married Marius, and these omens may be true of you and he, this truth was not something I foresaw.'

Rhia had assumed something similar of course, but to hear it said aloud by one so wise was not easy. Memories of Bevan and the child who'd never lived came flooding back to her and she felt her throat quiver and tears start to sting her eyes. But before they could fall she felt Reaghan's hand on her arm and a feeling of gentle warmth began to flow through her. Slowly the memories... they didn't exactly *fade*, but somehow they became less overwhelming, as if the images and the pain were being separated. She heard the old man speak quietly to her.

'I am sorry, child.'

The tears threatened to fall again, this time in gratitude as much as sadness, but Rhia held them back and tried to focus on what mattered here and now. It wasn't easy, but with the help of Reaghan's touch she pulled herself together.

'How then can the sorcerer be beaten?'

The druid rolled his shoulder a little.

'Our best hope is to face him with courage and the pure intent to defend our people, and to prepare ourselves for it as best we can.'

Rhia tried to hide her disappointment and failed.

'Is that it? What of your own magic?'

Reaghan sighed again.

'It is not easy for me to say or for you to hear, but the magic we might use against him is limited. In many ways the Luriae already use the ava without realising it, it is a part of the rituals of the Gadarim though they do not fully understand it. My brother druids and I have spoken and we are agreed that we will help the warriors by assisting in their rituals, and if the sorcerer attempts to cast his power at us we will dispel it if we must. Beyond that, we can only help by praying for your strength and courage.'

Rhia did her best not to sound petulant.

'But why?'

Reaghan locked his eyes on hers, and Rhia *felt* as much as saw the intent behind his gaze.

'Because to use the ava to kill is to pervert and deform it, and in time the user will be deformed along with it. To have power of any kind is to risk losing oneself in it, child. Long ago men used the ava for greed and murder and the world was almost destroyed as a result of their foolishness. Since then the druids have kept our endless watch, ensuring that such disaster is not wakened again.'

Rhia thought of the word 'waken' and remembered the tales of Mabonac, the green dragon beneath the earth. The

456

story was that he slept though the aeons, waking only when there was great evil to be defeated. If the gods truly were a part of the magic as Reaghan said, could it be that ill-use of it would awaken the dragon below? And if it did, would he know which men were wicked and which were good? His rage was quite literally legendary and if roused, who knew what he might do?

She found she had to look away before she spoke again. The power in those blue orbs was overwhelming. She took in a breath to ask another question but before she could say anything the door creaked open and Peira's face appeared around it.

'Forgive my interrupting father, but I had to come in.'

Reaghan rose slowly and gave her a gentle smile.

'I am a guest in your home child, if anyone is to apologise it should be me.'

Peira nodded her head and smiled a little shyly.

'As you say, father. I just thought you both should know that an outrider from the legion has crested the hill. The warriors are returning.'

*

Rhia and the druid entered the longhall together and despite feeling apprehensive at the prospect of bad news, she couldn't help but be impressed by the reaction of the people. She had never stood beside Reaghan as he walked into a room before and the effect he had on it was instantaneous. Though chatter continued among the people gathered there, it hushed considerably as the druid strode towards the high table, and not one pair of eyes failed to look to him with respect. Or with fear.

The tall man and the short woman had very different lengths of stride but Rhia managed to keep up with his long-limbed gait, resisting the urge to break into a trot.

Marius was standing before the high table, along with Gawan, Hefin and half a dozen other Gadarim. He looked tired and careworn but otherwise unhurt, and he smiled at her a little as she approached. For a second she felt awkward, not sure how to greet him in front of all these people, but then she remembered who she was and that she didn't give a damn, and she wrapped him up in an embrace and held him tight. Some of the headmen or warriors might disapprove of her showing overt affection to the Gaian but right now she would have struggled to care less. He was home and alive, and apparently not even wounded. If a wife could not embrace her husband on such a day, then there was something very wrong with the world.

Marius squeezed her back, his arms feeling strong around her waist, and Rhia closed her eyes and said a silent prayer of thanks. They broke off the hug after only a few moments and Rhia saw that Gawan was sneering in her direction. Clearly he would have loved to pass some comment or another, maybe about her lying with the enemy, or comparing her greeting to Marius now with her greeting to Bevan so long ago. Those cunning grey eyes glared at her from under heavy brows and she could feel his irritation at having to keep his mouth shut about it. The vicious bastard clearly longed to say something insulting to them both but he was standing in a room surrounded by the headmen of the Caderyn, and Rhia's father sat in his chair only a few paces away.

Rhia was tempted to wink or sneer back at the glowering Gadarim but she restrained herself for now and turned to hear her father speak.

'Welcome back to us, warriors of the Caledon.'

He had his arms spread open in obvious greeting and a moment later some women came forward with mugs of ale for the returning fighters. They took them with grateful bows, even Gawan nodded his head, and Carradan continued as they sipped.

'Later we shall feast you all more properly for your brave efforts, but for now I must ask; what is your report?'

Rhia saw Gawan step forward as if to speak but Marius got there first, causing the Gorvic's scowl to deepen even further.

'We have successfully prevented Lepidus from advancing far into Gorvicae land. We engaged an enemy detachment and forced him to reconsider his options and to consolidate, rather than push forwards. Many Gorvic people have now sought refuge in their mountains and hillforts, and the general is unlikely to pursue them with any great strength.'

Rhia was impressed, and not just at the success. Marius was clearly far more adept with languages than she was and had spoken eloquently, with barely a pause. The men around them were nodding in approval at the report and Marius continued before Gawan could jump in.

'Besides a few minor skirmishes the only real action fought was against the Third Cohort of the Fourteenth Legion. As suspected they have once more been... altered by sorcery and were inhumanly strong and fierce. Fortunately their fierceness has come at some cost to their discipline and our own cohorts managed to engage and defeat them, in the process gaining several hundred shirts of mail, as well as swords and shields for the Caledon Legion. A combination of good training, good planning, favourable terrain and advantage of numbers allowed us to destroy the unit entirely, with no survivors to tell of its fate.'

At this there came a cheer from those around them, though Rhia noted that the warriors who had been there didn't join in. Mostly they were looking tired and doing their best to hide it, but Marius and Gawan eyed one another with open hostility. Carradan raised his hand and the cheering slowly died down.

'I am glad to hear of it. What losses did you suffer in this battle?'

This time Gawan was first to speak.

'The Panther Legion had been strengthened by magics but we encountered no direct sorcery. Many fighters fell but our losses might have been worse. I would call the losses acceptable.'

The Gadarim of the Caderyn tribe glared at him as he spoke, though Marius was the one to voice their thoughts.

'Acceptable among your own perhaps, but the Caderyn cohort suffered far worse than your company did.'

Gawan shrugged indifferently.

'They were not fighting for their homeland, clearly their hearts were not so resolved as...'

The black-haired Gadarim got no further than that because Hefin leaped towards him with a curse on his lips, and only the restraining arms of Marius and the other Caderyn kept him from violence.

'Say that again you greasy dog and I'll cut your bastard heart out!'

The Leaping Wolf showed no sign of fear but his eyes widened in fury and his hand went to his sword.

'Make threats to me will you, boy?'

Rhia rushed forward ready to help Hefin if needed, but a deafening bang sounded from behind the chieftain's table and all eyes turned to see Reaghan, on his feet and with his staff in his hand. His face was stern and he slammed it down once again. The heavy oak thudded hard against the boards and another cracking bang echoed around the chamber. Silence reigned as all eyes turned to the druid, and when Reaghan spoke his voice made Rhia think of thunder somehow caged inside a bottle.

'Peace!'

He had not *shouted* exactly, but his voice rang with power and the warriors hastily backed away from one another. Even Gawan's sour face had a hint of fear in it and he raised his open hands in a gesture of submission. Reaghan nodded his head slowly before turning to his chieftain and Carradan addressed the warriors, his voice calm and commanding.

'Have you forgotten why we are here? We are here as one people. I will not have this alliance tear itself apart and save these Gaians the trouble.'

The silence that followed this stretched until Rhia was on the verge of saying something banal just to break the tension. Fortunately Marius saved her from having to, addressing the chieftain politely.

'As you say, father. Though it is true that more Caderyn fell in this assault than Gorvicae. And in my view,' he eyed Gawan but kept his tone carefully neutral, 'this might have been avoided.'

The Gorvicae's First Man sneered.

'We obeyed *your* plan, Gaian. We waited until you were engaged, softened their flanks with arrows and then fell upon their rear. It is no fault of mine if your company struggled to hold them.'

Hefin fumed openly and Marius was clearly holding back anger.

'You waited too long. The cohort that charged us was frenzied and you knew it.'

Gawan squared up to him but made sure not to raise his voice; Reaghan had returned to his seat but he was still watching them intently.

'I know their frenzy all too well, Gaian. I have seen it from this side before, as you recall.'

If Marius was put off by the reminder of his last campaign, he hid it well. Rhia couldn't help comparing the two grey-eyed men; the one full of sneers and blustering, the other maintaining a near-perfect mask of calm. But both angry. Angry enough that Rhia kept her hand close by her knife.

'Then you will know what a challenge it is for us to face them head-on for any protracted length of time. For all our training our shieldwalls are far from being legion standard, even when the rage causes the Gaians' discipline to erode.'

Gawan shrugged it off.

'We managed well enough didn't we? Neither my cohort nor your rabble broke under the strain.'

Marius took a slow breath through his nose and closed his eyes a moment. His mask was in danger of slipping and Rhia stepped in before he said something that might offend Reaghan or Carradan.

'*Managing well* won't be good enough when the Gaians come in force. This may have been a victory but you had every advantage over them. What happens when Lepidus comes down here with two legions and doesn't let us ambush him on the road? Then we will need discipline, and for orders to be followed.'

There were murmurs from around them, some of agreement, some of disapproval. Rhia noticed Baercban and Sedryn standing near the high table, both following the conversation with interest. Gawan turned his eyes from Marius to her.

'From someone who was back here washing skirts whilst we were…'

But Marius interrupted him.

'It does not take a war veteran to see the problem here. You should have advanced sooner, that is an end to it. I trust that next time you will follow my orders more closely.'

He spoke with the blithe confidence of a man who fully expects to be obeyed and Rhia was impressed once again by his bluff. He must have known the delicate line he was walking on, yet he affected that he had no concern at all about his authority. Gawan spun back to him, clearly keen on showing just how fragile that authority was, but Carradan spoke up before he could.

'Well, all is settled then.'

Rhia suspected her father had guessed what the Gorvic was about to do and had decided to preserve the image of Marius as a man to follow. Gawan settled for simply glaring at them both as the chieftain continued.

'And now we have more to do. Word from the east is that the Gaian enforcers have abandoned Nantwyn and we would be wise to secure the town before Lepidus marches down to us. Preparation for this will begin tomorrow. For today, I believe our warriors have earned a rest. Let food be brought, let us eat and drink together.' He stretched out his hands in front of him. 'Gawan, Marius, come and sit here with me and we shall talk more of this as comrades.'

The tension in the hall seemed to ease a little and a buzz of conversation began to circulate. The warriors in the middle of the room dispersed to the benches and the chieftain's men disappeared to fetch food and ale. Baercban and Sedryn moved to seats at the high table and Rhia began to move that way as well, Marius close beside her. On their way up to it, Gawan stepped close to her and spoke in a low whisper, quiet enough that only they would hear him.

'You might like the feel of him between your legs, but if your Gaian tries to shame me again I'll feed his liver to my dogs!'

Rhia closed her fist and made to rush him but Marius took her arm and held her in place. They were close to her father's table and no-one else had heard the threat above the chatter. She felt rage threaten to overcome her good sense but she forced herself to calm down and took a few slow breaths. Gawan seemed disappointed not to have provoked her into striking him and curled his lip a little as he turned away. Marius kept his hand firm on her arm until she nodded that she was alright. She was so angry, not just for his words but for the man's foolish ignorance. She had far more cause to hate him than he did to hate her yet she was willing to set that aside in the face of the greater threat. Could he not see the danger that they were all in, and that by causing strife between them they were all of them made weaker?

Rhia watched him walk back to Baercban and his coward of a son and saw a few words were exchanged, though she had no idea what they were. Hopefully Baercban might be talking some sense into him, not that Gawan seemed the type to take advice. She took another deep breath and tried to put him from her mind. Instead she turned back to face Marius. He was smiling in a way that said he sympathised with her perfectly and she managed a little smile of her own. She sighed. Her husband was safe. Lucan's father was back with his family. She had much to be thankful for today, she should focus on that. Rhia found Marius's hand and gave it a gentle squeeze. They could worry about Gawan and their other woes tomorrow. Right now there was drink to be drunk and food to be eaten, and one another's company to enjoy.

They took their seats at the high table and Rhia said a silent thanks to the gods in her head. Whether it had been Taran or Vulco or Camelas or Gron or some combination of them or a dozen others, it didn't matter. They had brought a victory to her people. And they had brought Marius back safely to her. That was what mattered right now.

Chapter 33. The First Setback

The next morning the Third, Fourth, and Fifth Cohorts were sent straight to Nantwyn, led by Madoc, Owain, and Kyran. Ossian, though no longer able to fight in the line, went with them along with Elfed and a company of archers. The remainder of the Caledon Legion would be following on their heels, but the First and Second Cohorts had earned a few days' rest and the Sixth and Seventh needed more training before they were fit for the field. Gawan had managed to bring some more Gorvicae down with him and these would have to be organised as well. Many would be used to fill the gaps left by the fallen in Gawan's cohort, and fresh Caderyn warriors would have to be placed into the damaged First Cohort as well. For all the talk of light casualties, many Caledon had still died, and their places in the line had to be filled.

Rhia tried not to think on that as she drilled the new units into shape, tried not to think about the families who would be missing sons and brothers, sisters and daughters. Instead she tried to focus on the positive; the banner of the legion was ready and the more experienced cohorts now had well-made and fresh-painted shields, and some even wore coats of iron mail. The training of the new fighters was going well and at least Gawan wasn't here to cause disruption. She'd have to see him later at a meeting of the tribunes but for now at least, the arrogant bastard was out of her hair.

She watched as the new cohorts switched from marching order into line of battle, and then back again at a barked command from Marius. Gadarim rushed along the lines straightening shields and giving encouragement, but the extra help was needed less and less with every drill. Rhia watched her husband, a new officer's sword at his hip courtesy of the Fourteenth's Third Tribune, gesturing with his baton and calling out new orders.

Lucan had been overjoyed to have his father back, and Rhia had been far happier than she admitted. They'd made love last night with an almost frantic passion and this morning it was difficult not to grin as she barked out commands. The fighters she was shouting at exchanged the odd smile about it but they were mostly Caderyn and she didn't really mind, especially if the humour kept their spirits up. The mood among the tribesmen had been oddly mixed since Gawan and Marius had returned, with half of them encouraged by the news of a victory and the other half dismayed and frightened by the descriptions of these sorcery-enhanced Gaians. And there was more bad news to add to that.

According to some of the Gorvicae scouts, Lepidus' legions now numbered four cohorts each instead of three. Rhia remembered the general petitioning to build up the size of his legion years ago, and apparently he now had the necessary authority. It meant that each legion would contain some seventeen hundred men, given that the First Cohort was always larger. The Caledon would still have the advantage of numbers, but that advantage was now significantly lessened. *And* we *don't have black magic to augment our strength.* Rhia briefly wished that Reaghan would use his magic to help them the same way, but then remembered the way his blue eyes had flashed at the concept of doing so. *You heard what he said; it corrupts the user to use the magic, this ava, to kill men.* But then she thought of little Lucan and wondered how much corruption she might risk if it meant keeping him alive and free. The line of thought was not a productive one and she tried not to dwell on it. The new cohorts seemed to be doing well enough and they had more people coming every day. There was still hope.

They drilled their new units for another hour or more before Marius called a halt for rest and water. Rhia would have loved to have slumped on the grass and joined the warriors in their respite, but she had other work to do and so gave Marius a weary smile and started heading off towards the longhouse. They would all be meeting there later to discuss when the new units would be ready to move out, but Rhia had supply problems to deal with on top of her training duties. A cattle trader from the south should be meeting her here later to negotiate a price for the herds he was bringing to help feed their newly-formed army.

Rhia had found plenty of employment for the semi-captive Gaian clerks at the governor's old house, putting her years of experience running a household to good use. Accounts were being carefully managed and where silver was unavailable, credit was arranged with everyone from merchants to blacksmiths to drovers. Even now wagons of grain were being brought from all over Caderyn land and beyond, even as far as the occupied Rydicae and Bearnicans. Word had reached their Lurian brethren of their plight and though few warriors had dared to come, they were doing their part by sending smiths and supplies along the less-used roads, evading the Gaian patrols to bring food and expertise to the beleaguered Caledon.

Rhia strode from the training fields towards the longhall and tried to make the calculations in her head of how much this brief war was going to cost in terms of supply. The short version of it was 'a lot'. Although the fact that more warriors kept coming to them was a blessing, it was also a curse in terms of logistics. There were still some clans of the Caderyn making their way to Bryngarth from across the territory, bands of Gorvicae were slipping past the Gaians in the north in small groups, and Ierryn had promised hundreds more Dariniae from Niswyn, though there'd been no sign of the islanders as yet. Rhia sighed as she went, thinking how much more it would cost in work, silver and credit to feed, train and equip these new men if they arrived, and a part of her almost wished that they wouldn't.

She exchanged nods and the odd greeting with friends as she walked through the town but mostly she focused on the task in hand, and it wasn't long before she reached the longhall. It was still some time before the other tribunes of the legion would get there, and she ought to have time to collect the ledgers she'd left there and get them to the clerks in their prison-office. Useful though they were, they still weren't trusted to wander about too freely, though they seemed to have no objection to remaining under token guard in Portunus' house. Some of them still feared reprisals for the death of Ewan.

Rhia walked in through the main doors to find the long hall empty but she spotted the leather-bound volumes beside her father's seat. Carradan had made the effort to learn the Gaian letters fairly well, but he had no head for figures and Rhia suspected he'd only asked to see them as a gesture, something to let her know he appreciated her efforts. She smiled a little. Even amidst all this he found the time to show love to his daughter. *But then, the old man is running short of children to show his love to.* The smile vanished as Rhia thought of Dane, and Gwen and Ewan. She bit her lip a little as her own grief threatened. *It must be so hard for him, but still he carries on. Losing my unborn child almost broke me, and if anything happened to Lucan... and he's lost three children that he's watched grow to adulthood.* Rhia sighed a little. The Charging Bull was strong in more ways than one.

She reached the high table and picked up the heavy book. There might still be time to run through some of it with the clerks before she had to be back. She had just turned to walk back along the hall when the sound of voices from the room beyond caused her to stop. One sounded like her father's voice, and it seemed he was having an argument. Rhia moved closer to the little door and the muffled sounds became discernible words.

'By your own man's word it was a success.'

The voice was clearly Carradan's, the tone calm but with an edge of frustration behind it. The replying voice was unmistakably that of Baercban.

'A success yes, but barely so. Gawan reported the Gaians are even more frenzied than before, and word is that they now come in greater numbers than we feared. We won on that day, but even your girl and the Gaian agreed that without numbers and surprise it might have been very different.'

There was an awkward pause before another voice, this one so weak and whining that it could only be Sedryn, broke the silence.

'We must send word to Lepidus. And negotiate with him.'

Rhia felt her fist clench and she shoved the door hard with her other palm. It banged loudly from the wooden tub leaning against the wall.

'Coward!'

All eyes in the room turned to look at her as she spoke. Along with Sedryn and the chieftains there was a fourth man in the room, a Gorvic warrior Rhia knew by sight but not by name. He was tall and looked fairly tough, but he had no battlemarks tattooed on him and she assumed he was a headman, or the son of one.

Sedryn's mean little eyes were blazing.

'Say that again you…'

But he caught himself in time before throwing insults at Carradan's daughter. Instead he addressed the chieftain directly.

'Your child does me wrong but I will forget it this once. The fact remains that the Gaians cannot be defeated by strength of arms and we have no choice, we must make terms.'

Rhia despised the man even more for letting such an insult go unanswered, and she started speaking at the same time as her father. She held back her anger and gestured for him to go first.

'It will be difficult Sedryn, perhaps even impossible, but this battle must still be fought.'

Rhia nodded in agreement.

'Lepidus and his sorcerer must be stopped or else who knows what their wickedness might lead to?'

She was thinking of Reaghan, and the earnestness of his warning. Sedryn looked between them both and turned to face his own chieftain.

'Father, you know I speak the truth.'

Baercban's expression made Rhia think of a dog chewing a wasp, but nonetheless he slowly nodded his head.

'The might of the Gaians cannot be challenged. We should show Lepidus that we are *able* to fight and then make peace with him. We may get good conditions if he believes us to be strong.'

Rhia felt her anger rise and she realised it was mainly because he was, at least partially, right. If they'd been talking of making war against the entire Gaian Empire than she would probably agree; there was no way to win. The resources of the Emperor were practically limitless and the best hope anyone had was to be on good terms with the Gaians when they came. It was a sad truth in a way, and were it not for men like Marius and Glaucus Rhia might have despaired at it, but it was the truth nevertheless and it was something they had to accept.

But they weren't fighting the Gaian Empire. They were fighting General Lepidus, and for all the threat that his legions and Praecus' magics might pose, he was acting almost independently, and he was playing a dangerous game. He had betrayed his own people's values, though doubtless *he* didn't see it that way, and was taking a great gamble in using sorcery so openly. If he prevailed in this campaign he might gain tremendous personal power, perhaps even enough to challenge Tiberian one day. But if things went badly he would lose not only men but reputation, and he risked having the greatest army in the world turn on him if he tried to go home.

'Lepidus does not wield the full might of the Gaians, and we have seen already that they can be beaten back with skill and courage.'

Her voice sounded far more petulant than she'd meant it to, and Baercban twitched his lip in annoyance.

'From one who has lived among them, I had thought to hear better wisdom.' He turned back to Carradan. 'We cannot fight this army and win, Carradan. We must seek terms.'

It was clear the Gorvicae chieftain was not happy about it but his tone was firm. Rhia's father spoke in a voice that was equally uncompromising.

'That is not an option here. Regardless of the Gaian general, Reaghan's council was clear enough; this sorcerer must be stopped.'

There was a jug of water and some cups on a table beside him, and Sedryn paced towards it as he spoke, his voice exasperated.

'You refuse to see reason, even right before your face?'

Rhia fumed at his blatant lack of respect but the Caderyn chieftain simply shrugged.

'I see no wisdom in your words, young man.' He turned to face his fellow chieftain. 'We would make ourselves slaves or worse if we sought a peace now. This Praecus must...'

But that was as far as he got. The moment he'd turned around Sedryn had drawn a knife from his belt, and by the time Rhia noticed the movement the young Gorvic had thrust the blade up to the hilt in her father's back. Carradan's eyes flew wide and he let out a choking grunt, and he was already falling as Sedryn withdrew the blade and struck again, up into the heart. Rhia's world turned red and she screamed and lunged at him, but the tall warrior was closer to her and he drew his sword and barred her way. The daughter of Carradan didn't pause for so much as an eyeblink, changing her direction and leaping at him instead.

The tall man had clearly expected her to back away and Rhia caught him off-balance. She grabbed him by the shoulders and flung her knee up between his legs. The kick barely connected, the tall man reacting quickly and thrusting his hips back, but it got the desired effect; it brought his head down to Rhia's more diminutive height, and with a quick jerk she pulled his shoulder one way and his jaw the other, exposing the front and side of his neck. White rage almost blinded her as she sank her teeth into the flesh and ripped away again in a welter of bloody gore.

The taste of his sweat mixed with the oddly metallic tang of blood, and Rhia felt him convulse and weakly try to back away. She held on long enough to ram her forehead into his nose and then let him crumple backwards, drawing her long knife as he fell. Her father was on the ground now, lying on his side with eyes open and staring, and both Sedryn and Baercban had drawn their swords. The older man was looking shocked, while the younger one seemed a mixture of scared and elated, his fingers twitching on Silverbite's grip. The Gorvic chieftain kept his eyes on Rhia as he hissed angrily to his son.

'What have you *done*?'

Sedryn tore his eyes away from his bleeding comrade, currently thrashing on the floor beside the unmoving Carradan, and flicked a quick glance at his father.

'He was never going to agree. We can send Lepidus his head as a token of goodwill.'

Rhia saw Baercban's fist clench tighter on his own weapon's grip.

'You thought to murder a chieftain of the Luriae? And in his own hall, in a town filled by his warriors?'

Sedryn shrugged a little, keeping his blade, *her* blade, levelled at Rhia as he spoke.

'We can get the body out quietly and make for Nantwyn with Gawan's men. From there we slip away to the Gaian lines.'

Baercban's jaw tightened in obvious frustration but Rhia didn't care. She kept her short knife pointed at them and all she could think of was how she was going to kill these men. Everything else, even the cold grief that clutched at her heart, would have to wait. She could still taste the tall man's blood in her mouth and she spat at Sedryn before menacing the father with her blade. She was easily out-ranged by both of them but neither one seemed over-keen to press in for the kill. Baercban slapped her blade aside and started circling to her right, trying to flank her. Sedryn, red flecks now showing on his sneering face, stayed where he was and spat back.

'This bitch will need to die first though, and fast.' His face formed a parody of a smile. 'Shame though, I'd have liked to enjoy myself with this one.'

Rhia growled and the young Gorvic faltered a little. To her right, she heard Baercban snarl at his son.

'Keep your noise and do it!'

The older man wasn't moving in at her, simply keeping her from escaping, and in a moment of clarity Rhia realised that he didn't really want to kill her, but that his son had left them with no other choice. *And still the little piss-drinker hasn't the balls to come for me!* Baercban seemed to have reached the same conclusion because Rhia felt him tensing to attack and she half-turned to face him, but Sedryn saw the opening and risked a quick dart forwards, forcing her to turn and parry his blade, no *her* blade, away. *He only attacks when someone's back is turned – a poor master for Silverbite! How in Taran's name did Baercban raise such a coward?*

Once again the Gorvic chieftain seemed to share her thoughts, and she saw his face twist into a grimace of shame. She tried to keep both of them in clear sight but it was difficult, and some detached part of her mind told her it would be only seconds before Baercban stopped waiting for his son to be a man and just ran her through himself. And the moment her back was turned, Sedryn would kill her as he had her father. The thought made her blood boil in impotent rage and she decided to do the only thing she could. If she leaped for Sedryn now there was a chance he wouldn't be able to back off quickly enough, and she could maybe take his throat before Baercban closed in. It wasn't a great plan, but she was dead either way, and this way at least meant justice for Carradan.

Rhia felt herself grow strangely calm, distancing herself from her grief and even from her rage as she readied herself to spring at her father's murderer. *Marius will take good care of Lucan, and at least I might see Gwen and my brothers on the other side of the bridge.* Rhia tried not to think of her dear boy growing up without a mother, and braced her legs ready to leap. She saw Sedryn's eyes go wide with fear and she felt a grin spread across her face. But apparently, she was not the only one who had come early to the longhall today.

The door behind her opened and instead of bounding forwards Rhia was forced to skip sideways to open up the distance between her and the newcomer. The man who walked in was heavy-set and strong, and was arguably the one man who could have made this situation worse. It was Gawan.

The First Man of the Gorvicae took in the scene at a glance, and his sword whipped from its sheath quick as lightning. His eyes went to his chieftain.

'What is this?'

Rhia spat out a reply before Baercban could answer him.

'This piss-licker just murdered my father and you're about to see me kill him for it.'

She nodded at Sedryn, who had taken advantage of the distraction to back away from her a little. With Gawan and Baercban on either side of her now, there was no need for him to put himself in danger. Rhia's contempt for him was growing by the second.

Gawan hadn't moved, and Baercban hadn't gainsaid her answer. The two men kept their swords levelled but neither one moved in for the kill. Gawan looked again at the body of Carradan, still staring off blankly into nothing. He addressed Sedryn this time.

'The wounds are in his back.'

He looked up and the younger man squirmed a little under his gaze, but he tried his best to sound unconcerned.

'No choice. We need to make peace with the Gaians and he would never have agreed to it. If we want a good deal for the Gorvicae we have to start talks with Lepidus *now*!'

Gawan said nothing and so Sedryn kept on talking.

'You know we cannot beat them but this fool wouldn't listen!'

Rhia snarled at him and he backed off another step, but she didn't dare follow up and show her back to the other two. She cursed inwardly, her teeth grinding together. Gawan was fast and Sedryn was now further away – the Gadarim would take her down before she got anywhere near her father's killer. *Father.* She knew she didn't have time to grieve but still it threatened to creep in and sap her precious rage from her. She gripped her knife tighter and tried to keep all three men in sight, her mind scrambling for some way to take at least *one* of them to the Otherworld with her.

As she did she noticed that Gawan wasn't really looking at her. His blade was still held ready but his eyes had gone back to the body on the floor, the pile of meat that had once been Carradan. The Gorvic's face was scowling but he nodded his head without looking up.

'You are probably right. The men we fought were strong, and the Gaian had a point about our discipline. We would be wise to seek terms with Lepidus.'

Rhia's skin felt suddenly cold as she anticipated his attack, and across from her she saw Sedryn's mean face smiling. He opened his mouth to say something but Gawan sighed and spoke before he could.

'But you should have stabbed him from the front.'

The smile left Sedryn's face as Gawan's eyes rose to meet his.

'Charging Bull deserved better than to meet his end at the hands of a worm like you, and you hadn't even the nerve to stand in front of him as you struck.' He turned to face his chieftain, his expression completely blank. 'He was Gadarim. I am Gadarim. If you try to interfere, I will kill you.'

Rhia's mind was racing faster than she could follow it but her eyes flicked to Baercban as the Gorvic chief replied, his own face and voice surprisingly calm, almost resigned.

'He is my son.'

Gawan paused for a second and a flash of regret crossed his features. His left hand unpinned the green cloak at his shoulder before drawing a long knife from his belt. The cloak fell to the floor and he nodded to his chieftain.

'Very well. May you cross the bridge unharmed.'

Rhia saw Baercban nod back to his First Man and then her eyes flew wide with shock as Gawan took a step towards her and offered her his sword, his voice flat and business-like.

'You will lay no hand on the chieftain.' He jerked his head towards Sedryn. 'But the coward is all yours, Wildcat.'

The young man's face drained of all blood and froze in an expression of horror. Rhia, without even thinking, switched her knife into her left hand and took the proffered sword from her enemy. The Gorvic Gadarim simply nodded before turning back to his chief, and Rhia fixed her eyes on Baercban's son. Sedryn's eyes flicked around him, clearly looking for a means of escape, but she was standing in between him and the nearest door, and the only other exit was the other side of the room. He licked his lips nervously and tried to set his face in a snarl, but the fear was almost pouring from him and a child would not have been fooled.

In the corner of her eye Rhia saw the other Gorvicae begin to move, but her focus was all for this one, this murdering dog of a man. On another day his obvious terror might have caused her to pity him, but today there was no pity in her soul. Back at Broken Stream she'd faced this man with the joy of battle pulsing through her veins. Today there was nothing but black rage and boiling hate, and she wasted no time with taunting or with threats. Rhia took a step forward and then lunged hard with the borrowed blade. Sedryn managed a panicked parry with Silverbite but she'd seen it coming and brought the heavy sword back in a level cut to his head. Her opponent cowered behind a hastily-placed block but he'd put no weight behind it, and the force of her cut pushed him off-balance. He swung wildly as he stumbled, hoping to deter her advance. But Rhia was in no mood for cautious fighting. She swayed a little on the spot and then slapped his blade aside, continuing its momentum and costing the coward his balance again. It was all the opening she needed. Without a second's hesitation she reversed her sword's direction and slashed the blade smoothly across Sedryn's exposed throat. The Gorvic gurgled and tucked his chin as his body buckled inwards, Silverbite dropping from his nerveless fingers. The iron clattered on the floor.

Rhia eyed her dying enemy for a heartbeat, watching the blood flow down his chest like a red waterfall, and then sprang forwards again, ramming her knife up under his ribs into his lungs. The coward would doubtless have cried out had he been able, but the best he managed was a weak, rasping cough from his ruined throat. Rhia let go of the knife, still lodged in her opponent's chest, and picked up his sword, *her* sword, with her free hand. It felt oddly comfortable to be holding it again, as if in this day of confusion and horror *something* right was happening.

Sedryn fell to his knees and Rhia didn't pause for a second. She swung Silverbite hard, putting all her weight behind it, and one side of the coward's head was crushed to splinters beneath the blow. Sedryn keeled over and struck the wooden boards, scarlet blood still pumping steadily from his neck. Rhia watched him for a moment, hypnotised, before remembering that she was still in very real danger, and she whipped her head around, both swords coming up to a guard. Gawan was watching her, his expression blank and remote, and behind him Rhia saw the corpse of Baercban. The High Chieftain of the Gorvicae lay unmoving on the boards, with a single red wound on the left side of his chest.

Rhia locked eyes with the Gadarim and for a moment felt the old spark of hatred and distrust in his gaze. Then it

478

seemed to fade away, replaced by... by nothing. She looked for any sign of his usual distaste or bitterness but instead saw just a plain mask that might have done Marius proud. There was a long moment of silence before he spoke, and Rhia heard the strain in the words.

'I do not like you, Wildcat. But what Sedryn did was worse than wrong, and Baercban would have tried to stop you taking what was yours.'

Rhia opened her mouth to speak, though what she'd have said she had no idea, but Gawan spoke again before she could.

'My people will not doubt me if I tell them the truth of what happened here. They will not like it but all know what kind of man your father was. And what kind of man Sedryn was. They will understand.'

Rhia's first thought was that it might not be quite that simple, then she remembered the word *father* and almost burst into tears. *My brothers, my husband, my child, and my sister – have the gods not taken enough from me already without taking him?* She wanted to break down and cry, to huddle in a ball under a blanket somewhere and never peek out from under it. But once again the tiny glowing coal of rage and pride kept her going, and she thought of Marius and of Lucan, and the work she still had to do for them and for her people. She straightened her spine and focused on the Gadarim before her. If he'd noticed how close she'd come to tears he didn't mention it. Rhia tried to keep the quiver from her voice.

'We can but hope.' She glanced down at Baercban. 'Assuming your people do not kill you for slaying your chieftain, who will lead them now?'

Gawan shrugged, his expression unconcerned, and he crossed the room to kneel down beside Carradan. Rhia felt a lump rise up in her throat as the warrior gently closed her father's eyes.

'We will likely be forgiven for slaying the murderers of Charging Bull.' She heard him whisper something under his breath before he rose from the body and continued. 'As to who leads us, someone will be chosen from the headmen at some point I've no doubt. Until then I am the First Man and we are at war. They will follow me.'

He said it with such casual confidence that Rhia couldn't help but believe his words. She had no reason to like this man but there was no doubt that the Gorvicae respected him. Rhia looked down again at the body of her father, which now looked almost as if the great man merely slept. Without him to lead them the Caderyn would turn to Madoc and to Reaghan, as would the Caledon in general, but though Reaghan would give council he doubted he would actively *lead* men, and Madoc was with his cohort at Nantwyn. Rhia squared her shoulders and took a deep breath through her nose. *And they will turn to me. They know who I am and what I have done. Olla might be the elder but she has no interest in war, and everyone has seen what Marius and I have been doing to prepare for this fight. They will look to me.*

She locked eyes with Leaping Wolf and held out his sword to him.

'Thank you for...?'

The Gorvic took the blade with a nod.

'Heartreaver.'

Rhia nodded back and spoke again, keeping her voice as calm as she could.

'For now my people will follow me. There will be much for us to do but we can leave that until later. Right now we need to tell the Caledon everything that's happened here.' She took a last look at her father and set her mouth in a grim line. 'And then we must get moving. Lepidus is coming for us, and we must be prepared to meet him.'

Chapter 34. Back to Nantwyn

'So you're saying the fort is useless?'

Rhia tried not to snap the comment at him but suspected she did a poor job of it. Tensions had been high enough on the long walk to Nantwyn without adding this new stumbling block to their troubles. The deaths of both Carradan and Baercban had come close to destroying the Caledon, and it had taken all the efforts of Rhia, Gawan, Marius and Reaghan, not to mention their old enemy Ierryn the Black, to keep the already fragile alliance from breaking apart. Their tireless work had left no time for her own grief and now, just as they had reached the hill-town and she might finally have found a moment to herself to mourn in peace, this latest bloody crisis had come up.

Madoc responded politely, though his own frustration was plain.

'For our original plan, yes. However it is still a place of refuge for those who cannot fight, and a strong place we might fall back to should we need to.'

Rhia was fairly sure that if they had to fall back to the extent of hiding here, they might as well cut their own throats and have done with it. She had arrived at Nantwyn only a few hours ago at the head of the remainder of the Caledon Legion, along with whatever other warriors they could bring. The journey had been hard and dismal, with none of the easy confidence they'd felt the last time she'd marched this way, and they'd arrived with not a moment to spare.

Hefin had been the first to spot the dark movements to the north, and a quick gallop in that direction had shown them that large numbers of men were crossing the hills. Gwydion, whose eyes were better than most, had described to them the Lion and Panther Standards of the Tenth and Fourteenth Legions, and Rhia and the Gadarim had galloped straight back to the town. Once there they'd found that Owain and Madoc had been hard at work, setting their cohorts to digging ditches and shoring up defences, ready to hold the town against the Gaians as a place of strength. The situation had seemed tightly-timed but otherwise favourable enough. The hill of Nantwyn was steep and the town stood like and island above the plains with no easy approach from any slope, and Rhia had been impressed with how much work had been done to strengthen it. But then the scouts who had been following the Gaians made their report, and Rhia had almost screamed in frustration.

It seemed that Lepidus, not wanting to become entangled in a prolonged siege, had decided to play on their sense of decency by a policy of pillage and murder. And worse. According to the scouts he was putting every village he passed to the torch and killing every tribesman he happened to find. He had made it plain that his intent was simply to butcher the general populace, and it had not taken Rhia long to work out why he was doing so. Lepidus knew that such wholesale slaughter would make the land he took less profitable, and so his only reason for doing it had to be to goad the Caledon into fighting him openly. *He knows we cannot match him shield-to-shield in a pitched battle, so he's denying us the chance to strike and run or force a siege. No warrior worth the name could hide on a hill while his people were slaughtered in their homes all around him.*

Rhia tried to keep her temper as she turned again to the First Man. They were meeting in what had been the longhall of the settlement's headman, though it had been utilised by Gaian enforcers since the first battle of Nantwyn. Joining them were the senior Gadarim, Reaghan and a few other druids, and the only High Chieftain still alive in their alliance; Ierryn of the Dariniae. The former common enemy of the Gorvicae and Caderyn had stayed quiet for most of the discussion, speaking only when he had a question, or had something of value to say. For all that she didn't really trust the man Rhia had a grudging admiration for him; he seemed at least to know what he was doing.

'A good place to have then, but of little enough value today.'

Rhia nodded her agreement.

'Falling back is not an option any more. We must face Lepidus now and crush his legions before they do more evil than they already have.'

There were a series of grim nods from around the room and Marius was the first to speak the obvious, if unpleasant, truth.

'Our legion is coming on well but to face the Tenth or the Fourteenth in open field? It is exactly what Lepidus would want.'

Gawan scowled at him.

'If you think it's so hopeless you can go back to them, Gaian.'

Rhia matched his scowl with a hard look of her own. They had enough problems here already without these two arguing again. Marius took a breath in to reply but Rhia beat him to it.

'He won't and well you know it. Shall we spend less time fighting amongst ourselves and more time preparing to fight Lepidus?'

Gawan didn't look contrite exactly but he grumbled something indistinct and started pacing the long hall. Rhia accepted that as the best she was likely to get.

'Marius makes a good point. Fighting a Gaian legion shield-to-shield is the worst thing we can do, but that is why Lepidus is forcing us to it. We have little choice but to meet him.'

There were concerned frowns all around and Ossian was the first of them to speak.

'Have we not the numbers on them still?'

He tried to put some optimism into his voice, though he surely knew better than most how little good numbers would do them. He had seen the Gaians in action the day they first took Nantwyn, and he'd fought them again as a Gadarim in the great battle that followed. Rhia remembered thinking he must have been killed that day, an Aboran having crushed his collarbone and half-severed his arm with a cleaver-like blade. But the Hawk of War had endured. His right arm now hung useless at his side and the slim man moved with obvious pain, but his eyes had lost none of their resolve. Rhia nodded to the broken warrior, trying not to slap his comment down too harshly.

'We have indeed, but not by so much as we'd hoped. Our only victory against a Gaian cohort was with a force almost twice their size, and that with the advantage of surprise.'

Owain cocked his head a little, aiming his question at both Rhia and Marius.

'Did you not say that their new frenzy can disrupt their discipline? Can that not be taken advantage of?'

Rhia shrugged and let Marius answer this time.

'Yes and no. Whatever the sorcery does to them it does seem to affect their self-control, but the strength that they gain in return makes up for it. Besides which we have the Aboran Destroyers to consider.'

Owain's lip twitched and Ossian hid his own fear well as both remembered the butchery they'd faced the last time they had fought the giant auxiliaries. Rhia tried to sound positive, someone had to.

'We know now how they are employed by the legions though, along with much of their tactical doctrine.' She nodded at her husband. 'And we do have some element of surprise. Lepidus knows that Marius is here and that he will tell us much, but remember Lepidus looks down on us as a mob of savages. Even if we understood what we were taught he'd never think we'd be able to use it.'

Marius nodded his agreement but the other men in the hall did not seem encouraged. Ierryn, his voice quiet but clear, turned to Reaghan.

'Druid, is there truly nothing your brethren can do to counter this magic?'

Rhia held back a sigh. They all knew that druids never used their skills in battle, though she had to admit, she had secretly hoped they might make an exception in this case. Reaghan shook his head slowly.

'The sorcery within the bodies of these men cannot be forcibly removed. It will be further cultivated by them or it will dissipate, but we cannot draw it out of them.'

It wasn't the answer that anyone wanted but it was one they had all expected. Ierryn however was not keen to take no for an answer. He kept his voice polite but the insistence in it was clear.

'There is no way in which your magics may help our people against this sorcery?'

Bael was looking uncomfortable but Reaghan answered straight away.

'You would have us enhance our own warriors as Praecus has done with his? Ierryn you do not know what you ask. I can bless our warriors, inspire and encourage them, and in this a portion of the gods' magic will enter into them. But to do what this sorcerer has done? Had I a moon's turn to do it and only men of righteous hearts, still I would hesitate to consider such a thing.'

Kyran, Ierryn's First Man, opened his mouth to speak but Reaghan simply raised a hand and the Darin kept silent.

'Should this sorcerer appear himself and attempt to cast spells at us directly then yes, my brethren and I are prepared to counter him. Beyond this you must rely on the courage and skills of our warriors. True magic has no place in war.'

As usual his words were spoken quietly but neither of the Dariniae argued further. There followed a few heartbeats of awkward silence before Madoc spoke up.

'Well then, we either need more men, more time to train those that we have, or a damned good plan that will work with what we have got now.'

Ierryn nodded his head.

'One of my Gadarim is bringing more fighters from Niswyn, he may even be at Bryngarth by now.'

Gawan ceased his pacing.

'Some bloody good he'll do us there, the Gaians are at our doors!'

Both Ierryn and Kyran scowled at him hard and Rhia noticed that the First Man bore an identical scar to his chieftain's, a thin vertical line just below his left eye. *Must be something their Gadarim do in their rituals.* The Gorvic glared back at the two scarred men, completely unafraid, and Rhia decided to say something before he caused any more trouble.

'Then we must hope they get here soon but not rely upon it. We must make a plan for meeting Lepidus in the field with what we have.'

Ierryn kept his eyes on Gawan a few seconds longer and then turned to face Rhia and Marius.

'We are in a solid defensive position, is there any way we might goad Lepidus into attacking the hill?'

Marius shook his head.

'The general is not a man easily fooled. He knows he has the advantage in the open and he knows we cannot let him butcher the towns and villages around us unchallenged. He has us where he wants us; he will not attack where he knows we can be strong.'

Once again the room was filled with silent frowns and this time it was Ossian who tried to think of a bright side.

'His scouting ability is lessened at least. Elfed led some men on a raid and killed many of their Nomad horsemen. They were camping some way from the legions and he took them unawares.'

Rhia would have preferred to hear that the Aborans had been killed in their camp, but she did her best to smile. They had little enough to feel bright about.

'Very good. The less he can see of us, the better.'

She took a deep breath and looked around her at the room of warriors. All of them, even Madoc and Ierryn, seemed to be waiting for her to speak again, and she did her best to sound calm and confident. *I'll never be my father, but I can damned well try my best.*

'We must form a plan before the legions can encircle us and so force us to adapt to their movements. Let us begin.'

She gestured towards the table and the men began taking their seats. A couple of them exchanged words with each other and Rhia took advantage of the buzz of noise to whisper an aside to her husband.

'Be honest, what are our chances?'

Marius kept a blank face as only Marius could, and turned his body to hide the conversation from the others. He barely moved his lips as he spoke.

'Our legion is good, but not good enough to face off with theirs. Unless we come up with something pretty damned good we won't come out of this alive.'

Rhia kept her fear controlled and quietly thanked the gods that she'd sent Lucan off with Olla and Siriol, though for how long they'd be safe out on the coast she had no idea. She forced herself to smile, even though she was certain Marius would see through it.

'Well, this plan had better be something pretty damned good then!'

Chapter 35. Textbook Preparation

The legions made camp on what high ground they could find, though the best they'd managed was a gently sloping hill. It was nothing to the size of Nantwyn's hill to the southwest but it was defensible enough and besides, the scouts reported tribesmen were still coming up from the west; they were unlikely to risk a serious attack tonight. Severus turned away from the town and watched as his legions pitched their clean white tents, each one set precisely at regulation distance. He took in a breath and felt the usual swell of pride at being the commander of the Tenth. He might be leading larger formations from now on, but always in his heart he was a man of the Tenth, and the Lion Standard was sewn into his heart. *The Fourteenth on the other hand... them I'll need to keep an eye on.*

His own legion had been enhanced by the sorcerer's powers but Praecus had explained that these things must come in stages. To give a man too much of the robus too soon could be dangerous; he had to be introduced to the power of it slowly. As such the Tenth were now far stronger, fiercer and more agile than they had been, but nowhere near as much so as the Fourteenth. The Fourteenth, as the initial experiment, were now nearing the level of power that the Aboran auxiliaries had, though Severus had noticed that their discipline had suffered as a result.

He fretted about that for a moment but then put it from his mind. Praecus had assured him that they would control themselves soon enough and that his later concoctions, or whatever it was he did, would address the problem now that he knew to look for it. Severus felt the old ache in his neck as he stretched it, and decided he would wait until it was perfected before he indulged in it himself. The idea had its appeal but Severus valued his sense of self control, and he was wary of anything that might compromise it. Especially now. The position he had made for himself had endless possibilities, limited only by his own sense of ambition. He would need his wits about him if he continued on this path.

He took a deep breath of the clear evening air and turned back again to face the enemy town. Some of the damn fools on his staff had suggested attacking now, clearly trying to impress him by their boldness. Imbeciles. Blundering into battle at night without need wasn't bold, it was stupid. The tribesmen might lack discipline but they knew their country and they had numbers. *Dis, they've already killed a troop of our Nomads by their stealth.* It was hardly a dent in his force but the horsemen were very useful to have and it had stung his pride a little to have lost them. No, movement by night was too risky, even for the legions. Much better to wait until morning for the fight. A battle in open field against not one but *two* robus-enhanced legions would be the worst possible nightmare for the Caderyn and their allies.

He was picturing the lines of attack on the plain below him when the sound of movement caught his ear and he turned to see Cadmus walking towards him. His First Tribune had always had good posture but tonight he seemed to somehow be walking straighter still, and his eyes seemed brighter and more alert than ever. The Tenth might only be at the first stage of their enhancement but nonetheless, the results were impressive.

The unofficial commander of the Tenth Legion snapped to attention and threw out his arm in a salute. The general returned it.

'All sentinels of the Tenth posted sir, and all preparations made.'

Severus nodded in acknowledgement, glad to see his legion's efficiency was not diminished. *The best damned legion in the whole damned Empire. And Cadmus will make a fine general of it.*

'Very well, tribune. Call stand to at dawn and we shall form up lines of battle at the base of the slope. There should be no need for a surrounding force, they'll be coming out for us in the morning.'

Cadmus nodded but he was frowning at the same time, and Severus suspected he knew why. Neither man was so naïve as to think civilians did not die in war, and more than once it had been necessary to send the enemy a hard message, but all this butchery of non-combatants had left a poor taste in his mouth, and he was fairly sure the tribune felt the same way. It was hardly soldiering. *But it is necessary.* Though he had seized his emergency powers legally, military actions on such a scale, with sorcery involved in it to boot, would be seen as a grey area at best should he ever be called to account in a court of law. Should he score a decisive victory the success would likely justify it, but if he became stuck in a protracted campaign or suffered heavy losses in a siege it would not look good for him should his powers be challenged later. And Severus Lepidus was not fond of taking risks. *A single great victory, one to cause a stir back in Tamora and beyond; that'll justify almost anything to pleb and patrician alike.*

He continued to Cadmus.

'We shall execute Standard Tactica Three as our primary plan, with Tactica Four as secondary and Tactica One as the tertiary. Any adaptations required will be signalled as usual. Circulate the orders amongst the men.'

Once again Cadmus nodded.

'Very well, sir.'

Severus returned the nod. So many generals gave orders only to their officers and kept the legionaries of the line in the dark. Most of those generals were high ranking patricians of course, and had an indoctrinated distrust of the lower orders. Fools. Keeping every man informed meant every man would know his part and be that much more prepared for what he had to do. *When I'm running the Empire I'll make that mandatory practice.* Severus caught himself at that. He'd not really thought in detail about such an ambitious plan, not beyond the odd daydream anyhow. To be thinking it so casually now was unnerving. And exciting.

He noticed that Cadmus was looking at him expectantly and the general made a casual gesture.

'You have something to add, Cadmus?'

The tribune nodded.

'I was wondering about young Dessida sir. If he is with them he may have whipped them into some shape, and he's familiar enough with the Tactica.'

Severus frowned a little at the thought of his old protégé. Antonius had shown such promise, it was a shame it had come to this.

'Even if he has tried, these barbarians have not the discipline to implement what he could teach them. What advantage he has in knowing the Tactica will be limited.'

Cadmus nodded, though Severus could tell he was still concerned.

'Though you may have a point even so.'

He thought of the one man he least trusted in this expedition, but without whom so little of it would be possible. He had to hold back a frown at the notion but it was probable he might give them a crucial edge in this battle, just in case young Antonius could find some weakness in their planning. There was no sense in taking risks without need after all. He nodded to Cadmus.

'A sprinkling of guile should counter any plan of his. Go and find Tribune Abellan. And send Praecus to me.'

Chapter 36. The Clash of Shields

Though the weather was mild Rhia felt a chill on the wind, and when she looked down onto the plain she saw grey mist floating in random clouds over the open ground. Not that it hid much of the Gaian army down there. She looked down at it from her position on the hill, some twenty paces outside of Nantwyn's perimeter ditch. Three grey rectangles were moving slowly across the open space, two more holding fast on the low ridge opposite, but clearly ready to move as needed. The seventh and eighth cohorts were likely held behind the ridge in reserve, ready in case the Caledon managed to flank the vanguard and threaten the high ground. It was a standard part of Tactica Three. The vanguard would engage heavily and the first reserve sections would then move around the flanks. *We should have the numbers to elongate our line though, maybe enough to threaten the Gaian formations on* their *flanks. But can we hold like that?*

Rhia couldn't help but think of the last time she'd watched Gaian formations from her own lines, preparing herself to charge down at them. *What a fool you were, so blindly confident of victory. What bloody fools we* all *were.* She ground her teeth a little, trying hard not to think of Bevan and Dane, and all the others who'd lost their lives that dreadful day. *Not this time.* This time they did not underestimate their enemy. This time they knew their methods and their capabilities. This time they were prepared.

She found herself remembering the old stargazer in Glyscoed Wood, and wondering for the hundredth time who he had really been. Earlier, from the other side of the hill, she'd seen the beginning of Glyscoed's trees over to the southwest. The old man had predicted their defeat by the Gaians, and a danger that would threaten them all. He had spoken of good and wickedness among their enemies, and how her son might bring peace and understanding between them. At the time she had thought so little of it, but now... could little Lucan really bring their people together someday? He was after all both Gaian and Lurian, and much of the rest of what the old man had said had come true. *But how will he unite us I wonder, as a proud ally to the Empire, or as a puppet chieftain to a Gaian warlord?*

She shook her head to clear it. This was no time for questions or doubts. Now was the time for battle. She looked to her left and shared a little smile with Meghan. They had already applied their battlemarks and the redhead's face was now daubed with blue swirls, the patterns snaking down her neck onto her shoulders and arms. She had never looked so strong, or so beautiful. Rhia wondered how *she* might appear if she looked at herself in her old glass back in Tamora. Nothing like a Gaian lady, that was for damned sure.

Beside Meg stood Owain, though he would soon be leaving to lead his own cohort. The stocky Gadarim looked fearsome, his beard gleaming with lime, his thick arms clinking with bracelets and his tattoos freshly painted over with bright blue woad. Though many warriors and Gadarim now had stolen shirts of mail, Owain had decided to fight bare-chested today, and his torso looked heavy with flat slabs of muscle, so different from the sculpted bodies of Gaian men. *Like Marius.* He shared a brief embrace with Meg before tipping Rhia a nod and then strode off to lead his company.

Rhia looked to her other side, where Marius stood beside her in the front line of the First Cohort. Like Rhia he was wearing mail and carried a Caderyn's blue and red shield, but Madoc and Owain had insisted that, as their effective commander, he ought to also have the honour of wearing

Caderyn battlemarks to war. How much Marius, who still wore his Vulco amulet, approved of that Rhia couldn't guess, but her husband seemed to suit the warpaint well. Rhia had been convinced she would find the look comical or embarrassing, but the simple lines drawn on one side of his face only served to make him look more like a warrior. Their strategy today was a simple one and so once again he had elected to fight on foot in the front line, and Rhia found herself looking forward to seeing her Gaian husband in action.

Up and down the line Bael and Reaghan were blessing fighters and weapons alike, their staffs jangling with iron rings as they called upon the gods, or the ava, and gave courage to the warriors. The elder druid passed by and blessed Silverbite for her before laying a gentle hand on hers, a solemn sort of smile on his kindly face. Once again she felt a warmth on her skin that seemed to travel all the way to her chest and then out to her limbs. It made her feel both safe and strong at the same time, both ready for war and yet strangely contented, and she knew that what she felt was the truest kind of magic, not the twisted spells of a sorcerer like Praecus.

All the way up the line other fighters were being gifted the same way, Reaghan and Bael moving through to the second rank once they'd finished with the first. Rhia noticed that when they blessed a Gadarim they seemed to whisper a few words, and Rhia hoped they were invoking Mabonac or Taran to protect their chosen warriors. She looked further along the ridge and saw the Gorvicae and Dariniae druids doing the same thing, scores of the holy men blessing hundreds, even thousands of Caledon fighters. Next along from her own cohort she saw a Gorvic druid blessing Heartreaver. Most of Gawan's long hair was now tied back behind his head but the hair on his crown was spiked into points, and all of it shining white with lime. His was one of only two complete cohorts of Gorvic warriors; what few others had made it there had been too late to be trained and too few to make a fresh company besides. Only one full cohort was made up of Ierryn's Dariniae, his promised reinforcements having still not arrived. For the most part, the fighting today would be done by the Caderyn. *As it should be.*

Rhia looked down at the plain again, where they would soon have to advance into bloody turmoil. Company pennants flapped in the breeze, along with the larger eagle standards of the Tenth and Fourteenth Legions. The Panther Legion was directly across from them, with the Lion Standard showing above the units to their left, slogging their way through the clouds of morning mist. She felt glad that they ought not to be fighting Marius' old comrades, though she hated to admit, she also felt a prickling of fear at the concept of fighting the more magically-enhanced soldiers. She took a slow breath. *Reaghan's blessings will make us strong, I can feel it now. And at least they are few enough Nomads there to shoot at us this time!* She managed a half-smile. The Nomads gave the legions vital fast-response troops and could manoeuvre far more quickly than their infantry counterparts. Thanks to Eogan and Elfed their numbers were severely thinned, and hopefully the Caderyn's own archers would be a fair deterrent to the horsemen.

She looked at the flapping standards and decided that now was the time. Now was the time to unfurl their own banner, to show the single symbol for their little army. She twisted on the spot and nodded to Bedwyr behind her. The young Gadarim returned the nod, and he and the man beside him unfurled the banner and raised it high above the cohort. Rhia looked up and screamed out the name of the Dragon God.

'Mabonac!'

The cry was echoed all around her as the great green dragon seemed to fly in the breeze, that same symbol that was copied over and over on the legion's many-coloured shields. She looked across to Gawan's cohort and saw they had raised their own pennant above them and were cheering the name as loudly as anyone. On their other side, Ierryn's Dariniae had done the same thing, and Rhia let herself smile in triumph. For all their differences there could be no doubt today that they were not three warring tribes any more. Today they were the Caledon. Today they were the Dragon Legion.

Rhia held up Silverbite and bellowed to the line, somehow making herself heard over the cacophony of warcries.

'Dragon Legion, First Cohort; for Nantwyn, for Taran and for the Caledon,' she pointed the blade down the hill towards the marching Gaian squares, 'forward!'

Whistles blew and bellows for Taran and Mabonac went up along the line as the warriors stepped forward as one, starting slowly down the slope and into the mist. Rhia felt her heart pounding in her chest and decided to embrace the feeling. Now was the time for racing blood and boiling rage. Today she would win freedom for her people, or else die in the attempt.

*

At the first Battle of Nantwyn, the meeting of the armies had been sheer bloody chaos, as Rhia, and doubtless many others there, could recall all too clearly. *This* time, the clash of lines could not have been more different. The Caledon cohorts had advanced in their old, seemingly scattered manner and then, as they came within twenty paces of the enemy, had formed into a solid wall of dragon-painted shields. Secretly Rhia had worried that the manoeuvre would prove too challenging, but the Caledon warriors had formed with a precision that would make any Gaian centurion proud. Rhia had seen the shock on the faces of the Gaians, even through their frenzied snarls, and when the shieldwalls had clashed, the Fourteenth Legion had been stopped cold.

Now warriors and soldiers hacked and stabbed around their shields, the wild strength of the Gaians countered by the momentum and surprise of the Caledon. Rhia saw a short sword come thrusting past her guard but she twisted on the spot and trapped the arm between her own shield and Marius' beside her. The soldier didn't seem to register the pain of cracking bone, and even when she lopped off his hand at the wrist, the berserk legionary merely grunted and stumbled. Rhia shoved him hard and he lost his balance, and the second rank men dragged him back into the formation, replacing him with a fresh soldier. That was alright by Rhia. He was at least out of the battle for now, and with only one hand he couldn't possibly fight in the line again. As far as his cohort was concerned, she might as well have just killed him. She grinned fiercely, and righteous fury lent her strength as she thrust out with her blade again.

Next to her she saw Marius cutting and thrusting methodically, barely seeming to think as he attacked and countered, his movements so well-drilled they were purely reflexive. A maddened legionary, frustrated by the defence, broke ranks to dart forwards at him, and Marius calmly ducked low and swiped a clean cut through his lead leg. The soldier seemed barely to feel it, but the blade had severed tendons and he began to topple sideways. From the Caledon wall two blades thrust out at once, one glancing from his mail but the other striking home into his neck. Blood gushed out and the man fell to the dirt.

All along the shieldwall men of the Fourteenth were breaking out of their formation in their fury to reach the enemy, and time after time Rhia saw them cut down from behind the dragon shields. Though the Caledon were far from getting it all their own way. Rhia saw the fighter beside Meg impaled on a Gaian sword, then heard him scream as the blade was twisted savagely in his guts. Meg cut at the soldier's arm but he wrenched the blade free quickly, drawing another horrible cry from the warrior, and the legionary began hacking at her shield. Meg ducked down and started thrusting back but she couldn't get around his defence. Elsewhere, Caderyn fighters were being pulled bodily from their line and hewn apart before their comrades' eyes. A blade came crashing down onto Rhia's shield and the strength of it dented the iron rim, but she somehow kept it up and stabbed forwards, forcing the maddened Gaian onto the defensive.

The pressure of the press was overwhelming, but though the Caledon's advance had been stopped, they weren't being pushed back either. Marius had been right; the soldiers of the Fourteenth were unbelievably strong, frighteningly so, but they lacked the cold discipline that made a Gaian legion unbeatable. The Dragon Legion was out-muscled, there was no doubt about that, but the long hours of training had paid off, and the Gaian's formation had lost vital cohesion.

Another heavy cut came at her shield and Rhia felt herself rocked back onto her heels. The Gaian followed up, shoving her shield with all his weight and strength, and Rhia fell to the grass with a thud. She felt a sharp pain in her tailbone and a surge of fright in her heart as the soldier moved forwards to finish her. She desperately raised her shield but before the Gaian could cut down at her, Marius' blade had found his ribs. The Gaian turned and cut for him but the veteran officer didn't try another counter. He simply took the blow on his shield and then turned to face the formation again. Rhia wanted to cry out to him but then two men from the second rank appeared, one dragging her from danger while the other rammed his sword into the legionary's neck. The soldier dropped and the Caledon fighter moved quickly into the gap in the line.

Rhia was pulled back into the fourth rank, still barely believing what she'd seen. Marius had such blind confidence in the other men of his cohort that he'd offered his back to an enemy in order to keep the main shieldwall intact, trusting the men behind him to deal with the soldier in the breach. It was an insane amount of trust to place in anyone, yet he'd done it without even thinking, and the fighters had come forward just as expected. Legion mentality; it was madness, but it worked.

Friendly hands helped her to her feet and Rhia took a moment to look around. She hadn't realised how hard she was breathing and she felt grateful for the respite. Over on the right she saw the Dariniae cohort, Ierryn himself front and centre, hammering at another company of the Fourteenth. Though their shields all bore the legion mark of the green dragon, the backgrounds of the Dariniae shields were still painted black, and their woad was such a dark blue as to seem almost the same colour. She saw their Gadarim, the lime streaks in their hair making her think of giant badgers, shouting out warcries and encouragement, and lending their strength and skills wherever the line appeared weak. Ierryn the Black, his own streaked hair blowing behind him in the wind, was moving with a speed Rhia would barely have thought possible, a maniac's grin plastered across his face as he butchered man after man, hacking and stabbing with barbaric glee.

To the left, Leaping Wolf was fighting with a grim determination, the Gorvicae company holding their own against another frenzied cohort of Gaians. Here too the discipline of the legionaries was being lost to their berserk attacks, and the green wall of Gorvic shields was holding well. Rhia felt elation swelling within her. They were winning. They were actually winning.

A shrill whistle from the Gaian squares sounded a retreat, and cries of victory were shouted all along the Lurian line, but Marius had anticipated this and the Caledon held their ground. The maddened Fourteenth men seemed torn between the instinct to follow orders and their lust for blood and death, and dozens were cut down as they ignored the retreating formation and attempted to carve their way through the Caledon shieldwall alone. Good warriors fell to their freakish strength but before long every Gaian not withdrawing had been cut down.

The soldiers backed up and Rhia elbowed her way to the front rank. Like everyone else she wished she could pursue them, but she knew that was exactly what they wanted. True enough, the legionaries had gone barely thirty paces when their lines opened up and Aborans poured forth from behind them, the giants bellowing strange warcries as they charged the Caledon line. Had they tried to press on they might have lost their cohesion and been close to the Gaian shieldwall when this happened. As it was, instead of battering straight into a loose mass of warriors, the giants were forced to run over a patch of open ground towards a solid line of dragon shields and unforgiving iron.

Rhia screamed out as the auxiliaries moved forward.

'Now!'

From the rear of their own ranks hidden archers sent shafts over their comrade's heads, while fighters at the front left second-long gaps in the shieldwall to let more bowmen shoot straight into the advancing Destroyers. Many arrows glanced from scale armour, but at such close range it was impossible to miss completely, and the archers at the front aimed for the exposed face and neck. Destroyers collapsed to the muddy grass, their insane power no match for an ash shaft through the skull, and by the time they reached the wall, more than a third of them were down.

Rhia felt a weight behind her as the second rank leaned their shields into her back, the third rank leaning into them, and when the Destroyers hit the wall, she was glad of it. One giant struck her with the strength of a raging bull, and even with the combined weight of three warriors behind her shield, she felt herself shoved violently backwards. Beside her, Marius cut at the Aboran's leg as he swung at her again, his tribune's sword hamstringing the huge man and unbalancing him enough to rob the second blow of its power. Rhia struck forward as he reeled and she sliced into his neck, though the cut was only shallow. It was enough however to keep him on the back foot, and Meg's blade thrust under his armpit even as Marius cut low again, shearing through his knee. Rhia seized the moment and Silverbite thrust up and under his guard, ramming through his unprotected groin. The Aboran actually cried out in pain and fell to the floor where Marius finished him off, his own warcry at strange odds to his fellows'. Not that anyone seemed to care.

'Gaivia Victor!'

All along the line Aborans, unable to break the wall and outnumbered by the weaker fighters, were cut down by Caledon warriors. The mighty Destroyers took their toll of course, and Rhia saw more than a few of her people hauled from the wall and chopped apart, but every time the wall reformed or else Gadarim, shining in blue and white, would dart forwards to distract or wound the giant, ducking back behind the shields once the moment had been gained.

All around her Rhia saw the monsters being felled, their massive strength bested by the unity and courage of the Dragon Legion. Her breath caught in her throat as she saw them fall. *Dear gods, we might actually do this!*

*

The sorcerer's fog was cold and unsettling, but Cadmus took care not to let his discomfort show. He was commander of the Tenth in all but name; he couldn't show fear about a little magic mist. The sound of battle to his left was deafening, but he couldn't see out of the grey cloud any more than the tribesmen could see in. The clash of iron, the odd battle-cry or scream, and the muffled trill of whistles all blended in to one messy mass of sound, and the First Tribune had no idea how things were faring. *Well enough, most likely. Though if Dessida's been working with them, these savages may be making us work for it.*

The First Cohort of the Tenth and the Second Cohort of the Fourteenth continued their slow pace, taking care to keep quiet, not that it mattered much in the mist. By Cadmus' estimation, based on a count of paces, they ought to have circled around the Caderyn's left flank by now. He signalled by gesture to wheel left and his company began to turn, Abellan's men following close on their flank. Sure enough, within a few steps he felt the gradient of the ground start to slope upwards.

According to Praecus the mist ought to hold until well after they reached the top, and by then it would be far too late for the tribesmen to do anything to stop them. They would enter the town almost unopposed, kill any druids they found and take Chief Carradan, alive if at all possible. With the town held and their chieftain a hostage, the barbarians would lose heart and probably start surrendering in droves. Cadmus wondered how merciful the general would be with them, and given the trouble they'd put him through, he decided the answer was 'not very'. Not that Cadmus objected. He'd disapproved a little of all this killing of villagers they'd been forced to, but the men on this field had opted to fight the might of Gaivia's military. They deserved everything they got.

He kept his footsteps soft, trying hard not to break into a run. The power the magicker had given them had made him keen for battle, ready and eager to fight in the front line. He felt stronger than he had in ten years, and the dozen aches and pains he'd simply accepted as part of life had disappeared. Even a day after the last ritual he could still feel the robus flowing like fire in his veins, urging him to use his new strength, to hack and tear and kill. Cadmus kept his breathing steady. Abellan and the Fourteenth boys had demonstrated already the danger of giving in to this power too early. *Keep your discipline, tribune. Keep it in you and in your men and we'll come out of this as conquering heroes.*

Despite himself, the habitually grim-faced man felt a smile spread slowly across his face. Battle was close, he could smell it, and the first tribesman he saw would feel the full force of his new-gained might. He'd have pitied the poor wretch... but the robus was singing through his body, and his strength was crying out for blood.

Chapter. 37 Second Nantwyn

Ossian watched the battle as it raged beneath him and once again felt the familiar surge of envy. Though he was in nominal command of the cohort stationed on the hill, and though he knew he was still seen as a Gadarim by his men, he would never fight again as one of them, and he knew it. Back at the first battle for this hill an Aboran Destroyer had crushed his shoulder and shattered half of his ribs. For several days his life had been feared for and one of the herbwives had suggested removing his arm. Ossian had refused. His right arm might be next to useless now, but damn it all, it was still his.

The fighting below seemed to be going well, though it was difficult to see through all the mist. It looked like the front Caledon cohorts had stopped the enemy advance and now the supporting companies were moving up to join the fray, both on their side and on the Gaians'. He wished more than anything that he was down there with them, standing shield to shield with his comrades as they fought for their tribe and their home. But wishes were for fools. There was honour enough to be had here, commanding the cohort of Caderyn left behind to guard the town. Should the worst come to the worst, they would fight a rearguard action as the townspeople fled west. Gaian scouts and Nomad horsemen might catch many of them of course, but if it came down to such a massive loss, their lives would be no safer staying put.

The Hawk of War looked to his section. Roughly two-thirds of them were men, the rest were women who had yet to become mothers. All were daubed with woad and carrying their new dragon shields, though they'd only had enough to equip the first two ranks of the cohort. *Hopefully we won't need to become engaged at all*, Ossian thought, and yet a part of him wished they would be, just so he could taste battle once more. He shoved the idea aside in self-reprimand. His pride was no reason to wish such a fate on his people.

Along with the Caderyn company he had been joined on the hilltop by a small mob of Dariniae. Ierryn's man had brought a few straggling Caderyn along on his way across their land, but most of the fighters with him were Niswyn men. Their leader was on the other side of town with the rest of his warriors, and for the hundredth time Ossian wracked his brains for why he'd seemed so familiar when they had met. He was of middling size, his hair streaked with stripes of white in the style of the Dariniae Gadarim, and he had a tiny scar below his eye. Ossian stroked his own lime-stiffened beard and pondered. It was difficult to tell under the thick beard and blue battlemarks, but the Hawk of War could have sworn he had encountered this man before.

He put the thought from his mind. The Dariniae were here and that was the main thing. They might not be drilled to fight as one as the legion had been, but they all seemed well-armed and fearsome enough, and many of those here looked as disappointed as Ossian was that they might not see combat today. Reaghan the druid was weaving in and out of them, nodding quietly or giving blessings before returning to the Caderyn. The old man had already given the cohort his encouragement, and Ossian could still feel the gentle warmth from the druid's touch.

Reaghan smiled a little as he approached.

'You are not too bored here, I trust?'

Ossian returned the smile.

'Eager to help but not so foolish as to try to, never fear, father. How are our omens?'

Reaghan shrugged his shoulders a little.

'It is difficult to tell. Last night we all of us saw portents of death and battle and great victory, but to which side it would be granted none are sure.'

Ossian frowned a little despite himself. Such portents were not much use to warriors. Reaghan saw his expression and smiled at him once again.

'Do not be too frustrated with us, young one. Should you truly wish it I can consult the gods again, though I warn you, their signs are rarely simple.'

The Gadarim blushed a little at the thought of having caused offence, and wasn't certain of the polite thing to say. If he told the druid not to bother it might imply he didn't value the offer, but if he said yes it might look like he was putting him to the test. In the end his curiosity won out over the worry, and he spoke as courteously as he could.

'I do trust your first readings father, but if you wish to ask again, I should be grateful to hear your thoughts.'

Reaghan nodded quietly. Doubtless he had seen the inner conflict that preceded the answer, but he was a kindly man and did not mention it.

'Very well.'

The old man closed his eyes a moment and took a deep breath in through his nose. He let it out slowly through barely-open lips and Ossian practically *felt* his concentration. A Gadarim had to be focused, it was a part of his testing after all, but when compared to the intensity of the druid's quiet thoughts, Ossian felt himself no more than a scatter-brained child. Reaghan stayed silent for a dozen heartbeats but then the lines of a frown appeared on his brow.

'Strange. Almost as if...'

Suddenly his eyes flew wide open and he spun in place to look down the hill. The morning mist was still patchy all over the ground and the druid turned to face the largest cloud of it, a thick grey mass on the north side of the hill. In an eyeblink Ossian saw the holy man's face go from curious to snarling. He brought his heavy staff up before him, pointed it at the mist and hissed out a strange word.

'Dagel!'

Ossian felt wind rush around them like a gale and the bank of mist in front of them disappeared before its power... to reveal two lines of Gaian infantry less than forty paces away, advancing slowly up the northern slope. Above the first section he saw a flapping lion pennant, the second one flying a panther. Reaghan stepped back to stand behind the line of shields and Ossian started bellowing out to his cohort, then remembered their procedure and blew three blasts on his whistle for good measure, two short, one long.

'Stand to!'

The warriors almost panicked at the sight of the enemy so close but they did as they were ordered and hurried to form up, facing the Gaians. Ossian heard the same orders bellowed by the Gaian commanders, but to his dismay he saw that they were practically formed already. He saw them lock their shields and heard another command to advance, and he began shouting desperately at his own company to form up. The Dragon Legion had trained hard for this, but they were having to move their whole formation to face at right-angles to where it had been, and the Gaians reached the line before the shieldwall was properly formed. The Lion cohort hammered into them like a bull charging a fence, enhanced strength and tight discipline smashing the badly-positioned Caledon.

Ossian screamed himself hoarse for the line to reform but it was far too late for that, and the Gaians hacked their way through warriors with barely a loss of their own. The Caledon fought hard to hold onto their ground but the Gaians kept shoving them back. Ossian called out to the

Dariniae behind them and more warriors came running to their aid. The Niswyn Islanders crashed into the fray and though each one of them fought like a madman, the Gaian advance was barely slowed.

Ossian wondered if he should signal for the other cohorts down below, but they were already entangled with the Gaian main force and if they turned their backs to them it would be slaughter down there. There were more warriors in the town and Ossian prayed they'd heard the commotion, but most were those who'd come too late to be trained to fight together, and would break upon a shieldwall like water on a rock.

The Gaian wall forged closer and Ossian drew his sword left-handed. His lack of shield meant he couldn't fight in a formation, but the ranks of his cohort had become a panicked mob and the battle had become a mess of cutting, stabbing, screaming warriors. A Gaian thrust a sword at him and he cut hard down on his wrist. The hand was half-severed and the sword thumped to the floor, and Ossian stabbed his blade forwards at the wounded legionary. His first thrust glanced from the rim of a shield but the second, by either skill or blind chance, slipped between the shields of the soldier and his fellow, and Ossian felt the blade sink deep into soft flesh.

But before he could draw back to either defend or attack again, the short blade of a Gaian in a crested helm was thrust into his midriff. The pain was indescribable, a vicious burning in his guts and the horrid, invasive feeling of the iron stuck in his belly. Ossian's vision began to swim and he felt his grip loosen on his sword. He felt himself slump forwards to lean on a shield, his head thudding hard against the rim. Black spots began dancing in front of his blurry world and for a moment Ossian forgot where he was. Then another blade hacked into his skull with crushing force, and the Hawk of War stayed down.

*

Rhia shoved hard at the Gaian in front of her, distracting him while Meg stabbed in around his shield. The soldier had sloppily moved forward from his wall and the gap was almost begging to be exploited. The broad blade entered at the armpit and the Gaian flinched but made no sound. He turned to face Meg but Rhia shoved his shield again and knocked his cut off target. Meg took it on her shield and swiped at the arm, her blade's tip cutting a chunk out of the muscle. The soldier's grip on the sword loosened but his face showed no sign of pain. Meg didn't wait for another chance and stabbed up into his face, the blade passing through nose and cheek to scrape the inside of his helmet. The legionary grunted and fell back into his comrades, who simply dragged him backwards in their eagerness to close in.

Rhia was tired, her arms and shoulders aching despite the white-hot rage of battle, and her shirt of mail felt as if its weight had trebled. They were holding them well enough but these maddened Gaians took a lot of killing, and they seemed both untiring and never-ending. After their Aborans had failed to break the Caledon line the infantry had engaged them again, and once more Silverbite was hacking and stabbing in the press. Their own reserve cohorts had come up to help them, but then so had those of the enemy, and the endless grinding slaughter showed no sign of slowing down.

Nonetheless, the feeling around her was one of confident determination. The last time most of these warriors had faced the Gaians, the shieldwalls had broken through them and the tribesmen had been scattered like Samhain apples in a gale. This time, though the fighting was hard, it was clear to both sides that the Gaians faced even odds, and that the united Caledon were not so easily crushed.

Another insanely strong shove pushed Rhia off balance, but the warrior behind her held her steady, and she ducked low to slash the soldier's leg while Marius stabbed at his neck. Her husband seemed to be just as tireless as the legionaries, calling out encouragement and fighting without pause, though Rhia knew his limbs too must be burning with fatigue. The man in front of them toppled, but he fell into Rhia's shield as he did so and dragged it from her grip, wrenching her shoulder horribly in the process. She cried out a little but stayed on her feet, and Meg stabbed down at him before he could do any more. Straight away she felt an arm behind her pulling her back, and another fighter stepped in to take her place, her own shield held ready.

Rhia took a breath, glad to be out of the fight again, if only for a moment. What respite they'd had when the lines had split had been all too brief, and Rhia felt herself gulping down air. At her height it was hard to see much of what was going on in the wider field but it seemed as if Ierryn and Gawan were holding as well as the Caderyn, and Rhia tried to take heart from that. They might not be truly *winning*, but they certainly weren't losing either. *And damn it, that's better than you feared!*

She was just thinking she ought to take someone's shield and return to the front line when a voice from behind her made her stop.

'Rhianwyn!'

She turned to see Bael, his white robe flapping around him, rush towards the formation and start shoving his way through it towards her. The druid's eyes were wide and he waved an arm back towards the town.

'Look – back on the hill!'

Rhia looked up and vaguely made out some movement up above them but the mist made it difficult to see. She heard Bael mutter something that sounded very un-druidlike, then saw him close his eyes and point his staff towards the slope, speaking again in what sounded like the Ancient Tongue.

'Dagel!'

The mist began to clear a little and Rhia saw to her horror what the young man had meant. Amidst the confusion of moving shapes up on the hill, she clearly made out a red pennant with a yellow-gold symbol sewn in its centre. Rhia felt as if she'd been doused in cold water. The Gaians hadn't kept their other cohorts in reserve. Praecus had hidden them in mist and now they were behind them. And the town was falling.

She whipped her head around to the press where still neither side seemed able to gain the advantage. Neither army was able to manoeuvre around the flanks, and the wild strength of the Gaians was being held off purely by the determination and discipline of the Dragon Legion. But only just. If she took warriors from the formation it might make the difference between victory and defeat. She gripped her sword tighter in frustration. There was a town full of people up there, mothers, elders and children, and what were they fighting for if not the future of their people, their way of life, who they were? Rhia bit her lip. She wanted to go back there and help but a part of her said to stay here. *What do I do?*

A tiny spark of hope came to her as she saw that Marius had been pushed back and replaced in the line and was now moving towards her, his breath coming out in gasps.

'It's damned hard work up there, but I think we may have them if we can keep this up.'

Rhia didn't waste time with chatter.

511

'We've been flanked! There are Gaians on the hill, look!'

She pointed to the slope and Marius looked up to it, his expression barely flickering as he took in the situation.

'We need to get men up there, there's no point driving this lot back if we're attacked from behind.'

Rhia was glad to hear her thoughts justified by another and started looking around for Madoc. She soon found him, standing behind their formation with some of his cohort, ready to provide warriors to plug any serious gaps. She elbowed her way towards him.

'Madoc – take command here, we need some of your company.'

He looked at her quizzically and once again she pointed up the slope.

'There are Gaians behind us. It looks like the Tenth's First Cohort and that means Cadmus will be there. He's a cunning bastard and we may need Marius.'

The fact that she would be staying with her husband went unsaid. Madoc looked for a moment as if he wanted to lead the fighters himself, but then he blinked and simply nodded.

'Go, I've near three hundred men not yet committed, Duran has a few more. Take them up the slope, I'll hold here.'

Rhia returned the nod and Marius called out some final words.

'If they pull back with order don't follow until they've opened more than thirty paces, then stay on them and maintain that gap. If their formation breaks send only one cohort to pursue, it may be a trap.'

Madoc nodded once again. No-one wanted to ask what to do if their own formation broke. Probably because there would be nothing *to* do.

Rhia started moving to the rear of the cohort, Marius and Bael following on. She found several ranks of fighters waiting to support as they were needed, and now that the mist was gone many of the warriors had seen the same thing they had and were pointing up at the slope. She called out as loudly as her dry throat would let her.

'Form up and follow me, pass the word on to the Gorvicae.'

The warriors started moving into position and passing the message down towards Duran's cohort, which was standing ready to support Gawan on the left. Rhia and Marius made their way to the rear, which would now become the front, while Bael disappeared among the ranks. She exchanged glances with her husband but he was keeping up his mask of a calm commander. For a second she was actually angry at him for staying so damned composed when innocents were likely being butchered up at Nantwyn, but then she scolded herself for thinking so. Marius was a good man and of course he cared about what was happening, but he was commanding in the only way he knew how. *And the warriors seem to like it; his mask may not be ferocious but it does make him seem fearless.*

They reached the front rank and someone handed Rhia a shield. She wasted no time with words and pointed her hard-won blade to the distant lion pennant.

'Forward!'

Warcries sounded from all around her as the mix of Caderyn and Gorvicae charged back up the hill, and Rhia tried not to think about what they'd find when they got there.

Chapter 38. The Final Battle

The hill of Nantwyn was steep and slippery and Rhia couldn't help but think, in some detached part of her brain, that this was part of what made it ideal as a place to defend. Had the Gaians been forced to climb up this thing under storm, with arrows and stones raining down and disrupting their formation, the Caledon would have stood a damned good chance of victory. The battle on the plain below had gone better than she'd dared hope, but with their reserve force now having to rush back up here she wished for the thousandth time that they had been able to fight defensively. *But that was never a real option to us. Lepidus' butchery of innocents saw to that.*

She was breathing hard, the air wheezing painfully out of her, and her wrenched shoulder was burning like fire. Just the weight of holding onto her shield was a nightmare and she hated to think of how it would feel when a magically strong Gaian started hammering down on it. *But once again they've given me no choice. It must be done.*

Her mixed cohort of fighters finally reached the hill's crest, and they took a few precious moments to reform their front two lines. It was as close to a rest as they were likely to get but to their credit, not one warrior dawdled as they formed their wall of shields. Ahead of them she saw warriors charging randomly at the Gaians, few if any of them taking soldiers to meet Annwn with them. The pennant over the shieldwall showed the panther of the Fourteenth but even had she not seen it, their fighting style made it obvious what they were. In the distance, to the right of the Panthers and a little further forward, she saw the tight and disciplined ranks of Cadmus' oversized First Cohort, clearly strengthened with misused ava. But that seemed as nothing to the frenzy of the Fourteenth.

While the Lions were using strength and tempering it with iron discipline, the wall of the Panthers was sloppy, and had the warriors charging at them maintained some order of their own, the legionaries might have found their hands were full. But these Caledon were fighters who had come too late to be trained, and they fought the Gaian line in the only way that they knew how. And it was slaughter.

Rhia called her section to advance towards them, thanking Taran and Camelas both that the soldiers were barely at the town. A few Aborans had broken off from the formation and were charging around hacking and killing, but for the most part the Gaians advanced slowly. The centre of the fighting was at the defensive ditch and only this small advantage, and the Fourteenth's lack of discipline, was allowing the Caledon to slow them down. Yet all the same the soldiers were advancing.

As her cohort approached the fray Rhia spotted Reaghan shepherding children and civilians away from the fighting. An Aboran approached the little group with a warcry on his lips, and Rhia's heart leaped to her throat as she saw the great sword swing. But the druid turned on him with an expression she'd never seen on him before: Fury. The old man brought up his staff and the oak simply stopped the heavy iron of the sword. Rhia stared. It stopped it *cold*! Such a cut should have cloven both staff and man in two, and the strength and weight behind it should at least have knocked him down. Instead the druid had stopped the blow dead in its tracks and in the moment of surprise as the Aboran stared at him, he whipped the oak in a graceful arc at the giant's armoured head. Rhia had no idea how old Reaghan really was, but men said his hair had been grey when her father was still young. Yet the blow of his staff crushed first the iron helm and then the skull within it, and the magically strong warrior dropped to the mud without a sound.

Rhia's eyes went wide but she had no time to stop and stare. She watched for half a moment longer as the druid called more townspeople to him, and then turned her full attention back to the legion. They were only a few long strides away and Rhia screamed out to her people.

'Kill them all!'

Cries of 'Taran!' and 'Mabonac!' and the occasional 'Caledon!' erupted from their throats as the hastily-formed cohort smashed into the Fourteenth's flank. For all their frenzy these men were still Gaian soldiery, and they turned their shields on them in an instant. The lines clashed and soon Rhia was hacking and stabbing away, probing into any gap she could see in the wall of shields. Silverbite glanced from mail and clattered from helmets but once or twice she felt it bite deep into yielding flesh, and the legionaries, though unperturbed by pain, found it harder to fight back with missing hands and spurting throats. A panther shield slammed hard into Rhia's flimsy defence and she felt the force drive through it to rattle her injured shoulder. She cried out as burning pain lanced through the joint, and it was only a quick stab from the man to her left that saved her from the soldier's follow-up. Unfortunately for him he over-extended himself as he protected her, and a hack from the Gaian's neighbour took his arm off at the elbow. He cried out and Rhia tried to intervene, but the warrior stumbled forwards and the next cut took his head.

To her right Marius had been forced to the defensive, the soldier in front of him hammering blows fast and hard onto his shield. A second glance showed her it was Abellan, the tribune she had seen coming out of the chamber where Nuallan was tortured. Rhia checked for a moment that a replacement was to her left, flicked a cut at the face of the man in front of her, then screamed as she drove her sword sideways beneath Abellan's arm. The mail didn't break completely, only a ring or two coming free, but the force of it drove hard into the tribune's armpit and his battering at her husband slowed for a moment. It was all the respite that Marius Dessida needed, and for all his berserk strength, the Second Tribune of the Fourteenth was no match for his counterpart. Marius made three quick stabs with classic legion technique; high, middle, then high again, the third one slicing home into the neck. Scarlet blood spurted and Tribune Abellan barely had time to stare at them before Marius' shield rammed into his head and his lifeless body crumpled to the dirt. Rhia turned her attention back to the man in front of her and couldn't help but feel a little proud, and not just because Abellan was dead at their hands. Marius' swordsmanship one-to-one might be basic, but in the confines of a wall her husband knew his trade better than anyone.

For a few more heartbeats the fight raged on, similar to that upon the plain. The difference here was that Rhia knew the men of the Tenth might well have reached the town by now, and with no cohort to engage them they would have almost free reign of Nantwyn. Rhia cursed and tried to push forward with her line but the attacks by warriors to their left had diminished, and the Fourteenth now brought their weight to bear on Rhia's company. Despite their best efforts they found themselves pushed back, and step by bloody step the Fourteenth Legion drove forwards. Marius and Rhia both bellowed out encouragement but the Caledon line was wavering, and Rhia panicked at the thought that it might break.

But then something strange happened. The pressure on her line became less all of a sudden, but her elation at the feel of it soon turned to sickened horror. Legionaries from the rear, clearly bored with merely adding their weight to the forward press, were deserting the cohort in twos and threes to sprint towards the town where they might satisfy their bloodlust more easily. Rhia called out to her section to push harder at the wall, desperate to drive them back and free up some warriors to go after them. The Fourteenth rocked back a little and Rhia ducked into the second rank, shouting out to Marius as she did.

'Hold them here!'

The Gaian simply nodded and Rhia gestured to the rear ranks.

'Back two lines with me!'

She raised her sword above her head and started moving towards the town, the warriors she'd called out to following after. The weight of her shield felt like lead on her arm and reluctantly she let it go, the heavy wood thudding to the ground. Her shoulder was in no state to use it anyway and besides, inside the town there would be little space for formation. Now they would fight in pairs or in small groups, and hope to all the gods it was enough to stop the Gaians. Their first clash showed her that it wasn't.

They had only reached the scattered outer buildings of the town when the first handful of legionaries turned back to hack at them, and Rhia realised that fighting out of the shieldwall was a mistake. All around her warriors were cut down where they stood, and though some scored wounds and even kills of their own, they simply hadn't the numbers to make a difference. *We can't save the town. No matter what happens on the plain, Nantwyn is lost.* She watched as a stray Aboran hacked a Gorvic fighter apart. *We are going to die here. And I'll never see Lucan again.*

The thought threatened to crush her spirit but just then a legionary charged her and she channelled her sadness into rage. The soldier rammed forward with his shield but Rhia twisted her body aside, stabbing her blade forwards towards his face. The legionary was too quick though, and he turned his shield to take the strike before lunging out, lightning-fast. Rhia threw herself backwards and avoided disembowelment, but her momentum carried her too far and she overbalanced. She threw out her arms but it was too late and she felt her legs go out from under her. She managed to get her sword up in time to half-deflect the next cut and by chance it glanced away, though the force of it shuddered through her arm and Silverbite dropped from her fingers.

Rhia twisted on the ground as a boot stamped down at her, then kicked out hard at the Gaian's knee. She felt the joint buckle but the soldier barely staggered and he shoved down at her neck with his shield's iron rim. Again Rhia twisted desperately out of the way but in the time it took her to move the Gaian had struck down again, this time ramming the shield's rim into her legs. She felt pain in her hip and thigh and tried to wriggle free of it, but his weight and strength was holding her pinned and she saw the sword rise above his head, a glint of pure insanity in his eyes.

Then something seemed to strike him in the back of his head and Rhia felt the weight leaving her legs as he toppled over. A man with lime-streaked hair followed up without a pause and thrust his sword straight down through the Gaian's neck. The soldier thrashed a few times and then lay still. A hand reached down to Rhia and she hauled herself up with an effort. The man looked at her with shock on his face and it took Rhia a moment to realise who he was. He was middle-sized and full-bearded, his long hair streaked with lime in the style of the Dariniae Gadarim. His face was half covered in battlemarks, the painted woad now smeared over his cheek, and she saw a tiny scar under his eye. But beneath it all she knew the face and recoiled despite herself. It was Delyn.

A wave of emotion hit her like a flood and it was all Rhia could do not to stagger and fall. Memories of her last battle came back in a wild rush. She saw Dane, an arrow still stuck in his chest as he was cut down by Gawan. She saw Bevan, his eyes wide as she drove a blade into the man she loved, and then saw him again as his life bled out of him in the barn. She saw Delyn, pulling her into the dark and taking down her trews… and she remembered the shame, the terrible, numbing, soul-crushing shame that had followed her since that day. The shame that had taken more than five years to die down and even with the love of a husband and child still plagued her sometimes at night.

All around them, black-clad Dariniae were charging from the town, crashing into the legionaries to wreak havoc and confusion. Rhia stared into the eyes of the man who'd both raped her and saved her and saw a brief reflection of her own shame in his eyes. He coughed a little and then spoke, his voice shaking.

'Rhianwyn… I…'

But before he could continue another soldier was upon them and he spun on the spot to clash blades with him, taking the blow at an angle. Rhia whipped free her long knife and pressed into the Gaian's flank, forcing her emotions down and away from her present thoughts. She cut into his leg and the soldier turned to face her but Delyn took the advantage and struck hard at his neck. The cut mostly glanced from shoulder-mail but it bit into some flesh too, and it was enough to make the soldier spin to take another swipe at him. Delyn sprang back and Rhia darted in again, this time slashing sideways with all of her weight and cutting through the soldier's calf. He collapsed to the floor with a grunt of surprise and Delyn took his blade two-handed and rammed it through the Gaian's face with a snarl. *Whatever else he's been doing, he's been practicing at warfare. The Delyn I knew had little love or skill for battle. This Gadarim is something else entirely.*

Once again Rhia felt herself distracted by roiling emotions, including shame of herself and blind hatred for Delyn, but there was no time for that now and she knew it. The Gaians still had men enough to do them serious damage but a glance across the hill made her hope start to swell, and she managed to forget her troubled thoughts for a moment.

Marius was coming up with half a cohort in his wake, and the Dragon Legion hit hard against the Gaians. Rhia cheered and started running to join them, Delyn and others following behind her. Marius' fighters were in a small but tight formation and they stood against the Gaians like a rock. Marius himself was at one end of the line and Rhia came to stand beside him, forgetting briefly that she had no shield. Her husband let a smile escape his face before turning it back to his usual blank mask. Delyn appeared beside them, a taken Gaian shield in his hand, and Rhia reluctantly stepped back to stand behind them. She was no use in the wall without her shield-arm.

More Gaians came at them and the Caledon stood firm, and Rhia let herself feel elated, the joy conquering her hate and shame. Though they still had to find and fight the dangerous men of the Tenth, here and now they were winning again. A grin spread across her painted face as more Gaian soldiers approached. But then it all went horribly wrong.

Three soldiers ran at the line and Marius deftly cut the arm of the first. The second engaged Delyn and shoved him with incredible strength. The third grabbed hold of Marius' shield and ripped the thing clear of his grip. Rhia heard him grunt with pain as his shoulder wrenched just as hers had done. He stumbled and struck out, stabbing the first man in the face, but the one who'd gripped his shield lunged forwards, and Rhia watched in horror as the blade plunged through his throat. Her husband staggered a moment and blood coughed from his mouth, then he dropped down to his knees before keeling over into the mud. He didn't move.

Rhia screamed and sprang at the Gaians, all fatigue and distraction forgotten as she hacked wildly at Marius' killer. The Gaian dropped behind his shield but Delyn hammered into his side, and Rhia sliced across his neck so hard the soldier was half-decapitated. All along the line the Caledon were moving forwards but Rhia was in no mind for such discipline. She leaped onto another man, bearing him to the dirt with just her weight. She pinned his arms to the ground with her knees and had she paused for even a second, the Gaian would doubtless have thrown her off. But she didn't pause.

Rhia stabbed down at his face, screaming wildly over and over. Marius was gone. Twice, *twice* the Gaians had taken her husband from her, both brave men who had cared for her and both struck down by the horror of this war. Tears poured from her eyes and ran in rivers down her cheeks, and Rhia kept on stabbing down hard at the Gaian's face. The line of Caledon passed by her, trying to drive the legionaries back and readying themselves for the charge of the Tenth, but Rhia didn't give a damn about that. The battle, the war, even her tribe had become nothing. Marius was gone. And these bastards had killed him.

The soldier's face was reduced to a red mess of blood and meat but still Rhia kept stabbing down. She felt a hand on her arm and looked up to see Delyn, a concerned expression behind his warpaint and beard. Rhia stared into his face. Delyn. Both times she'd lost a husband this man had watched it happen. Both times he had stood there when he might have helped to save them. And the last time this had happened, this man she had trusted had raped her while she lay dazed and helpless. Rage boiled behind her eyes and a new scream left her lips, and without even knowing it Rhia found she had sprung at him, shoving the Gadarim backwards. Her mind was filled with nothing but black fury as she drove the man backwards with all her weight. She wasn't even thinking as her knife thrust under his ribs.

The former Caderyn's eyes widened and he slumped forwards into her arms. Rhia took a step backwards and let him fall, and Delyn collapsed to the muddy ground and lay still. Rhia watched him for a moment and then sank to her knees, more tears flooding her eyes and blurring her vision. Shame, guilt, terror, pain and bone-deep fatigue rolled over her like an avalanche, and Rhia felt her body rack with sobs. Around her the chaos of battle still reigned, but the woman who was once Dessidus Rhianna neither knew nor even cared how it was going. She simply stayed there, kneeling down between a man she had loved and a man she had killed, and screamed as she wept her bitter tears.

*

The tribesmen were doing well, damn it they were doing far better than any could have expected, but victory for the Gaians was inevitable. Cadmus hacked down at yet another of their warriors, this time cutting through his shoulder, rending flesh and crushing bone. The man cried out but it was soon cut off as Lothar, standing beside him, thrust his own blade through his chest. The tribesman gurgled and fell as the cohort advanced, more blades stabbing down just to make sure. The company was advancing slowly over the ditch but nonetheless they'd not been stopped or even much slowed by their enemies.

Cadmus half-smiled as he launched another attack. He felt so strong! The robus of the sorcerer was still coursing through his body, and his cuts and thrusts had more power today than on any other he could remember in all the long years of his service. He felt young, but with the comfortable weight of experience to go with it, and not a single man or woman of this mob of savages had come anywhere close to touching him. To tell the truth, if he thought about it, the fury this strength gave him took quite a bit to hold in check. The raging storm inside him wanted to charge towards the enemy and tear them apart with his bare hands, but years of drilled-in discipline were still serving him well, and it seemed the same was true of most of his men. *Not like the bloody Fourteenth!*

Even as he thought it he saw another of the crazed soldiers trying to fight three Caderyn at once. He was strong and he was fast, even more so than Cadmus was, but he was fighting without thinking, slashing wildly at anything that moved. *Say what you will about these tribesmen though, they're bold enough bastards and they're cunning when they want to be.* He watched as the legionary swung and missed over and over, his anger only rising as he failed to score a hit. Had such power been in a shieldwall it might have been something impressive but out there alone, with three good fighters around him, it was just a recipe for disaster.

Cadmus wasn't surprised when the soldier was taken down, the three warriors working together to attack high and low to topple him. *Even these barbarians have learned to fight together, better than a legionary of Gaivia. Those Fourteenth boys should be ashamed.* He strongly suspected this was Dessida's influence and tried not to think about what would happen if they faced him. He was a good soldier but moreover he was well-liked by the legion, and to see him as their enemy might be bad for morale. Even Cadmus felt torn about him. Antonius Dessida had betrayed his legion, and for that he deserved a traitor's death, but he had been a good officer and had served well in his time. He'd been naïve and misguided certainly, but a fine tribune in his day.

The number of fighters before them began to dwindle, and as the last one was cut down Cadmus blew on his tin whistle. Two short blasts, one long.

'Stand to! Tidy up there and reform your line!'

The wall was fairly secure anyway but a quick re-shuffle to make it invincible was wise. They were practically into the town itself now and resistance was crumbling fast. A Caderyn cohort had come up from the battle below but they were busy engaging random Fourteenth men and Aborans, and a swift charge would scatter them to the winds. He raised an arm above him and whirled it round to indicate a turn. The company moved smoothly to face this new enemy and once again Cadmus felt contempt for the Fourteenth Legion. Those men not fighting were now pushing into the town, and what he saw there was frankly disturbing.

Soldiers in Gaian uniform were doing worse than killing civvies. He saw a legionary take a man by his silver beard and dash his head repeatedly against a wall. The old fellow looked frail and had been cowering from the soldiers, but the Gaian man was laughing as his blood and brains splattered everywhere. Further on he saw a man impale an infant on his sword and then hold it up above his head, and his comrades actually *cheered*. Women were weeping or screaming to the skies as they were dragged behind buildings or battered down with shields.

Cadmus turned to Lothar, who was also watching the carnage. The centurion swallowed a little before he spoke.

'Hardly soldiering, is it sir?'

Cadmus nodded slowly. A tiny part of him, the part he suspected was making him so strong, had a sudden urge to rush forward and join them, to grab his enemy by the throat and feel his flesh tear under his teeth. He shook his head. He'd killed civilians in his time but he was a soldier, not a beast. He watched two men who should have shared his attitude take a young man by his arms and try to rip them from their sockets. The man screamed as his muscles tore and his bones popped out of place. Apparently this process was taking too long for them because a third man, one of those freakish bloody Aborans, approached and calmly sliced off both limbs at the elbow. The legionaries laughed as they overbalanced, like a tug-of-war team when the rope had snapped. The tribesman fell to his knees and wept in agony, and the soldiers leaped back up and started battering him with kicks, chuckling uncontrollably as they did.

The First Tribune turned his face away. It was vile, but viler still was that part of him that wanted to do the same. He looked at Lothar and saw the same mixture of revulsion and fascination on his face. *This strength, this robus... is that what it does to us? Is that what it will do to me?*

A gang of warriors came charging from the west side of the town, their leaders wearing long streaks of white lime in their hair. They crashed into a group of the Fourteenth's men and Cadmus felt strangely happy as his fellow Gaians were cut down. The warriors didn't dare attack his solid cohort and instead focused their efforts on assisting their comrades. Cadmus' men weren't advancing on them yet after all, and there were things being done to their countrymen that no decent man could ignore.

Lothar pointed to the melee where the most fighters were packed.

'A good charge into that lot ought to scatter them like geese, sir.'

Cadmus knew that perfectly well himself but responded only with another quiet nod. He stood and watched the battle happening and couldn't help but feel impressed. And ashamed. Soldiers of Gaivia were fighting like a pack of rabid dogs while barbarian savages were fighting hard and bold. The tribesmen watched one another's backs and battled against opponents better armed and far stronger than they were. The Gaians flung themselves at anything they felt like killing at the time, and years of disciplined training had been forgotten in the slaughter. The Caderyn were fighting bravely. *But then they're fighting to save their people from monsters like that. I'd probably be doing the same thing. Dis below, I* know *I would!*

Once again Lothar spoke up from beside him, though Cadmus heard little enough conviction in his voice.

'Do we advance sir?'

Again Cadmus chose not to answer. Somewhere in that bloody mess he was sure he'd spotted young Dessida. He'd been fighting in a shieldwall, and a decent one at that. Underneath all that paint and beard he was still a soldier. Still a Lion, for all his betrayal. Where he'd got to now the tribune didn't know but he'd seen him alright, beneath a legion-style banner that showed a green dragon.

More men and women fought and died before them and the First Cohort simply stood and watched. Lothar actually plucked at his arm and spoke in a low, intense whisper.

'Sir, do we advance to support those soldiers engaged ahead of us?'

Cadmus took a long, slow breath and watched as those legionaries hacked wildly at warriors and children alike, watched as Caderyn fighters battled bravely to defend them, throwing themselves in fury at the robus-maddened men. He turned to face Lothar and locked eyes with him, seeing his own feelings reflected there. He spoke slowly.

'I see no soldiers ahead of us, Centurion Lothar. Only barbarians.'

The other man kept his face blank as he nodded, and Cadmus put his tin whistle to his lips. For half a second he almost stopped himself, that dreadful part of him longing to drive forwards and kill. But then the rest of him, the legion man, the proud soldier of Gaivia's Empire, shoved the sorcerer's unnatural frenzy aside and sounded three blasts on the whistle. One long, two short.

Beside him he heard Lothar bellow out the same order, and the Tenth Legion's First Cohort locked shields and started moving.

'First Cohort, fall back!'

Chapter 39. Retreat

For the first time in his almost thirty years of legion service, Severus Lepidus was running. More than once in his campaigns in Avidia he had withdrawn in the face of the enemy; several times he had fallen back as a feint or he had fallen back out of necessity. But every time it had been in good order, a deliberate retreat and not a rout. Today had been a new experience for him and frankly, he did not like it.

It had all seemed so simple; the bulk of the legions would advance in good form, admittedly with minimal cavalry support, and engage the enemy; driving them back while the flanking force stayed shrouded in Praecus' mist. Even if young Antonius *had* taught the Caderyn a few things, the weight and frenzy of the main assault would push them back eventually, and if that failed then the flanking force would take the town behind them. *So simple. What the Dis went wrong?*

He was riding his grey courser through the trees northeast of the field. With a little good fortune he would make it into Gorvicae land, where a company of enforcers could escort him back to the mountains. He hated to think what would greet him in Tamora. He could look forward to public disgrace at the very best, but right now mere survival was paramount, and he spurred his mount on to greater speeds. The greasy little magicker was struggling to keep up, and Severus was not the least concerned for him. His damned fool ideas might have cost him everything, and it was only out of habit that he'd let him come along. *But the first sign of his slowing me down and he's a dead man. Little bastard has more than earned it.*

His mind went back to the battle as he rode, still struggling to work out what had happened. Somehow, the Caderyn advance had formed up into cohorts and had

529

faced off with his legions shield-to-shield. He'd been surprised at their precision, but he'd been confident in his men. Both legions were made of veterans well-accustomed to the shieldwall, and both had been enhanced by Praecus' sorcery – the Fourteenth especially so. He had seen the effects of their amazing strength and he'd had no doubt that they would smash the tribes to kindling.

But they hadn't. Somehow the Caderyn and their allies had held their ground, remaining tight and disciplined while his own men lost their focus. He'd watched from the ridge as well-trained legionaries had reverted to mindless thugs, forgetting all they knew of tactics in a mad rush to reach the enemy. The men of the Tenth had done better than the others, but when the Fourteenth had collapsed they'd been forced to pull back or be flanked, and the last he had seen they had formed into squares, little islands of grey and red hemmed in by an ocean of tribesmen.

As for the flanking force he had no real idea. He'd seen the mist that hid them moving up the northern hillside, and then seen it blown away by some ill-timed gust of wind. Some Caderyn troops had then climbed the hill but he'd lost sight of them after they crested it. After that it had all been too far off for him to see anything, but the simple fact that he'd seen tribesmen coming back down the slope again was evidence enough that the attack had failed. *Cadmus will have kept them together though, even if those damned Fourteenth men lost their heads. If he lived through it he'll have kept good order. He may have his men pulling back this way even now.*

It was perhaps a little hopeful but he had to think on *something*. He was fleeing for his life towards an uncertain fate; he had to find something positive to focus on. He was still trying to find an up-side to all this when he spotted a handful of Gorvic scouts on the dirt track.

They were ahead of them and had probably cut through the denser woodland to get there. As they saw the two riders one of them called out and pointed, and three of the barbarians raised their bows. Severus kept his head down and dug in his heels, whipping his sword free from its scabbard. He'd no idea what Praecus would do and frankly, he didn't care. The sorcerer would either light them on fire, or something equally impressive, or else he would slink away in the confusion while they were distracted by the soldier. Severus' money was on the latter.

He felt the air whip by his ear as one shaft missed him by a hair, but the other two sank deep into his horse's chest and the animal screamed and faltered. Severus managed to keep his seat until he reached the scouts and he took the head of the first one while he was still in the saddle. Then his mount collapsed beneath him and he threw himself clear, landing on another man and hammering the sword's guard into his face.

Hands grabbed hold of his crimson cloak and he felt himself hauled backwards, but he spun even as he tumbled off-balance and swiped his sword low at someone's legs. A high-pitched cry pierced the air and a female fighter swung an axe at him, but her grip on the cloak was gone and Severus rolled out of the way. He saw only the injured woman and two other Gorvic warriors and, mercifully, only one of them had his bow. Like a fool he threw it down and drew a long knife from his belt, but Severus didn't pause to see what he did next.

A quick parry-and-thrust took the throat of the woman and when the next man charged in the general deftly stepped aside, sweeping a backhanded cut across his belly. The man cried out but Severus cracked his skull with the sword's heavy pommel, and the Gorvic crumpled to the dirt without a sound. He glanced around for the last man and saw him advancing on Praecus, who had been trying to ride around them and escape. *Coward.*

The tribesman lunged at the horse and the beast reared, and the magicker was thrown as the Gorvic moved in for the kill. The horse bolted back towards the south and Severus cursed before striding to Praecus' aid. He didn't like the sorcerer but it'd be poor form just to watch. *Yes, because after ordering good men murdered and playing about with sorcery, you truly are still a decent man!* He ignored his self-criticism and readied himself to strike. But he needn't have bothered.

Praecus simply raised his hand and opened it as if to grab an invisible cup. The Gorvic warrior stopped in his tracks and doubled over in pain. The sorcerer's fingers were closing slowly and the tribesman cried out, blood spitting from his lips. Severus watched in frozen horror as Praecus slowly drew his hand back and the warrior convulsed, dropping down to his knees and retching hard. He clutched desperately at his chest and throat, his eyes wide with panic, until Severus saw the magicker close his fist completely and wrench his arm back, a grin of harsh glee across his face.

The Gorvic gurgled pitifully and Severus had to look away as what looked like half his innards were dragged from his mouth in a welter of blood, and the unfortunate man fell to the ground, no doubt embracing his death. The general stared at the sorcerer but Praecus seemed unconcerned. He walked calmly across to the tribesmen that Severus had killed and relieved one of them of his green cloak before throwing it over his own shoulders. He nodded to another of the bodies.

'You should change out of that uniform. There are probably more of these scouts abroad and we'll need to pass unnoticed among them.' He put up his hood and glanced at Severus' legion-short hair. 'Make sure whatever cloak you get is hooded.'

The general bristled.

'I may have lost today but I am a man of the Tenth, not some damnable spy!'

Praecus sighed impatiently.

'Your precious legion has been scattered and defeated, and if the tribesmen catch you they will almost certainly kill you, and me with you. We must be sensible.'

Given what he'd just seen Severus was warier than he had been of the weak-looking man, but all the same, he had insulted the Lion.

'My legion is defeated because *your* sorcery failed them, and it turned the bloody Fourteenth into Dis-knows-what besides!'

The sound of voices nearby made him stop his admonishing and he listened out carefully for the language. For a second he'd hoped it might be Cadmus or the others but then the strange, lilting sound of the Lurian Tongue reached them, and Severus' eyes started scanning the woods as he brought his sword up to a guard.

'Get yourself a weapon. They're likely in a small group, we can...'

But he found himself stopping mid-speech. He couldn't move. His whole body suddenly felt cold and numb, and it shocked him that he was still standing upright. *Magic!* He turned his eyes to Praecus and snarled at the man.

'What are you doing you imbecile? You really think *you* can pass for a warrior? Damn it all Praecus...'

His words were cut off once again as he felt his lips and teeth being forced shut. A mix of fear and blind rage came over him and he desperately tried to will his limbs to move. Nothing happened. He saw movement in the trees ahead but the magicker threw off his taken cloak and then stepped in close, blocking his view. He spoke in barely a whisper, his voice changed to something very different to the cringing tones Severus was used to. It was deeper and richer, yet also harsher than before, and the words were fairly dripping with contempt.

'My name is Sarriban you impudent wretch! And a wiser man would have followed my advice.'

Through the numbness he felt the dagger's point entering his body, felt it drive under his armpit and into his heart and lungs. He felt mail rings part before the shocking strength and suddenly his body was moving again, but this time it was collapsing as the pain burned through his chest. He tried to speak but only blood came out and he toppled forwards with a grunt. Dimly, he saw Praecus produce a slave collar from his belt and throw it down at him as his voice lightened again, this time shouting in his native, Basian language.

'I'll not call you master again!'

He felt another hot pain in his back, up near his neck, followed by another, and then another, though by the fourth or fifth stab the pain no longer increased. General Severus Lepidus, Commander of the mighty Tenth Legion, thought back upon his life as it slowly bled out of him. He'd lived the life of a soldier since he could first lift a shield, and for the most part it had been a life of pride. These last few years had been set to be his greatest, yet a part of him regretted some of the things he'd been forced to do.

He had no chance to think on that further as his eyes began to dim, and the last thing he ever saw was the greasy-haired magicker, bowing low to a bunch of tribesmen and speaking quickly in a barbarian tongue.

'You saved me! Thank you so much gentle masters, thank you so very much!'

Chapter 40. The Dust Settles

Rhia was still kneeling among the corpses when a group of figures came walking up to her. She had no idea how long she had knelt there, only that she'd run out of voice and tears some time ago and was now simply stuck there, unable or unwilling to stand up. Marius, like Bevan and Dane, Gwen and Carradan and Ewan and all the others, was gone. Why bother standing up?

As they got closer Rhia recognised Reaghan walking at their head, his white robes stained with both blood and mud, his oak staff grasped in one hand. With him walked Kyran, the First Man of the Dariniae, supporting a slightly limping Ierryn. Though Reaghan looked at her with obvious concern, it was the island chieftain who spoke first.

'The Gaians are in retreat.'

Rhia didn't even nod. She just kept staring blankly into space. Kyran took over where his chief had left off.

'The maddened ones still fight but they do so without order, and our people are dealing with them in groups. We'll be blooded but we'll bring them down.'

Again Rhia did not react. Kyran looked concerned and continued uncertainly.

'The Lion Legion is moving back as well. We killed many, but many others kept together and made off east. Owain's cohort is following to make sure they keep moving.'

Rhia managed a dumb nod but that was it. Her grief and guilt felt like a heavy cloak on her shoulders, crushing her down beneath its weight. Ierryn jerked his chin towards the body of Delyn.

'A pity about him. He was once one of your tribe I think, though why he came to us I never knew. I didn't trust him at first but he proved his worth when my brother tried to fight me for my chair. After that I made him Gadarim.'

The Dariniae chieftain didn't seem exactly sad but he tilted his head a little in respect, hand over his heart.

'May he cross the bridge unharmed.'

The words were echoed by Reaghan and Kyran but Rhia remained silent. She didn't know if she really agreed with the sentiment. Had he really meant to force himself on her, years ago in a different life? Was he just a confused, love-struck young man who once made a mistake that he later redeemed? Or was he a manipulator, a rapist and a liar, who'd simply fled from justice and returned only because his chief commanded him? There was no real way of knowing now, and her crippling sense of grief was mixed liberally with the old familiar feelings of guilt and shame. Perhaps she had killed a man she had every right to hate, or perhaps she had killed one who might have been forgiven. She couldn't know. She would never know. But hero or villain the man who'd taken her in that barn was now dead by her hand. And it hadn't made that first pain go away.

Rhia honestly didn't know if she could live through this again. She had lost everything, even her sureness of herself, the pride that she had fought so hard to regain. So much was gone. Her eyes fell on a fallen knife and she wondered how it might be just to hold it in front of her and let herself fall onto it. She felt her fingers flexing. *Just reach out and take hold of it. What reason do you have to be here anyway? Just reach for it, fall on it, and be with your family again.* Her arm was stretching that way without her even thinking, and it was only Reaghan's voice that made her stop the movement.

'Child?'

She looked up at him and saw that kindly old face looking down at her. The tall druid was watching her worriedly, and Rhia saw what might have been the threat of tears in his eyes.

'Child, we must get you up from here.'

He stretched out his hand to her. Rhia looked at it, not really knowing what to do. She could get up, but what was the point? Why not just stay down here among the dead? As had happened so often, Reaghan seemed to read her thoughts.

'You have much to do Rhianwyn, people to gather and losses to count. And your son will want to hear of you. Lucan will want to know you are alright.'

Rhia blinked up at him, and it was as if suddenly the sun had come out from behind a cloud. The sound of Lucan's name somehow changed everything. In the grim blackness of her shame and despair there was suddenly a tiny golden light. She felt a warmness inside her as that light grew in brightness and realised for the first time how wrong she'd always been. For so long she had clung on to her rage, thinking it was what she needed to push past her darker emotions. The care and warmth of family had been a help to her, but mostly it had been anger and pride that had led her through the darkness, hadn't it? But of course, that had never been the case. It had always been the other way around. Her sense of pride as a Caderyn and her anger at her enemies had helped a little through her troubled times, it was true. But it was love, the love of her family, the love of her people, and her love for her child that had kept her sane. Kept her Rhianwyn.

She closed her eyes a moment and thought of Marius. Neither of them had ever said it, and she for one had never even *thought* it, but it was obvious to her now that he had loved her, and that she had loved him. It hadn't been the kind of love she'd shared with Bevan long ago but it had been real, and it had been strong. And it had given them Lucan. Or had it come *from* Lucan, *through* Lucan? Rhia really couldn't think and right now she didn't want to. The warm feeling she had at the thought of her son threatened to wither at the thought of her husband, still lying only feet away in the dirt.

Rhia risked a glance at him. He was face down, for which she was grateful, but there was still no mistaking who he was. *He'll need to be burned. It's how his gods like to greet their noble dead.* She tore her eyes away before more tears came. Rhia focused her thoughts on Lucan and looked up at the white-bearded druid. She nodded.

'Yes. Yes, we have work to do.'

Reaghan offered her his hand and she heaved herself up, unsurprised now at how strong the old man was. She swayed unsteadily as the blood began rushing through her legs, but Reaghan let her lean on him until she steadied.

'We can speak on things further in the longhall, my child.' He paused for a beat. 'Would you like a few more moments alone?'

Rhia found herself nodding quietly, and Reaghan and the Dariniae men bowed their heads and departed. Rhia stayed where she was and looked around her, taking in the full scene for the first time. Bodies were everywhere, both Gaian and Lurian, and tribesmen and women were flitting back and forth among them, putting soldiers from their misery or else helping wounded comrades. A glance behind her showed the plain below the town was equally littered, though it was too far off for her to make out details. A stench that she hadn't noticed before hit her nostrils in a wave of blood and offal, and she gagged and almost retched as it hit her throat. She straightened up and fought down the urge to vomit, and let her eyes lose focus as they stared across the carnage.

How long she stayed there she couldn't really have guessed but presently she heard footfalls coming towards her from the town, and when she turned her head she saw the last man she wanted to see. Gawan, though not exactly an enemy any longer, was hardly a man she wished to have as a witness to her grief. Rhia cleared her throat as she turned to him, trying her best to keep her face blank. The Gorvic didn't seem to care and instead looked beyond her at the field. His bleached hair and dark beard were both stained red with blood and the woad painted over his battlemarks was a smeared and blotchy mess. It probably was on her as well. She followed his eyes to where Marius lay and the Gadarim spoke three words.

'Shame about him.'

Rhia whirled on him, not sure if he was mocking her or not, but his face seemed serious enough. The Gorvic shrugged.

'He did a fair job – turning warriors into a legion. His damned shouting at us was wearying but the man had a point, and he fought bloody hard. He even helped my people when... well... after I've been discourteous to him. And to you.'

Discourteous was a bloody damned understatement, but Rhia could tell it hadn't been an easy thing for him to say. She nodded and spoke very calmly.

'Thank you.'

The Gorvic grunted and his brow furrowed as if he were thinking hard on something, then he stepped a little closer and spoke to her quite formally.

'This Gaian has proven his loyalty, his courage, his strength, his focus and above all things his will. Now and forever I say Marius son of Dessidus is Gadarim, and I name him the Roaring Lion. He lived and died with honour.' The Gorvic placed a hand over his heart. 'May he cross the bridge unharmed.'

Rhia wanted to weep, but not just out of sadness for him. In amongst the horrid grief was pride and gratitude. But

539

Gawan hadn't finished yet. He turned to face Rhia square on and looked straight into her eyes.

'And you... without a doubt you have all of these things and more. I am Gawan son of Dearg, the Leaping Wolf and First Man of all the Gorvicae, and I will prove with my life to all who would doubt that you too are Gadarim.' He placed a hand on her shoulder and Rhia found herself at a loss for words. 'Rhianwyn, daughter of Carradan, I name you the Fearless Wildcat. May you too live and die, and lead our people, with honour.'

*

The longhall of Nantwyn was packed to the rafters with more headmen and chiefs than Rhia even knew existed. Most were of the Caderyn, the Gorvicae and the Dariniae, but the three tribes of the Caledon were not alone. Breiryn from the south rubbed shoulders with Bearnicans and Rydicae from the east, and with Duronii and Averyn, the tribes of the Great River. Word of Second Nantwyn had spread far and fast, and every chieftain who had not come himself had sent along some trusted advisor. All were curious as to what would come now. Now that the invincible Gaians had been seen to bleed.

Rhia had spent the last five days sending messages back and forth, holding meetings with important men, and whenever she had time, grieving for the countless Caledon dead. She had taken care not to weep too openly about it, but it seemed like every day the dreadful tally grew ever larger as more warriors succumbed to infection or loss of blood. Like a fool she'd once thought that once a battle was done, it was done. The truth was a very different thing indeed. It was only once a battle was over that the real work could begin, and the real suffering could be fully appreciated.

Rhia was in danger of drifting off into despair again. Only the thought of Lucan, on his way here even now, along with the mountain of work she'd had to do, had kept the young woman sane the past few days. Left too much to her own thoughts they would stray back to blood and death, and she had to work hard to find her son's face in her mind to drive away the tide. *It will get easier, child.*

Rhia jolted almost out of her chair and glanced around to where Reaghan stood nearby. The old man had made no sound but she was sure it had been his voice. His blue eyes were unreadable and she tried not to stare. *Was that him using his magic? Or am I just hearing again something he has said before?* Whichever it was, the words had come at the right time. She'd been in danger of slipping away again and she was currently in the midst of something rather important.

The packed hall was thick with tension as the envoy of the Gaian Empire spoke politely before Rhia's high seat. In the absence of a male heir of Carradan, and with the support of Ierryn, Gawan, and most importantly of Reaghan, Rhia had been made temporary High Chieftain of the Caledon until a moot could be called to decide on the tribes' future. The thought of it was still very surreal. Almost as surreal as the swirling battlemarks she now wore tattooed around her left arm; a dragon and a lion, the one chasing the other around the forearm down to the wrist. *I am Gadarim.* It was even stranger than the notion of; *I am a chieftain.*

Rhia looked up from her arm and focused on their guest. He reminded her very much of Marius, though he was perhaps of slightly heavier build, and a little older than her former husband. He was tall and dark-haired, his features sharp and his voice educated. He was dressed in the familiar iron mail and leather breastplate of a Gaian officer, though the tunic and cloak were the black of the

First Legion, not the crimson of the Tenth. Marcus Galerius Gregorius, general of the First Legion, spoke on.

'...and any found to have been involved in that crime will of course be punished to the full extent of Gaian law.'

Rhia nodded slowly. She'd known Gregor and his brother fairly well from her time in Tamora, and the man had been friendly with Glaucus. If he said he was going to punish Lepidus' accomplices in the murder, then he meant it. A part of her was sorry that the bastard had already been killed, but another part of her was relieved. A public execution might have been satisfying to watch, for Rhia more than for most, but deep down she knew that it would have been sickening to the soul. Reaghan's words were hard to live by but the old man had a point; hatred and bloodshed only bred more of the same. And besides, it looked better to tell General Galerian that his former comrade had simply fallen in battle. *Even if it* was *while running away from it.*

The general paused a moment and Rhia looked around the hall. She saw a sea of faces she knew, though several were notable for their absence. Madoc had been killed chasing down the Gaian centre, making Owain the new First Man of the Caderyn, and Rhia tried to temper her sorrow with the sight of him and Meghan. The pretty redhead was leaning on the stocky warrior a little, and Rhia hoped they could at last be happy together. Ossian was gone too, the brave Gadarim whose rituals she had observed a lifetime ago, and which she still felt guilty for having spied upon. She no longer felt the gods had punished her and her people for it, but the memory of her irreverence still made her uncomfortable.

Rhia tried not to think of those who should be here and weren't; Madoc and Ossian, Dane and Ewan. Carradan. Marius. She forced the thoughts away, and resisted the urge to touch his Vulco amulet that she now wore on a chain around her neck. Enough were still here, alive and free, for her to be thankful for. And all were looking on in anticipation. Ierryn and Kyran stood to her left, while Gawan, Gwydion and Duran loitered to her right. Not one of those men would have hesitated for a heartbeat if she'd commanded them to kill the man in front of them right now. A couple were probably thinking about it already, but the fighting was over and Rhia planned to keep things that way. She spoke politely but stopped just shy of being too friendly. She might know and like Gregor but this was business, and they were still damned close to being enemies.

'I am grateful to hear it, General Galerian. But my own family affairs must come second to the concerns of my people.' Merwyn, the most senior of her Caderyn chiefs, nodded in silent approval as she went on. 'My people wish to know what has become of those soldiers commanded by the criminal Severus Lepidus.'

There were murmurs of agreement throughout the hall. The most sensible thing Gregor had done on his arrival was to announce that he had come in response to the acts of a criminal, and that Lepidus had been acting of his own accord. Since then he'd made clear, more than once, that the First Legion had come here to put down a rebellion by him, and that the Gaian Empire was in no way involved in this dreadful atrocity. It had the twofold virtue of lessening the odds of his men having to fight this new alliance themselves, and of making clear that the *Empire* had not been defeated; the loss was Lepidus', and his alone.

The crowd in the hall leaned forward to hear his reply, though he spoke clearly enough that there was no real need.

'The men of the Tenth Legion are on their way back to Tamora, under guard. Their acting commander brought them to us willingly and we shall, I hope, purge them of whatever taint this sorcerer has left on them.'

There were a few grumbles at that and Portunus, standing next to the general, looked nervous. Rhia wondered if the former governor was regretting coming with him after giving him the message about Lepidus. *Probably, but then there might have been something in it for him if he came along. Not that there will be.*

Rhia kept her tone courteous.

'And those men of the Fourteenth, and the auxiliaries? I trust we will not have to chase your rebels from our land ourselves, general?'

Gregor smiled with just his eyes. He knew the game Rhia was playing and he likely didn't mind. She had to appear aloof in front of the crowd and was doing so without being actively offensive. He could live with that.

'I would not wish to so burden you, Lady Dessida.' His face became more serious. 'Those men we have encountered were not keen to be taken in, nor were my men overly keen to capture them alive. All we have found we have slain, and any more who cross my path will meet the same fate.'

Rhia wasn't surprised by his grim enthusiasm. Lepidus had sullied the reputation of the legions, and that was something a man like Gregor could not forgive. He'd want to hunt down these sorcerous legionaries even more than she did. He would want to wipe away the shame. Rhia nodded again and allowed a little smile.

'We are all of us glad to hear it, another battle such as this would be... taxing.'

There were a few laughs from the crowd but Rhia took care not to take it too far. Gregor was a good man but he would have his limits. She continued politely.

'We are both of us committed to a lasting peace, I am sure. Has Tamora appointed a new governor yet?'

She could predict what his answer would be but she had to ask. Everyone needed to know how matters stood. Gregor shook his head.

'Not as yet. Until we can be sure of the damage done by Lepidus' dictatorship, I have taken temporary control of the region. For the time being.'

Rhia nodded. She had suspected this would be the case but it had to be stated aloud.

'I too am in temporary control of the Caledon Alliance. As such, I suggest we make an agreement between ourselves, here and now, before politicking can make the waters muddy.'

The hall seemed to approve of this in a quiet, mumbling way. The Luriae weren't exactly noted for their intricate politics but they were there nonetheless, and the situation in Tamora would be more complex still. Gregor nodded back.

'I agree, that would be best. What do you propose?'

His voice was calm and casual and his face a patrician mask, but Rhia knew he would be feeling tense. *He must be. I certainly am!*

'A simple arrangement between friends. Between *equals.*'

The emphasis was subtle but it was there, and everyone heard it. Rhia had already established that neither of them was more than a temporary war-leader and so the equality was already implied. Gregor tilted his head a little but said nothing and Rhia continued, trying not to show her nerves. She hated to think it but she missed her father, now more than ever before.

'We have no quarrel with you, nor with your Emperor. The source of our wounds is the same as the source of your shame; Severus Lepidus. Let us agree to live as we did before that man came to this isle; as neighbours.'

It was a half-truth but it served their purposes. The Gaian Empire would likely have expanded regardless of who'd been in command here, but that truth was inconvenient right now and Gregor knew it just as well as she did. Rhia continued, her confidence growing as both the Gaians and her own people seemed to follow her words closely.

'There is much that we can learn from each other, much benefit to be gained by mutual peace and trade. Let us agree, here before this assembly and before your own people,' she nodded to Portunus, 'to never again make war upon one other, and to respect one another's laws and territory. Let us agree to reap the rewards of peace and understanding.'

She waved a hand and Portunus' former clerks appeared from behind her. They looked weary but otherwise in full enough spirits and Gregor gave another of his tiny, silent nods as Rhia continued.

'I have had your loyal administrators draw this up in writing, as is tradition among the Gaians. Will you read this, General Galerian, and put your mark on it in the name of the Emperor?'

The silence in the hall was palpable, and Rhia suspected that Gregor played on it a little before he answered.

'I shall read your words Lady Dessida, and will of course be glad to sign if I find all terms to be acceptable. Which I am confident they will be.'

The longhall seemed to breathe out a little, some in disappointment at the lack of violence but most in sheer relief. They had seen enough of war. Rhia let Merwyn take over the talking, speaking in reasonably good Vulgare and letting the clerks fill in any gaps. There would be details to go over and Portunus finally started to look at home as he joined in the discussion. Rhia and Gregor exchanged a look of mixed amusement and relief before the general approached the table and started reading the documents. Rhia was fairly sure he would accept what he read there and so her mind began to drift again, swaying dangerously close to despairing grief once more. There was so much hope to be had in this room today, where a peace most thought impossible was now being forged, but still Rhia's mind couldn't ignore what all this had cost. *So much death. So much blood. So much shame.* The horrible, numbing grief might have swallowed her again, right then and there, had the great doors at the end of the longhall not opened inwards, and a familiar face appeared in the morning light. Rhia stood from her chair as the men beside her chattered, staring at the newcomers with a smile across her face. Olla and Siriol walked calmly into the room but Lucan, *her* Lucan, broke straight into the clumsy run of a child and Rhia almost burst out laughing. It was adorable. His face was beaming at the sight of her and in it she saw the shadow of both Marius and Carradan. Rhia forgot all about the solemn meeting going on and strode straight towards her son and lifted him up in her arms. He cried out with joy.

'Mama!'

Rhia held him close, so tight she feared she might be crushing him but she couldn't help herself. People were probably staring but she didn't give a damn about them. She didn't give a damn about the hard work she had ahead, or the nightmares or the grief or the worries that would dog her life, likely every day until her death. She forgot all about politics and warfare, about grief and loss and shame, about blood and death and fear. She had her son, and she loved him as he loved her. And as long as they had that, all would be well.

Epilogue

Lucan and Siriol had chased each other all around the little camp, but the cunning boy had finally found a decent hiding place. The camp they'd made, somewhere between the battle-hill and his grandfather's hill, was in the shade of a massive forest, and Lucan had scrambled across the open ground and up into the trees. Now just inside the wood, he was considering climbing up one of the smaller trees, the better to see where Siriol would be looking for him. It looked like it might be difficult to climb down again though and he stood and pondered it for a moment.

Without his wanting to, his thoughts turned to his father. Mother had told him that he had gone to be with his two grandfathers and that he wasn't coming back again. The thought made Lucan sad, as well as angry with him for leaving, and he did all he could to take his mind off it. Perhaps Father would grow bored of life wherever he had gone and he would come back someday? Lucan certainly hoped so. He missed him.

The boy shook his head. Right now he had hiding from Siriol to do, and he had to keep an eye out for her coming from the camp. He focused his eyes on the stretch of grass in front of him, the green almost glowing in the summer sunlight. He was so focused that he didn't see the man standing next to him until he spoke, his voice very low and calm.

'A fine day.'

Lucan almost jumped from his skin and stared at the old man. He held a staff in one hand and wore a cloak that looked at once dark green, and then brown, and then grey. His face was lined and bearded but his deep-set eyes seemed to shine, and though Lucan was afraid he did not run away. Somehow he felt the old man did not want hurt him. All the same he was a little frightening, and Lucan did his best to sound polite.

'Yes. A fine day sir.'

That seemed to be enough for the man in the cloak, who just stood in the shadow of the trees in silence, gazing out over the grass towards the camp. Lucan felt awkward and spoke quietly to him.

'Um, do you want to see my mother?'

The old man shook his head and spoke in his low voice again.

'I already have done, my boy. I came here to see you.'

A little breeze swept around him and the old man's face twitched a little. He nodded towards the camp.

'And to see them.'

Lucan was confused but he did his best to keep his manners.

'Can I ask why, sir?'

The man shrugged.

'To see them? Perhaps I am simply glad they are here. To see you?'

He looked hard at him and Lucan tried to hold on to his gaze. It was difficult.

'Perhaps I wanted to see if you will listen to what I say.'

Lucan had no idea what he was talking about but again, he tried to be polite. Both of his parents had been keen on his being mannerly, and one of his very first lessons had been to treat elders with respect.

'I will listen, sir.'

Once again the old man shrugged and seemed to speak half to himself.

'Perhaps. I have seen much that you may choose to do, my boy. I have seen you leading horsemen and I have seen you counting coins. I have seen you hold an iron horn, and I have seen you biting silver. I have seen you in white and blue and I have seen you in red and gold. I have seen you justly proud, little one. And I have seen you weep with shame. Nothing is certain.'

Lucan's confusion had only increased and he chewed his lip a little in concentration. The old man's voice became more direct.

'My words to you may change much, or else they may change nothing. But nonetheless I would have you hear them, child.'

Lucan nodded his head obediently, hoping he might understand the next thing that was said. The man in the cloak spoke earnestly, his bright eyes boring into Lucan's own.

'Remember who you are, Lucan son of Rhianwyn, Carradus Dessidus Lucianus. You are both men, and you must remember that. You must remember where you come from and it may help where you are going.' He shrugged once again. 'Or it may not. But my words had to be spoken and what you do with them is for you. Do you understand me, little one?'

Lucan was mostly still reeling in shock. How had the old man known his name? Known *both* his names? He calmed down a little when he remembered that the man had mentioned that he'd met his mother. *That must be why he knows me. He's a friend of hers and he wants to help me somehow.* He took a slow breath and tried to keep the nerves from his face. He was the son of Antonius Dessida after all. He mustn't show fear to anyone.

'I know who I am, sir. I can remember that.'

Truthfully, he wasn't all that certain what he'd meant. Who could forget who they were, after all? The old man seemed a little unconvinced himself but when he spoke he sounded casual enough.

'As you say. I care not.'

Once again a breeze went by him and he twitched his lip again.

'I care a little, child. Heed my words.'

Lucan nodded, still feeling very confused and wishing he was still just playing with Siriol. This man was unnerving him. He tried to keep his voice as strong as possible.

'I will, sir.'

The old man nodded slowly and turned his eyes back to the camp.

'Very well.'

He jerked his chin towards the grass and Lucan followed his gaze. Out on the open ground he saw Siriol, her blue dress bright against the green of the grass. He felt an urge to duck quickly behind the trunk of the tree but thought he ought to say something to the man first, to be polite. But when he turned back to face him there was no sign of the old man. And Lucan's fear and confusion only deepened.

About the Author

JP Harker is the pen-name of James Thomas, an obsessive martial artist and a committed geek of various types, who apparently didn't drive his wife mad enough with those things and so took up writing fantasy books as well. A proud Welshman with just enough Saxon in him to make things interesting, James hails from the beautiful county of Glamorgan in South Wales.

www.jpharker.co.uk

The Caledon Saga:

Wildcat

Leaping Wolf

Lion Cub

If you enjoyed this book, please tell everyone you know!

35508837R00327

Printed in Poland
by Amazon Fulfillment
Poland Sp. z o.o., Wrocław